CELIA'S JOURNEY

Key to the Past

CELIA'S JOURNEY

Key to the Past

by

Melissa Gunther

Hayes-Allan LLC
Colorado Springs, CO

Hayes-Allan LLC
www.hayes-allan.com
Hayes-Allan Internal ID: 71105-1207-352-3

ISBN: 978-0-9819470-5-1

First Paperback Edition, July 2012

To believing in what seems impossible

Table of Contents

Chapter One
Mail

Morning sun poured through the paned-glass window and spilled over the inert form buried under the covers on the bed. Birds chirped from the tree outside, but the heap on the bed simply rolled over to face the other direction, not realizing it was now facing the brightly shining sun. Eyes scrunched and there was a grunt, followed by a big yawn, and then the form on the bed sat up and stretched.

Celia Fincastle rubbed her eyes, looked out the window at the blue sky, and yawned again. She'd stayed up late the night before, opening all of the birthday cards and presents from her friends at her school, the Renasci Academy for Gifted Students. It had been the best birthday she could remember, even though it included heading back to Aunt Agatha's house after her first year at Renasci and despite the fact that Aunt Agatha hadn't even acknowledged her birthday.

Celia shifted to the side of the bed and slid her feet into her slippers. She stood and stretched, then went to her closet to get her robe. Seeing the collection of birthday cards lined up on her desk, she smiled, remembering all the friends she had made last year. She glanced at the clock and saw that it was still early, but she knew Aunt Agatha would be awake already. On her way to the door, she caught a glimpse of her reflection in the mirror and paused. She'd forgotten she'd worn the necklace to bed.

Professor Legaspi, one of her teachers and faculty mentors, had given her the necklace for her birthday. The round silver locket held pictures of her parents, whom Celia hadn't seen in ten years. She knew nothing about what happened to them, only that they disappeared just before she turned two years old. Soon after, Celia had come to live with Agatha Trowbridge, her distant but only remaining relative.

She opened the locket and studied the smiling face of her mother and the roguishly grinning face of her father. Looking back and forth between the pictures and her own reflection, she tried to figure out if she looked like either one of them. After a few minutes, she sighed, closed the locket, and headed downstairs for breakfast.

"Oh, good, you're awake," Aunt Agatha said as Celia walked into the kitchen. "We have a busy day today, so you'll have to eat quickly. No dawdling."

"What are we doing?" Celia asked, pouring herself a bowl of what looked like cardboard squares and rabbit food yet claimed to be cereal.

"I have some very important meetings to attend, and... Is that a new necklace?"

Celia touched the silver locket. "Yes, it was a birthday present from... a friend."

"How nice. What a delightful birthday... oh, no!"

"What?"

Aunt Agatha pressed a hand to her forehead. "Your birthday! How thoughtless of me! When was it again?"

"Yesterday." Did Aunt Agatha honestly think that she would believe that her aunt had forgotten when her birthday was? Until last year, Celia's birthday had been a celebration for

Aunt Agatha—one year closer to sending her off to boarding school. Celia bit her lip to keep from saying something that would get her in serious trouble.

"My goodness, I feel just awful that I forgot about your birthday! How terribly inconsiderate of me!"

"It's okay, Aunt Agatha."

"Oh, I must do something about this. I'll have to call all my friends and invite them over for tea. Yes, that would be splendid! We can have finger sandwiches and a prune tart. How delicious!"

Celia tried not to gag at the thought of a prune tart. Surely she wouldn't have to endure *that*. "Really, Aunt Agatha. You don't have to," she said, a note of panic creeping into her voice.

"Oh, and you can wear that delightful purple hat of yours. Everyone just loved that hat last year." She rose to her feet and swept from the room saying, "I must get working on this right away. There's no time to lose!"

Celia sighed as she dropped her cheek onto her hand. She hated that purple hat. Besides the fact that it looked like a chicken, it brought back memories of last year at school when someone had painted the mascot statues in the commons purple and dressed them in purple lion costumes. Celia had been framed for the prank and got stuck cleaning all the statues.

And *prune tart*!? It sounded awful. The chocolate and coconut cake she'd had with her friends on the trip home yesterday had been much better than that. She sighed again as she realized that she had the whole summer in front of her before she could go back to Renasci again.

"Hurry up, Celia!" Aunt Agatha called. "We have to leave in half an hour. Don't be late!"

Celia rolled her eyes and sighed for a third time. It was going to be a very long summer, indeed.

Chapter One

By mid-June, Celia had resigned herself to another six weeks of misery with Aunt Agatha. Every day was basically the same as the last, so the past two weeks felt like two months. Celia would get up and eat breakfast, when her aunt would announce that they were going to another one of her teas, luncheons, bridge club meetings, or some other collection of social gatherings. Since Aunt Agatha wouldn't let her wear anything "scruffy," Celia was forced to spend the vast majority of her time in uncomfortable and hideous dresses, usually accompanied by an equally uncomfortable and hideous hat of some sort.

Celia had been forced to endure the promised prune tart, which had been as horrible as it sounded, made worse by the collection of gossipy old ladies who had come over for tea. She found her mind wandering for much of the afternoon, thinking back to the birthday celebration she'd had with her friends from school. It wasn't much of a competition, that afternoon with her friends and the delicious cake versus this stuffy gathering of Aunt Agatha's friends and the disgusting prune tart, so Celia tried not to compare the two, but that didn't stop her from wishing she were anywhere other than where she was.

The only thing that had been worse than Celia's birthday tea was the Grandmother's Afternoon Tea, where all the ladies in Aunt Agatha's circle of friends brought their granddaughters for the event. It was designed to give everyone a chance to meet the granddaughters they all talked about so much so people could put a face with a name, but Celia had a sneaking suspicion that it was just an opportunity for everyone to show off their granddaughters and brag about how great they were, and she'd done her best to get out of the event.

"But Aunt Agatha," Celia had said, using what she hoped was her most persuasive voice, "I'm not *really* your granddaughter, so I don't think I should be going with you. Won't everyone else decide that they should be able to bring someone other than their granddaughter?"

"Oh, pish posh, Celia. I'm not about to let everyone else show off their granddaughters while I sit in the corner and watch. You're going, and that's final."

"Couldn't I—"

"Absolutely not. I said you're going, and I don't want to hear another word."

Try as she might, Celia could not convince Aunt Agatha to let her skip the tea, so she was forced to endure three hours of listening to snobby girls who were being groomed to become identical copies of their snobby grandmothers, who each thought her granddaughter was the greatest thing since sliced bread.

"Oh, my Abigail is just the smartest little thing! You should see how her teachers rave over her."

"Well, my Veronica has the best voice you ever heard. I always say that she's going to sing at Carnegie Hall someday."

"Have you seen little Penelope? She's so adorable! I've told her parents they should send her pictures out to an agent and get her into modeling."

"Well, *my* mom says that the people who go to *my* school are the best students because we go to the best school."

"Yeah? Well, *my* daddy says that I'm his little princess, and everyone else isn't good enough for me."

"I've never *heard* of your school. RAGS? How appropriate. Is that what you wear for your school uniforms?"

She'd figured that no one there would have ever heard of her school, and that was just fine with her. Renasci wasn't the average school, and the students who attended the school were not your average students, either. The school was for people with very unusual talents and abilities, or gifts, which let them do things that most people could only dream of attempting. Even though the people at Renasci didn't try to keep their school a secret, most people refused to believe that such abilities existed, so they had never heard of the school.

Collapsing on her bed after that torturous afternoon, Celia was certain that was the last straw. If she had to go to another one of Aunt Agatha's meetings, her brain was going to explode. She rubbed her eyes and studied the constellation stickers on her ceiling. How she missed her bed at school, with the windows that let her see the stars, which were brighter and more numerous than here at Aunt Agatha's house.

Sighing, she glanced around the ceiling, then bolted upright, her heart pounding with excitement. For the stars on her ceiling were glowing blue, and that could only mean one thing: someone from the demesne was trying to contact her.

She looked over at her desk, then scrambled to her feet and hurried over to see what had arrived. She found two envelopes sitting there, and grabbed the ivory-colored one that was sitting on the top. "Celia Fincastle" the envelope said, and she quickly opened it and pulled out the letter.

Dear Celia,

I trust you are doing well at home with your aunt and enjoying your summer break. It occurred to me that you haven't learned how to send mail in the demesne, so you have no way of contacting any of us. To remedy that, I have enclosed an address where you can send correspondence. Should you need to reach anyone, simply send out a letter to that address and someone will make sure it reaches the correct individual. However, please be sure that your name and address are not visible on the outside of the envelope when you mail it.

I am assuming your aunt will not wish to act as your guardian for this year either, so I will be contacting her about my position as temporary guardian again, if that is acceptable to you. Should she agree, I will perform the same duties as last year, signing your ERs and handling any necessary disciplinary action (although I don't anticipate that being a problem for you this year).

Sincerely,

Higby

Havensmoor via A-BUS 3rd Station

Despite the fact that the letter said nothing about getting her away from Aunt Agatha, it was nice to hear from someone in the demesne, and Celia was quite excited about being able to send mail out to other people.

She turned her attention to the second envelope, this one plain white. "Celia" was printed in silver ink on the front in even letters. The back flap on the envelope was stamped with the image of a silver eagle. She carefully opened the envelope and pulled out a sheet of light gray paper.

Dear Celia,

I hope you are having a good summer holiday. We heard from Maddie that she's heading to camp in July, and both we and she wondered if you'd like to go with her. She should be sending you a note soon with the rest of the information about the camp, in case your aunt is curious. The camp runs the two weeks before school starts, so you'd head straight to school from camp. I know it's not much of a help to get you out of the house right before you'd be leaving anyway, but I guess two fewer weeks is better than nothing.

Your packet of information for this school year should be heading your way soon, but don't worry about getting all of your books and things. We'll make sure you have everything you need when you get here. See you then!

Warmest wishes,

Professor Legaspi

Summer camp? Celia had never been to camp before. Was the camp just for kids with unusual abilities, or was it for everyone? Did it matter? She could get away from Aunt Agatha a whole two weeks early! To make it even better, she'd get to see Maddie, too! Madelia Hannagan was her best friend, an energetic blond-haired girl who often talked before she thought. They'd met on the way to school last year, and had been friends ever since.

She carefully folded the letters and returned them to their envelopes, then put them in her closet with the pile of birthday cards she'd set on a shelf. She couldn't ever remember getting mail before, other than last summer when she first found out about Renasci, so it felt kind of special to get *two* letters, even if they didn't come in the regular mail.

For the next week and a half, Celia waited every day for the mail to arrive, hoping she'd hear something from Maddie. She sat outside on the front steps, watching carefully for the mailman, then stood, shifting from foot to foot with anticipation, while he retrieved their mail from his bag. She flipped through the mail, her hope fading with each item not bearing her name, until she reached the bottom of the stack and still had nothing from Maddie. Then she'd drop the mail on the sofa table and hurry upstairs, thinking maybe something had appeared on her desk, only to be disappointed when she saw her empty desktop.

Finally, on a Friday near the end of June, Celia saw a bright pink envelope in their pile of mail and knew it had to be from Maddie. Sure enough, it was addressed to "Miss Celia Fincastle" in Maddie's curly handwriting. Celia rushed inside, leaving the rest of the mail in the parlor, and headed up the stairs two at a time. Once she was safely inside her room with the door closed, she opened the envelope and pulled out an equally bright green piece of paper.

Dear Celia,

I hope you are not too bored at your aunt's house this summer. My annoying siblings have been up to their usual trouble, making my life miserable the way they always do. My little brother decided that it would be a good idea to smear toothpaste all over the mirror in my room and my sister thought it would be fun to use my clothes to play dress-up. I never thought I'd say this, but I can't wait to go back to school!

Professor Legaspi heard about the camp I'm going to next month, and she thought you might like to go, so I'm officially inviting you to come to camp with me. I sent the brochure, too, so your aunt will know that the camp really exists and she's not sending you off to who-knows-where (not that it sounds like she'd care). I really hope you can come. It would be so much fun to have you there.

I'd better go - my brother is trying to tie all my shoelaces together.

See you soon (I hope!),

Maddie

Celia laughed out loud at the antics of Maddie's brothers and sister. She could see Maddie getting really irritated with her younger siblings, particularly when they tried something like tying her shoes together. But although she found the descriptions funny, what really put a smile on her face was the actual invitation to go to camp with Maddie. It meant she only had to endure three more weeks with Aunt Agatha.

She spent the rest of the afternoon studying the camp brochure, looking at the pictures of the pine trees, lake, and cabins, and reading the descriptions of the activities the camp offered. By the time Aunt Agatha called her downstairs for dinner, she was excited about going to camp and hoped Aunt Agatha wouldn't object.

She waited until the meal was almost over before she brought up the subject. "Aunt Agatha?"

"Yes?"

"I...uh..."

"Don't stammer, Celia. It's terribly impolite."

"Sorry. I just wanted to let you know that my friend invited me to go camp with her."

"Oh? What friend is this?"

"Her name's Maddie. She's in my class at school."

Aunt Agatha pressed her lips into a thin line. "And just how will this interfere with my plans?"

Celia's eyebrows rose. "What plans?"

Agatha let out an impatient sigh. "I am a busy woman, Celia. I have many things on my schedule, and I cannot take the time to drive you around to who knows where!"

Celia swallowed a laugh as she recalled Maddie writing that exact phrase in her letter. "I...think someone would give me a ride," she said cautiously.

"Oh. Well." She patted her hair. "How long will you be away?"

"Almost two weeks. But then I'd go straight to school from there."

"And when would you leave?"

"Three weeks from tomorrow."

"Hmph." She tapped a finger on her cheek. "Very well. If it won't inconvenience me, you may go."

"Thank you, Aunt Agatha."

Agatha shook her finger at Celia. "Just don't be bothering me if you get homesick and want to come home. I shall be too busy to put up with such nonsense."

Celia wondered why she would get homesick after only two weeks at camp when she spent ten months at school last year without any problems, but decided it would be wise to keep that thought to herself. "I won't."

"Oh, and make sure that Mr. Snodback or whatever his name is will be responsible for you while you're at this camp."

Celia frowned. *Mr. Snodback*? "You mean Higby... *Snodridge*?"

"Yes, that's it. I can never remember his name."

She recalled Higby's letter from a couple weeks ago. "I'm sure he won't mind."

"Excellent."

Celia was so excited she nearly squealed, but figured Aunt Agatha wouldn't approve, so she smiled to herself instead.

Aunt Agatha might see it as getting rid of her earlier, but Celia saw it as gaining her freedom earlier. She couldn't wait.

A few days later, Celia was cleaning up her room, per Aunt Agatha's orders, while she thought about what she and Maddie might do at camp.

"Celia!" Aunt Agatha called from downstairs. "The mail is here. Would you please bring it inside?"

"Yes, Aunt Agatha," Celia said, slipping her shoes on her feet and heading downstairs. She went to the front door and collected the mail from the box mounted on the side of the house, spying a large envelope at the bottom. Coming back inside, she flipped through the stack, finding nothing of any interest to her until she reached the large envelope, which she noticed with excitement was addressed to her.

"Here's the mail," Celia said, setting it on the table beside Aunt Agatha, who was sitting in the back parlor, working on her needlework.

"Oh, good. I've been waiting for it all day," Aunt Agatha said. "Is that big envelope for you?"

"Yeah. It's from school."

"Ah, of course."

Celia opened the envelope and pulled out a small stack of papers. Year-long Assignment for Sixth-Year Students the top of the first page read. *Homework?* Celia thought with disappointment. She'd been hoping to hear something about a summer program that could get her out of this house or maybe even something about her classes for the next year—anything that would give her a reason to believe that this mind-numbing summer would eventually come to an end.

She sighed and kept reading.

> Sixth-year students at Renasci must complete a year-long assignment about their

family tree. The purpose of this assignment is to help you learn about your relatives who have attended Renasci or other schools for gifted students so you can learn more about your own abilities and talents. In addition, you may find that there are people in your family tree who have been gifted even though they never attended a school to receive training for their abilities. These individuals, just as those who did receive training, are important to your family history of people with exceptional abilities.

Enclosed you will find the assignments you will need to complete before your return to school on August 1st. There will be many more assignments throughout the coming year that will help you produce a finished product that will serve as a reference tool for yourself and others.

We look forward to seeing what you discover this summer and hope that the remainder of your holiday is enjoyable.

Warmest regards,

The Sixth-Year Faculty and Staff of the Renasci Academy for Gifted Students

Her disappointment faded slightly. Yes, it was still homework, but maybe she'd find out something about her parents by doing this assignment. And maybe she'd find out that someone else in her family had been incredibly gifted, which would explain the unusual success she had during her first year of school. Celia had been just as surprised as everyone else when she had received perfect marks on most of her exams.

"Did your school send you anything important?"

"Just a big assignment with some stuff to work on this summer. We have to learn about our family tree."

"How splendid! I just love studying genealogy. I'm sure I can show you the books in the library that have information about my ancestors. They're a fascinating group, I assure you."

"Um...well, okay." She didn't think that any of Aunt Agatha's family would be part of the family tree that Celia needed to research, but she thought maybe the books Aunt Agatha had might mention the rest of Celia's family, or perhaps she might find a book she had overlooked. Celia had looked for information about her parents before, but she'd never found anything, even though she'd searched the entire house from top to bottom.

"We'll start tomorrow."

The following day was a disaster. Aunt Agatha was excited when they first went into the library, a cozy, wood-paneled room next to the back parlor. She quickly pulled a small pile of books off the shelves and opened them up to show Celia all of the interesting people in her family tree. She was so proud of the nobility and important people she was related to, and she took great delight in pointing out all the accomplishments and acquisitions of all of them. But then Celia pointed out that she wasn't on Aunt Agatha's family tree, and that was where everything started to go downhill. Since Celia was only related to Aunt Agatha through marriage, none of Aunt Agatha's ancestors were directly related to Celia, a fact which disgusted and distressed Agatha so much that she developed a roaring headache and had to lie down in her room for the afternoon.

Celia cleaned up the library, reshelving books and collecting all the papers spread out on the table. She grabbed her notebook, which had nothing written in it yet, and trudged upstairs to her room, where she flopped on her bed. While Celia didn't really care that she wasn't related to all of the important people in Aunt Agatha's family, she was disappointed that she hadn't found out any information about her own family. She'd grown up without knowing anything about any of them, and it had only been in the past year that she'd learned a few snippets about her parents.

She wasn't sure how she was supposed to research her family tree when there was no one left for her to talk to. It seemed that everyone else was going to have a big advantage, since they all knew at least one person from their family. Other than Aunt Agatha, Celia hadn't seen anyone else even remotely related to her since she had been two, and she certainly didn't remember any of them from that long ago. She hoped Professor Legaspi or Higby would be able to help her, but that wouldn't do her any good for the portion of the assignment that was due at the start of school.

Celia sat up and pulled the assignment out again. Her first task was to write down as much information as she could about the people she was closely related to, such as parents, siblings, grandparents, aunts, uncles, and cousins. Following that, she was to interview at least three of them about their schooling and abilities. She huffed and tossed the paper on her bed. The first part was the easy part; she'd write nothing because she didn't know any information about anyone. But how could she interview three people when she didn't even know one?

She thought about writing to someone, but she'd already asked people about her parents, and they'd all said that they had simply disappeared and no one knew what had happened. And the library in town wouldn't be any help at all—it probably didn't even mention the demesne or Renasci. Celia figured there had to be information about her family somewhere in the demesne, since they had been chosen as the Overseer's princeps twice now.

That part was still unsettling for her. It had been almost a year since the trip to school where Celia had learned that she was some sort of important person in the other world, or demesne, that contained Renasci. She didn't understand all of it yet, just that the supremely powerful Overseer had for some reason picked her family, and specifically her, to be leaders over the demesne. It was, apparently, the second time Celia's family had been chosen for the position, so she assumed there had to be information about the previous princeps somewhere, but she didn't have the faintest idea where to look.

Not for the first time, Celia closed her eyes and tried to fight off tears. It just didn't seem fair that other people had so many relatives to talk to when she had none. There was no way she could study her family tree, and she'd end up getting a bad grade for something that wasn't her fault. But more than that, Celia's tears fell because it was in times like these that she felt the absence of her parents so deeply.

When Aunt Agatha called her for dinner, Celia wiped her face and headed downstairs, but her appetite was rather meager. She asked to be excused early and headed back up to her room, where she fell into a restless, lonely sleep.

Chapter Two

Free!

"Celia! Are you ready yet?"

Celia rolled her eyes at the screech that carried up the stairs. After so many years of admonishing Celia to not yell in the house, Agatha should have known better than to do so herself, but it seemed she definitely followed the "do as I say, not as I do" way of thinking. "I'm just getting my last things packed, Aunt Agatha," she called back.

"Well, hurry up. What time is your ride coming?"

"I still have half an hour."

"Just make sure you're not late. Think how I would look if you weren't ready on time!"

Three weeks had crawled by at slower than a snail's pace. Every time Celia looked at a calendar, it seemed to her that someone must have added days before her departure for camp. The only good thing that had happened was that Celia's family tree assignment gave her a much-needed excuse to avoid going to Aunt Agatha's utterly boring social events.

Now, finally, it was time for Celia to head off to camp for two whole Aunt Agatha-free weeks. Of course, right after that, she was going back to Renasci for ten whole Aunt Agatha-free months, but that was just icing on the cake for Celia. She'd gotten a letter from Maddie a few days ago that said she'd be getting a ride from Maddie's family, as long as she could put up with the obnoxious siblings. Quite frankly, Celia thought she could have put up with riding with Aunt Agatha if it meant leaving her behind once she got to camp.

Celia took one last glance around her room, making sure she hadn't forgotten anything. She glanced in her closet and nearly gasped when she saw an old book sitting on the shelf. She couldn't believe she'd almost forgotten *that*!

The large, leather-bound book had been her first introduction to the world of Renasci last summer, when she'd found it while cleaning the attic. Mr. Morven, her academic advisor last year, had made a point of mentioning its importance to her and reminded her many times to keep it in a safe place. Grabbing the book off the shelf, she stuffed it in her backpack and headed downstairs. She'd opted for her backpack instead of her duffle bag this time, figuring it would be easier to carry and perhaps she would need it at camp.

"Well, it's about time!" Aunt Agatha blustered once Celia had lugged her trunk onto the front porch. "I didn't think you would make it."

"I still have fifteen minutes before they're supposed to get here, Aunt Agatha."

"That doesn't matter. The proper thing to do is to be ready early and never be tardy."

Celia sighed, resigned. "Yes, Aunt Agatha."

Maddie's family showed up exactly on time, pulling in front of the house and parking their white minivan. The side door flew open and Maddie jumped out, running up the path to give Celia a hug. The rest of her family followed at a more restrained pace, and Celia couldn't help but notice that her parents looked less than thrilled.

"Good morning," Aunt Agatha said as they all approached the porch. "I'm Agatha Trowbridge. It's so nice to meet one of

Celia's friends and her parents. I like to stay involved in her activities, you know."

Celia heard Maddie snort beside her and mutter, "Oh, brother," before Celia nudged her with an elbow.

"Aunt Agatha, this is Maddie and her parents..." Celia trailed off. The polite thing to do would be to introduce everyone, but she had never met Maddie's family, so she didn't have a clue what their names were. "Um, Mr. and Mrs. Hannagan," she finished lamely.

"I'm Bob," Maddie's father said, holding a hand out to Aunt Agatha, who plastered a smile on her face and shook it politely. "And this is my wife, Annette, and our kids, Maddie, Huxton, Sabrina, and Dairek." He pointed to each, in descending order, as he said their names.

"Wonderful to meet you," Aunt Agatha gushed. "I can't thank you enough for giving Celia a ride. I'd do it myself, but I'm just not as young as I used to be, and it's so hard to ride in the car these days."

"It's not a problem, Mrs. Trowbridge," Mrs. Hannagan said. "We were headed right past here anyway."

"It's '*Miss*' Trowbridge," Agatha corrected.

"Oh, I'm sorry," Mrs. Hannagan said, looking properly chastised.

"Well, I suppose you'd better get on your way then," Aunt Agatha said, pushing to her feet in a way that contradicted her comment about getting old.

Mr. Hannagan looked at his watch. "Yes, we really should. The sooner we get to camp, the sooner we can head home." He looked over at Celia's trunk. "Is this your stuff?"

Celia nodded. "Just that and my backpack, but I can carry that."

"All right, then, let's get it loaded."

Within minutes, everyone was loaded in the van and ready to go except Celia, who was saying good-bye to Aunt Agatha.

"Well, Celia, I hope you have a good year. I guess I'll see you next summer," she said, then held out her hand for a handshake.

Celia shook her hand awkwardly, remembering a similar situation last year, and said, "All right. Good-bye."

"Yes, good-bye."

Celia turned and climbed into the backseat of the van, taking the last seat beside Maddie. Mr. Hannagan closed the sliding door, walked around the van, and climbed in the driver's seat. "All set?" he asked.

"Yes!" everyone in the back chorused.

"Then let's go."

Celia turned to wave at Aunt Agatha, but once again, she was already walking through the front door and didn't even notice that they were pulling away. She sighed, relieved that she was finally away from the woman.

"So you're really Celia Fincastle?" Maddie oldest younger brother asked from his seat on the other side of Maddie.

"Huxton!" Maddie cried. "That's rude!"

"It's okay," Celia said. "Yeah, I am."

"Wow."

"Huxton," Mrs. Hannagan said sharply from the front. "That's enough."

"Sorry," he said.

"How old are your brothers and sister?" Celia asked Maddie quietly.

"Huxton's ten; he'll turn eleven in August. Sabrina's seven and Dairek's six."

"Are any of them coming to camp with us?"

Maddie shook her head. "No, thank goodness. Mom doesn't let us go to overnight camp until we're eleven."

"I forgot to ask before—is the camp part of the demesne, or is it for everyone?"

"It's for kids in the demesne, mostly."

"So everyone there will be from Renasci?"

Maddie shook her head. "No. There are lots of other schools in the country for gifted kids; Renasci's just one of them. The best one, if you want my opinion, but maybe I'm a little biased."

Celia chuckled. "A little? Well, I guess I would agree, but I didn't know there were other schools. Where are they?"

She shrugged. "I'm not sure."

Celia nodded. "So, Mr. and Mrs. Hannagan, are all of your children going to be attending Renasci?" she asked, trying to make conversation.

"Looks like it," Mrs. Hannagan replied. Celia could almost feel the cold breeze coming from the front of the van.

"Wow," she whispered to Maddie, "what did I say?"

Maddie shook her head. "Nothing. I told you, they have this weird idea about you. . . . I don't know what it is, but it's like they have something against you. Don't worry about it."

"Oh." Celia shrunk back in her seat and looked out the window. It seemed her reputation preceded her yet again, only this time is was working to her disadvantage before she even said anything.

"Ouch!" Maddie cried. "Huxton! Stop poking me!"

"I didn't!"

"Yes, you did. Like this," she said, jabbing him in the side with her finger.

"Ow! Hey!" Huxton reached over and pinched Maddie's arm.

"Stop that!"

"You started it!"

"I did not! You poked me first."

"Did not!"

"Did too!"

"Did not!"

"Kids!" Mr. Hannagan bellowed from the front seat. "Do I have to stop this car, or can you figure out how to get along?"

"Sorry," Maddie and Huxton muttered.

Celia watched the whole thing with wide eyes. She'd heard about road trips and phrases like, "Do I have to stop this car?" but she'd always thought they were just something someone had made up. Suddenly she giggled.

"What?" Maddie asked.

"Nothing. I just realized how nice it is to be out of Aunt Agatha's stuffy old house and around normal people for a change."

"Celia, if you think this is 'normal' then you're in for a big surprise," Maddie said.

Sabrina and Dairek, sitting in front of them in the middle row, starting whining and arguing at that moment, and Mrs. Hannagan leaned over in her seat to stop their fussing. Huxton scowled at Maddie from the far corner of the seat where he had scooted to get as far away from her as possible.

Celia looked at all of it and decided that even if it wasn't normal, she'd take this any day, and she settled in to enjoy the ride to the camp.

Three hours, five rest stops, and fifteen arguments later, they pulled through a wooden arch proclaiming the entrance to Camp Altohodos. Just inside the arch, a series of wooden signs appeared on the side of the road, saying "Welcome to Camp Altohodos—please proceed to the main entrance," and "All unattended campers will be fed to the bears."

"That means younger brothers, too," Maddie said, nudging Huxton.

"Yeah, right," he said, his voice muffled because he was leaning on the windowsill with his chin in his hand.

"Mommy?" Dairek piped, a note of panic in his voice. "Are they going to feed me to the bears?"

Chapter Two

"No, Dairek, they won't feed you to the bears."

"But Maddie said..."

Mrs. Hannagan turned to give her daughter a look. "Your sister was just teasing. Weren't you, Maddie?" Her tone suggested that Maddie had no choice but to agree.

Maddie ruffled her youngest sibling's hair. "Just joking, Dare. Don't worry."

They ended up in a long line of traffic a few moments later, and everyone started getting antsy. After such a long car ride, the younger kids wanted to run around, and Celia was afraid Maddie and Huxton were going to come to blows soon. She studied the trees out the car window, thinking it reminded her a little of the area around Renasci, which sat in a forest in the Rocky Mountains.

They inched their way forward, until eventually they reached a man directing traffic to a field for parking, where they bounced over the uneven ground and finally came to a stop in front of a line of pine trees. "Everyone out!" Mr. Hannagan announced.

Sabrina and Dairek scrambled out of the van and started running in circles, while the occupants of the back seat took a little more time crawling out. They all stretched, then headed in the direction of a large crowd of people on what looked like a basketball court, looking for check-in and cabin assignments.

"Check-in, this way!" someone called, and they followed the voice to the end of a long line that snaked around the basketball court. Taking a position at the end, they crept forward little by little. Mrs. Hannagan sent Huxton off with the two younger kids, reminding him to "keep a close eye on them!" Finally, they reached the front of the line, and took a spot at a table opposite a woman wearing a polo shirt with a nametag that proclaimed her to be "Daisy."

"Hi, there, folks," she said. "Checking in a camper?"

"Two of them, actually," Mrs. Hannagan said.

"Names?"

"Madelia Hannagan and Celia Fincastle."

"Fincastle?" Daisy glanced up and looked between Maddie and Celia. "Really?"

Uh-oh, Celia thought. She hadn't thought to ask if people would know her name here, and it appeared that they did. She said nothing, but hoped the woman wouldn't make a big deal out of her being there.

"Well, you're both right here on the list, so I'll need signatures verifying that you dropped them off, here," Daisy said, pointing to a spot on the clipboard, "and here." She shuffled through a pile of papers to her left. "It looks like you girls will be in the Hedgehog cabin, which is right here," she said, setting a map of the camp in front of her and pointing to a little square indicating the cabin's location. "You can head out there now, or you can hang around here for a bit. They're doing the official camp opening in a few minutes."

"What should we do with their trunks?" Mr. Hannagan asked after signing the clipboard.

"You can just unload them by the mess hall, and someone will take them to the cabin later."

"Oh-key dokey."

"*Dad!*"

"Sorry."

Daisy smiled. "Here are your lists of activities, girls," she said, handing them each a sheet of paper. "You'll have to talk to your counselors and find out if your cabin is planning any group activities, but otherwise you're free to participate in any activity listed on that sheet." She checked her clipboard again. "You'll have a cabin meeting at eleven-thirty when your counselors will go over the basic schedule for meals and so forth, so make sure you've made it to the cabin by then. Otherwise, I think you're all good to go!"

Chapter Two

"Can we go ahead and leave?" Mrs. Hannagan asked.

"I don't see why not. If we need anything else, we'll contact you."

"Okay. Thanks." Mrs. Hannagan ushered them off to one side and rounded up her other kids. "Time to say good-bye, everyone. Maddie's staying at camp and we're headed home."

"Bye, Mom. Bye, Dad. Bye, annoying siblings," Maddie said, giving each one a hug as she said their names. Celia covered a smile with her hand when she saw Huxton make a disgusted face as Maddie hugged him.

Mrs. Hannagan turned to Celia. "Well, it was...um, nice...meeting you, Celia," she said, holding out her hand much like Aunt Agatha.

Celia shook it politely. "Thank you for inviting me and giving me a ride, Mrs. Hannagan."

"Oh! Um...you're...welcome." In spite of her words, she acted more like Celia had the plague and she couldn't wait to get away from her. She recalled Maddie mentioning something about her parents not being big fans of hers last year, but she hadn't really thought about it much until now. She wondered what had happened to make them dislike her before they had even met her.

"Okay, guys, time for you to leave," Maddie said, turning her sister toward the car and giving her a gentle shove.

"All right, all right!" Mr. Hannagan laughed. "We're going!" He gave Maddie one last hug as Mrs. Hannagan herded the kids toward the van. "Have a good time."

"Thanks for the ride, Mr. Hannagan," Celia said.

He looked at her as if he had forgotten she was there. "Oh...um...right. No problem." He gave her a half-hearted wave and then turned to follow the rest of his family.

"Sorry about that," Maddie muttered as they watched them all load in the car.

"What?"

"My family. I told you, they have this...*thing* about you. They won't tell me why. And my brothers and sister...well, they're just plain annoying."

"They're not so bad."

Maddie shot her a look of disbelief. "Try spending twenty-four hours a day with them."

Celia shrugged. "They're better than Aunt Agatha."

Maddie chuckled. "Well, let's forget about them for right now. We're finally at camp, and we're *free* from all of them!" she said, throwing her arms out wide and spinning in a circle.

"Attention! The opening ceremony will begin momentarily at the fire pit."

"Come on," Celia said, slinging her backpack on her shoulder. "Let's go!" She linked arms with Maddie and they followed the crowd to the fire pit, which was across the way from the basketball court.

The official opening was a ceremonial lighting of the campfire, followed by a rousing rendition of the Camp Altohodos song. Laughter rang out as everyone followed the camp director in the official camp handshake, which included "shake your head" and "shake your tail feathers." The director, called "D.B." by the campers, an energetic black man with a big, bouncy Afro, then dismissed the campers to go to their cabin meetings, which began in about twenty minutes.

The large congregation of students split and went in different directions, all heading to their various cabins. Celia looked at the camp map again to find the Hedgehog cabin, which she finally located tucked at the edge of the woods near the Arts and Crafts building. It was one of the furthest cabins from the main center of the camp, which included the Activities building and the Mess Hall.

"Do you know where we're supposed to go?" Maddie asked, watching the crowd of kids zigzagging around them.

Chapter Two

"I think it's that way," Celia said, pointing off to one side where a group of kids were heading.

"Okay. Let's go."

They went back towards the center of camp, and Celia pointed out the Mess Hall as they went past. Maddie's stomach growled and they laughed, as they both knew that she was always hungry. They headed up a hill and past a couple of cabins for younger kids, then went around the Art building. They stopped to look at some of the artwork that was hanging in the windows of the building, and a couple of groups of campers went by behind them. They seemed to be whispering excitedly about something, and Celia thought it was great that so many people were so happy to be spending time at camp. That is, until she heard someone whisper something about "princep" and "Fincastle."

"What are they talking about?" Celia asked Maddie.

She shrugged. "Got me. I haven't been paying any attention."

"What's going on?" Celia asked one of the girls who was heading past them.

"Didn't you guys hear?" she asked.

"What?"

"Someone told me that Celia Fincastle is at Camp Altohodos this summer! Can you believe it?" Excitement shone in her eyes. "I hope I get to meet her." She ran off.

"Here we go again," Celia groaned. "Hey, Maddie?"

"Yeah?"

"How would you like to be me for the next two weeks?"

Maddie's eyes widened. "What!?"

"Have you been to this camp before?"

"No, not this one. Why?"

"So no one knows you, then." Celia shook her head. "I don't want to have everyone staring at me the whole time I'm here," she said. "I just want to have fun and be a normal kid. So if you pretend to be me and I pretend to be you, then—"

"*I* can have everyone staring at *me*?" Maddie interrupted, coming to a stop.

Celia turned to face her, giving her a weak smile and then shrugging. "You're right. Never mind. It was a dumb idea, anyway," she said, walking on ahead.

"Now, wait a minute," Maddie said, catching up and flinging an arm around her shoulders.

"Just forget it," Celia said. "We'd never be able to pull it off, anyway."

"Why?" she challenged. "Because you don't think I can be a good enough 'you'?"

"No, because I don't have as big a mouth as you," she teased.

"Hey!" she cried, bumping Celia with her hip.

"Just kidding!"

"I think we should do it."

"I don't know, Maddie."

"Come on. I think it would be so much fun! What's the worst that could happen?"

Even though it had been Celia's idea, she had a horrible feeling in the pit of her stomach that told her the worst that could happen could be quite terrible, indeed. But then another group of kids came up behind them, all of them talking about Celia being at camp and wondering who she was and what she was like, and she started to feel sick to her stomach at the thought of everyone watching her every move.

Neither Celia nor Maddie said anything as the group passed by them. "Well?" Maddie asked when they were alone again.

Celia sighed. "I don't know. It seems like a good idea, but I'm just not sure about it."

Chapter Two

"Look, if anyone finds out, then we'll just tell them the truth. How else are you going to get away from all your adoring fans while you're at camp?"

She threw her hands up in surrender. "Fine!" she laughed. "We'll give it a try. But if it doesn't work . . ."

"Don't worry so much. I'm sure it will be fine."

"We'll see . . ."

They marched down a slight hill and then saw the edge of the woods in front of them. A couple of cabins were tucked into the trees, so they headed in that direction. "Which one is ours?" Maddie asked.

Celia glanced at the map again. "The one in the middle, I think."

"Okay."

They reached the wood-sided cabin a few moments later, noticing the sign that said "Hedgehog" over the door. A covered porch ran the length of the cabin in the front, with a couple of benches and chairs, all of them unoccupied at the moment.

"Here it is," Maddie said, heading up the steps onto the porch. She knocked, then opened the screen door when they heard, "Come in!" The two of them walked inside.

"Hi!" said a short girl with dark brown hair. "I'm Marisol. Who're you?"

"Uh, I'm . . . Maddie, and this is . . . Celia," Celia said, tripping over the words.

"Welcome to Hedgehog cabin. We're gonna start the meeting in a few minutes," Marisol said. "Those two bunks over there are still empty, so you can pick which one gets the top," she said, pointing at a set of bunk beds in the far corner.

"All right. Thanks," Maddie said.

Maddie decided she wanted the top bunk, so Celia took the bottom. She slipped her backpack off her shoulders and set it in the back corner of the bed. Since the book was still in her bag, she hoped it would be safe there.

"See?" Maddie whispered. "No one's ever going to know we've switched places!"

"Okay, okay! It might be fun," Celia admitted.

"Hi," someone said from behind them. They turned to see a tall blond standing nearby. "I'm Bernadette, but everyone calls me Bernie," she said, holding out her hand.

Maddie shook it vigorously. "Hi, Bernie. I'm Celia, and this is Maddie."

"Have you been to camp before?" Both girls shook their heads. "Well, you're going to have so much fun here. There's always something to do, and it's just... well, a lot of fun!"

Celia grinned. She was starting to think it might be just that: a lot of fun. For the first time since she found out about her fame in the demesne, she wasn't worried about people giving her funny looks and whispering about her as they walked by. She looked at Maddie out of the corner of her eye. That was all going to be her problem for the next two weeks.

In the next few minutes, they met the remaining four girls in the cabin and one of the counselors. Besides Marisol and Bernie, their cabin mates were Tabitha, a quiet girl with curly brown hair, glasses, and freckles across her nose; Stephanie, who had spiky black hair and a dark suntan; Keely, a bubbly girl who wore brightly-colored nail polish; and Arletta, a statuesque black girl with long cornrows that fell to her waist. They shared the space with two counselors, one of whom was Ashleigh, who wore cargo pants and a tank top and had her blond hair up in little knots all over her head. The other counselor had apparently gone to pick up the final cabin assignment list and was on her way back.

It took no time at all for the girls to become friends. No one seemed to be grumpy or obnoxious, and Celia's hopes for the next two weeks rose a little higher. While they were all waiting for the other counselor to return, they stood around and chatted about what they wanted to do while they were at camp and how much they were looking forward to having a good time.

The screen door slapped shut and they saw the outline of a person coming into the room, but the sunlight behind the figure kept them from seeing her clearly. She headed over to Ashleigh, saying, "I've got the list," and Celia felt a little prickle on her spine. When she turned to face the group, Celia gasped quietly and grabbed Maddie's arm.

"What?" she said, giving Celia a funny look.

"Look!" She spun Maddie around so she could get a good look at their second counselor.

"*Doxa*!?"

Chapter Three

Camp Altohodos

Celia's hopes for her two weeks at camp crumbled around her. She could not believe it. Of all the people in the world, she had to get *Doxa* as a counselor?

Doxa had been a roommate last year at Renasci. A first-year, finishing up her last year of school, Doxa had gone out of her way to make things difficult for Celia and the other seventh-years in the room. She'd been particularly nasty to Celia, even going so far as to help with a plan to frame her to try to get her expelled. She wasn't exactly on Celia's list of favorite people.

Ashleigh declared the start of the cabin meeting and everyone gathered in a circle on the floor. Celia tried to stay out of Doxa's sight, but with only eight of them, it was a bit difficult.

"All right, girls," Ashleigh said, looking around the circle. "Our first order of business is to go over camp rules." She read through the list of do's and don'ts. "Any questions?"

"Do we have to go swimming?" Tabitha asked quietly, twirling a strand of her curly hair around her finger.

Ashleigh nodded. "You have to at least try everything we do as a cabin. If you don't like it, you don't have to participate the next time." Tabitha looked relieved. "Any other questions?" She looked around the circle again. "Okay. Our basic schedule around here is pretty easy to follow. Breakfast is at seven-thirty." She held up a hand at the groans that met her statement. "I know, I know. But trust me, you'll all be up in plenty of time and you'll never even notice. We sit together as a cabin, and we'll show you where our table is in the Mess Hall when we head over for lunch. You have free time after breakfast until eleven-thirty, when lunch is served. After lunch, we'll do structured activities, either as a cabin or with other cabins or dividing into interest groups, until three-thirty. Free time until dinner at six, then campfire at seven-thirty. Most days, that will be it, but on certain days we'll have night-time cabin activities."

She held up a piece of green paper. "This list will be posted by the door each week. It has any important information you might need to know for the week, including the meal menu, the meeting times for certain activities, and who is in charge of clean-up. Each cabin does clean-up for the Mess Hall for three days, and there will be no excuses for avoiding your clean-up duty."

"What if you're sick?" Bernie piped up.

"Then you'll be in the infirmary and we'll have a note from the camp nurse," Ashleigh said matter-of-factly.

"Oh."

"Any other questions?" After a moment of silence, she continued. "Most nights we'll have what we call a huddle-up just before lights-out. That's when you'll have a chance to talk about what you did during the day, bring up any issues you might have, and go over the schedule for the next day. If there are any new announcements, we'll tell you then. Understand?"

Celia nodded her head with the rest of the girls.

"Great! I think that covers everything we needed to go over, so I'll let you all get to know each other a little bit better, and we'll head over to the Mess Hall for lunch in a couple minutes."

Everyone pushed to their feet, and they started chatting again. Doxa went over to a couple of the girls and introduced herself, and Celia started to get nervous. What if Doxa blew their cover and she and Maddie had to switch back to themselves again? She dreaded the thought of spending the two weeks of camp with everyone staring at her and trying to talk to her.

It seemed Doxa was saving Celia for the end, and after working her way around the rest of the cabin, she finally turned in their direction. "Hi," she said, coming up to them. "I'm Doxa. And you are . . . ?"

Celia gulped. "I'm . . . Maddie, and this . . . is, uh, Celia."

Doxa gave her a long look, then shifted her gaze to Maddie, who lifted her chin a bit higher and stared back. "Maddie and Celia?" She nodded slowly, sliding her hands in her back pockets. "Nice to meet you," she said finally, eyeing Celia curiously.

Celia could hear her heart pounding in her ears. Would Doxa say anything?

"Is this your first time at camp?" Doxa asked.

Celia nodded hesitantly. "Yes."

"Well, I hope you have a great time . . . Maddie." She turned to Maddie. "You, too . . . Celia."

"Hey, wait," Arletta said from behind Doxa. She poked her head over Doxa's shoulder. "Did you say your name was Celia?" When Maddie nodded, she said, "I heard that Celia Fincastle is supposed to be here. Is that you?"

"Um . . . y-yeah."

Arletta's eyebrows flew up. "Really? Wow. I never thought I'd get to meet you!"

The other girls in the cabin overheard the conversation and were now gathering around. Celia could feel her heart pounding again, and noticed that Maddie was shrinking away from the rest of the girls, trying to hide behind her.

They were saved by Doxa announcing, "Time to go to the Mess Hall, everyone. Let's head out." A flurry of activity followed her words, and Celia breathed a sigh of relief. As she walked out the cabin door, she felt Doxa's gaze on her, and she glanced back. Doxa had an odd look in her eyes, but Celia couldn't figure out what it was.

They made it to the Mess Hall just in time for lunch, which was served cafeteria-style, table by table. Celia made sure she was sitting at the opposite end of the table from Doxa, and she spent the entire meal listening to people pepper Maddie with questions while Maddie tried valiantly to keep her mouth full of food so she wouldn't have to answer.

"Still sure you want to do this?" Celia leaned over to whisper at one point.

"Don't worry about it," Maddie mumbled back. "It's fine."

When the meal was over, the counselors announced that there were no official activities for the afternoon, so everyone could do whatever they wanted with their free time. They all headed outside and went in different directions, and Celia and Maddie decided they'd head back to the cabin to unpack a little. As they walked in that direction, Doxa came up beside them.

"Ah . . . Maddie, could I speak with you?"

"Uh . . . sure . . . Doxa." Celia looked at Maddie, who gave her an uncertain shrug.

"Would you like to take a walk with me?"

"Um, I guess."

They turned and headed out on the path that went around the lake.

"So, *Maddie*, I guess I'm not exactly your best friend right now, am I?"

"Um..."

"It's okay. I understand. I just wanted you to know that I talked with my parents and learned some stuff, and...well, I guess you could say that things have changed. I've changed." She sighed. "I don't expect you to believe me or anything, but..."

"What stuff?"

"Hmm?"

"You said you learned some stuff. What stuff?"

She sighed again and looked out over the water. "Celia—" She glanced sideways at her. "Er, *Maddie*, I...I'm sure you get this all the time, and you're probably really sick and tired of hearing it, but I really can't tell you."

"Oh."

"Can I ask you a question?"

"I guess."

"Why the switching places?"

Celia thought for a moment, then shrugged. "I just wanted to be a normal kid for a little while. We didn't figure it would hurt anything."

Doxa chewed her bottom lip. "I don't...I'm not so sure, Cel—, uh, Maddie."

"Why?"

Doxa was quiet for a minute, then shook her head, saying, "Never mind. If this is what you want, then I'll go along with it for now."

They walked in silence for a ways. "So..." Celia said. "Did you, uh, get to graduate?"

Doxa nodded tersely. "Headmaster Doyen let me finish my schooling at home. I came back after everyone went home to take my exams and they gave me my diploma." She spoke with little emotion in her voice, as if she were recounting a news story with detachment. Suddenly she stopped walking and put a hand on Celia's arm. "Look, Celia, I know I've said I'm sorry and I know that's a measly offering for what I put you through last year, but I hope you can forgive me and at least give me a chance. I don't expect you to become a close friend or anything, but at least let me show you that I've changed."

Celia looked at her. It was so different from the Doxa she'd known last year. That Doxa wouldn't have cared what someone else thought of her, unless it was someone she was trying to impress. But now she sounded almost...*desperate* to prove that she was a different person.

"I..."

"Just give me a chance?"

"Um..." Celia fidgeted nervously. She wasn't ready to trust Doxa after the events at school last year, but try as she might, she didn't have the heart to say no to her. She couldn't in all honesty act like Doxa hadn't done anything to her last year, but she figured she could at least give her a chance to show that she'd changed. "I-I'll try."

Doxa studied her for a moment. "Okay," she said, nodding. She turned down the path again and Celia followed, wondering what had happened to change Doxa so much in such a short time. "So I suppose you'll be working on your family tree, huh?"

Celia nodded. "Yeah. It's not exactly easy when I don't have any relatives to talk to, but..." She shrugged helplessly.

Doxa looked at her in surprise. "I hadn't thought of that."

Celia looked away. So many people never stopped to think about how much they already had just by having their family around. "It's okay."

"What are you going to do?"

"Got me. I guess I'll just do what I can and hope I don't get a bad grade."

"Hmm."

They were most of the way around the lake, and although talking with Doxa wasn't anywhere near as bad as it had been at school last year, Celia was glad their chat was coming to an end.

"Well, I'll let you head off and do your own thing, then," Doxa said, tucking her hair behind her ear. "I'll see you later."

"Okay."

Doxa gave a wave as she set off toward their cabin. Celia turned to see if she could find Maddie. She headed past the Mess Hall and noticed a large group collected around the base of a tree. She wondered what everyone was doing, so she went to see.

"Is it really her?" someone asked as Celia got closer.

"I think so," someone else replied.

"I can't believe I got to see Celia Fincastle!" another said excitedly.

"Oh, no!" Celia said under her breath. She pushed her way through the crowd toward the tree. It took quite a bit of effort, but she finally reached the center of the crowd, where she found Maddie pinned against the tree trunk by the kids surrounding her. People were calling out and trying to talk to her, and Maddie looked a little overwhelmed. Celia couldn't blame her. She'd had people make a fuss when she showed up at school last year, but it hadn't been anything like this.

"Celia?" she called.

"M-Maddie? Is that you?" Maddie answered.

Celia reached over and grabbed her arm. "Okay, everyone. Give her a little space, will you?" She practically dragged Maddie back through the crowd until they finally reached the open air outside the mob. "Run!" she yelled.

She and Maddie took off across the camp, heading for their cabin. She could tell by the sounds behind her that people were actually running after them as they tried to escape. They sprinted past all the buildings, people shouting and calling behind them, and Celia thought she had never been more relieved than when they finally spied their cabin. She saw Doxa walking toward the cabin, but she turned when she heard the noise behind her. Celia nearly laughed when she saw the look on Doxa's face as she took in the scene in front of her. She could just imagine what it must look like, with everyone running after them across the camp.

"Get in the cabin! I'll take care of it," Doxa called as they dashed past her.

Maddie reached the door first, and she yanked it open and hurtled inside. Celia rushed in behind her and slammed the door, leaning back against it and gasping for air. After a few moments of trying to catch their breath, Maddie suddenly started laughing.

Celia looked at her in amazement. "What?"

"I was just thinking," Maddie said. "That was *so* funny!"

"Are you kidding!? It was not!" She stared at Maddie, who was doubled over in laughter. "What would you have done if I hadn't come to find you?"

Maddie waved a hand. "But everyone following us all the way to our cabin! It's just so funny!"

Celia shook her head and peeked out the window. Doxa was turning everyone around and sending them away. A few campers were trying to sneak past, but she caught them all before they reached the steps. Celia had a sneaking suspicion that Doxa was using some of her gifts to round up the kids, but she wasn't sure.

"I mean, they were just, like, 'It's her' and then they went crazy!" Maddie was still going on about the kids, trying to get her laughter under control.

"Maddie, it's not funny."

"Oh, come on. It was, too."

Celia pushed away from the door and walked over to her bed. She didn't find it at all amusing that people were so obsessed with her. She found it irritating and tiresome.

The door opened and Doxa came inside. "Anyone else in here?" she asked.

Maddie, who apparently still didn't trust Doxa, refused to answer, her laughter finally under control.

Celia shook her head. "I don't think so."

Doxa took a deep breath. "Girls…that could have been dangerous."

"Oh, please," Maddie scoffed.

"I'm serious," Doxa said, and Celia could tell by her tone of voice that she was. "Something has to change."

Celia felt her stomach jolt. She didn't like the sound of that. "What?"

"If people find out that you switched places…"

"*Honestly*," Maddie groaned. "I don't mind taking Celia's place. It's no big deal."

Doxa pressed her lips into a thin line and looked carefully at Celia. Celia stared back, wondering what was going on. "I'm sorry," Doxa finally said, shaking her head, "but I can't just let you two wander around camp on your own anymore. It's not safe. We can't have this kind of thing happening."

"Why?" Celia asked.

"It's just not safe," Doxa repeated, still looking at her. "I'm sorry, but you'll just have to try to understand."

Celia let out a sound of frustration, pushing off the bed and walking across the room to the window on the other side of the room. She was tired of people keeping secrets from her. She knew there was more going on than anyone would say, and she was really tired of people telling her only that they couldn't tell her anything. She stared out the window, feeling like a prisoner. Even switching places with Maddie wasn't going to let her be a normal kid.

She felt a hand on her shoulder and glanced over to see Doxa standing next to her. "You okay?"

Celia shook her head and shrugged, saying nothing. No one would understand.

She heard Doxa sigh. "Look, I'm not saying you have to switch back or anything, but I don't think it's a good idea for you to be going around camp without a chaperone, just in case."

"Fine," Celia sighed. But it wasn't fine. Not at all.

Despite her reservations, Celia actually found herself enjoying her time at camp. Doxa acted as their chaperone, escorting them across the grounds whenever they wanted to go somewhere and observing while they participated in activities. Even though she'd expected it to be uncomfortable, it was actually a bit easier knowing that someone was watching out for her and making sure that she didn't have to deal with all the other kids "going crazy," as Maddie said.

After the first couple of days, things quieted down and people stopped staring at Maddie all the time. By the end of the first week, only a couple of campers came up to her each day, so it was a lot better.

Celia tried every possible activity at camp, even if she thought she would be terrible at it or that it wouldn't be something she would enjoy. Aunt Agatha had limited her to what she had deemed "proper activities for a lady," and Celia relished the opportunity to do very un-proper and un-ladylike things. She rode horses, tried archery, participated in a mud fight, went swimming and water skiing at the lake, worked on ceramics and painting in Arts and Crafts, played Soccovolle (a game played in the demesne that was a combination of soccer and volleyball), attempted the ropes course, went on an overnight camping trip in the woods, and a whole host of other things that Aunt Agatha would never let her do in a million years. Even though she was still awful at sports, she wasn't the only one, and she tried to make up for her lack of skill with enthusiasm and enjoyment.

She was afraid that Maddie's trip to camp would be miserable, dealing with everyone thinking she was really Celia Fincastle, but Maddie seemed to enjoy playing the part. They tried hard to avoid conversations about the subject, but a few were inevitable, especially among their cabinmates. Every once in a while Celia would feel a little bad that they were misleading so many people, but when she saw how much Maddie was enjoying the attention and how much she could do without worrying about everyone watching her, she felt a little better.

Although Celia had been worried about running into some of the students from Renasci, since they knew who she really was, she never saw anyone she recognized. She was surprised to learn that the campers were all students at other schools for gifted students, located all over the country. She hadn't realized that the demesne was as big as it was, and it was interesting to hear about the other schools.

At the start of the second week, Celia's cabin had planned a campfire by the lake, and everyone in the Hedgehog cabin was excited. Ashleigh and Doxa told them to dress warmly, since it was a little chilly by the lake after dark, and to make sure they had fresh batteries in their flashlights. By dinnertime that evening, their table was buzzing with anticipation.

"All right, everyone," Ashleigh said, getting their attention. "We have about two hours before we can head to the campfire site at the lake, so we're going to do some other cabin activities. Let's head back to our cabin, grab our gear, and we'll head out."

Chapter Three

They walked as a group to their cabin by the woods.

"Hey, Maddie," Marisol said, coming up next to Celia. "Do you know if Celia likes s'mores?"

"S'mores?" Celia had never heard of them before.

"Don't tell me you don't know what s'mores are!?"

Celia shrugged. "Sorry."

"Hey, guys! Maddie doesn't know what a s'more is!"

"You're kidding!" Arletta said, spinning around in front of them and walking backwards. "Oh my gosh, you're going to *love* them!"

Bernie frowned. "I've never had one, either. What's a s'more?"

"They're a sandwich made with graham crackers, chocolate, and toasted marshmallow," Stephanie explained. She rolled her eyes. "I could eat a million of them."

"Yum," Celia said. "Sounds good. Are we going to make some at our campfire?"

"I hope so," Marisol said. "Hey, Ashleigh?"

"Yeah?"

"Are we gonna make s'mores tonight?"

Ashleigh laughed. "Are you kidding? Of *course* we're going to make s'mores. It wouldn't be a campfire without s'mores!"

"YAY!" everyone chanted.

Their counselors took them into the woods for some trust exercises before heading out to the lake. They brought them to a clearing with a tree stump standing in the middle, and set them up for trust falls. Keely went first, as she stood on the stump with her back to the rest of them and her arms crossed over her chest. As the counselors counted to three, she fell backward onto the arms of the other girls. One by one, they all took their turns on the stump. Celia was a bit nervous when she went, but they caught her just fine. When Maddie took her turn, she heard someone whisper that they hoped they didn't drop the next princep, but she couldn't tell who had spoken. She idly wondered what they would say if they knew *she* was really Celia and not Maddie.

After their trust falls in the woods, they headed to the Mess Hall to raid the kitchen for s'mores ingredients. With their arms loaded with graham crackers, chocolate bars, and marshmallows, they walked the path to the lake. They picked out some sticks for roasting marshmallows, and then the counselors got the campfire going in the fire ring.

When the first marshmallow was perfectly toasted, someone said, "Celia gets the first s'more!"

Celia watched with mixed emotions as Maddie carefully bit into her marshmallow sandwich. Somehow it seemed that the one time being Celia Fincastle was an advantage was when Celia wasn't being herself. Maddie licked the marshmallow off her lips, saying, "Mmmm," and Celia looked down at the sand. It wasn't that she felt jealous of Maddie getting the attention or even the perks, it was just...well, she wasn't really sure.

"You doing all right?" Doxa asked softly from beside her.

Celia glanced over and nodded, returning her gaze to the sand.

"You sure?"

She nodded again.

Doxa gave her a one-armed hug and rubbed her back. "I know it's hard," she said in a voice barely over a whisper.

"How would you know?" Celia asked quietly, unable to keep the bite out of her voice.

Doxa sighed. "It's a long story," she said.

"Um, Maddie?"

Celia looked up and saw Maddie standing in front of them, looking back and forth between them. She held out a s'more to Celia. "Here. For you," she said.

"Thanks," she said, taking the s'more.

"Hey, Celia!" someone called from the other side of the campfire. "Come sit with us."

"Just a minute," Maddie called back. "You want to come with?" she asked Celia, still glancing back and forth between her and Doxa.

"No," Celia said wearily. "You go ahead."

"Well, fine."

Celia sighed as she watched Maddie flounce off.

"She doesn't like me very much," Doxa said, watching her as well.

"Can you blame her?" Celia asked.

"No," she admitted. "I was pretty nasty last year." She sighed as she pulled her hand back and intertwined her fingers on her lap.

"Can I ask you something?"

"Sure."

Celia watched the flames flickering in the campfire. "Why are you here? Why did you decide to be a counselor this summer?"

"Easy answer? I needed something to do."

"And the hard answer?"

Doxa glanced at her. "Let's just say that I felt it was an important role that needed filling and leave it at that, shall we?" She pushed to her feet and walked over to Ashleigh, leaving Celia frowning in confusion.

Celia didn't talk to Maddie much the rest of the evening, she was so busy with everyone trying to spend time with Celia Fincastle, a.k.a. Maddie. Celia ended up talking with Tabitha some of the time, and the rest of the time she sat by herself and watched the flames shoots sparks up into the night sky. By the time Ashleigh and Doxa put the campfire out and had them start back toward the cabin, Celia was more than ready to call it a night.

"Hey, stranger," Maddie said, running over to her. "I didn't see you much tonight."

"Yeah, imagine that."

"What do you mean by that?"

"Nothing. Just that you seemed to have other people you wanted to spend your time with. It wasn't like you tried to spend any time with me."

"That's because you were spending all your time with your new best friend: Doxa!"

"At least she was talking to me! You were so busy with your fan club that you didn't even notice that I was there."

"If that's the case, then why did I bring you a s'more? I kind of had to notice that you were there to do that, didn't I?"

"Not that you stuck around after that."

"I invited you over with me. *You* turned me down."

"Why would I want to sit there and listen to everyone oohing and aahing over the 'next princep'?"

"Look, it's not *my* fault. And maybe if you had been there, I might have been able to talk to someone who wasn't busy oohing and aahing."

"It sure didn't seem like you wanted me there."

"I told you—you were talking to Doxa."

"Come on, M—, uh, Celia."

"No, *you* come on, Maddie. You're just jealous that everyone wanted to spend time with me."

"I am not. I couldn't care less."

Maddie suddenly stopped and looked at her carefully. "Are you okay?"

Celia closed her eyes. "I'm fine. Just…forget it, okay?"

"Come here," Maddie said, pulling her into a hug. "I'm sorry. I should have come over and talked with you."

"No, I'm sorry," Celia said, hugging her back. "I was just…in a bad mood, I guess."

Maddie stepped back and they started walking again. "Friends again?"

"Of course."

"I can't believe you've never had a s'more before," Maddie teased.

"Hey! It's not like Aunt Agatha would let me build a campfire in the backyard. And, of course, it's not proper to go tromping around in the woods, so I haven't been allowed to go to camp before."

"Oh, that's good!" Maddie laughed. "I can just see your aunt's face if you asked to build a campfire in the backyard."

As they made their way back to the Hedgehog cabin, their laughter rang out through the trees.

"Can you believe that we have to leave tomorrow? I wish we could stay with the rest of them," Celia said, folding a shirt and setting it in her trunk.

"I know," Maddie agreed. "How come we have to start school so early?"

Celia shrugged. "Got me."

"Oh, well," Maddie said, tossing down a pair of shorts. "I guess that's the price we have to pay for going to the best school in the demesne!"

It was Thursday, the last day of July, and they were packing because they had to leave early the next morning to catch the BUS to Renasci. The session didn't officially end until Saturday, but some of the campers had to be at school on August first, so they were leaving a couple of days early.

At the campfire that night, D.B. led them all in a good-bye song for those campers who would be leaving the next day. Since the camp wasn't officially closing yet, they didn't put out the campfire, but they did go through a closing ceremony so the people leaving early wouldn't miss out. They ended with another round of the camp handshake, and Celia couldn't help but giggle as D.B. told them to "shake your tail feathers" one last time.

Huddle-up that evening was full of people exchanging addresses with Celia and Maddie. They handed out their address at school, but Celia didn't really figure she would hear from any of them. She was fairly certain that, while they had been friendly and everything, they would probably stay in touch with Maddie, who they thought was Celia Fincastle, and not her friend, who wasn't as important in their eyes.

As the lights turned out in the cabin, Celia stared at the bottom of Maddie's bunk above her. It had been an amazing two weeks at Camp Altohodos, and she was glad she had been able to come with Maddie. For the first time in the past year, she'd felt like she could just be herself, without worrying about everything that went along with being Celia Fincastle. Yes, she'd had Doxa following her around, but even that hadn't been as bad as she'd expected. She was beginning to think Doxa really had changed, and that was probably the biggest surprise of all.

Her eyelids grew heavy as she thought about everything that had happened while she had been at camp. It had been a real eye-opener for her to learn about the other schools in the demesne, and an even bigger eye-opener to realize they all knew who she was, too. Of course, they had only known her by name, and now they knew her as Maddie, but, well, that wasn't something she was going to think about for now.

Despite the difficulty of changing places with Maddie and her mixed emotions about Maddie enjoying it so much, camp had really been a good time. Celia yawned and rolled over on her side. As she drifted off to sleep, her mind kept replaying all the good memories, and she fell asleep with a smile on her face.

Chapter Four
BUS Ride

Doxa shook her awake before the sun came up the next morning. "Come on. Get up! Time to get moving!" she said quietly.

"Mmphf."

Celia heard a chuckle. "Nice try, Fincastle. Out of bed," Doxa whispered.

Celia flipped back her covers and heard Maddie make a similar sound as Doxa woke her up. A little while later, still yawning, they were sitting in the Mess Hall having a bowl of cereal while they waited for their ride.

"Who's coming to get us?" Celia asked, her head propped up on her hand.

"Mr. Morven."

She brightened a bit. "Really?"

Doxa nodded. "He's bringing a van and taking you to the A-BUS. That will take you to the C-BUS station, so you can get to the school."

"Huh?" Celia had ridden the BUS, the Belowground Ushering System, to Renasci last year. But she'd never heard of the A-BUS before. "What's an A-BUS?"

"There are multiple BUS routes around the country. The A-BUS runs north-south along the eastern edge of the country.

You'll take that to the station where you pick up the C-BUS, which runs east-west through the middle of the country. That takes you to Renasci," Doxa explained.

"Oh."

Maddie, who was practically falling asleep in her cereal bowl, didn't say anything.

Doxa glanced at her watch. "You'd better hurry up. Mr. Morven should be here soon."

They rushed to finish their breakfast and then waited by the front driveway. A few other campers were sitting by the driveway, most of them looking as drowsy as Celia felt. As the sun was just beginning to peek over the lake, a white van pulled into the loop and stopped in front of the bench where they were sitting. Celia nudged Maddie, who had dozed off leaning against her shoulder, and watched as a slender man with wire frame glasses climbed out of the driver's seat. He walked around the front of the van and smiled when he saw them.

"Good morning, ladies," he said.

"Hi, Mr. Morven," Celia said. She had met Mr. Morven last year, and he had been the one to get her both to and from school last year. No matter what he was wearing, he always managed to look quite presentable, as if he were stepping off the pages of a fashion magazine.

"Hmphf," Maddie muttered as she stretched.

Mr. Morven turned to Doxa. "Hi, Doxa."

"Hi, Mr. Morven. The girls are all set. I made sure that *Maddie* has her backpack and *Celia's* things are all packed in her trunk." Celia noticed that Doxa made an effort to stress their switched names.

Mr. Morven looked at them in confusion. "Oh-kay," he said slowly.

"Should we load their stuff in the van?" Doxa asked,

hitching a thumb over her shoulder in the direction of their trunks.

Mr. Morven looked between them, trying to figure out what was going on. When he turned to Doxa, she tilted her head in the direction of the other campers on the benches nearby, and although he still looked confused, he said, "Yeah. We'd better get on our way."

In a few moments, Celia found herself sitting next to Maddie in the middle seat of the van, their trunks packed into the back. Mr. Morven beeped the horn as he shifted the van into gear, and Celia waved to Doxa as they pulled away. Maddie leaned against the window and fell asleep almost instantly, and though Celia was tired, she didn't feel very sleepy, so she watched the scenery as it went past.

Mr. Morven glanced in the rearview mirror and saw she was still awake. "Did you have a good summer, Celia?"

"It was okay. Camp was fun."

"That's good." He tapped his fingers on the steering wheel. "Um, mind if I ask why Doxa was calling you two the wrong names?"

Celia shrugged. "We just thought it would be fun to switch places while we were at camp. It gave me chance to just be a normal kid for a couple of weeks."

"Oh." He shrugged, too. "Well, I guess. Was Doxa your counselor?"

"One of them."

"Hm."

They rode in silence for a few miles. "How far are we driving to the BUS station?"

"Oh, it's not very far. The BUS, as you know, travels much faster than this van, so we'll take it as much as possible."

"Oh." Celia well remembered how fast the BUS traveled—it made her feel extremely nauseous last time.

Chapter Four

The hum of the tires on the road and the noise of the engine lulled Celia back to sleep, and she didn't wake up again until they were pulling into a dirt parking lot. A glance at the clock told her she'd only slept for about fifteen minutes. She looked around, but all she saw were pine trees.

"Where are we?"

"The BUS station," Mr. Morven said, turning off the engine.

Celia figured it wouldn't do her much good to ask any more questions. The BUS stations all seemed to be in unusual places and never looked like what they were. She poked Maddie, who hadn't woken up yet, and climbed out of the van. Mr. Morven went to get a cart for their trunks, and she tried to see what was behind the cluster of trees he'd walked toward. A little bit later, they left the van and headed for a path that curved around through the forest. The trees were too thick to see through, so it was a big surprise when Celia found herself in a big clearing with an old-looking train depot standing in front of her.

They walked through the front doors and into the building, and Mr. Morven ushered them over to the ticket counter. He bought three tickets to the C-BUS station, and asked when the BUS would be pulling in.

"Any time now," the ticket seller replied, an older man with bushy white eyebrows who was chewing on an unlit cigar. He pulled the cigar out of his mouth and held it up to them. "My wife made me quit some twenty years ago, but she let me keep a few just for the memories," he said, winking at Celia, who grinned back at him. "Are you heading back to school?"

"Yes, sir," Celia replied. "We're students at Renasci."

"Ah, fine school, fine school," he said. "My kids went there. Well, you all have a good trip."

"Let's head out to the platform," Mr. Morven said, steering his cart toward the doors on the back side of the building.

Only a few minutes after they sat down on a bench, a bright yellow streak pulled up along the tracks in front of them. As it pulled to a stop, Celia noticed that it looked exactly like the BUS she had ridden last year, only that one had been blue. The sunshine yellow vehicle looked like an enormous caterpillar sitting there, it's round cars lining up like marbles, with windows in the compartments and a door every few cars.

They waited for the passengers to leave the train, then the conductor called for boarding and they loaded on. Mr. Morven picked a compartment midway through the train, and loaded their trunks under the gold-colored benches. They settled into their seats as he slid the compartment door closed, and soon they were on their way.

"You might want to look out the window while you can," Mr. Morven said. "We'll head underground pretty soon. The A-BUS travels underground most of the way."

Celia watched out the window, but she noticed that Maddie went back to sleep. In very little time, they did head underground, and the view out the window switched to a dark wall. The lights on the train lit up the inside, and Celia was pleasantly surprised to find she didn't feel as sick as last time.

"So, did you work on your family tree this summer?" Mr. Morven asked her.

Celia was glad to finally talk to someone who understood her predicament. "I tried," she said, "but it's not like I can just ask my parents about the rest of my family. I don't have anyone to interview."

He nodded. "We figured as much. A few of us are working on something, so don't worry about it."

"But I didn't finish the assignment."

He looked at her with understanding. "I know. But trust me, your professors will understand. And unless I'm very much mistaken, they'll probably cut you a little slack. You'll still have to finish your family tree, mind you, but given your situation I would imagine that they'll give you a little extra time to use the library and some of the other resources at the school."

"But how am I going to find anything on my family?"

"Well, it will be difficult to find information on some people, but I would think there should be some information about your parents and grandparents in the library, since your grandmother was princep before you."

"She was?"

His eyebrows rose. "You didn't know?" He rolled his eyes. "Well, of *course* you didn't know," he said to himself. "How *would* you know?" He shook his head. "I'm sorry, Celia. Forgive me for being so dense. Yes, your grandmother was the princep before you were chosen. She served as princep for nearly forty years before you came along."

"Really?"

"Absolutely. So I'm sure there's information about her somewhere in the library." He crossed one leg over and rested his ankle on his other knee. "I think Professor Legaspi was working on pulling together some information for you, as well."

"What was my grandmother's name?"

"Violet..." He shook his head. "Her last name escapes me at the moment. But I'm sure you can find that out easily."

Celia nodded. "I still can't interview anyone."

"True," he agreed, "but I don't think any of your professors will hold that against you, given the circumstances."

"Won't all the other kids complain?"

He winked at her. "That's one of the advantages of being the Overseer's princep."

Celia sighed and looked down at her shoes. Sometimes she wondered what would happen if she didn't want to be princep. Would people be upset that she had gotten so much special treatment and then not taken the job? And how was she supposed to know if she wanted the job in the first place? No one else she knew was trying to figure out if they wanted a job that everyone already assumed they would take.

"Don't worry about it, Celia. Everything will work out." Mr. Morven set his attaché case on the bench beside him and pulled out a stack of papers. "Mind if I get some work done?" he asked. Celia shook her head. "I guess there's not a whole lot for you to do, since you already ate breakfast and Maddie's asleep." He checked his watch. "We have about an hour until we get to the station, and then you could get something to do at one of the rathskellers," he said, referring to the shops at the platform for the C-BUS.

"I think I might take a nap and try to catch up on some sleep," Celia said.

"That might be a good idea."

Celia scrunched up her sweatshirt in the corner between the seat and the outside wall and used it as a pillow. She dozed on and off, at one point noticing that Mr. Morven was talking on a cell phone, but she didn't wake up enough to pay attention to his conversation. She did wake up, though, when Mr. Morven shook her shoulder.

"Come on, girls," he said, shaking both Celia and Maddie to wake them up.

Celia yawned as she sat up and stretched. She looked out the window and saw that they were pulling into the platform she had been to last year.

"We have to get off the train before it leaves again. They stay here for a little bit longer than some of the other stations because it's a major stop, but we can't just sit around here all day," Mr. Morven said, gathering his papers and putting them away. "Can you girls grab your trunks?"

Chapter Four

They dragged their trunks along behind them as they left the BUS and stepped onto the platform. Celia noticed the same rathskellers were still located across the platform from the tracks, and her stomach started to growl when she smelled something delicious in the air. Breakfast seemed like it had been a long time ago.

"We'll just sit here until the C-BUS gets in," Mr. Morven said, stopping at a bench near the end of the platform on the far side from the stairs.

"How long until the BUS gets here?" Maddie asked, still yawning.

"The A-BUS leaves in twenty minutes and the C-BUS should pull in about ten minutes later. They change the schedules a bit on starting days for the schools, in order for everyone to make it on the BUS and off to school." He looked over at the rathskellers. "Did you want to get anything to eat while you're waiting?" Maddie's stomach growled and they all laughed. "I guess so."

"Maddie's always hungry," Celia teased.

"I can't help it," Maddie said.

"Come on," Celia said, grabbing her hand and pulling her to her feet. "Let's go get something for snack. Are you staying here?" she asked Mr. Morven.

"Sure," he said.

"Thanks." They headed down the platform and stopped at the one selling sopapillas. "You want some?" Celia asked Maddie.

"What are they? I've never heard of them."

"They're really good." A few minutes later they were wandering along, munching on their sopapillas and checking out the other rathskellers. "I stopped in here last year," Celia said, pointing to the book and magazine rathskeller. "Want to check it out?"

Maddie shrugged. "Sure." As they headed into the stall, Maddie squealed and ran over to a display of magazines. Celia, rubbing her now-aching ear, followed her over. "Look!" Maddie said, holding the magazine out to her. "It's Ed Bornhoft!"

"Who?"

"*Celia!*"

"What? I don't know who you're talking about."

"Ed Bornhoft! I told you about him last year, remember? He's, like, the best Soccovolle player ever. And look at him!" she cried, shoving the magazine under Celia's nose. "Don't you think he's cute?"

Celia looked at the curly-haired young man on the cover. No, he certainly wasn't ugly, but she didn't think he was worth going so crazy about. Maybe she was missing something. "Um, yeah, he's okay."

"I *have* to get this," Maddie said, digging in her pocket for her money. When she pulled out a fistful of bills and coins, Celia looked at them in amazement. As Maddie counted, Celia studied the collection of money over her shoulder.

Last year she'd learned the demesne used a different kind of currency, called a konig. But she had never actually *seen* a konig before. "What *are* all those?" Celia asked, her curiosity finally getting the best of her.

"What?" Maddie asked. Seeing Celia looking at the money in her hand, she said, "These? Haven't you seen money before?"

"Well, yeah," Celia said, feeling a little stupid. "But not in the demesne."

"Really?" Maddie sifted through her money and pulled out a gold octagon-shaped coin. "This is a konig. The bills are for twenty, fifty, one hundred, five hundred, and one thousand konigs, not that my parents gave me that much. The other coins are for one, five, and ten konigs, and one, five, and ten reynas, and there are fifty reynas in a konig."

"Why don't you just use dollars and cents?"

Maddie shrugged. "Got me. That's just the way it's always been, I guess." She went back to counting out her money. The coins in her hand were all different colors, some of them red, some of them green, others blue, purple, or silver. Although she was interested in the different money, Celia was glad she didn't have to worry about it. Mr. Morven had given her a card last year that worked like a credit card to pay for all her purchases.

Celia looked over when she heard a whistle and saw the bright yellow A-BUS moving out of the station. Only a few more minutes and they could get on the C-BUS and grab a compartment.

"Are you getting anything?" Maddie asked her, carrying her now-paid-for magazine in her hands.

"No, that's okay."

"You can look through my magazine, if you want."

"Thanks."

"Celia?" Both girls turned toward the platform when they heard someone call. "Hey, Celia! Is that you?" They headed out toward the front of the stall. "Maddie! Celia!" They noticed someone waving from across the platform, so they headed in that direction.

"It's Josh!" Celia said as they got closer. "Hi, Josh!"

"Hi!" he replied, coming over to meet them. Josh Rumbles was one of their classmates, a member of their coterie, the groups into which all the students at Renasci were divided. He had spiky hair and an athletic build, which made sense since he was an exceptional Soccovolle player. "How was your summer?"

"You mean, besides dealing with my siblings?" Maddie asked.

"Well, yeah, I guess."

"Not bad. Camp was *great*. You should have seen it. Celia and I switched places and everyone went crazy. It was so funny."

"It wasn't *that* funny," Celia said. "How was the Summer Tournament?"

Josh made a face. "Lousy. It rained a lot, and we lost all our matches."

"Oh, that's too bad. I'm sorry."

He shrugged. "Oh, well. Hopefully we'll make it back there next year and do better."

"Is anyone else here?" Maddie asked, referring to the rest of the kids in their coterie.

Josh looked around. "I haven't seen anyone, but I just got here. The A-BUS was a little late."

"You took the A-BUS, too?" Maddie asked.

"Yeah, from Florida. We ran late, so we had to stop at the second platform and lug all our stuff over here."

"Is there more than one BUS for each route?" Celia asked. She'd assumed there was just one train for each line, but if Josh had taken the same route they had, there was no way he'd been on the same train.

"Yeah," Josh answered. "I think there're two for each line, but I'm not sure. Usually they pass about midway, but I guess the schedules get a little mixed up for the schools."

Their conversation was drowned out by the sound of the C-BUS arriving. Celia watched as the vehicle pulled in, looking identical to the A-BUS only colored vivid blue instead of yellow.

"I guess we'd better get our stuff loaded," Celia said. "Do you want to share a compartment?" she asked Josh.

"Sure. I'll let Heath know if I see him," he said, referring to another one of their friends.

"Okay. See you in a bit."

She and Maddie headed back over to the bench where Mr. Morven was watching their trunks. They quickly picked a compartment and loaded their things onto the BUS.

"I'll let you girls ride on your own this time, if that's all right," Mr. Morven said, tilting his head toward the front of the train. "If you need me, I'll be a few compartments that way."

"Thanks, Mr. Morven," Celia said.

"There they are," Celia heard someone say from the other direction. She turned and saw Josh and Heath making their way up the aisle toward their compartment. She smiled when she saw Heath, whose blond hair still looked like he hadn't combed it when he got up that morning. He always reminded Celia of a surfer or a skateboarder, and his laid-back attitude matched his look.

"Hi, Heath," she said.

Maddie stuck her head out the door over Celia's shoulder. "Heath! How was your summer?"

"Totally churry," he said, flipping his hair out of his eyes.

"Um…is that good?" Celia asked. She still had a little trouble with the slang in the demesne.

"Better than good," Josh said.

"Oh. Well, great!"

Before long, they were talking and laughing and didn't even notice that the time had flown by until they heard the "ALL ABOARD! ALL ABOARD," announcement over the loudspeakers. They watched the confusion on the platform as everyone hurried to get to where they belonged, whether on or off the train. There was a whistle and a loud hiss, and then the vehicle lurched into motion. They waved at everyone on the platform, although they couldn't make out any faces after the first few seconds, and then they sat back for the long ride to their school.

The conductor, a tall, skinny man named Zosimo Bearden, came around and punched their tickets. When they were aboveground again, Josh pulled out a deck of cards and they played a couple of hands of rummy before Maddie's stomach started to growl again. Since it was getting close to lunchtime, they decided to head back to the dining car to get something to eat.

It wasn't easy to walk on the BUS while it was moving, as it traveled at a tremendous rate of speed, so they bounced their way back with their hands out to the side in case they had to catch their balance. They sort of fell into the dining car, and Celia looked around with a smile on her face. She *loved* the dining car. It had round booths along one side, and a counter with stools on the other side that curved around and ran the length of the car. It was all decorated in blue, like the rest of the BUS, but it had the feel of an old-fashioned soda fountain.

They grabbed one of the round booths and tried to figure out what they were going to order. The dining car could serve anything you wanted, no matter what. After changing their minds many times, they finally decided on their choices, and Josh offered to head up to the counter to give their order to the man behind the counter.

While they were waiting for their food, two girls came up to their table. Both were tall and slender and they looked nearly identical, but while one had very pale eyes and hair, the other had equally dark eyes and hair. Celia recognized them immediately. Odette and Odile Signus had been some of the first people to befriend her at school last year.

"Hi, guys," she said.

"Hey, everyone. How was your summer?" Odile asked.

"Good." "Great." "Not bad." "Awesome!"

"Did you two do anything interesting?" Celia asked.

Odette nodded. "We spent a couple weeks at Uncle Ezra's house. It's such a neat place, so that was fun. Otherwise, we did a summer ballet program, and a couple of intense training classes, but that was pretty much it."

"Sounds like you were busy," Maddie said.

Odette shrugged. "A little, I guess."

When the man behind the counter called their order number, Odile and Odette left them to eat their meal. A few other people stopped by their table to say hello to Celia, and she remembered with fondness the time at camp when she hadn't had to deal with all of that. Looking around the dining car, Celia noticed a few new kids, which she assumed were the incoming seventh-year students. Some of them were already talking with their new friends; others were sitting quietly by themselves watching their surroundings with wide eyes. She remembered how overwhelmed she had been last year and felt a little sorry for those kids.

Their stomachs full, Celia and her friends headed back to their compartment. When they were all sitting down again, Josh asked, "So, did you guys finish your family tree assignment?"

"Yeah," Heath said. "It was pretty easy, since my brother had to do his a few years ago. He did most of the work for me."

"Heath! I seriously doubt that your professors are going to let you get away with just using the stuff your brother did," Maddie said.

He shrugged. "Well, it's not like my family changed any since then, other than getting older, I mean."

Maddie shook her head. "No way am I letting Huxton mooch off of my work. He'll have to do all the research on his own, just like I did."

"I thought it was kind of interesting," Josh said. "I've already learned about some really cool people on my family tree."

"Really?" Celia asked.

"Yeah. Like this one guy, my great-great-great-great...I don't know how many 'greats' grandfather. He was the official record keeper for the princep. Isn't that neat?"

"Wow," Maddie said. "I wish I had some interesting people in my family. They're all so boring."

"I'll bet your family tree is really cool, Celia," Josh said, looking at her.

"Um...well, I haven't gotten very far yet." She couldn't very well say that she hadn't been able to do anything.

"Yeah, there are probably tons of cool people in your family," Maddie said.

Celia said nothing, as she didn't know what to say. How could she tell them that she didn't know anyone on her family tree other than Aunt Agatha, who wasn't even an aunt at all? They would never understand what it was like to have no idea about your family, not even your parents.

The conversation moved on to all sorts of different topics, like what classes they might be taking that year and what the new seventh-years would be like, but Celia stayed fairly quiet. A little while later, they had all dozed off and slept most of the remainder of the journey. Even if Celia hadn't been tired, she probably would have tried to sleep once they reached the mountains. The BUS climbed the mountains underground through a series of switchbacks, which made Celia's stomach very queasy. She woke up briefly when they announced that they were approaching the mountains and everyone needed to stay in their seats, but she fell back asleep quickly.

When she woke up next, she saw that Heath was awake and looking out the window at the scenery, which now looked much different from the plains they had been traveling across before. High, jagged mountain peaks towered around them, and they were surrounded by tall pine trees.

"We must be pretty close to school, huh?"

"Yeah," Heath replied. "They just gave the ten minute announcement."

Celia looked over at Josh and Maddie. "I guess we'd better wake them up."

As the BUS pulled into the station, they heard, "We are approaching the Renasci Station," over the loudspeaker. "Please remain in your seat until the vehicle comes to a complete stop, then proceed in an orderly fashion to the nearest exit. Your belongings will be delivered to your quarters. Seventh-years should gather on the right side of the platform, as indicated. Thank you."

Celia looked out the compartment door and laughed as she saw all the people filling the aisle, just as they had last year. And, just like last year, they all fell forward when the train jerked to a stop and had to scramble to get back on their feet. "You'd think some of them would learn, wouldn't you?" she said.

The rest of them laughed, too. "Or maybe at least learn to listen and pay attention," Maddie said.

Once the aisle had cleared out, Celia grabbed her backpack and they made their way out of the compartment and down to the nearest door. Stepping off the train brought them onto the bustling platform. They jostled their way through the doors of the station at the back edge of the platform, then through the small building and out the other side. As they stepped through the doors, Celia smiled as she looked up at the huge building in front of them, it's massive beams, large granite steps, and oversized wooden doors looking very welcoming and comforting to her.

She'd finally made it back to Renasci.

Chapter Five

Return to Renasci

"Come on," Celia said, rushing toward the double doors in the center. She couldn't wait to get back inside and see everyone again. She took off, not looking to see if anyone followed her or not. Weaving her way through the crowd of students, she made her way into the antechamber and then through past the double curved staircases that led to the second floor. Stepping into the enormous room that was Main Hall, she spun in a circle and took a deep breath. Somehow it even *smelled* better here.

"Celia!" she heard someone call. Looking over to where the voice had come from, she spied a woman with curly reddish-blond hair and bright green glasses heading her way.

"Professor Legaspi!"

The woman rushed over and stood in front of Celia, smiling as she studied her. "Oh, who cares," she finally said, and swept Celia up in a hug. "It's so good to see you," she said.

"You, too," Celia said. It was kind of strange, she thought, that her professor felt more like an older sister or maybe an aunt than any sort of...well, teacher. But Professor Legaspi had taken more of an interest in Celia than most, since she had been close friends with Celia's mother.

Chapter Five

"I hear it's been a rough couple of weeks," Professor Legaspi said quietly.

"Kind of," Celia admitted.

Professor Legaspi stepped back, glancing over at some of the other staff members across the room. "We'll talk later, okay? Right now I have to go meet the new students."

"All right."

Maddie, Josh, and Heath caught up with her as she watched Professor Legaspi walk away. "Should we head up to quarters?" Celia asked.

Josh shrugged. "Why not?"

Main Hall was just as busy and loud as last year, with everyone saying hello to each other. The four of them made their way toward the opposite end of the room, and Celia looked at the wall of windows at the end of the room with delight. She'd never get tired of seeing that view.

They turned and headed down a hallway, through a few doors, down another hallway, and through a few more doors. Halfway down the next hallway, they turned through a set of doors that led to the stairs. Two flights later, they found themselves in front of a pair of elaborately carved doors bearing lions and crowns which were flanked by two lion statues.

"Here we are," Josh said, pushing the door open.

Celia stepped through the doors and immediately felt like she was home. The lounge sat directly in front of her, with its comfy chairs and couches, and as she turned to the left, she saw the door to her room at the end of the hallway in front of her. The boys went down the hallway to the right to their room while Maddie followed Celia into their room.

The walls in the room were covered with the same ornate purple and gold wallpaper that covered the rest of the walls in the Mensaleon quarters. In the center of the room was an area rug with a collection of armchairs. Large lanterns hanging from the ceiling acted as chandeliers and gave off a cozy glow.

"My bed!" Maddie cried dramatically, flinging herself at the unit she had occupied last year.

The beds at Renasci were very unusual. The bed itself was located high in the air, like a bunk bed. Underneath was a column of drawers and a desk. At one end was a bench and some hooks for hanging coats, and the other end had a ladder going up to the bed. Each bed had two windows with bookcases in between and at each end, and thick purple curtains that pulled around to close off the bed from the room and cover the windows.

The best part of all was the large walk-in closet located under the bed at the back. The door would only open for the owner of the closet, so Celia headed over to her closet and set her backpack inside before closing the door again. She looked over at the beds on the other side of the room, remembering Doxa and her groupies staying there last year. Now that the new seventh-years would be coming in, Celia and her classmates would be the older kids in the room for the rest of their time at the school.

"Did you want to change your bed, now that the rest of them aren't here?" Maddie asked, walking over to the bed Doxa had occupied.

Celia shook her head. "No, I like looking out at the woods instead of the commons." Her bed sat along the outside wall on the far corner of the building. She looked out at the trees that surrounded the school and had a view of the stars in the sky each night. The beds along the inside wall looked toward the commons, a grassy open area between the buildings that curved around from the main building. While the commons were nice to look at, with mascot statues for the coteries and picnic tables for when the weather was nice, Celia preferred not to look at the side of the other buildings.

"Yeah, I think I like my bed, too," Maddie said.

There was a slight commotion at the door, and both girls looked over to see an Asian girl and a girl with blond hair come into the room.

"Libby! Galena!" Maddie said. Libby Cresswell—the blond girl—and Galena Zwingle were the other two girls in their year.

"Hi, Maddie! Celia!" Galena said, waving to them as she walked across the room. "Have you met the new seventh-years?"

Maddie shook her head. "Nope. They haven't shown up yet."

Libby and Galena looked at each other. "Do you think we can switch beds?" Libby asked.

Celia shrugged. "Try the closet and see," she said.

Galena walked over to the bed on the same wall as Maddie's. "Not that I didn't like my bed, but since it's on the inside wall, I didn't have any windows," she explained. She disappeared into the corner and came out a moment later. "It opened!" she said.

Libby hurried over to the bed sharing the same corner. "This one's mine, then," she said, hanging her sweatshirt on one of the hooks.

Galena walked over to her old bed. "The door won't open anymore," she said after trying to get into the closet.

"Guess you're stuck with your new bed," Maddie said.

"Hey, fine with me!" She looked around the room. "When does our stuff get here?" she asked.

Celia shrugged. "I don't know."

"Well, I'm gonna go catch up with my brother. Want to come with, Libby?"

"Sure."

"I think I'll stay here until my stuff and the seventh-years get here," Celia said, sitting down in one of the cushy armchairs in the center of the room.

"Okay. See you later."

Maddie flopped into the chair next to Celia. "I hope we get some good roommates."

"Me, too."

There was another commotion at the door and they looked over to see a pile of trunks and luggage coming through the doorway with only a pair of feet sticking out of the bottom. The pile fell to the floor with a loud thump, and they saw a burly boy grinning at them. "Hi, girls," he said. "Here's your stuff."

"Thanks," Celia said, standing up. "Did you carry it all the way up here?"

"Yeah, but it's no big deal," he said. "I'm in Corpanthera."

"Oh. Well, thanks."

"No prob."

All the students at Renasci were divided into coteries based on their strongest abilities. Celia was in Mensaleon, which had students who had gifts of the mind, but she still remembered her surprise last year when the book that divided everyone out said she could be in all five coteries. Students in Corpanthera were the ones whose strongest gifts were exceptional physical feats, such carrying ridiculously heavy loads of luggage. The other coteries were Tattotauri, for students with the gift of touch, Sprachursus, for students with the gift of tongue, and Aquilegia, for students with the gift of sight. Each coterie had a dean, and Professor Twombly was the dean of Mensaleon, while Professor Legaspi was the dean of Aquilegia.

Celia and Maddie pulled their things out of the pile of luggage and started unpacking. Just as Celia pushed her trunk into place in her closet, she heard voices in the room. Coming out of her closet, she saw Professor Twombly, with her brightly-colored clothes and her short flame-colored hair, surrounded by eight slightly scared-looking kids.

Chapter Five

"Oh, hi, girls," Professor Twombly said when she saw Celia and Maddie. "Everyone, these are two of our sixth-year students. Girls, these are our new seventh-years."

"Hi," Maddie said, waving at them.

"Girls, you'll be in here with Maddie and Celia, so you can go ahead and pick beds and get your things unpacked. Boys, if you'll follow me, I'll show you to your room." She turned and left the room, the four boys following her, leaving four girls with very wide eyes standing just inside the doorway.

"I'm Maddie," she said, introducing herself. "Welcome to Renasci. What are your names?"

"I'm Tiffany," a girl with big brown eyes and dark blond hair said.

"Jenilee," said the girl next to her, who had very long brown hair and soft green eyes.

"Caydi," said the next girl, with black hair and very pale skin.

"Audra," said the last girl, a short girl with brown hair and bright blue eyes.

Celia looked at her. "Audra," she repeated, placing the name. "You're Blaine's sister." When the girl nodded, she said, "I'm Celia. I don't know if Blaine mentioned me, but he said you might end up in Mensaleon."

Audra brightened. "Oh, yeah! Blaine did tell me about you. He said you were a really cool person, just like another little sister."

Celia laughed. "Yeah, Blaine's a cool guy. I wish I had a brother like him."

"Hey, wait," Jenilee said. "You're Celia Fincastle, aren't you?"

"Guilty," Celia said, resigned.

"Oh, wow. Neat!" "No kidding!" "Cool."

"Can we please not make a big deal about it?" Celia pleaded.

"Oh, sure." The girls all nodded.

"We're in these beds," Maddie said, indicating the beds behind her, "so you can pick from those four over there."

As the girls pulled their things out of the luggage pile, Audra leaned over to Celia. "Which bed is yours?"

"That one," Celia said, pointing to her bed.

"Can I have the bed next to yours?"

"I don't see why not."

Audra grinned. "Great."

There was a short discussion amongst the newcomers, and then they all dragged their things over to their newly-chosen beds. While the new girls began unpacking and settling in to their new home, Celia and Maddie decided to head out to greet the rest of the kids in the coterie. "We'll be out in the lounge," Maddie told them.

"Okay. See you later!"

As Celia stepped into the lounge behind Maddie, she heard someone call her name once again. A bubbly redhead ran over and gave her a hug. "Hi, Celia!"

"Hi, Merry. How was your summer?" Merry was Celia's student mentor, and Celia didn't think she had ever met a more cheerful person in her life.

"Oh, it was great! I got to help out at my parents' coffee shop and bakery, and I met the most amazing guy. He has these cute little dimples and he's just so sweet!"

"Sounds great," Celia said.

Merry gave her another hug. "Oh, it's just so great to see you again!"

"All right, everyone!" Professor Twombly called from the entryway. "It's time to head down for dinner. Seventh-years, please follow me. The rest of you can go on ahead."

"Great. I'm starved!" Maddie said.

"*Maddie!*" Celia rolled her eyes and laughed. They followed the stream of people heading out the door and down to the refectory. Since the first meal was done differently from the rest of the year, they all sat divided by coterie and year, so Celia and Maddie sat with Libby, Galena, Heath, Josh, and the other Mensaleon sixth-years, Burnsy Nesbit and Kittrick Borega.

Headmaster Doyen, a slightly pudgy, balding man with two patches of hair just above his ears, stood at a podium at the front of the room and called for attention. The room quieted slowly, as everyone turned to listen. "Welcome back, everyone, to another year of learning at Renasci. I hope you all had a nice summer holiday and are ready to get back to class." A loud groan rose from the students, Celia included, as they followed the tradition repeated every year. "Ah, yes," Headmaster Doyen said. "The obligatory groan. Ah, well, so goes another year. Before we begin our meal, I'd like to take a moment to introduce the newest member of our staff, Mr. Bazemore, who will be taking the position of Vice-Chair of Student Affairs. Mr. Bazemore comes here with his son, Quiroz, who will be joining us as a student. I hope all of you will make them feel welcome."

There was a smattering of applause, but it seemed most people were too interested in dinner to pay much attention to most of what Headmaster Doyen was saying.

"One last reminder for all of you, and then we can begin eating. I'm sure you're aware that today is Friday, which means you have an extra two days over the weekend before classes begin on Monday." A cheer rose up from the tables. "And on that note, I believe we will start eating. Servers, if you will..." The headmaster sat down at the staff table and fourth-year students all over the room jumped up to collect the dishes of food off the back tables and distribute them among the tables for their coterie.

"Mmm. Chili, cornbread...It all smells great," Maddie said, serving herself a big bowl of chili.

"Oh, wow," Celia said after taking her first bite of chili. "We've had chili at home before, but it never tasted like this! I think Aunt Agatha needs to hire a better cook."

"You have a *cook* at your house?" Kitt asked incredulously.

Celia shrugged. "Aunt Agatha refuses to make anything harder than toast, and she won't let me try."

"My mom would be so jealous," Heath said. "She hates to cook. Good thing my dad doesn't mind helping out or they'd probably have pizza a lot."

"Hey, Heath, is your brother back at school this year?" Celia asked.

Heath nodded, his mouth full of food. "Last year, too," he said, his voice muffled by the huge bite he had taken.

"He's a first-year? I didn't know that," Maddie said.

"Is he on the Soccovolle team again?" Josh asked.

" 'Course."

"Good. I'm looking forward to a rematch," Josh said. "I'm sure we can beat them again this year."

"Don't be so sure, man," Heath said, shaking his head. "They were pretty mad they lost last year on a tiebreaker. They're out for revenge."

"Ooh, I'm so scared." Josh laughed. "Bring it on."

"Does that mean you're gonna wear your...um, *colorful* match attire, Heath?" Maddie asked.

"Yup." Since Heath's brother was in Corpanthera while he was in Mensaleon, Heath wore the colors for both coteries at last year's matches. It made for a rather interesting look, with his odd combination of blue and purple.

"Oh," Maddie said. "Great." She didn't exactly sound enthusiastic.

"Hey, Burnsy," Libby asked the red-haired boy on her left. "How was your drama camp this summer?"

"Fine," he said quietly, his face glowing bright red. Burnsy was a really nice kid, but he was painfully shy. He was quite unusual, though, since he was a wonderfully talented actor. He barely said anything around school, but when he got up on a stage, he just seemed to come alive. He'd played the lead in the school play last year, and everyone had been amazed at how spectacular he'd been.

"Did you have a good time?"

"Yeah. It was fun."

"What do you guys think about the genealogy project?" Galena asked.

"My parents are being no help at all," Kitt complained. "They won't tell me anything. I ask them a question about one of my relatives, and instead of giving me the answer, they make me call them up or write them a letter. It's so annoying!"

"Yours, too?" Libby said. "That's what my parents are doing. It takes forever."

"I found this guy that was the official record keeper for the princep in my family tree," Josh said.

"Oh, neat," Galena said. "I'll bet your family tree has lots of interesting people on it," she said to Celia.

"Well . . ." Celia sighed. "It's a work in progress, but, yeah, I guess so. Doesn't everyone have someone interesting in their family?"

Maddie snorted. "Not me. My family is dull as dirt."

"Oh, come on. I'll bet that if you do a little research you'll find someone really interesting."

"Yeah, I'll believe *that* when I see it."

The servers brought dessert out to the tables and Celia's mouth watered just looking at the delicious confection. Mini tiered cakes covered with ribbons of frosting were given to each person, and in no time at all the cakes had vanished.

"Oh, that was so good," Kitt said, sitting back from the table after licking his fork clean.

"Too bad we don't have that every day," Josh said.

Celia felt a touch on her shoulder and looked up. "Hi, everyone," Professor Legaspi said as she stood between Celia and Maddie, a hand on each of their shoulders.

"Hi, Professor Legaspi," everyone at the table chorused.

"Welcome back," she said. "Did you all enjoy your meal?"

"Um-hm." "Yes." "Definitely." "Totally!"

"Great! Well, don't let me stop your conversation. I just came over to chat with Celia for a moment." She squatted down between the chairs. "Can you come up to my office just before breakfast tomorrow?" she asked Celia quietly.

"Sure."

"Okay. We'll talk then, all right?"

"All right."

"See you all later," she said, standing up and giving them a wave as she walked off.

Headmaster Doyen dismissed them soon after, and everyone filed out of the refectory and headed off to their quarters. Celia's feet were dragging by the time she made it to the top of the stairs at the Mensaleon quarters. She and Maddie had gotten up very early and it had been a long day.

A couple of the first-year guys held the doors open for all the students, and Celia muttered, "Thanks," as she walked through.

"Oh, look. The mail came," a third-year student named Rebecca said, heading over to a detailed metal box on the side of the lounge. "Hey, Celia," she said. "There's something in here for you."

"What's Aunt Agatha sending now?" she said as she walked over to take the envelope. "Last year she sent me a letter telling me to leave her alone the whole year. I can't imagine what she wants this year. Thanks," she said when Rebecca held it out to her.

She carried it into her room, noticing that the handwriting on the envelope wasn't Aunt Agatha's writing. It looked more like someone her own age, since the "i" in her name was dotted with a heart. She sat down in an armchair and tore open the seal. After scanning the first few lines of the letter, she held it out to Maddie. "Here," she said. "It's for you."

"What? It's addressed to you."

"I know. But this letter is definitely not for me."

Maddie took the letter and started reading, then burst out laughing. "Oh, I hadn't thought about that," she said. "When we gave everyone at camp our address, I didn't think that they would still be writing to the switched Celia and Maddie."

Celia shook her head. "Who's it from?"

"Arletta," Maddie said, glancing down at the bottom of the page. "She says she just wanted to keep in touch."

"Maddie, we left this morning. They just saw us last night."

"I know."

"Which reminds me, however. How *does* a letter get here so fast? There's no way she sent that a few days ago."

Maddie waved her hand, distracted, since she was trying to read her letter and talk with Celia at the same time. "Something with the blue light. I forget the name of it. My grandmother uses it all the time."

"Oh." Maddie didn't say anything more, so Celia said, "Well, I'll leave you to your letter and get ready for bed. I'm beat." Maddie nodded, but she was so busy reading that Celia was pretty sure she didn't even know what was going on.

Celia quickly got ready for bed, fighting to keep her eyes open. She was glad they didn't have to go to classes tomorrow. A couple of days to catch up on sleep and settle back into the school sounded like a great idea to her. She wished everyone in the room a good night and then climbed up into her bed. After pulling her thick curtains around her bed, she left the outside window curtains open and looked out at the stars.

It felt good to be back at school. When she'd come last year, she'd felt overwhelmed and out of place. But by the end of the year, she'd made a lot of friends and found people who cared about her. True, there were still people who only wanted to talk to her because of who she was, but there were many more who had looked past all of that and seen her as a person.

She thought about the letter "Celia" had gotten from Arletta. A lot of the people at camp had been the type who were only interested in knowing someone famous, which Celia was starting to find annoying. They didn't really want to know her, or the "Celia" that they knew, anyway. They only wanted to be able to say that they were "friends" with Celia Fincastle.

Celia rolled over onto her side and sighed. She wondered what the coming year would hold. She had a feeling that something exciting waited just around the corner. She only hoped it would be a good surprise this time.

She reached over and pulled the curtains across the windows and settled back on her pillow. It didn't take long at all for her to drift off into a deep sleep.

Chapter Six
Back to Class

Although Celia slept quite well, she managed to wake up on time and be over at Professor Legaspi's office right before breakfast.

"Hi, Celia," Professor Legaspi said, coming out of a door on the side of her office. "Close the door and take a seat." Once she saw Celia was sitting in one of the silver chairs in front of the desk, she asked, "How was your summer?"

Celia shrugged. "Not bad." Professor Legaspi raised an eyebrow at her as she settled in her own chair. "Okay. It was kind of difficult. But camp was fun."

"I heard about camp," she said dryly.

"How?"

She lifted one shoulder in a shrug. "Doxa, Mr. Morven... they told me about it."

Celia wasn't sure how she felt about that. It wasn't the first time she'd gotten the feeling that an awful lot of people seemed to have discussions about her without her knowing about it. "Oh."

"So, did it work, switching places with Maddie?"

"You heard about that?" When Professor Legaspi nodded, she said, "Well, I guess it worked. It was kind of nice to be the plain one for a while instead of the one everyone knows about."

"I would imagine that Maddie didn't complain either."

"I guess not."

"Hm." She shifted in her chair. "Well, I wanted to talk to you about your family tree assignment. How's that coming along?"

"It's not," Celia muttered dejectedly.

"Yes, that's about what we expected. I'm afraid that it might be a little bit longer before I can give you a hand with that."

"Why?"

"There's a box..." she said, waving her hand in the air, "...somewhere, but I can't for the life of me find where I put it."

"A box?"

She nodded. "Your mother gave it to me, just before she...well..." She cleared her throat. "Anyway, she gave me explicit instructions to give you that box when you started working on your genealogy project."

"Wait, she knew something would happen to her?"

Professor Legaspi shook her head and sighed. "No, not that she told me. But I wonder sometimes if she suspected something. She seemed to have an instinct about things.... Elle always seemed to have a hunch, and it usually proved correct."

"Elle—was that her name?"

Professor Legaspi looked at her with surprise. "My goodness, you don't even know their names?" she asked incredulously.

Celia shook her head. "Aunt Agatha wouldn't talk about them by name." She sat in anticipation, hoping Professor Legaspi could tell her something about her parents. She'd had so little information up to now, and she literally sat on the edge of her seat, waiting to see what she would say.

"Oh, Celia...If I'd known..." She glanced at the locket that Celia had put on that morning. "Had you seen pictures of them before you opened the locket?" Celia shook her head, her throat too tight to say anything, and Professor Legaspi closed her eyes briefly as she placed a hand on her forehead. "I'm so sorry," she said, looking at Celia again. "I wish I had known." She gestured to the locket. "Your mother's name is Adelle, but her friends and family called her Elle. Of course, when she married your father, her name changed to Fincastle, but her maiden name was Hilleman. Your father's name is Jacob."

Celia swallowed hard. "N—...No one knows what happened to them?"

Professor Legaspi dropped her gaze to her desk and shook her head. "Apparently there was very little evidence to work from when they disappeared. Of course, there were searches, but no one ever found anything."

There was silence in the office for a few moments.

"Professor Legaspi?"

She raised her head again and looked at Celia. "Yes?"

Celia licked her lips. She wasn't sure if she should ask the question, but she had to know. "Do...do you think they're...dead?" Professor Legaspi flinched when she said the last word.

She sighed again and shook her head helplessly. "I honestly don't know, Celia. It's been so long, and there's been no trace of them...but...well, I guess I just can't fathom...I don't want to believe that they're...gone...but I suppose some would say that it's foolish to think otherwise, since they haven't been seen in such a long time."

Celia nodded but didn't say anything. In some ways, she thought it might have been better if she'd known that they died, because then at least she would know what happened to them. But this way... ever since she could remember, every day of her life she wondered what had happened to them.

Professor Legaspi looked at her watch and pushed to her feet, clearing her throat. "Anyway, I just wanted to let you know that I'm still working on finding that box, and I will give it to you just as soon as I can. In the meantime, now you have some names to work with, and maybe you can find something on your own. However, breakfast started fifteen minutes ago, and I don't know about you, but I'm getting hungry, so I say we head down to eat." She turned to the doorway. "Oh, I almost forgot. The deans are handing out class schedules to everyone except the seventh-years today, but you won't be getting one. Mr. Morven and I will meet with you later to go over your class assignments. I believe he'll be setting up a time to meet with you."

"Okay."

Professor Legaspi opened the door. "After you, Miss Fincastle," she said, gesturing through the doorway. They walked down to the refectory in silence, each lost in her own thoughts. When they reached the bustling room, they each collected a plate of food and went in separate directions. Celia found Maddie, who had saved her a seat, and watched as Professor Legaspi sat next to Mr. Morven at the staff table.

She turned her attention back to her table and her own breakfast, which looked far more appetizing than the cold cereal she'd had the last couple of months with Aunt Agatha and at camp. She listened to the conversations going on around her, but didn't join in. When she had finished eating, she glanced around the refectory again and noticed Professor Legaspi and Mr. Morven talking with their heads bent close together, and Celia knew it was another discussion about her.

Her eyes roamed the staff table and she saw Mr. Bazemore sitting next to Headmaster Doyen. His dark hair was streaked silver at his temples and he looked like a very intimidating man. Celia wasn't sure if she liked him or not, but she figured she'd give him a chance before deciding. She moved down the tables, past a few of the teaching assistants she hadn't yet met, until she reached the end of the table. She frowned and looked quickly through the staff members again.

"Hey, Maddie?" she asked, nudging her friend on the arm.

"What?"

"Have you seen Higby? I don't see him with the rest of the staff."

Maddie turned in her chair and looked, too. "You're right. No, I haven't seen him this year."

"Did he do orientation for the seventh-years?"

Maddie shrugged. "Got me."

Celia glanced around and saw Audra sitting at the next table. "Hey, Audra?" she called.

"Oh, hi, Celia."

"Come here," she said, waving her over.

Audra jumped out of her chair and hurried around the table to Celia's chair. "What is it?"

"Just wondering about something. Did Higby take you guys through orientation yesterday?"

Audra shook her head and frowned in confusion. "Higby? Who's he?"

"Never mind. Who did orientation?"

"The new guy, Mr. Bazemore," she said, pointing over at him.

"Really?"

"Yup."

"Okay, thanks, Audra."

"Sure, Celia. See you later."

Celia turned back to the table. "Where do you suppose Higby is?"

"Don't know," Maddie said. "What's his job, anyway?"

She thought for a moment. "I don't know," she finally answered.

"So what did Professor Legaspi want?"

Celia turned to her with wide eyes. "Oh, I almost forgot. She asked me about my family tree."

"And?"

"She said she had a box of stuff my mom gave her to give to me when I started working on it."

"No kidding? Why would your mom do that?"

Celia shrugged, still trying to fit all the pieces together in her mind. "She said my mom might have had a hunch. Anyway, she told me my parents' names. Isn't that great?"

Maddie looked at her like she'd just grown ten extra arms. "You didn't know your parents' names?"

She held her hands out in a gesture of question. "How would I? Aunt Agatha wouldn't talk about them."

"Oh, right. Sorry," Maddie winced. "But how did you do any work on your family tree if you didn't even know your parents names?"

"I, uh, well..." Celia sighed. "I haven't really done anything for my family tree," she confessed.

"Celia!"

"Shh!"

"Sorry," Maddie said, lowering her voice. "What are you going to do?"

"I don't know. But it's not like I have tons of family members running around that I can just talk to when I need information."

"True. Can Professor Legaspi help?"

"I hope so. Like I said, she told me my parents' names."

"So, what did you find out?"

"Well, my mom's name was Adelle, but she was called Elle, and my dad's name was Jacob. Oh, and Mr. Morven told me that my grandmother's name was Violet, and she was princep for almost forty years."

"No kidding?"

"That's what he said."

"Well, I guess that gives you a place to start, then, doesn't it?"

"Guess so."

People were starting to clear their dishes and leave the refectory, so they joined the crowds and headed out to Main Hall.

"Hey, there's Higby!" Maddie said, pointing across the vast room.

Celia looked over and saw Higby standing with Professor Legaspi. She was talking quickly to him, and he had his head bent down to hear what she was saying. As Celia watched, he snapped his head up and looked at Professor Legaspi in surprise. She nodded tersely and began talking again, this time gesturing with her hands. Higby said something back and nodded his head. He looked over and spotted Celia watching them, so he smiled and waved. Celia expected him to come over and say hello, but he turned and guided Professor Legaspi through a door on the other side of the hall and they disappeared from view.

"What was that about?" Maddie asked.

Celia shook her head. "I don't know. But I think I'm getting really tired of people talking about me without including me in the conversation."

"Come *on*, Celia," Maddie said, rolling her eyes. "You don't really think that was about you, do you?"

She shrugged. "Just a hunch."

"A hunch? Like your mom had a 'hunch'?"

"Maybe."

They turned and headed up to quarters, where a group of kids had gathered to plan their day's activities. Some of them wanted to go play Soccovolle, others wanted to sit in the lounge and watch a movie. In the end, they decided to split and do both, with the remaining kids choosing to do their own thing. Maddie decided to stay in her room and write a few letters to her friends from camp, which left Celia trying to decide what to do.

"You coming to play Soccovolle, Celia?" Josh asked, nodding his head toward the door.

Celia laughed. "Me? I stink at Soccovolle."

"I told you," he said, coming over to rest an arm on her shoulder, "you just need a little practice."

"Yeah. Right."

He laughed and began pushing her to the door. "Come on. You won't get any better if you don't try."

"What if I wanted to watch the movie?"

"Do you?"

"Well, no."

"Then you're coming outside and playing Soccovolle."

"Fine, fine!" Celia said, giving up and going willingly.

A few hours later, they all came back inside for lunch, tired and hungry, but happy. It had been a lot of fun to play with all the kids at school, and since some of the kids from the other coteries had joined in, it had turned into a bizarre version of the game, but lots of fun nonetheless. They'd had too many players, so they played in shifts, with team members rotating through and changing often. The result had been closer to utter chaos than any sort of organized game, but everyone got to play and had a good time. Celia even managed an assist on a goal near the end. Josh had given her a high-five and a "Told you so" as they rotated players.

Most of the people who had played outside during the morning decided to stay indoors for the afternoon, and the time passed quickly. Before Celia knew it, it was time to get ready for bed again, and she was yawning and struggling to keep her eyes open.

"Okay, everyone. I have your class schedules, so I'll bring them around to your rooms," Professor Twombly called from the foyer.

"Oh, I don't even want to think about classes yet," Maddie said from up on her bed where she was fluffing her pillow. "It was bad enough having to go buy all my books before we went to camp. Hey," she said looking down at Celia. "Did you get your books?"

"Professor Legaspi said they'd take care of it."

"Huh. Must be nice."

Professor Twombly knocked and came in the room. "Good evening, ladies," she said, going over to Libby's desk. Although Professor Twombly always wore interesting outfits, her weekend attire was particularly noteworthy. Today she had donned a lime green sweat suit and a matching headband. It competed in intensity with her hair and her long, bright pink earrings.

"Now, of course," she said, addressing the younger girls, "seventh-years have an assembly Monday morning for your schedule and books, so you'll be waiting 'til then. For the rest of you," she said, turning back to the sixth-years, "I have your schedules here." She flipped through a small stack and pulled out a few pieces of paper. "Libby, here is yours.... Galena, this is for you.... Maddie, here's yours...." She stopped when she reached Celia. "Oh, Celia. Um...I'm afraid..." She flipped through the stack again. "I don't seem to have..."

"It's okay, Professor Twombly," Celia said. "Professor Legaspi said Mr. Morven would meet with me and give me mine."

"Oh, good. Well, then, good night, girls," she said, and swept out of the room.

"Hey, look," Maddie said, studying her schedule. "I actually got two classes with the deans. The rest of mine are with the assistants."

"Really?" Galena said. She looked at her own schedule. "I only got one class with a dean, and it's with Professor Twombly."

"That's not so bad," Libby said. "At least that's your coterie."

"What do you suppose is going on with your schedule, Celia?" Galena asked.

"I don't know. I just figured it had something to do with being out of the demesne all summer," Celia said. "You know, because I couldn't buy my books."

"I guess," Maddie said, putting her schedule on her bookcase. "But don't you think they could have just left your books on your desk for you?"

Celia shrugged. She was saved from saying anything by Professor Twombly calling for lights out, and everyone hurried into bed. As she lay on her bed, Celia began to wonder what *was* going on with her schedule. She hoped there wasn't anything wrong.

"Come on in, Celia," Mr. Morven said the next morning when she knocked on the door. Professor Twombly had handed her a note that morning on the way down to breakfast, asking her to come to Mr. Morven's office at ten o'clock.

"Hi, Mr. Morven."

"Grab a chair. Professor Legaspi should be here any minute."

"Can I ask you a question?"

"Certainly."

Chapter Six

"Why are you meeting with me? I thought you were the seventh-year and new student advisor."

"I was. But Headmaster Doyen changed things around a little. He thought it would be smarter to have each class stay with an advisor all the way through their seven years instead of switching to new advisors every year. I was the lucky one who got to move up first."

"Oh. So you'll be our advisor the rest of the time?"

"That's correct."

"Knock-knock," Professor Legaspi said, coming in the door and closing it behind her. "Good morning, Celia."

"Hi, Professor Legaspi."

She took the chair beside Celia and crossed one leg over the other. "We wanted to talk to you about your classes for this year."

"What about them?"

"Well, as you know, your final exams last year and the ALPHAs help us determine what classes each student takes this year."

"Yes."

"Your exam scores were phenomenal, Celia," Mr. Morven said. "I've never seen a seventh-year score so high."

Celia started to feel queasy. This wasn't sounding good. She didn't want to be the super-genius student again this year. Last year had been bad enough. "Okay," she said shakily.

"Based on your finals and your ALPHAs last year, your professors have decided that you need to be taking fourth-year classes this year," Mr. Morven said. "Now, I know that sounds like a big jump, so they're recommending that you take both the fourth-year classes *and* the sixth-year classes with the rest of the students your age. How does that sound?"

Celia was flabbergasted. "Uh…" Fourth-year classes? She didn't even know what to do in her seventh-year classes last year. How would she possibly keep up with fourth-year classes?

"I won't lie to you; it's going to be a lot of hard work. You'll basically have a double load of classes, and since you tested high in every area, you won't even get a break in one subject."

"I..."

"Tell you what," Professor Legaspi said when Celia hesitated. "Why don't we try it for a few weeks and we'll see how you're doing. We can kind of take it day by day, and if we need to change something, then we can. Does that work?"

"I guess," she said weakly.

"You're sure?" Mr. Morven asked, sounding uncertain.

"I'll do my best," she said, sounding more confident than she felt.

"Good for you," Professor Legaspi said. "The other deans have agreed to give you any help you might need, so if you need anything, just ask, all right?"

"Okay."

Mr. Morven picked up a sheet off his desk and held it out to her. "This is your schedule, then. We went ahead and got all your books for you, so I'll get someone to run them up to your room later today."

"Thanks." Celia looked at her schedule and thought it was the most jam-packed agenda she had ever seen. She had classes all morning, every morning, and nearly every afternoon. She counted the classes listed. Fifteen! She groaned silently at the thought of the mountains of homework she was going to have this year.

"Do you have any questions?" Celia shook her head. "Well, good luck, then. And if you need anything from me," Mr. Morven continued, "you know where to find me."

"All right."

Once Celia was back out in the hallway, she let out a deep sigh. She studied her schedule closer as she made her way back to her quarters. She had the standard sixth-year classes: Basic Skills I for Mind, Body, Touch, Vision, and Speech. A note at the side said she was taking all five as "S" level classes, whatever that meant. In addition to those, she had ten classes listed, two for each subject area, for what she assumed were her fourth-year classes. All of those were marked with an "S", as well.

"Did you get your schedule?" Maddie asked when Celia walked in the room.

Celia nodded and handed it over for her to see. She sat down in a chair next to Maddie while she read through her classes.

"Celia! How many classes are you taking?"

"Fifteen."

"What?...How?...Huh?"

"I'm taking a full load of sixth-year classes, but I also have a full load of fourth-year classes."

"*What!?*"

Celia nodded. "I guess I did well on my exams," she said lamely.

Maddie rolled her eyes. "Now, there's an understatement." She sighed and looked at Celia's schedule again. "Well, I guess the good news is that we've got two classes together. We're both in Professor Twombly's Basic Mind Skills and Professor Legaspi's Basic Vision Skills classes. But it looks like that's it."

"Well, I'm sure we'll still see each other."

"Oh, I know. But I'm going to miss having you in my classes."

"What does the 'S' stand for?"

"Skill. You can either be in Skill level or Core level. Skill level classes are the ones you're most gifted in, so you have to do more work. Core level just means you have to learn the theory for everything but don't have to actually be able to do any of it."

"Oh."

Maddie handed back her schedule. "How are you going to keep up with all the homework?"

Celia sighed. That was her question, too. "I have no idea."

Monday morning, Celia headed to her first class of the day, Introduction to Languages with Professor Perrin, the dean of Sprachursus. Celia picked a seat far off to one side of the room and hoped people wouldn't notice her.

It didn't work.

People whispered and pointed as they chose their seats; some stopped in the middle of the doorway when they saw her. Professor Perrin smiled at her when he came in, but didn't make a big deal about her being there. He was fairly young, and although he wore a dress shirt, he almost always had the sleeves rolled up to his elbows. He was always friendly and cheerful, and was a favorite of many of the students at the school. Maddie claimed he looked just like Ed Bornhoft, but Celia couldn't really say one way or the other.

Celia hunched over in her chair as she felt the stares of her new classmates on her back. She knew it was unusual to have someone taking classes outside their year, and of course there was the fame factor, but was it really that big a deal?

When Professor Perrin clapped his hands to signal the start of class, Celia hoped that would be the end of the curiosity and they could start focusing on class work.

"Welcome back, everyone," he said, stepping around to the front of his desk and leaning back on it. "I trust you all had an enjoyable summer?" Murmurs and nods followed his question. He chuckled. "And now I see that you're all super-excited to be back here at school." He rubbed his hands together as the class grumbled. "I suppose we might as well deal with the elephant in the room right off the bat." He held out his hand to Celia. "As many of you have noticed, I'm sure, Celia has joined your class for the year. I expect you all to treat her like any other student, and I hope that is the last I have to say on that subject for the rest of the year."

Celia felt her face grow warm and tried to sink down in her chair.

"Now," Professor Perrin continued, "as most of you know, fourth-year classes mark the start of a change in your academic career. You have reached the midway point at this school, (*Except for me,* Celia thought) and are now starting to narrow down your focus and develop your strengths. Since you can now choose some of your classes, the expectation is that you will have more interest in the subjects you are studying. As a result, we expect more from you on every level. Your work will be harder, more intense than last year.

"Those of you who are taking this as a skill level class will have practical assignments and exams along with the written components given to everyone. For those of you taking this class as a core subject, that does not mean that it will be easy. There is a lot of information and material to cover, and you will be required to learn all of it."

If Celia had been nervous before, now she was terrified. Did they really think she could do this? How was she supposed to keep up with a class of fourth-year students when she had no idea what they were talking about? All her classmates had studied this stuff for three years already.

Her stomach churned as Professor Perrin handed out a syllabus that laid out the planned curriculum for the year. Her head spun as she looked at all the topics they were going to cover, most of which she had never heard of before. By the time class was dismissed, she felt exhausted, and she still had four more classes to go to that day.

Somehow she made it through the rest of the day, and the day after, and before she knew it, she had reached Friday afternoon. It had been a grueling week. In an odd way, her sixth-year classes were a welcome break from the intensity of her fourth-year classes. Besides the fact that the material was easier and the professors had lower expectations, she was in with kids her own age, which made things a lot smoother for her.

All ten of her fourth-year classes had been a near repeat of her first class with Professor Perrin. Everyone in the room had stared at her and whispered to each other until the professor started class, at which point they all called attention to her being in the class, and Celia blushed and tried to disappear under her desk. She'd only known one person in any of her fourth-year classes, a Mensaleon girl named Victoria, who had been the only one to come over to her desk and say hello to her.

Since Maddie was only in two of Celia's classes, she felt very alone most of the time. Very few of the kids that had been in her classes last year were in her classes this year. She assumed that now that they were divided out by level, she might have classes with these kids more over the next few years, but then she realized she might not be in many classes with them if she ended up taking harder classes every year.

On top of all that, she had to get special permission from all her professors for an extension on her family tree assignment. They all understood her predicament, but they still required her to fill out a form asking for the extra time. Each one required her guardian's signature, but since Celia hadn't seen Higby since she saw him talking with Professor Legaspi, she had to take all of them to Mr. Morven, who said he'd take care of it for her.

"How are your classes going?" he'd asked before she left his office.

"Okay, I guess."

"What's wrong?"

Celia sighed and shook her head. "Nothing. It's just . . . "

"Hard?"

She nodded.

"I'm sure things will get better."

"I know."

"Just tired of being the one singled out?"

"I guess so."

"I know it's little consolation for you at the moment," he said, "and it sounds like a trite motivational speech, but so much is asked of you because you have been exceptionally gifted. And I'm not only referring to your talents, but also to the position for which you have been chosen."

"Sometimes I wish I was just like all the other kids."

"I know. But that would be a tremendous loss for the rest of us." He turned back to his paperwork. "Hang in there, Celia. I'm sure you'll do just fine."

By the end of the week, she had been to all of her classes, some of which met more than one day a week. In addition to her Basic Skills I classes and Introduction to Languages, she also had Basic Cryptanalysis and Beginning Dream Interpretation with Professor Twombly; Introduction to Locks and Study of Touch with Professor Mesbur, the dean of Tattotauri; Camouflage I and Speed & Strength I with Professor Spadaro, the dean of Corpanthera; Basic Cryptopicts and Beginning Night Vision with Professor Legaspi; and Basic L'Auzzulla, also with Professor Perrin. She'd had no idea what L'Auzzulla was when she headed to that class, but she'd actually been excited when she found out that it was the communication through the blue light that Maddie had told her about before.

Dropping her bag by her desk on Friday evening just before dinner, Celia looked over and saw Maddie working on homework at her desk. "Hi, Maddie." She collapsed in an armchair.

She looked over and smiled. "Hi, stranger. How was your first week of classes?"

"Long. Tiring. Hard."

Maddie gave her a sympathetic look. "I'm sure. Well, cheer up. It's Friday and you have the whole weekend off."

Celia huffed. "Not with my ten tons of homework to finish."

She wrinkled her nose. "Ugh."

"Yeah."

"Well, come on. Right now it's time for dinner, and you can leave all of your books and homework here," Maddie said, dropping her pencil on her desk and walking over to Celia's chair. She tugged on her arm to try to get her to stand up. "Move it, lazybones."

"Lazybones!" Celia protested. "I'm hauling fifty pounds of textbooks all over school. That's not lazy."

"Sorry. But you still have to get up and go down to dinner."

"Fine. Just as long as it doesn't mean more homework..."

Chapter Seven
Inside the Box

By the middle of August, Celia had settled into a routine at school. Her classes were hard this year, much harder than last year, but she guessed that was to be expected since she had basically jumped ahead by two years. If not for her speed reading and writing abilities, she never would have been able to keep up with all the homework her professors assigned. They handed out assignments on the assumption that people had no more than three areas of skill level classes, so for most students, the workload was bearable. For Celia, however, who not only had five areas of skill level classes but also two full loads of classes, it was an unbelievable amount of work.

She had hoped she could avoid all the stares and whispers from everyone this year, but that wasn't meant to be. As soon as word got out that she was taking every fourth-year class offered, people started pointing in the hallways and whispering as she walked past. Most of the time, she just gritted her teeth, lowered her head, and kept moving, but sometimes it was difficult. Her professors did what they could, deflecting attention when they noticed something in the hallways, but they weren't always around, and some of the older kids took the opportunity to tease her about being some kind of freak.

Things weren't loads better in her sixth-year classes, as the kids all found out that she was taking fourth-year classes, too. There were mixed reactions: some kids were jealous that she was in with the older students, some kids were jealous that she was so gifted, some kids suddenly wanted to be friends with the girl who knew all the fourth-year kids, and some kids were just tired of hearing about Celia Fincastle. Celia found it sort of funny that she was in the same camp as the last group—she was tired of hearing about Celia Fincastle, too.

Since her extension for her family tree assignment ran out at the end of the week, Celia was in the library one afternoon, trying to find information about her relatives. She'd found a fair amount of information about her grandmother, Violet, but mostly lists of data pertaining to her years as princep. There was very little personal information about her in any of the books Celia looked in, and she couldn't find anything about her parents, so she was starting to get a little frustrated.

"Psst! Celia." She looked up and saw a skinny boy with short black hair standing by her table in the library.

"Oh, hi, Eliot," she said. Eliot Paulden was a sixth-year student in Aquilegia. Celia had a couple of classes with him last year and he was in a few of her classes this year, too.

"Professor Legaspi sent me to find you," he said. He handed her a folded note. "She wanted me to give you this."

"Oh. Thanks."

"Sure." He turned around and left, so Celia turned her attention to the note. It was written on light gray paper and when she opened the note she saw the silver-inked writing of Professor Legaspi.

Celia,

Success! I finally located the box I was telling you about. I'm teaching all afternoon, but I have a few minutes to spare just after dinner tonight, if you can make it. If not, we'll try for tomorrow.

Professor A. Legaspi

Celia glanced at her watch. It was only two-thirty and she had a class at three o'clock. She didn't know how she was going to pay attention in class, knowing that Professor Legaspi had found the box from her mother. Somehow she managed to sit still through her class and even eat dinner without bouncing out of her chair with anticipation. As soon as she saw Professor Legaspi get to her feet, she jumped out of her seat and hurried to the door.

Professor Legaspi saw her waiting and smiled at her. "A little anxious?" Celia shrugged helplessly. "That's okay. I understand. Come on. It's up in my office."

The walk to the Aquilegia quarters seemed to take hours, and although Celia wanted to run the whole way, she tried to calm down a bit and walk at a sedate pace. Professor Legaspi unlocked her office door and stepped inside, told Celia to wait there, and went through the other door. Celia stood, shifting from foot to foot, until she came back carrying a box about the size of three stacked textbooks.

"Here it is," she said, setting it on her desk. "Your mother sealed it before she gave it to me, and no one has opened it since." She opened a desk drawer and pulled out a pair of scissors. Holding them out to Celia, she asked, "Would you like to do the honors?"

Celia swallowed and took the scissors. She turned the box and carefully cut the tape on one end and then the other, and then ran the scissors down the seam in the center. Setting the scissors back on the desk, she delicately opened the outer flaps of the box and then lifted the inner flaps. Her breath caught in her throat when she saw what was inside.

The box was full, piled right to the top. Sitting in the center of the pile was a picture of a couple, which Celia recognized as her parents, and a child, which Celia could only assume was her. Her parents were smiling as they watched Celia playing with a doll that was lying on her lap. Her father had his arm around her mother, who was leaning against his shoulder. They all looked happy and peaceful, apparently unaware of what waited in their future.

"Oh, Celia, look at all those pictures," Professor Legaspi said, peering over the edge of the box. "There must be something in there that can help you with your family tree."

"I hope so."

"Well, I'll let you take it back to your quarters and look through it on your own. Good luck."

"Thanks, Professor Legaspi," Celia said, picking up the box. When she made it back to her room, the rest of her roommates had returned from dinner and were working on homework.

"Look, Maddie," she said, coming up next to her desk. "Professor Legaspi found the box from my mom."

"Oh, wow! What's in it?"

"Pictures. I don't know what else."

"Let me see!" Celia took out the picture on the top and held it out to her. "Is that you?" she asked, pointing to the girl with the doll.

"I think so. Those are my parents, so I'm guessing that has to be me."

"Oh, you were so cute!"

"Give me that," Celia said, swiping the photo out of her hand.

"Aw, come on. I want to see some more pictures."

"Maybe after I look at them."

"Okay. That's fine. I'll let you look through them on your own."

"Thanks, Maddie." Celia took her box and climbed up the ladder to her bed. After pulling her curtains, she turned her attention to the box, and carefully started taking things out one at a time. There was picture after picture, most of them labeled on the back, stating who was in the picture and when the picture was taken. After a while, Celia started getting tired, so she decided to call it a night. When she glanced at the pile in front of her, she saw that she'd barely made a dent in the collection in the box. She could hardly wait for the next day when she could continue her discoveries.

By the end of the week, Celia had learned enough information to just squeak through the requirements for the first assignment of the family tree. It was a huge relief for her, since she hadn't been at all certain she would be able to complete the assignment on time.

Every spare second she had she spent on her bed, looking through the pictures in the box. She'd found a pile of old black and white photographs, which said they were snapshots of her grandmother. Since Maddie had been so patient, Celia let her look at some of the pictures on Saturday afternoon.

"Is it kind of weird to basically be seeing your parents and grandparents for the first time?" Maddie asked, studying a family picture from a holiday party.

"A little," Celia admitted. "It almost feels like I'm looking at pictures of someone else's family. I have to keep reminding myself that I'm related to all these people."

"Who's the guy in the wheelchair?" Maddie asked.

"I don't know. Does it say on the back?"

She flipped it over and shook her head. "Nope. It just says 'Christmas, 3rd Year'."

Celia shrugged. "I don't have any idea. I haven't seen any other pictures of someone in a wheelchair."

"Hey, look at that. You look just like her!" Maddie said, pointing to the picture of Violet.

"Really?"

"Yeah. Well, okay, not exactly like her, but really close."

"You think so?"

"Here, look at this one," Maddie said, holding out a photo. "You two look really similar."

Celia took the picture and studied it. Violet and a group of her friends were sitting on a blanket on the grass, obviously having a picnic and enjoying a sunny day. She looked fairly young, somewhere in her teens, and she and her friends were laughing and having a good time. A bunch of guys were off to one side, eyeing the girls. Celia did a double-take.

"Is that Higby?" she asked, squinting at the picture. "Did he know my grandmother?"

Maddie looked over the edge of the picture. "It kind of looks like him."

"Maybe he could tell me something about Violet."

Maddie shrugged. "It's worth a try."

Celia tracked Higby down in Main Hall after dinner.

"Good evening, Miss Fincastle," he said in his proper manner. "I must apologize for not catching up with you before now. I've been incredibly busy. How was your summer?"

"It wasn't too bad."

He smiled. "Enjoyed your time with your aunt, did you?"

Celia made a face. "You try eating prune tart."

His face showed disgust. "I'm sorry, did you say 'prune tart'?"

"Yup."

"My dear, that is the most horrific thing I have heard in a long time. You have my deepest sympathies." He gave her a slight bow of condolence. "Now, was there something you wished to discuss with me?"

"I'm trying to do some research for my family tree project. I saw this picture and thought that man looked a little like you."

Higby took the picture and grinned. "Oh, I remember that day." He chuckled. "A group of us had gone to the park for a picnic, and we just happened to find this group of lovely young ladies. At the time, none of us knew that the new princep was among them." He paused, studying the picture. "But I'm afraid the man in the picture is Sebastian Hilleman, the man who eventually married your grandmother."

"Oh. Like I said, he looked a little like you, so I thought...but I guess not. But if you were there, did you meet my grandmother?"

"Yes, actually, I knew Violet Hilleman relatively well," Higby said, a note of fondness in his voice.

"Will you tell me about her?"

He smiled. "She was spunky, quite stubborn and determined, but she was one of the nicest people I ever met. As princep, she didn't tolerate any foolishness, but she always believed in second chances."

"Did she go to Renasci?"

"Yes, I believe she did."

"What coterie was she in?"

"Well, I imagine that there must be some record of that, her being princep and all."

"Oh, right. What about her husband?"

"Ah..." He thought for a moment, then shook his head. "I'm sorry, Celia, but I can't help you with that."

"That's okay. You knew my parents, right?"

"That I did."

"What were they like?"

"Well, let's see. Your mother was a delightful woman, always had a smile on her face. Your father...I seem to recall that he had a keen wit; he liked to make your mother laugh."

Celia sighed. "I wish I remembered them."

Higby gave her a look of understanding. "So do I. It seems incredibly unfair."

"Well, thanks for your help," she said, taking the picture back from him.

"You're quite welcome. I wish I could be of more assistance."

"Well?" Maddie asked when Celia met up with her at the other end of Main Hall.

Celia shook her head. "It's not him. But he did tell me a little about her and my parents."

"Well, that's something, I guess."

"Yeah, I guess."

She headed to the library the next day, hoping to find some more information about Violet. After much searching and skimming, she finally came across a short biography, which talked about Violet's time at Renasci and a little bit about her family. Excited, she went to check the book out so she could study it more carefully.

"Oh, my," Mrs. Romanaclef, the librarian, said when she saw the book. "No one's checked this out in quite a while. Is there a particular reason you're interested in Violet Hilleman?"

Celia nodded and opened her mouth to answer, but Mrs. Romanaclef continued.

"I'll bet it's because you were chosen as the next princep, isn't it? I suppose if I were you, I'd want to learn about the ones who came before me, too. I was always a big fan of Violet

Hilleman. She just seemed like a very refined lady." She shook the book at her. "You'd do well to follow the example of such a sophisticated woman."

"Well, actually, Mrs. Romanaclef, Violet was my grandmother," Celia finally managed to say. "I'm doing research for my family tree project," she explained.

"Why, really? I don't think I knew that. Or perhaps I did and I just have forgotten it over the years." She shrugged and handed the book over to Celia. "Well, either way, I hope you enjoy reading about your grandmother. As I said, she was a wonderful lady."

"Thanks."

She spent the rest of the day curled up on her bed, hungrily reading everything in the book. It talked about Violet's family, her parents and brother, and her years as a student at Renasci. Violet was the youngest in the family, and her brother, Tarver Kunkel, was ten years older than her. Her parents, Theodore and Winigan Kunkel, and her brother had also attended Renasci, and they were apparently a very powerful and influential family. Violet had been an excellent student, a member of Tattotauri who also had an aptitude for the gifts of speech.

Celia smiled as she looked at some of the pictures in the book, which showed Violet when she was very little, getting all dressed up for holidays with her family. Tarver, who seemed to always have a mischievous grin on his face, was often seen giving his sister bunny ears in the pictures. There were fewer pictures of Violet after she went off to school, and no pictures of Tarver after he was about fourteen years old, but Celia thought maybe that was just because they were both off at school and weren't around for as many pictures.

"Hello? Earth to Celia?"

Celia pulled her eyes away from the book and looked over the edge of the bed where Odile and Odette were standing.

"Oh, hi, guys."

"Wow, must be a fascinating book," Odette said. "We called you three times."

"Sorry. It's about my grandmother."

"There's a whole book about your grandmother?" Odile asked skeptically.

Celia nodded and held it up for them to see. "She was the princep."

"Okay, now it makes sense," Odile said.

"Hey, wait. Is that Violet Hilleman?" asked Odette.

"Yeah. Why?"

"Our Uncle Ezra worked for her for about ten years," Odette said.

"Really?"

"Yeah. He said it was the best job he ever had."

"What did he do?"

The two girls looked at each other and frowned. "I don't know, do you, Deel?"

Odile shook her head. "I don't think he's ever said *what* he did, just that he worked at the palace."

"There's a palace?"

"Of course. It's . . . " Odile waved her hand. "Somewhere. I don't really remember where. You didn't know that?"

"No."

"Well, anyway," Odette said, "we were just coming to get you for dinner. Maddie said she'd tried to get your attention for ten minutes and she finally gave up."

"Oops." She set the book on her bookcase. "I guess I was too busy reading," she said as she climbed down the ladder. "I didn't want to speed-read my way through it, so I was trying to take my time and really concentrate on everything."

"I guess it must be kind of weird to be learning about your family from books, huh?" Odile asked as they walked down to the refectory.

Celia shrugged. "I guess. I don't really have anything to compare it to, since I haven't learned anything from Aunt Agatha."

"Really?" Odette asked. "Why not?"

"She doesn't know much. She didn't really know my family, and she was out of the country when they disappeared, so... Besides, she isn't part of the demesne, so she would have no idea about any of this."

"Oh."

"Good evening, ladies," a deep voice said from next to them, and all three of them jumped.

"Oh, my gosh!" Odile said, putting a hand on her chest. "Mr. Bazemore, you nearly gave me a heart attack."

"I'm so sorry," he said smoothly. Celia looked up at him, her heart still pounding from being startled. She hadn't had much of a chance to see Mr. Bazemore yet, but she still thought he looked quite intimidating. Now that she was standing next to him, she discovered that he was very tall, and she had to crane her neck to look at him.

"We were just heading down to dinner," Odette said, inching toward the doorway.

"I really am sorry for scaring you," he said. "I've been told before that I don't make enough noise when I walk. It appears they were correct." He held a hand out toward the dining room. "After you, Miss..." He trailed off, looking at Odette.

"Signus," she said.

"And you?" he asked Odile.

"It's Signus, too."

He looked surprised. "Sisters?"

"Twins," Odile said.

"Really? Fascinating." He turned to Celia. "And you, Miss..."

"Fincastle," Celia mumbled, hoping he wouldn't hear clearly.

"Did you say Fincastle?" he asked, leaning one ear closer.

"Um, yes."

"Ah, well, I must say your reputation precedes you, Miss Fincastle. It's quite an honor to meet you."

"Um, yeah." She wasn't sure what she was supposed to say.

"Shall we head in to dinner?" He followed them into the refectory and headed up to the staff table while they went over to a table where Maddie had saved them seats.

"I don't think I like him much," Odette said, sliding into her chair. "He gives me the creeps."

"Who?" Maddie asked.

"Mr. Bazemore," Odile said, putting her napkin on her lap.

"Oh."

"Have you guys met him?" Celia asked.

Maddie nodded. "He stopped by my Basic Touch Skills class last week. He seems kind of... mysterious, I guess."

"I agree," Odette said.

"I don't know," a boy said from the other side of Odile. Celia recognized him as one of Odile and Odette's classmates, Rowel. "I don't think he's so bad. He's just quiet, I think."

"I don't know," Odile said.

The three second-year students started talking, and Celia turned to Maddie. "I'm sorry I wasn't paying attention when you called me for dinner," she said.

"That's okay." She still looked a bit miffed.

"No, I was just so busy reading my book. I found something in the library about Violet. It had all sorts of information about her family and her time at school. She was in Tattotauri."

"Really?" Now she looked excited. "That's great, Celia!"

"I know. I was starting to wonder if I'd ever find anything about my family."

"Too bad you already turned in your last assignment."

"I know."

"Mr. Dorset told us we're getting our next assignment for it next week."

"Who's Mr. Dorset?"

"The teaching assistant for Professor Perrin. He teaches my Basic Speech Skills class."

"Oh."

"Trust me, I'd rather have Professor Perrin, even if it meant more work. Mr. Dorset is about a hundred and fifty years old. He's so boring."

"So what's our next assignment going to be?"

Maddie shrugged. "Don't know. I hope it's something easy, but it probably won't be. I really wish I had some more interesting relatives."

"Are all your relatives part of the demesne?"

She shook her head. "None of my dad's family is."

"Really? How'd that happen?"

Maddie frowned in thought. "I'm not exactly sure, but something happened with my grandfather. No one ever talks about it, and my grandfather gets really upset if you ask him. But whatever it was, he refused to let his kids be part of the demesne while they were growing up. My mom married someone outside the demesne because she didn't know anyone in the demesne."

"That doesn't seem very fair."

"I don't know," she said with another shrug.

Celia remembered hearing about gifts fading without use and training when she first came to Renasci. "But then your mom never learned how to use her gifts? So she can't do anything?"

"I don't know. It's kind of a touchy subject around our house."

"Oh." Celia chewed a bite of food. "But, Maddie, if all that was going on in your family, don't you think that something interesting had to happen?"

"Maybe, but I'm not getting in trouble by asking about it."

"But if it's for school…"

"I don't know, Celia."

"You could at least try. If your grandfather won't talk about it, maybe your grandmother would. Didn't you say she went to RAGS?"

"Yes, but—"

"So maybe she could help."

Maddie sighed. "I'll think about it."

They ate in silence for a few minutes, listening to the conversations going on around them.

"Can you believe this is the last week of August already?" Maddie asked. "It seems like the time is flying by."

"Yeah, but that means that midterms are flying closer every day."

"Oh, like you have anything to worry about," she said sarcastically.

"Like taking exams for fourth-year classes?"

"Okay, maybe," Maddie conceded.

"Well, I'm not thinking about it yet. We're only three weeks into the semester, so I have plenty of time to worry about my exams later."

"I agree."

On Monday morning a student aide dropped off a note for Celia while she was in her Cryptanalysis class. Opening it, Celia read:

Celia,

We'd like to meet at the end of the week

to discuss your academic performance since that will be the end of the first month of classes. After checking everyone's schedule, it looks like the only time we all have available is during lunch on Friday. If you can come up to my (Mr. Morven) office at noon on Friday, we'll provide a meal for you while we review your classes. If that doesn't work for you, please let one of us know.

Mr. Morven

Professor A. Legaspi

She'd forgotten about their scheduled meeting, she'd been so busy keeping up with all her schoolwork. She wondered if they thought she was doing well in her classes or not.

All her professors handed out big assignments that week, so she had very little free time to keep working on her family tree and sorting through the box from her mother. By Friday, she was very tired, but she'd managed to finish all her homework for the week and only had one more class that afternoon before she could relax for the weekend.

She headed up to Mr. Morven's office just before noon, and took a chair in the waiting area outside when she found his door closed. Professor Legaspi showed up a few minutes later, and she glanced at the closed door, too, before sitting down next to Celia.

"Hi, Celia. I'd say I haven't seen you in a while, but that wouldn't be true," she said. Celia had been in her Night Vision class that morning. "I hope Mr. Morven brought a big lunch. I'm starved." To punctuate her statement, her stomach growled.

Mr. Bazemore walked past them and nodded. "Hello, ladies," he said.

"Hello, Mr. Bazemore," Professor Legaspi replied amicably.

As he headed around the corner, Mr. Morven's office door opened and Higby came out. "Hi, ladies," he said. "Sorry to keep you waiting."

"Oh, no problem, Higby," Professor Legaspi said. "It gave me chance to catch my breath. I've been running around all morning."

"If you'll excuse me, I have to be going," Higby said, nodding to them and then walking off.

"Come on inside," Mr. Morven said. "I asked one of the aides to run down to the kitchen and get us some lunch. They should be back any minute."

They chatted aimlessly until the aide brought their food, and then Mr. Morven closed the door and they got down to the real reason for their meeting.

"So, Celia," Mr. Morven said, twirling spaghetti on his fork. "How are you doing in your classes?"

"Okay, I think."

He nodded. "Do you feel like it's too much for you?"

She shrugged. "It's hard, but..."

"I talked with the other deans," Professor Legaspi said, "and they all had nothing but good reports."

Mr. Morven nodded again. "That's what I heard. From an academic standpoint, for now, at least, you're doing fine." He looked at her carefully. "What about the other kids?"

Somehow Mr. Morven always seemed to know what the real issue was. "They're..."

Professor Legaspi took a deep breath. "I should have known."

Mr. Morven exchanged a look with her. "Are they giving you a hard time?" he asked, looking back at Celia.

"A little," she admitted.

Mr. Morven leaned back in his chair and it gave a loud squeak. "Sorry," he said, wincing at the noise. "Has it gotten better since the beginning of the year?"

Celia had to slurp a noodle before she could answer. "Yeah," she admitted.

"Well," he said, tenting his fingers in his lap, "I guess it's up to you. Do *you* want to stick with your schedule?"

"I..."

"Celia, to be honest, you don't have to take all of those classes this year if you don't want to," Professor Legaspi said. "But after much discussion and debate, we thought it would be best if you worked up to your potential and got as much training as quickly as possible."

"Why?"

Again they exchanged a look. "Um, should you choose to become princep," Professor Legaspi said carefully, "it would be best if you were fully trained and prepared for anything."

"You mean because the Coridans don't want me to be princep."

"Not entirely, but, yes, that's part of it."

Mr. Morven cleared his throat and sat forward again. "The main question, Celia, is whether you want to continue taking a double load of classes. If you feel like you're still doing all right, then we can stay with the wait-and-see approach and meet again later to reevaluate at that time. If at any point you feel like you don't want to continue, we can change your schedule. Is that what you want to do?"

"I guess so."

"You're sure?" Professor Legaspi asked.

"Well, I mean, yeah, it's hard, but so far it hasn't been too bad, so I guess I might as well keep going."

"All right," Mr. Morven said. "We'll meet again after midterms and see how you're doing then."

Celia couldn't decide if she'd just given herself a huge challenge or set the stage for her own downfall.

Chapter Eight
Camouflage

August turned into September and Celia spent the vast majority of her time working on homework. Somehow she managed to keep her head above water, but it wasn't an easy feat. More than once, Maddie had interrupted her studying to tell her it was getting late and Professor Twombly had already called for lights out.

As the middle of September drew near and the leaves outside changed to golden yellow, the talk around school turned to something that Celia had paid little attention to the previous year: the fall dance. Seventh-year students weren't allowed to attend the dance, a fact that Doxa and her friends had tried to rub in their faces last year. But this year, as sixth-years, Celia and her friends were able to go for the first time, and that had everyone buzzing.

Celia herself was ambivalent about the dance. It wasn't as if she had a boyfriend or even someone who had a crush on her who would ask her to the dance, so she wasn't expecting an invitation. Shc guessed that if someone asked her, she might say yes, but since she didn't really think that would happen, she wasn't going to worry about it.

On a Tuesday in September, Celia was sitting in her Dream

Interpretation class, listening to Professor Twombly lecture. When her professor wrapped up her talk, she announced that they would be starting projects the next week.

"You'll be divided into pairs," she said, "and each pair will have a different topic to research and report on. I will be picking your partners (groans rose from around the room) and will post the list next week. It will be up to all of you to arrange meeting times with your partner outside of class to finish your work on the project. Are there any questions?" She looked around the room. "Good. Class dismissed."

Celia collected her books and left the classroom, heading back to her quarters to get her books for her next class. Idly she wondered who her partner would be, and she mentally ran down a list of the kids in the class. She still didn't know many of them. It had been hard to learn so many names in such a short time. She had new classmates in her sixth-year classes whom she hadn't known from last year, and then all the kids in her fourth-year classes, whom she didn't know at all.

"Hi, Celia," Audra said as Celia walked into the room. "How's your day going?"

"Not bad, Audra. How about you?"

She shrugged. "Pretty good. I got a letter from Blaine."

"Really? What's he up to?"

"I don't know. He didn't really say."

"I thought he had a couple of jobs lined up or something."

"I guess. He didn't say that he wasn't working, just didn't mention it at all."

Celia frowned. "Did he think about going to college or anything? *Are* there colleges in the demesne?"

Audra giggled. "Of course there are."

Celia shrugged, feeling her cheeks grow warm "Sorry, I'm still getting used to everything."

"That's okay. But I don't know if Blaine thought about college or not."

"Hm." Celia glanced at her watch. "I'd love to stay and chat, Audra, but I've gotta get to class."

"Okay, sure. See you later."

Celia hurried to her next class, her Basic Body Skills class with Professor Spadaro. While it wasn't really one of her most favorite classes, she found it a nice break from some of her other classes. Professor Spadaro was the dean of Corpanthera, and his classes were always very physically active lessons. They didn't get to try as many things this year as they had last year, but it was still nice to be able to get up and do something instead of trying to think so much like the other subjects.

Celia had Professor Spadaro for two other fourth-year classes, Camouflage and Speed & Strength. He was a tall man with very pale coloring, except for his vividly blue eyes. He moved smoothly, gliding everywhere in a very graceful and fluid manner. In some ways, his appearance belied his abilities, because he appeared to be weak and fragile, when in reality he was capable of some amazing things.

Unfortunately, it was in Professor Spadaro's classes that Celia felt most inept. She was quite intimidated by the Corpanthera students who made up the majority of the classes, as they were all very physically oriented. She was not. She had never been very good at sports of any kind, and it didn't seem like that had changed. Professor Spadaro pushed her hard, too. Sometimes Celia felt like he picked on her more than the other students, although she was pretty sure her professors wouldn't do something like that.

On this particular day, Celia was glad it was her last class of the day. She was also glad that she was in Professor Spadaro's Camouflage class, since they were doing an introductory unit about camouflage and today was a practical lesson.

"Hi, Celia," the boy who sat next to her said as she slid into her seat. He'd introduced himself the first week of classes as Gage Nalcrest.

"Hi, Gage."

"Are you ready to try camouflage?"

Celia decided it might be best if she didn't mention she'd been studying it for six weeks in her other class. "Um, I guess. Do you know what we're going to be doing?"

Gage shook his head. "I haven't heard anything."

Celia sighed. "I'm sure I'll stink at it."

"Aw, come on. You'll do just fine."

"I don't know."

Professor Spadaro stepped to the front of the room. "If you all will grab your books and follow me," he said, "we'll be heading down to the gym for our lesson today."

There was a slight stampede as people rushed for the door, but Celia hung back and waited for the pandemonium to die down before following at a more relaxed pace. She noticed a couple of other girls doing the same thing, so they formed a quick alliance and grouped together for the day.

Once inside the gymnasium, which took up the two lower floors and half the building underneath the Sprachursus quarters, Professor Spadaro gathered them around one end of the room.

"Now, behind this curtain," he said, pointing to the fabric hanging from the ceiling just behind him, "I have set up a series of backgrounds and situations in which you will attempt to camouflage yourself. Keep in mind the points we have covered in class and do your best—remember that good camouflage often takes years to perfect."

He led them around the end of the curtain and gave them a minute to look around. There was a background that looked like the forest around the school, another one that looked like the beach, one that looked like a city sidewalk, and another that looked like a desert. There were also stations set up that looked like a living room, a classroom, an office, and a BUS compartment.

Chapter Eight

"Um, Professor Spadaro?" one of the girls asked.

"Yes?"

"Well, I know we've studied *how* to camouflage yourself, but I was just wondering *why* you'd want to camouflage yourself."

"Good question. Can anyone think of any time when you would want to be camouflaged?"

"When someone's chasing you," one of the boys called out.

"If you're undercover!" "To spy on your big brother!" "To sneak out so you don't have to eat your broccoli!"

Professor Spadaro laughed along with the rest of the class. "Those are all good answers, although some of them are probably more practical than others. The main thing, though, is that you would want to camouflage yourself in any situation where you don't want to be seen."

"Oh."

"Any other questions?...Okay, who'd like to try first?" The hand of every boy in the class shot in the air. "All right, Gage, we'll start with you. The rest of you can line up and we'll take turns."

Over the next hour, Professor Spadaro had them stand in each situation and see if they could camouflage themselves so they couldn't be seen. However, since it was a difficult thing to do and they were only sixth-year students, he said he was really seeing if they could change even one small thing about their appearance in each case. It ended up being a funny show to watch.

The boys were the most enthusiastic, scrunching up their faces and fisting their hands trying to get something to change. One of them managed to get his legs to turn orange in front of the sand on the beach, but it didn't camouflage him much at all. Another turned his hands green in front of the trees, but they were lime-colored instead of leaf-colored.

None of them managed to accomplish anything in the room settings, although a few of them thought that their exceptional ability to lounge on the sofa in the living room should count for something.

The girls went after the boys, and they didn't do any better. One of the girls changed the pattern on her skirt from stripes to flowers, but it changed back quickly when she looked down with wide eyes.

Celia took her turn toward the end, and she swallowed hard as she stepped in front of the first background, the forest. She concentrated on changing her appearance, trying to use some of the lessons she learned in her fourth-year class, but she didn't see any changes in her appearance. She moved on to the beach and tried again, but still nothing. The line had slowed down in front of her, so she waited by the beach setting for the next background to open up so she could move on.

"Hey, look!" she heard someone call, and with a start she saw one of the boys pointing at her. At his call, a whole group gathered around her.

She looked down to see what they were looking at and was startled to see that her feet and shoes had changed so that they matched the sand exactly. She moved them this way and that, but it was nearly impossible to see where her feet were.

Looking up again, she saw the entire class staring at her with wide eyes and open mouths. Professor Spadaro stood off to one side, watching her with an odd expression on his face. She thought it was a combination of surprise and approval, but it almost seemed like something else lurked underneath. Before she could figure it out, he stepped to her side.

"Well, well, Miss Fincastle. It seems your record is intact," he said, studying her sand-colored feet. "Very nicely done. Everyone," he said to the class, "this is what you want to do, blend into your background so the average observer cannot tell the difference between you and your surroundings." He looked at his watch. "I'm afraid that we've run out of time, so class is dismissed."

Everyone headed over to the bleachers on the side of the gym to collect their books. As Celia stepped away from the background, she was relieved to see her feet return to normal. She saw a few of the boys throw her looks as they gathered their things and left the gym. Apparently they weren't taking their failure and her success very well.

Celia sighed and trudged toward the door.

"Hey, nice job, Celia," Gage said, passing her on his way to the exit.

"Oh, thanks, Gage, but I really didn't do anything."

He shrugged and walked backwards to he could talk to her. "Well, it sure didn't seem that way. Take it easy!" he said, spinning around and waving offhand behind him as he walked off.

Celia pulled the gym door open when she reached it and stepped into the hallway. She was glad her classes were over for the day. She wasn't sure she felt up to dealing with her classmates anymore.

"How'd she do it?" A group of boys from her class were huddled in the hallway outside the gym.

"Beats me. She must have had help from someone. How else would she know how to do that?"

"But I heard she doesn't have any relatives in the demesne."

"So? She doesn't need relatives to give her extra help—everyone wants to kiss up to the next princep."

Celia tried to keep her head down as she walked past.

"Look, there she is."

"Hey, Celia. How'd you do it?"

Celia stopped and turned towards them. They'd turned to face her, a small mob of disgruntled faces staring at her. "Do what?"

"Who showed you how to do camouflage? No way you could do it on your own."

"Yeah, maybe you stole someone's paper, just like last year."

Celia didn't respond, turning and walking off instead.

"What's wrong? Afraid we might have found out your little secret?"

"Gentlemen," a deep voice interrupted. Celia spun back around and saw Mr. Bazemore standing behind them in the hallway. "I believe you owe Miss Fincastle an apology."

"What for?"

"For making an incorrect accusation," he replied smoothly. "From what I understand, those responsible for last year's problems admitted to everything. Miss Fincastle's name was completely cleared," he said, walking slowly up to meet them. The boys bunched together and stood as close to the wall as they could get. Safety in numbers, Celia assumed. "I also understand that Miss Fincastle is an exceptional student, if your headmaster is to be believed."

Celia stood with her mouth open. Mr. Bazemore was the last person she expected to defend her. The boys stood with open mouths, too, only for a very different reason. Mr. Bazemore exuded an air of authority without even trying, and she could see a couple of the boys swallowing hard, their gazes darting around nervously.

"I'm waiting…" Mr. Bazemore said calmly.

"Sorry." "Yeah, sorry, Celia." "Mmbf." "Mrrmmr."

Mr. Bazemore studied the group of boys. "I don't want to hear that this happened again. Do I make myself clear?" The boys nodded, looking like bobble-head dolls. Celia had to bite her lip to keep from laughing. "Good. I suggest you all find somewhere you need to be."

"Yes, Mr. Bazemore," they chorused as they split and fled in different directions.

Chapter Eight

Mr. Bazemore watched a few of them as they hurried off, then turned back to Celia with a sly smile on his face. "Best part of my job," he said with satisfaction.

"Um, thanks, Mr. Bazemore," Celia said.

He smiled at her, and Celia felt a shiver go up her spine. "You're quite welcome, Miss Fincastle. No one should have to put up with that kind of treatment, and it is my pleasure to defend such an illustrious student."

"I, um...I'd better get going," Celia said, taking a few steps backwards.

"Of course. Have a good evening."

Celia nodded, then turned around and practically ran the other way. She wasn't sure what it was, but something about Mr. Bazemore just didn't seem right to her. Something in his eyes, maybe. Whatever it was, Celia was now very confused about him, since his defending her didn't fit into the impression she had of him so far.

The next week, she headed into her Dream Interpretation class and noticed that everyone was crowded around a spot on the wall.

"What's going on?" she asked the girl at the desk next to her.

"Partner assignments."

"I completely forgot about that." She headed over to the sheet tacked on the wall and searched for her name. She'd been paired with someone named Cynnamyn Vandeau. Walking back and sitting down at her desk, she tried to figure out if she knew who her partner was.

"Hey, Celia," a girl with short curly brown hair said as she came over to Celia's desk. "It looks like we're partners for the project."

"Hi."

"I'm Cynnamyn Vandeau," she said, pronouncing her name "Van-doo" and holding her hand out, "but everyone calls me Cyn."

"'Sin'?" Celia repeated. She shook her head. "I'm sorry. I guess you already know I'm Celia," she said, shaking Cyn's hand. "Nice to meet you."

Cyn laughed. "Don't worry about it. Yeah, my name's a little weird, but I'm used to it. Nice to meet you, too."

"So, I guess we have to figure out when to get together to work on this project, huh?"

"Seems like it. When do you have free?"

Celia laughed humorlessly. "Um... never?"

Cyn looked at her with concern. "You aren't going to be one of those partners who doesn't do any work, are you?"

"Oh, no, no, that's not what I meant. It's just that I have a pretty busy schedule. It might be kind of hard to find a time we're both available."

"Oh, good." She looked relieved. "For a second there I was really worried." She looked over as Professor Twombly walked in the room. "Oops. Better grab my seat. We'll talk later."

Celia settled into her chair to listen to Professor Twombly talk about symbols in dreams, their topic for the day. Dream Interpretation seemed a little like guesswork to Celia, and she supposed that sometimes people guessed correctly but often did not. Perhaps it was just that she hadn't met many people who could interpret dreams well. Oh, who was she kidding—she hadn't met *anyone* who could interpret dreams at all before she came to Renasci.

Cyn caught up with her later as they were walking through the hallway. "How about if we meet during dinner and figure out when we can work on our project?"

"Sure. Sounds good."

"Okay, see you then."

Celia was sitting at a table with her friends when Cynnamyn came over. "Hi, Celia."

Chapter Eight

"Oh, hi, Cyn. I saved a seat for you," Celia said, moving her sweatshirt off the chair next to her.

"Thanks."

"Cyn, this is Maddie, Josh, Heath, and Kitt. Everyone, this is Cynnamyn. She's in one of my classes."

"Hi, guys. Nice to meet you."

"You, too." "Same here." "Ditto."

"So, Celia, it sounds like your schedule is probably more packed than mine, so when do you want to work on this?"

"If I could choose any time I wanted, I'd probably pick the weekend, 'cause my weekdays are almost full, between classes and homework."

"Wow. I don't think I could handle that much. How do you do it?"

Celia shrugged. "I'm not really sure. I'm just trying to get everything done, that's all."

Maddie leaned over. "Yeah, with her amazing speed-reading and -writing, that's all."

"Really?" Cyn took a sip of milk from her glass. "I'm in Sprachursus, so I'm not very good at either of those."

"I can't write faster than a snail," Maddie complained. "But at least you get to take classes with Professor Perrin, since you're in his coterie. I'm stuck with Mr. Dorset."

Cyn made a face. "I'm sorry. I've heard he's really dull and really strict."

"You're telling me," Maddie said, turning back to her own dinner.

"So how about Saturday morning?" Cyn asked.

"Um...yeah, that should work. I'll bring my notebook. And I promise I won't be a slacker. I might be busy, but I won't leave you with all the work."

"I believe you."

"So, Cyn," Maddie said, turning back to her, "what are

you doing in Celia's Dream Interpretation class if you're in Sprachursus?"

Cyn laughed. "Well, my mom was in Mensaleon and my dad was in Sprachursus, so I guess I take after both of them. I do pretty well at mind talents, if I do say so myself, but I'm definitely better at gifts of the tongue."

"Tuh. Not me," Maddie said. "I can muddle my way through Professor Legaspi's vision classes, but I'm hopeless at all the others."

"You should have seen me in my seventh-year finals," Cyn said, shaking her head. "I was miserable at Professor Spadaro's section."

"Did you have to do his jousting thing, too?"

"Yeah, but I hear it changes a little each year. Not that it mattered," she added. "I didn't even make it two steps before I fell off the plank. Every single time. I think he took pity on me and let me quit before my time ran out."

"Really?" Josh asked. "I actually made it over to Professor Spadaro, but I couldn't get past him."

"No way, dude," Heath said. "You'd never know my brother's in Corpanthera. I hit the foam *way* too much."

"Ask Celia how she did," Maddie said innocently.

"Maddie!"

Kitt gave her a speculative look. "How *did* you do, Celia?"

"I, um . . . well, fine."

Cyn looked at her sideways. "What's 'fine' mean?"

"Um, well, you know, I didn't do too bad."

"She whacked Professor Spadaro into the foam," Maddie stated.

"*Maddie!*"

"You didn't!" "No way!" "*Cool!*"

Celia sighed. "Yes, I did. Can we not make a big deal out of it?" She looked at her watch. "Oh, look at the time!" she said quickly. "I've got a ton of homework to do," she said, scooping up her dishes and standing up. "I'd better get to work. See you, guys." She heard laughter as she walked away from the table.

Even though she was keeping up with her classes fairly well, things went steadily downhill for Celia over the next few weeks. She and Cyn worked on their project as much as possible, but when it came time for their presentation, Celia caught a cold and lost her voice, so she couldn't speak. She'd written thorough notes, so Cyn had been able to fill in her part of the presentation, but Celia still felt bad about it. Professor Twombly had been sympathetic, but said new strict grading policies had been implemented and she had no choice but to dock a few points from Celia's grade, despite the circumstances.

The boys in her Body Skills class had gotten worse instead of better, now teasing Celia because Mr. Bazemore had stepped in to defend her. When Professor Spadaro wasn't looking, they gave her dirty looks and made comments under their breath. Gage had heard some of the remarks and was doing his best to stop them, for which Celia was grateful, but before long they turned their attention to Gage, teasing him about being Celia's boyfriend.

By the beginning of October, most of the school was talking about one of three things: midterm exams, the Fall Soccovolle Tournament, or the fall dance. Celia, for one, wished she had never heard of any of them. Except maybe the tournament, which she was kind of looking forward to watching.

Midterm exams were held the Thursday and Friday of the second week of October, just before the Fall Tournament, which was held over the weekend. Since she had so many classes, and therefore so many exams, Celia had to make special arrangements for her midterms. The only way for her to complete her exams was to have shortened exam times and cram as many of them into the two days as possible. Her professors put together a grueling schedule where she had to leave one exam early and get to the next exam late and try to finish her exams before her time was up. Just looking at the schedule made her exhausted.

Due in part to her heavy schedule and the upcoming marathon midterms, Celia had paid very little attention to the last topic of conversation, the fall dance. She knew her classmates were all discussing their dates and their outfits, but she just didn't have time to worry about it. That was, at least, until all the girls started asking her if she was going to the dance.

The first had been Libby and Galena, who hadn't meant anything by their question. They'd asked both Maddie and Celia one evening in their room, and Celia had exchanged a glance with her best friend and said something like "We're not sure yet."

"One of the guys in my Speech class asked me," Galena said. "We're just going as friends, but still..."

"Aric, one of Galena's brother's friends, asked me," Libby said. She giggled. "He's pretty cute."

"Oh, um...that's...great," Celia said, pasting a smile on her face. Had she missed something this summer? Something that said she was supposed to fall madly in love with some boy just because she turned twelve, maybe?

Somehow in the last two weeks of September, it seemed that everyone had decided that a person's worth was determined by their date—or lack thereof—for the dance. Those who had dates were now considered cool kids, and those who didn't have dates were now considered the geeks of the school. Celia figured that given everything else surrounding her time at Renasci, she wasn't really too concerned with being thought of as a geek.

"Hey, ladies," Heath said, coming up and sitting with Maddie and Celia at breakfast one day. "Are you as tired of hearing about this dance as I am?" he asked with a roll of his eyes.

"You said it," Maddie said. "Am I a failure as a person if I don't have a date for the dance?"

"According to the rest of the students here," Celia said, "yes. But don't worry, Maddie," she said, patting her shoulder patronizingly. "You're not alone."

"Yeah, I'm in your camp, too," Heath said.

"So why don't you ask someone?" Celia asked.

He looked suspiciously between the two of them, and they both laughed. "Don't worry, Heath," Maddie said. "We're not fishing for invitations."

He looked relieved. "Phew. For a second there… Anyway, I guess I just don't want to have to spend an entire evening getting all dressed up just so I can stand around and feel uncomfortable," he said.

"I agree," Celia said, nodding her head. "Maybe we should throw an anti-dance."

"That's not a bad idea," said Maddie.

"Well, I'm just glad to hear that I'm not the only one who isn't going dance crazy. It's like an epidemic around here," Heath grumbled.

As Celia lay in her bed that evening, she couldn't help but start to wonder if she was missing out on something. For starters, why wasn't she more enthusiastic about going to the dance? And why didn't she care a whole lot that she didn't have a date? But more than that, was she some kind of hypocrite because she didn't really care whether she went to the dance or not, even though she secretly wished someone would ask her to go? And what would happen if no one asked her? Would she still be able to go to the dance? Would she even want to?

In the midst of all of the fuss about the dance, she'd almost forgotten about her family tree assignment and the box from her mother, which was still sitting in her closet, waiting for her to get back to it. Her professors had all reminded their classes that their next assignment was due just before midterms, and Celia hadn't been able to find any more information yet.

Thoughts of the dance now replaced with worries about her family tree, Celia stared at the ceiling. She'd thought at the beginning of the year that something would happen this year, she just hadn't been expecting all of this. A long while later she finally succumbed to exhaustion and dropped off to sleep.

Chapter Nine
In the Infirmary

"What do you mean, you can't hand in your family tree assignment?"

Celia had set up a meeting with Professor Legaspi on Monday of midterms week. She had done as much research as possible, but there was no way she could write a three-page summary of her family's gifts and abilities. She didn't even know what coterie her father had been in when he'd attended Renasci, so how was she supposed to know what his gifts were?

"I've tried to do research, but no one has any information, and there isn't much in the library," Celia explained to a concerned-looking Professor Legaspi. "I just can't write three pages about people I don't know who don't have any information written about them."

She rubbed her forehead. "We can try for another extension, but I'm not sure that more time will be any help for you. I confess, I'm really not sure what you're going to do."

"It's not fair," Celia complained, slouching in her chair and swinging her foot. "Isn't it bad enough that I grew up without my parents? Why do I have to get bad grades because of it, too?"

"I'm really sorry, Celia. I wish I knew what to do. It doesn't seem fair, but this is the way it is, so we'll have to figure out how to deal with it."

"But how am I supposed to interview my relatives and things like that? It's impossible."

"I agree."

"And everyone else has an unfair advantage, because their parents are right there for them to talk to. I don't even have grandparents or aunt or uncles or cousins or anything."

She sighed. "I understand, Celia. But it *is* a mandatory assignment for all sixth-years. You can't get out of it."

Celia frowned and looked out the window. What was she supposed to say?

Professor Legaspi pushed to her feet. "Well, just keep doing your best," she said. "I guess if it comes down to it, you'll have to get a guardian signature for your poor grades, and I'm fairly certain that you shouldn't have any trouble with that."

"Yeah, I know. So I work my tail off to get good grades and in return I fail because I don't have any relatives," she muttered. "That really seems fair."

"Keep your chin up. Everyone knows it's not your fault."

Celia walked back to her room with her hands stuffed in her pockets. She'd spent as much time as possible either in the library or looking through her mother's box of pictures, but it wasn't doing her any good. Since her mother hadn't been selected as princep, there wasn't any information published about her, and there certainly wasn't any infor-mation about her grandfather or her father's family, since they married into the family. Her mother's pictures, while fascinating to look at, didn't have any information besides names and dates, so those weren't any help, either. She'd hit a dead end. And now it looked like she had no choice but to get zeros on her assignments because she didn't have enough information to complete them.

She sighed. For a while, it had seemed like she was juggling everything and doing fairly well. Now it looked like all the balls were falling down around her, and there was nothing she could do about it.

Although she had studied hard and felt fairly confident that she knew the material, Celia woke up on the first day of midterms with a nervous knot in her stomach. She nibbled on a piece of toast at breakfast, but she didn't have much of an appetite. Her schedule over the next 36 hours was daunting. She had four exams before lunch today, five after lunch, four before lunch tomorrow, and four tomorrow afternoon. She would get half an hour for lunch today and an hour for lunch tomorrow, otherwise every minute of her day from 8 a.m. to 5 p.m. would be spent taking an exam.

As she walked into the room for her first exam, she took a deep breath and let it out in a loud sigh. She just hoped she made it through the next two days.

Her first exam was for Professor Perrin's Introduction to Languages class. He'd prepared a written exam for everyone and chosen not to have practical exams for the "S" level students. Celia was quite thankful for that. She was busy scribbling away on her final answer when Professor Perrin tapped her on the shoulder and indicated her time was up and she need to get to her next exam.

She hurried through the hallways, trying to get to her next exam as fast as she could. She headed around a corner and bumped smack into someone.

"Oh!"

"Miss Fincastle?" Celia looked up with trepidation and saw Headmaster Doyen frowning down at her. "What are you doing in the hallways? Shouldn't you be taking exams?"

"I'm heading to my second exam, sir."

He squinted at her. "The second exam period doesn't begin for another hour. What are you talking about?"

"Um, I have too many exams to fit them in the normal exam periods, so my professors are letting me double up and take only an hour for each. I really need to get to my exam or I won't be able to finish." She fished in her pocket. "See, I have a hall pass and everything."

He glanced down at her pass and looked at her suspiciously, but said, "I'll be checking your story, but for now, you may go."

"Thank you, Headmaster Doyen."

After last year's fiasco, Celia wasn't one of the headmaster's favorite students. He'd spent the year accusing her of making trouble, and when he'd had to eat his words and apologize at the end of the year, he hadn't been very pleased. It seemed his dislike hadn't diminished any over time.

Celia scurried to her next exam, quietly sneaking into her Basic Mind Skills class and getting an exam from Professor Twombly, who gave her an encouraging smile.

She was pleasantly surprised to find that her sixth-year exams seemed much easier than her fourth-year exams. With fifteen minutes to spare after handing her exam to Professor Twombly, Celia tried to take a few deep breaths and calm herself down. Before she knew it, however, she was on her way to her next exam, and hurrying to finish in time again.

Her only reprieve over the two days came Friday morning, when she had two of Professor Mesbur's exams back to back. Professor Mesbur, the dean of Tattotauri, was built like a professional wrestler, but he had the personality of a teddy bear. Although he seemed big and burly, he was actually quite gentle. He kindly let her take both exams in the same room, despite the fact that her second class was in a room across the school. It saved her a few minutes' time and gave her another chance to catch her breath after she finished.

Chapter Nine

By the end of the two days, Celia felt like she'd run a marathon. Her brain was fried and she was so tired, she thought she might drop. Dragging herself into her room, she climbed up the ladder to her bed and collapsed in a heap. The next thing she knew, Professor Twombly was gently shaking her awake.

"What?" she murmured as she sat up and looked around. It was dark in the room and her stomach was growling.

"You slept through the Start of Tournament Banquet," she said.

"I did?" She still felt a little disoriented.

She nodded. "I brought up a tray of food for you. It's in the lounge, if you want to grab something to eat before you head to bed...or back to bed, I suppose."

"Okay. Thanks."

Celia dragged herself to the deserted lounge and scarfed down the plate of food. Professor Twombly gave her a sympathetic look as she headed to get ready for bed. She staggered back and dropped onto her bed, and that was the last thing she remembered for the night.

Since she had been too tired to pull her curtains, she woke up early as sunlight filled the room. Rubbing the sleep from her eyes, she climbed down her ladder, pulled on a robe, and went out to the lounge. She was surprised to find Josh sitting on one of the couches, reading a book.

"Hi," she said, taking a seat on another couch and tucking her feet under her.

"Oh, hi," he said, looking up and seeing her. He was wearing a warm-up suit and a pair of slippers and looked a little tired. "I heard you had a long two days."

She yawned. "You don't know the half of it." She frowned at him. "How come you're up so early?"

He shrugged. "Couldn't sleep."

"Why not?"

"Nerves. It always happens before a big game."

"Oh. Well, I'm sure you'll do fine."

"Thanks."

"How was the banquet?"

"Nothing special. Just the usual, I guess."

"I slept through it."

He tried not to smile. "Really?"

"Go ahead, laugh. I still can't believe it."

"I'm not laughing, it's just…you must have been pretty out of it."

"I guess."

"So how come you're up so early?"

"I was too tired to close my curtains. The sun woke me up."

"Oh."

Celia pushed to her feet and yawned again. "Well, I'm gonna go get dressed and leave you alone. Good luck this weekend," she said.

"Hey, thanks." He went back to his book but called her back when she got to the door. "Oh, Celia?"

"Yeah?"

"Heath, Kitt, and I were wondering if you and Maddie might like to go to the dance as a group. We kinda don't want to ask anyone to go as a date, but we thought it might be fun to go with a group of friends."

"Sounds good to me. I'll ask Maddie."

"Okay."

Celia headed off to get dressed, and when she stuck her head back in the lounge, it was empty, so she decided to go ahead down to the refectory. It was still quite early, and the refectory wasn't open yet, so Celia sat down in one of the chairs in Main Hall, facing out the huge wall of windows that looked out at the mountains. She slouched down so her head rested on the back of the chair and waited for someone else to show up.

"...but I don't care what he says. I'm tired of having people interfering at my school!" Celia heard voices moving into the room.

"Then show them they can't tell you what to do. Be firm and don't let them get away with anything."

There was a sigh. "But it seems almost cruel, doing that to a student."

Celia's eyes widened. She was pretty sure it was Headmaster Doyen and Mr. Bazemore, but she couldn't turn around to see without them finding out she was there.

"Do you want your school falling into anarchy?"

"Absolutely not."

"Well, then, that's your answer."

"I suppose you're right."

"You're not going out of your way to make things difficult, merely enforcing the rules that are already in place. No one could begrudge you that."

"True."

"Besides, I've heard that a few too many people bend over backwards for..."

The voices faded as they left the room on the opposite side. She wasn't sure what they were talking about, but she had an uneasy feeling that it would eventually have something to do with her.

A little while later the kitchen staff opened the refectory and set out breakfast. Celia was the only one in the room for about ten minutes until a few other early risers came in for their meal. When Maddie showed up, Celia was just finishing her juice.

"Boy, you were out of it last night," she said. "I tried to get you up three times, but you didn't even move. I had to check to make sure you were still breathing."

"Long day," Celia said.

"Obviously. Did you get dinner?"

"Yeah, Professor Twombly brought up a tray."

"That was nice of her."

"Yeah." Celia set her napkin on her plate. "You ready for a full day of Soccovolle?"

"You bet. Just as soon as I polish off my breakfast," Maddie said, digging in.

The Fall Tournament was the first of two tournaments that determined the school's winning Soccovolle team. Whichever team won the overall title got to play in the Summer Tournament, which featured teams from schools around the country.

After donning purple streaks on her cheeks and a purple metallic fringe scarf, Celia followed the rest of the coterie out to the Soccovolle stadium, which stood past a collection of pine trees off to one side of the school. Mensaleon wasn't playing until after lunch, so they weren't really rooting for anyone that morning, but that didn't stop anyone from displaying their coterie pride.

The first match of the year pitted Sprachursus against Aquilegia, and as the green-clad players of Sprachursus ran onto the field, everyone started cheering with excitement. By the time the silver-colored jerseys of Aquilegia made an appearance, the roar in the stadium was deafening.

Coach Jeuset-Partie came out to start the game and the match began.

Soccovolle was played like volleyball when the ball was in the air and soccer once the ball touched the ground. Players could bump, set, or spike the ball until it touched their feet or the ground, at which point they could no longer use their hands and they had to play the game like soccer. There were tall rectangular nets for scoring goals, and if a player managed to get the ball through the gold hoop at the back of the net, it scored three points instead of the usual one.

Each team had seven players on the square-shaped field: one guard to cover the goal, three protectors to play defense, and three attackers to play offense and score goals. The game was very fast-paced and the ball moved around the field at an alarming speed. Celia could only imagine what the professional matches were like; the amateurs at Renasci were amazing to watch.

On this chilly fall morning, the Sprachursus players seemed to take control of the match early on. They outran their Aquilegia opponents and took many more shots on goal. By halftime, they were leading four to nothing. The fans in the stands were cheering loudly, although Celia had to wonder if it was because they were really rooting for the teams or if it was just to keep warm. When the whistle blew for the start of the second half, the players ran back out on the field.

Either the Aquilegia team had a major boost at halftime or the Sprachursus team had worn themselves out in the first half, but the second half of the game looked very different from the first. The players in the green jerseys seemed to drag around the field and couldn't keep up with the silver jerseys. Within a few minutes, Aquilegia had scored two goals.

After that, the Sprachursus team perked up a bit and managed to fend off the shots, but in the final few minutes of the game, Aquilegia got control of the ball. They moved it down the field toward the Sprachursus goal, and one of the attackers went to take a shot. She spiked the ball at the net and everyone in the stadium watched as it bounced off the ground, hit the shoulder of the guard, and then dropped smoothly through the gold hoop at the back of the net.

The Aquilegia fans in the stands cheered wildly as their team celebrated on the field. The game clock ticked down and Aquilegia was declared the winner of the first match, five to four. By that time, even with the snack vendors handing out food to the fans, everyone was getting hungry, so they headed inside for lunch.

By the mid-afternoon game between Mensaleon and Tattotauri the weather had warmed up some. Celia sat with the rest of her purple-clad coterie members, all cheering loudly for their team. She saw Josh warming up for the game, but she wasn't familiar with the rest of the players. Across the field, the Tattotauri team warmed up in front of the red-clothed fans filling those bleachers. Coach Jeuset-Partie called the teams to the field, tossed the ball in the air, and the game began.

The teams were evenly matched, and it was a tough battle. Every time Celia thought her team was going to score, the Tattotauri guard deflected a shot or caught it in her hands. The fans spent the entire game on the edge of their seats, ready to jump up and cheer or waiting nervously for the shots to be blocked.

Partway through the second half, the score was tied at two. Mensaleon had control of the ball and was kicking it down the field. Celia saw Josh, who was filling in for a teammate in the attacker position rather than playing his usual protector position, get the ball and dribble up to a Tattotauri protector. He spun around to avoid the other player, and continued toward the goal. As he went to pass to a teammate, he collided with another protector in a hard crash. Both players fell to the ground as everyone in the stands gasped and rose to their feet.

Coach Jeuset-Partie hurried out to check on the two players, who had at least rolled over on the grass, but neither had gotten to his feet yet. He knelt next to them and talked to them, and soon the Tattotauri player carefully sat up and then got slowly to his feet. All the fans cheered as he waved and walked gingerly to the sidelines.

Celia cheered, but she was still worried about Josh, who hadn't gotten up yet. Coach helped him sit up, but they seemed to be checking his leg carefully. It looked like he was grimacing in pain and wasn't moving his left leg.

"Oh, no," Maddie whispered as the coach called for a stretcher to come to the field. Everyone watched as they lifted Josh onto the stretcher and carried him off the field toward the school. He waved to them and everyone cheered, but he was definitely not going to be playing anymore.

"Where are they taking him?" Celia asked.

"The infirmary. Dr. Spedacura will take care of him," an older girl in front of them explained.

"Where's the infirmary?"

"On the top floor of the main building, above the library."

"Oh."

"Don't worry," the girl said. "I'm sure he'll be fine by tomorrow."

Celia looked at her in confusion. She'd never seen someone recover from an injury that quickly, and she was pretty sure they were going to find out Josh's leg was broken.

The game continued, but without Josh on the field, the Mensaleon team seemed to be struggling. His replacement obviously wasn't as comfortable on the field, and he didn't seem to attack the ball the way Josh normally did. Things started going downhill for Mensaleon, and by the end of the game, they were behind 6 to 3. The final seconds ticked off the clock and a groan rose from the purple stands as Tattotauri scored once more, giving them a very lopsided victory.

Everyone filed back into the school to get ready for dinner and then the night match between Corpanthera and

Aquilegia. Celia and a few of her friends decided to try to find the infirmary to check on Josh before dinner, so they dumped their coats and headed off to the main building. They walked up the curved staircases in Main Hall and marched along the side balcony to the back side of the building. After going down a hallway along the side of the commons, they reached a staircase that took them up to the top level. A set of carved doors proclaimed the entrance to the infirmary, so they carefully pushed the door open and stepped inside.

"Hello?" a voice said, and they saw a man step through a doorway on the right. He looked older, with a pair of reading glasses perched low on his nose. He wore a bright red lab coat and was wiping his hands with a cloth as he came closer. "Can I help you?" he asked. "Another injury?"

"No," Celia said. "We were just wondering how Josh is doing."

"Josh . . . ah, yes. He came in a bit earlier. Oh, he's doing fine now that I amputated his injured arm."

"You *what!?*" the group of them chorused.

He looked at them in surprise. "You didn't hear? Yes, there was nothing more to be done, of course."

"But—you—he—" Celia spluttered.

Suddenly he chuckled. "Sorry, I couldn't resist. My wife says I have an odd sense of humor. Josh is doing just fine. His leg should be better by morning."

Celia could hear all the sighs of relief around her. "Can we see him?"

"Sure. He's right this way," the man said, leading them towards a door across the room. "By the way, I'm Dr. Spedacura. You must be Josh's friends."

"Hey, Doc, have you ever really amputated anything?" Heath asked as they approached the door.

"Oh, heavens, no. Never had to. Well, except that one time when someone came in after doing too much homework. Had to cut the pencil out of his hand." Celia looked at him with a raised eyebrow. "Hah! I see I can't fool you, young lady. I can tell you're a smart one." He pushed the door open and held it as they walked through. "Here you go, Josh. Company's here."

Celia and her friends stepped into the room and saw Josh sitting up in a bed near the window. His face lit up and he smiled when he saw them. "Hi, guys! Thanks for coming."

"Are you okay?" Maddie asked.

"Oh, sure. Dr. Spedacura fixed me right up."

"What happened?" Kitt asked.

"Broke my leg when I ran into Jim," he said, obviously referring to the player from Tattotauri.

"Ouch," Heath said.

"Yeah, no kidding."

"Where's your cast?" Celia asked.

"Cast?" Everyone looked at her with confused looks.

"Um, for when you have a broken bone?" When they still stared at her oddly, she gave up. "Okay, how do you fix a broken bone in the demesne?"

"Doc's a healer," Heath said.

"Well, yeah, all doctors are healers. So?"

Maddie shook her head. "No, he means a real healer. He heals with his hands."

"Are you saying...you mean..." Celia waved helplessly in the air. "He fixed your broken leg with his *hands*?"

"Yeah."

"But I...how...Okay, this is just too weird."

Maddie gave her a smirk. "Any weirder than you turning your feet into sand?"

Celia's mouth dropped open. "How did you hear about that?" She shook her head. "Never mind. It's...I..."

"Don't worry, miss," Dr. Spedacura said, walking up next to her. "A lot of people have trouble with it when they hear about it for the first time. You must not be familiar with the demesne."

"Um, no, not really."

"It's quite simple, really," he continued. "Healers are exceptionally gifted with their hands. It's the highest level of talent for those with the gift of touch."

"Oh."

Dr. Spedacura poked Josh's leg. "How's it feel?"

"Way better than before. Can I play tomorrow?"

"Absolutely not. But you can go watch the game by then. You'll be out of here by breakfast." He winked at Celia. "Good thing, too. Otherwise he might have to stay even longer after eating my wife's special sickbay meals."

Celia laughed, giving up on wrapping her mind around the idea of healing injuries with bare hands. After everything else she'd come across, why not that, too?

Maddie stomach growled. "I guess we'd better get down and have dinner. I'm starved."

"Maddie—"

"I know, I know. I'm always hungry. Get better, Josh. Too bad you can't play tomorrow. We needed you out there."

"Who won?"

"Um, Tattotauri," Kitt mumbled.

"Oh, man. All that for nothing."

"Well, just stay here and rest," Celia said. "We'll see you tomorrow."

"Okay. Thanks for coming up, guys."

"Bye, Dr. Spedacura."

"Nice to meet all of you."

They trooped down to the refectory and ate their dinner, then joined the crowds getting ready for the night match. As the sun dropped behind the mountains, the temperature outside dropped as well, so everyone bundled up to keep warm. Since his brother was playing, Heath decided to wear blue that evening to support him, and he stood out like a sore thumb amidst the purple outfits surrounding him.

Since Aquilegia had the unlucky position of playing two games in one day, the night match wasn't a particularly competitive game. The Aquilegia players were obviously tired, and Corpanthera dominated the play. It was an easy win for the team that lost last year's overall title in a tiebreaker.

Mensaleon played in the morning game on Sunday, and, just as Dr. Spedacura had said, Josh had been back at the table in the refectory for breakfast that morning. He'd said his leg was sore, but not too bad. He wanted to be out on the field, but wasn't really feeling up to that much, so he sat on the sidelines and watched.

Playing against Sprachursus, the Mensaleon team looked good, and easily won the match to give them a 1-1 record. Tattotauri won a surprise victory against Corpanthera that afternoon to put them in the lead with a 2-0 record.

The Fall Tournament wrapped up with an End of Tournament Banquet, which Celia enjoyed thoroughly since she'd missed the starting banquet. There was tons of food and everyone was in a good mood, but as the evening wound down, people started to realize they had to go to classes the next day and get their midterm scores. Celia was a little nervous about her grades, since she'd had such a jam-packed schedule. She just hoped she didn't fail miserably.

Chapter Ten
Envelope

Celia was pleasantly surprised by her exam scores. She hadn't gotten perfect scores like last year, but she hadn't gotten anything lower than an A-minus on any exam, a feat she thought was pretty spectacular, considering her hectic exam schedule.

There were mixed reactions around the school, as some people were relieved to have done well on their exams and others were dreading the reaction they would get when their parents saw their ERs, or Evaluation Reports, which would be sent out later that week.

Celia wasn't worried about her ER, not only because she had done fairly well on her exams, but also because she knew her guardian wouldn't have any problems signing her ER without giving her any lectures. Higby had never said anything about her grades, other than that she was doing well and to keep up the good work.

By midweek, the only thing anyone was talking about was the fall dance, which was being held that Friday. It seemed everyone wanted to know who everyone else had chosen as a date, what they were going to wear, or even if they were going at all. Even the seventh-years, who weren't allowed to attend, were curious.

Chapter Ten

"Are you going?" Audra asked Celia Wednesday evening in their room.

"Yeah, some of us are going just as a group of friends. It should be fun."

"It sounds like it."

"Who all is going?" Libby asked, walking over.

"Um, me, Maddie, Heath, Josh, and Kitt, so far. Who knows, we might add a few more by then."

"Oh. It sounds like you'll have a lot of fun."

"You can come with us."

"No, I'm going with Aric, Galena's brother's friend."

"Oh, that's right. Well, I'm sure you'll have a good time with him."

"Yeah..."

"I wish I could go," Audra said.

"Last year we all played a game of charades. It was loads of fun," Celia said. "I'm sure you guys will have a good time. Maybe even better than the dance."

"Yeah, maybe."

The next day at lunch, a bunch of the older girls were talking about the dresses they had bought for the dance.

"How do they buy clothes on campus?" Celia asked no one in particular.

"They don't," Odile said.

"Then how do you get a new dress for the dance?"

"Starting fourth year, you're allowed off campus during certain weekends," Odette explained.

"You are? How come I've never noticed that?"

Odile shrugged. "Because you're too busy doing homework?" Celia gave her a look. "Sorry, but it's true. Last year you spent most of your time in the library, avoiding Doxa. This year, you're always doing homework."

"You make me sound like a geek."

"Well, if the shoe fits..."

"Hey!"

"We're just kidding," Odette said. "We know you have a lot on your plate."

"But didn't you ever wonder how we were keeping up with our ballet while we're at school?" Odile asked.

"Well, now that you mention it..."

Odette laughed. "We got special permission for the first three years. It's been easier now that we don't have to do that, but we head off to special training sessions every month."

"Oh"

"For someone so incredibly gifted," Maddie said, "Celia tends to get a little involved in what she's working on. She doesn't seem to notice everything going on around her."

"I guess not," Odile said.

"Are you two going to the dance?" Maddie asked them.

"Yeah, Rowel finally got up enough courage to ask Odette to go," Odile said.

"And Odile's going with a first-year guy," Odette said.

"Well, I hope you two have fun," Celia said.

"It sounds like you two should have a pretty good time yourselves," Odile said.

"Why?"

"Everyone in the coterie is talking about your big group friends date. It sounds like a really good idea."

Maddie shrugged. "It wasn't my idea."

"Actually," Celia said, "the guys thought of it."

"Really? Too chicken to ask you to go as dates?"

Celia and Maddie looked at each other and burst out laughing. "Somehow I don't think any of them would be the type I'd be interested in," Maddie said, giggling.

"Yeah, they're more like brothers than...boyfriends." Celia choked on the word.

Chapter Ten

"We just thought it would be fun to go and not worry about all that boyfriend-girlfriend stuff," Maddie added.

"Hm, maybe you're onto something," Odile said. "I've noticed a lot of people getting way too stressed out over a school dance."

"Not us. We're just going to enjoy it."

Celia was surprised at the way they had gone from zeros to heroes in such a short amount of time as word spread throughout the school of their plan. Everyone thought it was a great idea, and a few people even came up to them to tell them they wished they had thought of it before agreeing to go as someone's date.

On Friday evening, Celia and Maddie put on their dresses and were ready to go in a short amount of time. They spent a little while watching everyone else on the girls' side of the coterie primp and preen in preparation for their dates, but finally decided they were getting tired just watching all of the running around.

Walking into the lounge, they noticed that it was filled mostly with guys, all apparently waiting for their dates to get ready.

"Um, hi," Maddie said hesitantly when every head in the room turned their way.

"You're ready already?" one of the guys asked.

"Yeah," Celia said.

He looked at her. "You guys look fine. What's taking the rest of them so long?"

They both shook their heads. "We have no idea."

After a little while, a small group of students were ready to head down to the refectory, where the dance was being held. Celia and her friends were, of course, among them. Josh and Kitt looked about the same as the rest of the guys, but Heath had decided to wear a bright, flashy Hawaiian shirt. There was no way he was going to get lost that evening.

The refectory had been decorated with streamers and balloons, and the lights were dimmed to create an entirely different feel. The tables had been pushed to the sides of the room, and a mirror ball hanging in the center of the room sent out sparkles of light. The guys immediately headed over to the snack table, filled with finger foods and other snacks and a huge punch bowl.

The room filled up fast, and a few brave souls decided to start the dancing, so the rest of the crowd joined in. Celia and her friends, who weren't officially there as dates, sat out most of the slow dances, choosing to enjoy people-watching or just sitting and talking, but they had a lot of fun dancing during the faster songs.

"How's your leg doing, Josh?" Maddie asked as they returned to their table for another slow dance.

"Great. Can't even tell that anything happened."

"Dude, do you think they'll do the limbo?" Heath asked.

They laughed, and Kitt slapped Heath on the back while he suggested, "Why don't you go ask them?"

Celia noticed that some of her classmates looked like they felt a little awkward, and she was glad she'd chosen to go with friends instead of trying to find a date. Not that she didn't like her guy friends, she just didn't... *like* them, like them.

Their table laughed even harder when Heath actually got up and went over to the disc jockey to request the limbo. They watched with curiosity as he gestured and the disc jockey shook his head vehemently. Heath said something else, and the disc jockey shook his head again, so Heath headed back to the table with slumped shoulders.

"He said no."

"Aw. I'm sorry, Heath," Maddie said.

"How come?" Josh asked.

Chapter Ten

"He said we're about out of time and he was going to do a final dance next."

"Oh."

Sure enough, the disc jockey announced the final dance and put on another slow song, so Celia and her group decided they didn't really need to stick around. They headed back up to their quarters to get ready for bed.

"How was the dance?" Audra asked, coming out of the lounge.

"Fun." "Good." "Not bad." "No limbo."

"What?"

"They wouldn't do the limbo for Heath," Maddie explained with a laugh.

"Oh."

Celia yawned. "I don't know about the rest of you, but I'm beat," she said.

"Yeah, I think it's time to hit the hay," Josh said.

Maddie and Celia each hugged their friends and thanked them for a fun evening, and then they all went to bed.

The next day, Celia had finished all her homework and was sitting on her bed, sorting through the box from her mother, hoping she would find something useful. She stretched out the information she'd found before and managed a decent grade on her last assignment, but if she didn't find something soon, she was going to be stuck for the next part, too.

She picked up another picture, looked at it, and set it aside. So far she'd found a lot of pictures, but not a lot of information about her family members. After that first book she'd found in the library, she'd found nothing more—not even a tiny tidbit. Hopefully that would change as she worked her way through the box. She turned back to the box and gasped. The next thing on the pile was a teal-colored envelope with very neat handwriting on the front. It said simply *Celia* in black ink.

With trembling hands, Celia picked up the envelope. Could it be that her mother had written her a note and left it for her to find, like a note in a bottle? It wasn't Professor Legaspi's handwriting, and she'd said no one had opened the box since Elle had given it to her.

Celia carefully flipped the envelope over to the back and saw a seal with the image of a stylized ram pressed into the wax. She knew that symbol. It was the same as the one on the card Mr. Morven had given her, the image he said represented the Overseer's princep.

Her heart racing, Celia carefully pried the wax seal open and slid out a folded sheet of teal paper. She thought her heart might beat right out of her chest it was pounding so hard. She couldn't wait to see what her mother had written. Carefully unfolding the paper, she held her breath as she opened the final fold, scanned the paper, and let her breath out in a whoosh as her shoulders slumped in disappointment.

The paper was covered with unreadable marks that looked like they might be pieces of writing, but never an entire word or even letter. A couple of marks at the top of the page were thicker than the rest, but nothing made any sense to her. It was impossible to tell what it was supposed to say, and no matter how hard she tried to figure it out, she couldn't read even one single word.

She fell back on her pillow in defeat. Just when she thought she was going to learn something, she ran into another roadblock. She was beginning to wonder if there was some reason she wasn't supposed to learn about her family.

An idea popping into her mind, Celia sat back up and turned to the box. Maybe there was something else in the box that told her how to read the letter. She quickly took the entire pile out of the box and flipped through. There were pictures and more pictures, but she didn't take the time to look at them. Halfway through the stack she came across a partial family tree, what looked like a rough draft from her father's sixth-year assignment. She set that aside to study it later and went back to the pile. Picture after picture went back into the box to be examined later. Celia held her breath as she flipped through the last few pieces, but let it out in a deep sigh when she reached the end and still had no clue how to read the letter.

She was still looking out the window, wallowing in disappointment, when Maddie came in the room a while later.

"Hi, Celia."

"Hi."

"What's wrong?"

Celia lifted her hand, still holding the letter, then dropped it back to her lap.

"What's that?"

"A letter."

"From who?"

"Whom."

"Huh?"

"It's 'from whom,' not 'from who'."

Maddie rolled her eyes. "Whatever. Who wrote the letter?"

"Don't know," Celia said, lifting one shoulder.

"Um," Maddie said carefully, walking over to Celia's bed, "can I come up there?"

"Sure."

Maddie climbed up the ladder and sat on the other end of the bed. "Now, what letter is this? Did someone else from camp write to you, uh, me?"

She shook her head.

"What's going on?"

Celia sighed and turned to her. "I found this in the box of stuff from my mom," she said, holding the envelope out for Maddie to see.

"Did your mom write this?"

"I don't know. I guess so."

"Why don't you know? Didn't the letter say who wrote it?"

"I don't know. Look." She thrust the letter under Maddie's nose.

"Oh."

"Yeah."

Maddie took the letter and studied it. "This doesn't make any sense," she said. "There's no way you can read this."

"I know."

"Well, why would your mom... or someone... leave you a letter you can't read?"

"Got me."

Maddie set the letter down and noticed the partial family tree. "Well, what's this?"

"I don't know. I haven't looked at it."

"But, Celia, this looks like your dad's family tree. Won't that help you?"

"I guess."

"Okay, what's wrong? You should be excited about this," she said, holding up the paper.

"Why? Because I get another little nibble of information about my family but can't read the words my mother wrote? Whoop-de-do."

"You don't know your mother wrote that."

"Professor Legaspi said my mother gave her that box to give to me and that no one had opened it since. Who else would have written it?"

"I don't know. I'm just saying."

Celia turned back to the window.

Chapter Ten

"Hey, there's a lot of information on here, Celia," Maddie said, studying the family tree. "It's a good thing you found this."

"Why?"

"Because our next assignment is to fill in the background for one of our parents, remember? You can start with your dad. You'll have plenty of information with this."

"I guess."

"Fine," she said, putting the paper down. "Sit up here and pout. See if I care. I'm not staying here so you can be a grump."

Celia sighed. "I'm sorry, Maddie. I'm just frustrated, and . . . disappointed."

Maddie reached over and gave her a hug. "Oh, I know. You get your hopes up thinking maybe you'll get to hear something from your mom, and all you find is this."

Celia tried to swallow the building tears.

"I wish I could help, but my grandfather won't let anyone talk about you . . ." She trailed off and bit her lip. "I probably shouldn't have said that."

Celia looked at her, confused. "Why would your grandfather have anything against me?"

"I don't *know*, Celia. My grandmother knows something, but she won't say, and my grandfather knows more, but he acts like I'm not talking whenever I ask him."

"And since your parents weren't part of the demesne . . ."

"They know absolutely nothing. At least, not firsthand."

"What do you mean?"

"Well, I mean, my mom obviously knows something from my grandfather. Otherwise, why would she dislike you so much? She wouldn't know anything about you if it weren't for her parents."

Celia sighed and leaned her head against the window. "It's so unfair."

"What is it my grandmother used to say? 'Fairs are for pigs and cotton candy'?"

Celia groaned. "Maddie, that's horrible."

"Sorry." She tapped the family tree. "But you should really look at this, Celia."

"Why?" she asked, reaching over to pick it up.

"Because it has your father's entire family on there. Or, at least, most of them."

"Look, my father had a sister, Emily."

"Did you know that?"

Celia thought for a moment. "I don't know. I don't think Aunt Agatha ever mentioned it...but then, she didn't talk about my family at all."

"How, exactly, is Aunt Agatha related to you?"

"Um...something with her nephew..."

"Was her nephew related to your parents?"

"I don't know."

"Maybe you should write and ask her."

Celia gave her a look. "Right. I'm sure she'd really be happy that I interrupted her time away from me and bothered her with another one of my selfish requests."

Maddie shrugged. "So put it in a way she can't refuse."

"What do you mean?"

"Ask her to send you her own family tree. Somehow she seems like the type that doesn't have a problem talking about herself."

Celia giggled. "Have you been spending time with Aunt Agatha behind my back? You seem to know her pretty well."

"It's a gift," Maddie said, buffing her fingernails on her shoulder in mock pride.

Celia sighed again. "Thanks for cheering me up, Maddie."

"No problem. What are friends for?"

She reached over and gave her best friend a hug. "You have to help me write a letter to Aunt Agatha."

"Sure. That'll be fun."

Celia spent the next week looking over her dad's family tree. She found out her dad had a sister who was about six years younger than he was. His parents, Greta and Reddick, were also listed on the family tree, but since her father had worked on it during his sixth-year at Renasci, there wasn't any information about what had happened to any of them since December some thirty years earlier, the date scrawled at the top of the page in very messy handwriting. She did learn from the assignment that her father had been in Sprachursus, so she now knew the coteries for both of her parents.

A little while later, not long after Celia sent a letter to her aunt, a large envelope addressed to her arrived in the mail.

"Look, Maddie," she said, waving the envelope as she walked into their room. "She took the bait."

"Open it! I want to see what she said."

Celia wrestled with the tape holding the flap closed, and finally managed to get the envelope open. Pulling out a thick stack of papers, she found a note card sitting on the top.

Celia,

I am delighted you are interested in the very distinguished ancestry of the Trowbridge family. We are, as I told you last summer, a family of very important and powerful people.

I have enclosed a complete genealogy of the family for your assignment; I am certain your professors and classmates will be suitably impressed with your pedigree. Should you require any additional information about any of these notable figures, I would be thrilled to assist you in any way possible.

Sincerely,

Agatha Trowbridge

Celia and Maddie cracked up when they read the note. "Oh, I can just picture your aunt saying that," Maddie said, laughing hard.

"Look at this thing," Celia said, hefting the genealogy Aunt Agatha had sent to her. "I don't need all of this. I just need to know how I'm related to her."

"Well, I guess we sit down and start reading," Maddie said, rolling up her sleeves.

A long time passed while they studied the immensely intricate family tree, which included inane details such as when people lost their first tooth or how tall they were on their fifth birthday.

"This guy had six toes on each foot," Maddie said.

"Oh, gross!" Celia looked back at her page and pointed to someone. "Her brothers called her 'Pig' as a nickname."

"That's terrible!"

"And this lady worked as a chamber maid in a castle."

Maddie laughed. "So much for the 'distinguished Trowbridge family'," she snickered.

Finally, Celia managed to find Aunt Agatha in all the mess.

"Look, there's Aunt Agatha," she said, pointing to her name. "Right there next to William. That must have been her brother."

"Who are we looking for?"

"We don't know, remember? I don't know how the two families are related."

"Well, William had a son, Charles."

"That's Aunt Agatha's nephew. She used to talk about him a lot."

"Where is he now?"

Celia shrugged. "I don't know."

Maddie looked at her with raised eyebrows. "It doesn't say he died, does it?"

"No, but that doesn't necessarily mean anything. Maybe she just stopped talking to him. Or maybe *he* stopped talking to *her*. I mean, you've met her, so you see how it could make sense."

"True." She looked back at the page. "Look, it says he got married."

"That's odd. His wife just has a first name... Maddie! That has to be it!"

"What?"

"Every single person on here has tons of information, even the people who married into the family. Everyone except Charles's wife!"

"What's her name?"

"Emily."

"Is there an Emily on your dad's family tree?"

"Yes, remember? That was my dad's sister's name. That must be my aunt!"

"You're right!"

"So my aunt married Aunt Agatha's nephew."

"Well, you've figured that out, then."

Celia frowned. "But what happened to my aunt, then? And my uncle, I suppose, since she was married to Charles."

Maddie shrugged. "I don't know. It doesn't say."

"No, and there's no way Aunt Agatha's going to tell me anything about that."

"So, we know that your aunt married your Aunt Agatha's nephew, but we don't know what happened to them. We also know the names of your father's parents, but again, we don't know what happened to them. We know what coteries your parents were in, but we don't know anything about what happened to them, either. I'd say you're in great shape, Celia."

"Gee. Thanks."

"Well, okay, at least you can fill in the blanks for your father's family tree and turn in that assignment. Mr. Dorset told us that once we hand that in at Thanksgiving, we won't have another one due until February. That gives you a little time to figure something out. Maybe by then we'll figure out what to do with that letter."

"Yeah, maybe." She didn't really hold out much hope.

Chapter Eleven
Unreadable

Thanksgiving crept up before Celia even realized it. She spent all her time either in class, working on homework, trying to research her family tree, or trying to figure out how to read her mysterious letter. With all of that going on, she barely even noticed that time was flying by and the holidays were approaching.

Professor Legaspi and Mr. Morven called her in for another meeting after midterms, once Higby had signed and returned her ER. Since she had survived her first quarter with high marks and was still reasonably sane, they decided to stick with the status quo and reevaluate again after semester finals.

Celia was still having a little trouble with some of her classmates, since they were still giving her a hard time every once in a while, but as time passed, the novelty of teasing her was starting to wear off and they were moving on to new targets. As they got further into the school year, Celia was finding her fourth-year classes more and more difficult, and her sixth-year classes seemed easier and easier. It helped that the topics they were studying in those classes were the same ones she was covering in her more advanced classes, but no matter the reason, she was relieved to find her sixth-year homework taking less and less time.

As the week of Thanksgiving approached, Celia and Maddie were discussing the letter she had found in the box from her mother.

"Do you have any other ideas?" Maddie asked, studying the letter again.

Celia shook her head, leaning back in the armchair and staring at the ceiling. "I tried everything I can think of. Unless there's something I'm missing, I can't read it. It's not a language I can understand and I can't see any hidden messages in it or anything."

"Maybe you have to fold it."

Celia sat up and looked at her. "Fold it?"

She shrugged. "Well, maybe it's like two halves of a letter and you have to fold it over itself to put the words together."

"I guess it's possible. But there are only the fold marks from when it was in the envelope."

"So maybe you have to fold it on one of those lines."

"Let's try," Celia said, holding her hand out for the letter. Maddie handed it to her and she walked over to a window. She folded the paper in half and held it up to the light. There were no obvious words jumping out, so she tried folding the paper lengthwise. Disappointed when nothing appeared that way either, she shook her head and slumped back into the chair. "No luck," she said, dropping the paper onto her lap.

Maddie sighed. "How are you going to read it?"

"I don't know."

"Have you asked any of the professors about it?"

She shook her head. "No. I thought about it, but..."

"But what?"

"I don't know. I just kind of wanted to read it for myself, I guess. If it really is from my mom, I'm not sure I want someone else reading it to me."

"Well, it won't do you any good if you can't read it at all. I think you should ask Professor Legaspi."

"I guess I could try."

Celia tried to set up a meeting with Professor Legaspi at the end of class the next day, while she was collecting all her books and everyone was filing out the door.

"I'm so sorry, Celia," she said. "I'm terribly busy right now. Can you just talk to me now?"

"Um...I'd rather not."

She looked up with a concerned look on her face. "Is something wrong?"

"No, no. Nothing's wrong. I just wanted...Well, it can wait, I guess."

"Are you sure?"

"Yeah, that's okay."

"Like I said, I'm really sorry. But I have a big project I'm working on and I'm right in the middle of it. Perhaps after Thanksgiving?"

Celia nodded, trying to keep the disappointment off her face. "Yeah, that's fine."

"Is it something Mr. Morven could help you with?"

"I...I don't think so."

Professor Legaspi studied her again. "You're sure it can wait?"

"Yeah. Really."

"All right. I've got to run. I'll see you, Celia."

"Okay," Celia said, watching with drooping shoulders as Professor Legaspi hurried out of the classroom.

"Well?" Maddie asked at lunch.

"She's busy. She said maybe after Thanksgiving."

"Oh. I'm sorry, Celia. I know you want to read that letter."

"Not much I can do about it now," Celia said, digging into a serving of macaroni and cheese with little enthusiasm.

Thanksgiving at Renasci was a real celebration. Decorations covered the school, giving a feeling of fall with colored leaves, ears of dried colored corn, scarecrows, gourds and pumpkins, hay bales, and corn shocks embellishing the entire campus. The cooks in the kitchen seemed to take Thanksgiving dinner as a challenge, preparing a mind-boggling array of delicious foods for the feast. The school started smelling of tasty aromas a few days before Thanksgiving, making it hard for everyone to concentrate on schoolwork.

On Thanksgiving, classes were cancelled and everyone enjoyed the brief respite from studying. Dinner was served a little earlier than usual, which was a very good thing, considering the smell of roasting turkey that was filling the halls. Since it was a special occasion, they served the meal the same as the opening dinner, with platters of turkey, heaping bowls of mashed potatoes, and loaded plates of rolls all served to the tables. After stuffing themselves with the turkey, potatoes, rolls, corn, cranberry sauce, stuffing, gravy, sweet potatoes, pumpkin pie, and pecan pie, all the students headed to bed with very full stomachs.

With no classes the next day, either, it was a day to celebrate, as well. It was too cold to play Soccovolle or football outside, since winter had arrived a bit early, but a few groups went to the gym to play basketball. Most of the students sat around enjoying the fireplaces that now had roaring fires in them, which were located all over the school. Main Hall was the obvious choice, as fireplaces lined the walls of the huge room, but the lounges in each coterie had a fireplace, too, so everyone could choose where they wanted to spend the day.

The Monday after Thanksgiving marked the first day of December, and that meant all the fall decorations on campus were replaced with Christmas decorations. Celia loved all the Christmas decorations. An enormous tree took up residence in Main Hall, standing in front of the huge wall of windows, it's star-capped tip nearly brushing the ceiling five stories up. With its ribbons, bows, and hundreds of lights, it looked quite festive, and filled the air with the scent of pine. Weekends meant the lights in Main Hall were dimmed in the evenings, leaving the room lit by the glowing lights on the tree and the numerous candles that appeared around the room.

Garlands of greenery and holly berries draped across the ceiling and matching smaller versions in the other hallways brought a holiday atmosphere to the entire school. Twinkling lights in the quarters gave the rooms a cozy feel each night, and Celia enjoyed spending her evenings with her curtains open so she could see the glow of the lights on the ceilings, just as she remembered from last year.

Professor Legaspi set up a meeting with her on Tuesday evening, and Celia was anxious to see if she could figure out the letter. Even though she'd waited this long to hear something from her mother, now it felt like each day was an eternity, knowing that the letter was sitting there but not being able to read it.

They got their grades for the next piece of their family tree assignment, the one they'd turned in just before Thanksgiving. Celia had done surprisingly well, thanks to the discovery of her father's family tree. She was dreading the next piece, which was going to be filling in the other half of her family tree, but since that wouldn't be due until March, she didn't have to worry about it yet.

The professors started talking about semester finals, which were only two and a half weeks away, and that made everyone a little nervous. Midterm scores went onto ERs, but semester final grades went onto permanent records, making them more important and more nerve-racking. For Celia, it meant another round of utter chaos, trying to fit all her exams into two days and rushing around like crazy again.

She tried not to think about that as she headed up to Professor Legaspi's office in the Aquilegia quarters on Tuesday. For now, she wanted to focus on the letter, held tightly in her hands, and her hopes that Professor Legaspi might be able to figure out what it said.

"Hi, Celia," Professor Legaspi said when she knocked on her office door. "Come on in." Celia closed the door behind her and took a seat in one of the silver-colored chairs. "So what's up?"

"I was sorting through the box my mom gave you to give to me," she said. "I found this." She held up the letter.

Professor Legaspi's eyebrows rose in surprise. "A letter?" Celia nodded and turned the envelope so that the front was facing her. "For you?" She frowned. "Is it from your mom?"

"I don't know. I can't read it."

Professor Legaspi looked at her with confusion. "What do you mean, you can't read it? Why not?"

"It's in some kind of code."

"I see. So, why haven't you decoded it?"

"I've tried everything I can think of, but I can't figure out what it says."

"I guess I don't understand. You're taking S-level classes in everything. It shouldn't be that hard for you to figure out how to read a coded letter." She held out her hand. "May I take a look?"

"Sure," Celia said, leaning over to hand her the envelope. Professor Legaspi took the paper out of the envelope and carefully unfolded it. Celia watched as she scanned the paper and a look of understanding came over her face.

"Ah, now I get it. This isn't a standard code." She frowned at the paper. "I'm not sure I've seen anything like this before." She glanced up at Celia. "Have you checked for hidden messages?"

Celia nodded. "Maddie suggested folding it, but that didn't work either."

"And it isn't in another language?"

"Not that I can figure out."

"Hmm." Professor Legaspi tapped a fingernail on her lip. She picked up the envelope again and studied the writing on the outside. "Well, I'm not sure if this helps or makes it worse, but the writing on the envelope is definitely from your mother."

"It is?"

She nodded. "I'd recognize her handwriting anywhere. It was almost disgusting how neat she always wrote."

"What do you suppose she wrote to me about?"

Shaking her head, she said, "I haven't the slightest idea. It could be almost anything."

"Oh."

"If I had to guess—since she specified that you were to receive the box at the start of your sixth year—it might be information about your family tree, but I could be completely off base on that."

"Do you know how to read it?"

"Not off the top of my head. Let me look at it a minute." She mumbled something as she frowned at the paper, her eyes darting around the page. After a few moments, she stared at it intently, and Celia guessed she was trying to look for something hidden either in the paper or behind the other writing, or perhaps some other kind of hidden message. She tried turning the paper in all different directions, flipping it around and looking at the back, curling it into a tube, and lining up different lines of text, but every time she shook her head and looked more confused.

"Let me try..." She leaned over and rummaged in one of her desk drawers, coming up with a large sheet of some sort of clear material. She set the letter in front of her and carefully laid the clear sheet over the top, checking every corner of the page, but then shook her head again. "Nothing. Strange."

"What?"

Professor Legaspi looked up, startled, as if she had forgotten that Celia was still sitting there. "Hm? Oh, well, it's just that Elle was in my coterie; we were both in Aquilegia. I would have figured that if she were going to write a coded message, she would have used something from that discipline as the means for encoding. It was, after all, her strongest ability, and it seems a little odd that I can't read this. But maybe..." She trailed off, frowning in thought again.

"What?"

Professor Legaspi looked at her again. "Do you happen to know what coterie your father was in when he was here?"

"Um, yeah. He was in Sprachursus."

"He was? I didn't know that."

"It was on the sheet I found in the box."

"What?"

"I found a piece of my father's family tree from when he worked on it during his sixth-year. It said he was in Sprachursus."

"Wow. Wait. That's how you managed to finish your last family tree assignment, isn't it?" When Celia nodded, she said, "Well, that was good timing, I guess, to find that when you needed it. I guess I've been a little busy, since I wasn't even aware you'd found it."

"That's okay."

Professor Legaspi turned her attention back to the letter. "Well, I suppose it's possible..."

"What?"

"If your mother was concerned about someone else finding this letter, then she would have made every effort to be certain it was encoded in such a way that the average person would not be able to read it. Even the average person in the demesne," she added.

"So how am I supposed to read it?"

"Well, it's possible that she asked your father to help her encode it, using sort of double coding, if you will."

"Double coding?"

She nodded. "Um-hm. She may have asked your father to translate it into some other language, since he would have been better at that and therefore known some rare language to use which wouldn't be widely known. There might be a message encoded in that translated messaged, and therefore double coded."

"Oh. But I tried reading it, and I couldn't."

"True. And you do have the gift of tongue. But..." She bit her lip in thought.

"What?"

"Well, it's possible that you just haven't had enough training yet." She tapped her fingernails on her desktop. "Do you mind if I ask Professor Perrin to take a look at it? Maybe he can help us."

Celia shrugged. "I guess not."

"Let me see if he can come up here." She turned to the phone on her desk and picked up the receiver. After pushing a few buttons, she put the receiver to her ear and waited. "Lee, could you come up to my office?... Thanks." She hung up the phone and turned to Celia. "He'll be right up." She went back to studying the letter while they waited.

Not long after, there was a knock on the door. "Come in," Professor Legaspi called. The door swung open and Professor Perrin came in.

"What did you need, Anne?"

"Celia and I need your help with something," she said, gesturing to Celia.

Professor Perrin turned to her. "Oh, hi, Celia. What's up?"

"Celia found this letter and we think it might be a big help with her family tree assignment, but she can't figure out what it says. We suspect it might be double coded, but we're not sure."

His eyebrows rose. "Double coded? Must be really important."

"We don't know. We're pretty sure it's from her mother," Professor Legaspi said, giving him a pointed look.

"Ooohhh," he said knowingly. "Well, let me see if I can give you a hand." He took the paper and studied the markings. "Wow, this is really unusual," he said. After looking at it for a few minutes, he shook his head and handed it back. "I'm sorry, Celia, but I've never seen anything like that before. I don't know that writing."

"Oh. Well, thanks anyway."

"Nothing?" Professor Legaspi asked. "Not even a hint?"

He shook his head. "I've studied an awful lot of languages, and I don't recognize that at all. It's been a long time since I came across anything in another language that I couldn't read. It's possible that it's some kind of language that she invented, but that still shouldn't be that hard for me to figure it out."

"So no clues at all?"

"Sorry, but no."

Professor Legaspi sighed. "Well, thanks for trying, Lee."

"Sure thing. See you both later," he said, heading out the door and closing it carefully behind him.

Silence fell over the office. Celia studied the carpet, growing more discouraged by the second. If her professors, who had gone through extensive training and were some of the best in their fields, couldn't figure it out, she was pretty sure there was no way she ever going to be able to read that letter. Her mother might have had an important message for her, but if she couldn't read it, it wouldn't really matter what the letter said.

"You tried codes and things like that?" Professor Legaspi finally asked.

Celia nodded. "I didn't find any sort of pattern. There aren't any markings that are exactly the same, and it's not likely that a message wouldn't have any repeated words."

Professor Legaspi nodded, but didn't say anything for a minute, and the office was silent again. "And you tried using touch? Like on your ALPHAs last year?"

She nodded again. "There's nothing there."

She sighed and folded the letter. "I'm completely stumped, Celia. I can try asking a few people who might be able to help, but if we can't figure this out, I'm not sure that they'll be any better." She tucked the letter back in the envelope and slid it across the desk. "I'll keep working on it, do some research, see if there's any information out there, but it doesn't seem likely. I wish I had better news."

"That's okay," Celia said, taking the letter back. Her throat felt tight and she just wanted to get back to her room and go to bed.

"No, it's not," Professor Legaspi said quietly. "I know it would mean so much for you to be able to hear from your mother, and I'm sure it's frustrating and disappointing to get this far only to hit a roadblock."

Celia lifted one shoulder in a shrug. "Thanks for trying."

Professor Legaspi gave her a small smile. "Sure."

She got to her feet and headed to the door. "Good night."

"Night, Celia."

Celia managed to make it back to her room and get ready for bed before the tears came. She'd really hoped that Professor Legaspi would be able to figure out how to read the letter. She wanted so badly to read her mother's words, and it was almost cruel to get this close only to be denied the opportunity. Wiping away tears as she looked at the stars through her window, Celia sighed with disappointment. She might never know what her mother had written to her, and for all she knew, that might have been her last chance to ever hear from her mother.

Celia tried to put the letter out of her mind and focus on her schoolwork. She spent some time in the library, trying to find more information about her mother's family, but she had little success. She'd learned quite a bit about Violet, but very little about the rest of the family, which she supposed was understandable, since Violet had been princep and therefore attracted more attention than the others.

The last weekend before finals, a pile of mail arrived for Celia. She set the stack on her desk, wondering who would be sending her this much mail.

"Who are they from?" Maddie asked.

"I don't know. I don't see any return addresses."

"Return addresses?"

"Yeah, you know, so they can be returned to the sender if they don't make it to where they were supposed to go?"

"What are you talking about?"

Celia looked up at Maddie. "Let me guess," she said. "Mail never has a problem getting anywhere in the demesne, and you've never heard of something being returned to the sender?"

"Yeah. Why bother sending something if it's just going to come back to you?" Maddie asked, a confused frown on her face.

"It's not that you *want* it to come back to you. Sometimes the postage…" At the bewildered look on Maddie's face, she gave up. "Never mind." She picked up the first envelope and opened it. After pulling out a Christmas card, she stared at it in shock. "A card? No one's ever sent me a card."

"Who's it from?"

Celia opened the card, then handed the card to Maddie with a disgusted look on her face. "It's yours," she said.

"Mine? Why—Oh."

"Yeah, oh."

She opened the rest of the pile and handed them all over to Maddie. Every single card in the stack was from someone at camp, addressed to Celia, but intended for "Celia" as they knew her.

"Well, I can leave them here over break so you can enjoy looking at them," Maddie offered in a cheery voice.

Celia gave her a stony look. "So I can look at the cards for me that really are for you?"

"Well, yeah?" She sounded uncertain.

"Thanks, but no. That's okay."

"Sorry, Celia. I didn't think about cards and stuff..."

Celia waved her off. "Don't worry about it. It's starting to get kind of funny. If anything comes for me, uh, *you* while you're gone, I'll just save it for you."

"I don't know," Maddie said, setting the cards on her desk. "I'm feeling kind of unpopular. No one's sent anything to me...um..." She trailed off, looking over at Celia.

"I knew they wouldn't."

"But..."

Celia shook her head. "Is it like this for you when we're at school?" she asked.

"Like what?"

"Does everyone pay attention to me and treat you like chopped liver?"

"Chopped liver?" She shook her head with confusion.

"Sorry. It's just an expression. It means, um, something useless, I guess."

"Oh. Well, kind of, I guess," she admitted.

"They do?"

"A little. It's not as bad as camp, I'll say that. But, yeah, people do kind of make a fuss over you and totally ignore me."

"That's so unfair!"

"Yeah, but you're really good at making sure I'm not left out. I guess I didn't do that so well at camp," she said, looking down at her feet.

"Don't worry about it. I asked you to take all the attention so I wouldn't have to."

"Well, yeah, but I kind of ignored you sometimes."

"Really, Maddie. Don't worry about it. Think of it as payback for all the times people pay attention to me and ignore you."

"And make you chopped liver?"

They both laughed. "Exactly," Celia said.

The last week of the semester was an extremely demanding week for Celia, filled with review, studying, and exams. She felt fairly confident about her exams, but still a little nervous, and the thought of trying to repeat the exam schedule from midterms was intimidating to say the least.

Much to her surprise, many of her professors had chosen practical exams for their S-level students, which worked out to Celia's advantage. While the C-level students took another written exam, the professors had the others work through a series of tasks that required application of the lessons they had studied that semester. They were graded on their ability to finish the tasks and how well they applied the techniques.

While Celia enjoyed practical exams more than written ones anyway, it was even better this time. Her professors graciously let her go first, allowing her to finish each exam quickly so she could make it to her next exam earlier than she anticipated. It made her exams much easier to survive, instead of the marathon session of written tests she'd had in October.

The school turned into a buzz of activity after the last exam, as everyone hurried to get on the BUS to go home for break. Celia, who, of course, was not going to spend the holidays with Aunt Agatha, was staying at the school again this year, and she sat in one of the armchairs in the center of the room and watched her frantic roommates. While she'd been the only one staying in the room last year, Audra was staying for break with her this year, and she sat in another armchair and watched the goings-on around her, too. They weren't sure who else in the coterie was staying.

As the girls in the room filtered out the door one at a time, they all wished the two of them a merry Christmas as they exited. Maddie was the last to leave, and she gave Audra a hug before turning to Celia.

"Have a good Christmas, Maddie," Celia said.

"You, too, Celia."

"Say hello to, um, your family, if that won't ruin the holidays for them."

Maddie laughed. "I will." She reached over and gave Celia a hug. "I'll see if I can find anything out while I'm there," she said.

"Don't get yourself in trouble," Celia warned.

"I won't. See you next year," she said as she headed out the door.

Celia and Audra watched until they couldn't see her anymore, then turned and looked at each other. "Well," Celia said, "want to go see who else is staying?"

"Sure."

They headed out to the foyer on their way to the lounge and saw Heath coming from the other side of the quarters.

"Hey, Heath, are you staying this year, too?"

"Oh, hi, Celia. Naw, actually, I forgot something. My parents wouldn't let me get out of going to great-aunt Mildred's this year." He sighed. "My cheeks hurt already."

Celia laughed, remembering he'd said his great-aunt pinched his cheeks every time he went to see her. "Well, good luck with that," she said. "Have a merry Christmas."

"You, too," he said as he walked out through the heavy wooden doors leading out of quarters.

"Let's go see who's in the lounge."

They were surprised to find the lounge deserted.

"Do you think we're the only ones staying?" Audra asked.

"I wouldn't think so," Celia said. "Let's check out the other rooms."

They headed for one of the other girls' rooms, over near the door to their room. Audra walked in front of Celia, but when she went to walk through the doorway, she bounced backwards into Celia. "Ouch!"

"What happened?"

"I don't know." Audra reached out and touched the open doorway. Her hand hit an invisible barrier in midair, as if a clear wall had been put up across the opening. "What's that?"

"I don't...Oh, wait. I know what that is," Celia said. "Last year, Doxa told me that no one can go into a room unless someone from the room is in there. She said they can't get past the doorway."

"Well, I guess we know there's no one in there," Audra said, rubbing her nose where she'd hit the barrier.

Celia tried to swallow a laugh, but couldn't, and soon they were giggling as they checked the other girls' room. This time Celia put her hand out and felt the doorway before they tried to walk in, and felt the same barrier on that door.

"I guess we should check the boys' rooms," Audra said.

Chapter Eleven

The three boys' rooms had the same barrier in the doorway, so they headed back to their own room. Audra put her hand up in front of her and stepped tentatively toward the door, but they walked in without a problem. "So, we're it?" she asked.

"Seems like it," Celia said. "It's kind of creepy up here without everyone else around."

They both froze in place when they heard a deep voice calling from the foyer. "Hello? I know you're in here."

Chapter Twelve

An Unexpected Christmas Gift

"Who's that?" Audra whispered, her eyes wide.

"I don't know," Celia whispered back.

"Where are you?" the voice called.

"What should we do?"

"I don't know!"

"Celia! Audra!"

"He knows our names! We're the only ones here!"

"Come on," Celia said, pulling Audra over to her bed. She yanked open her closet door and pushed Audra inside in front of her, pulling the door closed except for the last crack.

"Hello? I know you're here," the voice said again. Celia thought it sounded like it was coming closer. Audra clung to her arm, fingers digging in. Celia thought she heard her whimper.

"You can come out, now," the voice said, sounding very close. "I know you're in this room somewhere, 'cause I made it through the door."

"Oh, no!" Audra squeaked.

"Celia? Audra? It's okay. You can come out."

"Girls?" another voice—this one feminine—said. "Where are you?"

Chapter Twelve

"That sounds like Professor Twombly!" Celia said. She pushed the door open and peered around the corner of her bed. She nearly collapsed with relief when she saw Professor Twombly standing in the middle of the room, looking around with concern. "Come on, Audra. It's okay."

"What were you doing in your closet?" Professor Twombly asked. "Didn't you hear us calling?"

Celia licked her dry lips. "We, um, we heard a man's voice... and..."

"Oh, I'm so sorry," the man's voice said, and Celia saw a tall man step out from behind Professor Twombly. "I didn't mean to scare you."

"It-it's... um, okay." Celia's heartbeat was starting to return to normal.

"I didn't even think of that," Professor Twombly said. "Girls, I'd like you to meet my husband, Mr. Twombly."

Husband? Celia hadn't known Professor Twombly was married. "Um, nice to meet you," she said.

"You must be Celia," he said, smiling at her. "It's quite an honor to meet you."

"Uh, thank you."

"And you must be Audra," he said.

Audra blinked her wide eyes and swallowed hard, but when she tried to speak, no sound came out.

"I'm really terribly sorry for frightening you. I should have realized you might be afraid."

Celia took a deep breath. "It's all right. Really." She looked between the two adults. "Do, um, do you work at the school, too, Mr. Twombly?"

"Oh, no. I have a job at a company a little ways away. I commute to work."

"So you live here?"

"Yes, but you probably have never seen me before. I try to stay out of the way." Now that Celia wasn't completely petrified, she took a moment to study Mr. Twombly. He seemed to be almost the opposite of Professor Twombly, wearing neutral-colored clothes and a conservative haircut. He had plain features, with no particular attribute standing out as note-worthy.

"Girls, we were just coming to tell you that you're the only ones staying here for break," Professor Twombly said.

"We noticed," Celia said, and she saw Audra rub her nose.

"Well, Mr. Twombly and I are going on vacation over break, so I won't be staying here with you," she continued. "You can stay here and someone else will come up to stay with you, or you can go stay in one of the other coteries. It's your choice."

"Um..." Celia looked at Audra, who looked back at her.

"I think I'd rather stay here," Audra said quietly.

"That's fine," Professor Twombly said. "I'll find out who will stay with you and let you know."

"Okay."

They left the room and Audra collapsed into an armchair. "My heart is pounding so fast!" she said.

"I know."

A few minutes later, Professor Twombly came back to let them know that Professor Legaspi would be coming to stay with them. "She'll bunk down in our quarters," she said.

"Okay."

"Well, have a very merry Christmas," she said, heading for the door. "I'll see you girls next year."

"Bye, Professor Twombly."

A little bit later, Professor Legaspi showed up with a small bag in her hand. "Hi, girls," she said, sticking her head around the door. "The rest of the kids are down in Main Hall, if you want to go join them."

"Okay."

Chapter Twelve

There were about as many kids staying over Christmas this year as there had been last year, but where there had been more Mensaleon students staying last year, this year they had the fewest. The other coteries had at least five kids staying, and Aquilegia had the most with eight.

Christmas break had been Celia's favorite time at school last year. She and the rest of the kids from her coterie had spent the time playing games, watching movies, and just having a lot of fun. She hoped this year would be the same.

The small group of students ate dinner in the refectory and headed up to bed, all of them pretty tired after two days of exams. The next morning they were up fairly early, and everyone was delighted to find out it had started snowing overnight. They played in the snow for most of the morning, having snowball fights, making snowmen and snow angels, and attempting to build a snow fort, which ended up collapsing before they finished it.

When Christmas Eve rolled around, they gathered around the tree in Main Hall and drank hot chocolate while they enjoyed the glow from the lights. When they all grew tired, they headed up to their rooms to go to bed.

Celia tossed and turned while she slept, having very vivid and unusual dreams. She saw herself standing in front of a tall bookcase, so tall she couldn't even see the top. Somehow she knew that the book she wanted was up at the top, but every time she tried to climb the ladder next to the bookcase, it seemed like the bookcase grew taller. She climbed higher and higher, until she was up in the clouds, and birds started flying past her, their wings flapping as they went by. A few of them brushed up against her, and she shooed them away. When her hand hit one of them, she realized they weren't really birds, but sheets of paper flying around.

She reached out to grab one of them and found herself

falling off the ladder she had been climbing. Down, down she fell, floating through the air, snatching one of the paper birds on her way down. When she finally landed back on the floor again, she looked at the bookcase and saw an old, leather-bound book on the bottom shelf. She picked up the book and flipped it open, turning pages without paying much attention. The paper bird in her hand turned into an envelope, and the flap opened and another paper bird flew out. Snatching the bird out of the air, she held it up to the book and the paper turned into a real bird and flew off.

Celia sat straight up in bed, wide awake. She couldn't shake the feeling that there was something in that dream she was supposed to pay attention to, something that would help her. Trying desperately to remember every detail of the dream, she closed her eyes and searched her memory. There'd been a tall bookcase, maybe from the library? But she'd searched the library all over and hadn't found anything. And the paper bird...it had turned into an envelope...her mother's letter! Her heart pounding with excitement, Celia somehow knew that was the answer. Her dream had something to do with that letter. But what?

She thought again, and recalled what she had dreamed about after she'd caught the paper bird. She'd fallen to the floor...and there was an old book...The book! Why hadn't she thought of it before? Maybe it had something that would help. She scrambled out of bed and down the ladder. Closing her closet door behind her, she turned on the light and grabbed both the book and the note. Her fingers tingled when she picked up the book, and she felt a jolt of antici-pation run through her. She carefully opened the cover of the book and then flipped past a few pages. Her pulse raced as she tried to compare the markings in the book with the note from her mother she held in her hand.

Chapter Twelve

Lifting a hand to flip a few more pages, she felt the book begin to vibrate on her lap. The pages started to quiver and she pressed her back against the wall of the closet, trying to move away. A wind rushed through the closed space, and she felt the hairs on the back of her neck prickle. Just the same as the last time she had opened the book and felt that wind, it blew the pages until they stopped about a third of the way into the book.

Celia waited, expecting the blue light that had appeared from the book the last time, but no light ever appeared. The wind died down, but the pages still seemed to quiver. Slowly, carefully, she leaned forward and looked at the pages of the book. Her hands began to shake as she saw markings that looked very similar to the ones on her mother's letter. This had to be the key to reading the note, but what was she supposed to do with it? The book wasn't any more readable than the letter, so it wasn't the key to a code or anything like that.

She leaned her head back against the wall and closed her eyes, thinking hard. As she concentrated, she had a faint memory of the rest of the dream she'd been having just before she woke up. She'd been holding the book, and then...and then she held the note up to the book!

Her eyes popped open and she studied the letter. She wasn't sure that was going to do any good, since the letter was written on thick paper that wasn't even translucent. She glanced back at the book with it's still-quivering pages. It seemed almost to urge her on, so she decided to give it a try.

She set the letter on the left-hand page of the book and tried to line something up so she could read the writing, but she couldn't see anything through the thick teal paper. She sighed, getting a little discouraged, and shook her head. She had to be crazy, thinking this would work, but she slid the paper over to the right-hand page anyway. She shifted the sheet around and gasped when it moved on its own and seemed to melt into the page of the book, the markings of the bottom page bleeding onto the teal paper and lining up with the ink already on the letter.

The thick lines at the top of the page became the same stylized ram that had been on the seal of the envelope, and the remaining markings turned into the same exceptionally neat handwriting that was on the envelope. Celia sat breathing hard for a few moments, completely overwhelmed at everything. She had finally figured out how to read the letter. After more than ten years, she would finally get to hear something from her mother, even if it had been written long ago.

Wiping a tear from the corner of her eye, she took a steadying breath and started to read.

My darling daughter Celia,

If you are reading this, it is because our worst fears have come true and we are not with you. While my heart aches at the thought of being separated from you, I am encouraged to know that you have made it to this point and are reading this letter.

Per the instructions I left, you should be reading this as you are a sixth-year student at Renasci and working on your family tree. I write not only to help you with that, but also for a more urgent and pressing matter.

I have left for you an object, hidden in the school, which will help you with your genealogy but is vital to your role as princep. I cannot tell you where it is hidden for fear it might be discovered; you will have to find it yourself through the clues I have left you. I have no doubt that you are a very intelligent girl and am confident you will succeed.

One note of caution: Should this object fall into the wrong hands, it would mean certain disaster for you and the demesne, so be careful whom you trust.

As always, my precious little girl, I love you. Good luck.

Your loving mother,

Elle

Clue #1: The roots grow deep - 77 feet to be exact. But the third branch is the most important. For at its center is the answer you seek.

She read it three or four times, trying to soak in every word. Giving up, she carefully set the book on the floor beside her and scrambled to her feet. She grabbed a notebook off her desk and hurried back into the closet, where she carefully copied the words of the letter. When she finished, she studied the letter, trying to figure out if she was supposed to leave it in the book or take it back out. If she left it in the book, then anyone who came across that page would be able to read the entire letter, and her mother had written a clear warning. But how was she supposed to get it off the page?

She spied a loose corner at the bottom of the letter, so she slipped a fingernail under the edge of the teal paper. The corner lifted, and the ink faded from the page as if dissolving in water. As she lifted the rest of the page, the paper separated from the page in the book and the ink markings disappeared, leaving only the original marks on the paper.

Celia carefully folded the letter and tucked it back in the envelope. She closed the book, noticing its pages were no longer quivering, and set both the book and the letter on a shelf in the closet. Grabbing her notebook, she reread her mother's words. Just when she figured out one mystery, she ran into another, and this time it wasn't just a question of figuring out how to read a letter. Now she had to go on a hunt around the school.

Leaving the notebook in her closet and closing the door behind her, Celia climbed back up into bed. Glancing at the clock on the bookshelf next to her bed, she saw that it was after two in the morning. Smiling to herself as she fell back asleep, she thought it might have been the best Christmas present she'd ever received.

Chapter Twelve

"How did you ever figure it out?" Professor Legaspi asked, studying the copied words in Celia's notebook the next morning.

Celia had woken up early and found a pile of presents for Audra and herself tucked under the tree in their room. They'd carried them into the lounge and opened their presents in front of the fireplace, their feet tucked up under their robes because it was quite chilly that morning.

Celia had received a framed family tree from Aunt Agatha, who had apparently decided that she was fascinated by the Trowbridge family genealogy, never mind that Celia wasn't even *on* the family tree. Maddie had given her a leather-covered journal—purple, of course. She'd gotten a pile of candy from a group of her friends, including Josh, Heath, Odile, and Odette, which she promptly shared with Audra because there was no way she could eat that much without getting sick.

When Professor Legaspi woke up, she joined them in the lounge, sipping from a mug, while she watched them open the rest of their presents. When Audra went to take a shower and get dressed, Celia told her about the letter, prompting her professor's question.

Celia bit her lip. "This might sound strange, but... I had this dream, and..."

Professor Legaspi shook her head, a smile on her face. "Not strange at all, Celia." She waved a hand at the richly-decorated purple-and-gold wallpaper on the walls around them. "You're in Mensaleon, and you definitely have gifts of the mind. Your dreams are a way for you to learn information you can't learn any other way."

"Really? I mean, I'm taking Dream Interpretation, but we've just been working on other people's dreams."

"And you think your dreams don't work just as well?" She shook her head. "I would venture to guess that *your* dreams in particular, Celia, have a much greater meaning." She glanced at the clock on the wall. "You'd probably better go get ready if you want to eat breakfast. We can talk about this more later."

The table in the refectory was loaded with sweetened breads and rolls and all sorts of scrumptious-looking delights. The small group of students loaded their plates and sat down to enjoy their meal.

"Wow, I wish my mom could make these," someone said.

"I wish we could have this every day!"

Agreements sounded from all around the tables.

In a rather short amount of time, the group polished off every last piece of pastry and then headed off to enjoy all their Christmas presents. Professor Legaspi and Celia retreated into Professor Twombly's office to talk about the letter.

"So your mother hid something at the school," Professor Legaspi said thoughtfully.

"Do you know anything about it?"

"Unfortunately, no. There were many areas of her life which your mother was not able to discuss with me."

"Why?"

She sighed. "Things were... difficult, Celia. Casimir... I'm not sure how much I should tell you. I'm not sure how much I *can* tell you."

"Why?" Celia asked again, feeling a little like a broken record.

"Well, I was good friends with your mother, but I wasn't really part of her life at the palace. I was finishing my schooling and then..."

"They disappeared."

"Yes."

"As far as I understand, the situation was tense, and no one was sure what Casimir was doing. Most people didn't know anything about it, and I'm not sure I understand all the reasons for that yet, but the few who did know about Casimir were trying very hard to make sure that information stayed where it belonged. So your mother wasn't able to tell me much of anything, I'm afraid."

"Oh."

"Do you have any ideas about the clue?"

Celia shook her head. "I guess maybe some sort of plant, with the roots and everything. But I don't know how you would find out how deep any of the roots are on any plant, never mind one that has three branches."

"Yes, it's a rather tricky clue. I wonder…"

"What?"

"Well, you know what coteries your parents were in, but I wonder if your mother had some mind abilities from her parents."

"Violet was in Tattotauri. I don't know about my grandfather, Sebastian."

"Hm." She didn't say anything more.

"Celia? Professor Legaspi?" Audra called from the foyer.

"We'd better go out there," Professor Legaspi said, rising to her feet. "I suggest you keep that in a safe place," she said, indicating the notebook with the words from the letter. "If your mother went to so much trouble to protect the contents of that letter, it's probably wise for you to do the same."

When the mail came later that day, Celia wasn't really surprised to find an envelope with her name on it. She figured it was likely another card for the other Celia from one of the girls at camp. It *was* a card, but she was surprised to find it was actually for her, not Maddie. The front had a winter scene that looked like it was from the Victorian era, with a candle in the window of a house. When she opened the card, she found this message:

Dear Celia,

I am quite certain that you are spending your Christmas at Renasci, and thought you might enjoy a card. I hope you have had a wonderful holiday.

I also hope you have had a good year so far, and that things are a little easier for you this year than they were last year.

Know that you are in my thoughts. Have a great holiday.

Warm wishes,

Doxa

Surprised, Celia read the note again. Either Doxa was putting on the biggest act she'd ever seen, or she really had changed. She still wasn't quite sure which was the case.

Over the next week, Celia and Audra spent time with the rest of the kids that had stayed at school, playing board games and watching movies. It was too cold to do much outside, so they usually picked a lounge and gathered there before deciding what they wanted to do.

Celia had been in the Aquilegia quarters and the Sprachursus quarters, but only as far as the deans' offices. It was a little odd to go into quarters for the other coteries. The layouts were similar, but not identical, so it was easy to get confused about which way to turn. Each coterie had a similar décor, much like the purple and gold theme in the Mensaleon quarters, but since each coterie had a different color, the quarters reflected that. Corpanthera's walls were blue and gold, Sprachursus had green and gold, Aquilegia had silver and gold, and Tattotauri had red and gold, all of them using their coterie color as the main color for furniture, curtains, and carpet. A quick glance into some of the rooms revealed the same beds as those of Celia and her roommates, only the thick curtains that pulled around the bed were made of blue, green, silver, or red material, depending on the room.

A few evenings, Celia and Audra stayed in their room and played backgammon with the set Blaine had given his sister for Christmas. While Celia had played backgammon before, she discovered Audra was a cunning and capable player. After losing ten times in a row one evening, Celia cried uncle and pleaded for mercy.

New Year's Eve found everyone gathered in Main Hall to count down to midnight. As the clocks in the school chimed twelve o'clock, everyone cried, "Happy New Year!", tossed confetti and streamers, and blew on paper horns or spun noisemakers. As the break wound to a close, everyone tried to squeeze the last few drops of fun out of the remaining days. On Sunday morning, the mood in the refectory was gloomy, as everyone realized that the rest of the students would be returning that day and classes started again the next day.

Celia, however, couldn't wait for Maddie to get back so she could tell her all about the letter. She played backgammon with Audra a few times, but her mind wasn't really on the game and Audra won easily. (Celia didn't want to admit that the outcome probably wouldn't have been much different if she *had* been paying attention, however.) Finally Audra said she was going to head down to Main Hall and wait for some of her other friends to get there.

Celia waited in an armchair, thinking about the clue from her mother's letter. She still hadn't come up with any good ideas. When she finally heard people coming into the quarters, she jumped to her feet and went out to the foyer. A stream of people came through the door and split in different directions as everyone headed back to their rooms. Finally Celia saw Maddie come through the door. She hurried over to where Celia stood and grabbed her shoulders.

Both of them spoke at the same time. "Guess what!?"

Chapter Thirteen
Answers and Questions

"You first! No, you!" They laughed and headed into their room.

"Tell me your news," Maddie said, setting her bag down next to her bed.

"I figured out the letter," Celia said quietly.

"No way!"

"Yes, way!"

"That's great! What did it say? Was it from your mom? How did you figure it out? Was it a code?"

"Slow down!"

"I want to know!"

"I'll tell you. Just be patient. What's your news?"

"Oh, I talked to my grandparents. I have some information for you."

"Will it help me finish my family tree?"

"Probably not. But it might help us figure out why my parents don't like you."

"Oh. Well, that's good."

"Let me get my stuff unpacked and then I want to know what was in that letter!" She tossed a backpack up onto her bed and took her other bag into her closet. A few minutes later, she returned. “Come on. Climb up on my bed. We can pull the curtains so no one can hear.”

“Okay.”

Once they were safely tucked inside the sound-proof curtains surrounding Maddie’s bed, she turned to Celia. “Okay, so how did you figure out the letter?”

“Well, this is gonna sound kind of weird, but I had a dream about it.”

“A dream? Cool.”

“It was Christmas Eve. I woke up thinking that my dream had to have something to do with the letter. So I headed into my closet to check it out.”

“And?”

“And the book went to the right page, just like last time.”

“Book? What book?”

“You know that big book I showed you last year, the one Mr. Morven told me to keep in the closet?” When Maddie nodded, she continued. “I saw that book in my dream. So when I went to check the book, it opened to the page I needed. I guess you kind of had to be there to understand that,” she said when she saw the disbelieving look on Maddie’s face.

“Okay. So you had the book open, but how did you know what to do?”

“My dream, again. In my dream, I held a piece of paper up to the book, so I tried that with the letter. It didn’t work on the left page, but when I put it on the right page, it sort of melted into the book and the ink markings on the page in the book seeped through onto the letter, and then I could read it.”

“Wow. That’s really neat! And on Christmas, too. What a great present! So what did it say?”

Celia held out the notebook she had brought up with her. “Here. I copied it down.”

Maddie took the notebook and read the contents of the letter. “Oh, wow. It’s like a treasure hunt!”

"Yeah."

"So have you figured it out yet?"

Celia gave her a droll look. "Do I look like I figured it out?"

"Okay. So you have another puzzle to solve. I'm sure you can solve this mystery, too."

"So tell me what you found out."

"It was tricky, but I talked to my grandmother when we were visiting over Christmas."

"And?"

"And she said that she couldn't really tell me much, since it wasn't her business to go blabbing it all over the place, but she'd try to get my grandfather to talk to me. And yes, that's pretty much exactly how she said it."

"Your grandmother sounds like a fun lady."

"Yeah, Grand-ma-ma's pretty cool. So, anyway, I guess she talked to Grandfather and convinced him, because he sat down the next day and told me a little bit. He said he couldn't tell me everything, because he'd made a promise not to talk about some things, but . . . "

"So what did he tell you?"

"Well, you know about Violet's brother, Tarver, right?"

"Yeah. He was her older brother."

"I guess my grandfather was really good friends with him."

"With Tarver? Really? Did he know Violet, too?"

"Yeah."

"You're kidding! Can I interview him? Maybe he could tell me something about them or my parents."

Maddie winced. "I don't think so."

"What? Why not?"

"See, Tarver was older than Violet, and I guess maybe he thought he should have been chosen as princep or something. Whatever it was, my grandfather said that it was really tough on Tarver when Violet was picked as princep."

"Oh."

"Yeah. And since my grandfather was friends with Tarver, he sort of...well, he's not exactly Violet's biggest fan."

"Oh."

"He said I was too young to hear some of it, but I guess there was a really rough time around when Violet was chosen and when she actually took the position of princep. He said not to bother checking the library here, because it wasn't something they wanted kids reading about."

"That doesn't sound good."

"No. It seemed like it was really bad."

"But why does he dislike Violet so much?"

"Celia..."

"Just tell me. Please."

"Okay. My grandfather said that it was Violet's fault that Tarver ended up in a wheelchair."

"A wheelchair? What happened?"

"I told you—he wouldn't tell me everything. But somehow Tarver was injured, and it left him paralyzed and in a wheelchair."

"Oh, that's terrible."

"Grandfather sort of went off on a rant when he said that. Something about a wedding and being selfish and 'you'd think after paying that kind of price'. I couldn't really follow what he was saying."

Celia thought for a moment. "So that's who the guy in the picture is...the one in the wheelchair. It was Tarver."

"Oh, yeah. We wondered who that was."

Celia frowned. "But I don't understand what all of this has to do with your parents not liking me."

"Well...Apparently my grandparents aren't *your* biggest fans, either. Or, at least, my grandfather. I'm not as sure about my grandmother."

"Oh."

"So my grandfather passed his dislike of Violet on to my mom, and they've sort of stretched it out to include you, I guess. It's possible that my grandfather just has a thing because you're princep, the same as Violet, but I'm not really sure."

"It's so unfair."

"I know. But since my dad wasn't part of the demesne when he met my mom, he's gotten all his information from her, and she's always gotten along better with my grandfather than my grandmother."

"So I didn't have a chance."

"Basically." She smiled. "But look at it this way—at least you know that they don't like you because of something you have no control over instead of disliking you for you."

"Oh, that's a whole lot better," Celia said sarcastically.

Maddie's stomach growled and she looked at her watch. "We'd better get ready for dinner," she said.

As Celia lay staring at the ceiling that night, she thought about what Maddie had told her. She wondered what had happened to Tarver, how he'd been injured, and why his friend, Maddie's grandfather, had come to the conclusion that it was all Violet's fault. Had Violet done something to Tarver? Somehow, Celia just didn't think that was possible. She'd seen the pictures of Violet and her family, and they certainly didn't seem to be enemies or anything. In fact, she recalled all the pictures where Tarver was giving his little sister a hard time—pulling her hair or poking her in the side. They were always laughing, that was for sure.

She remembered Maddie saying there had been a rough time when Violet had been picked as princep. What had that meant? Had it just been rough for the family? She didn't think so, since Maddie's grandfather had mentioned that there wouldn't be information in the school library. Why would he tell them that if there wasn't a record of it somewhere? And how was Celia supposed to find out what happened to her family if there wasn't any information in the school library? No wonder she'd hit a dead end in her research.

And how unfair was it that Maddie's parents didn't like her even before they had met her? Celia wondered how many other people had that opinion of her. Would she spend her entire life trying to convince people that she wasn't what they thought she was? She smiled in the dark as she remembered Maddie quoting her grandmother. "Fairs are for pigs and cotton candy." Maddie's "Grand-ma-ma" seemed like a great person to know. She wished she had known her grandparents.

That got her thinking about her family, and how little she knew about what happened to them. She assumed her grandparents had died, otherwise she wouldn't have gone to live with Aunt Agatha. Surely her grandparents would have chosen to take her in if they'd been around when her parents disappeared. And something must have happened to her aunt, her father's sister, otherwise she assumed she would have offered to take care of Celia. Of course, without any family members left, it was impossible for her to know what had happened to all of them. She might never find out.

She did know that Violet and Sebastian only had one child, her mother, because one of the books she'd found in the library had mentioned that. Without any other aunts or uncles, there would have been very few options for Celia once her parents disappeared. She thought about Higby, Mr. Morven, Professor Legaspi...any of them could have raised her, but she guessed they all figured she'd be better off with a relative, even a distant one, than a stranger. Celia wasn't so sure.

Rolling over on her side, Celia sighed. Oh, well. She couldn't change the decisions other people had made for her so many years ago. And she supposed she couldn't really change the opinions people had about her now, no matter how unfair and uninformed they might be. Drifting off to sleep, her last thought was of her family tree—how much she had filled in already, but also how many huge holes still remained.

"This assignment is due on January 30th, so plan your time accordingly."

Celia looked at her calendar and groaned silently. Professor Mesbur had just assigned a huge paper and it was due the same week as three other huge assignments for her other classes. Did her professors get together and decide to make everything due at the same time on purpose? It was only the end of the first week after break, and already she had homework piling up on her desk. She could just imagine what it would be like in a few more days, once she had assignments for the rest of her classes.

She gathered up all her papers and books after Professor Mesbur dismissed class and slung her bag over her shoulder. Weaving her way through the hallways, she noticed a lot of happy faces, since it was Friday afternoon. When she made it back up to quarters, she found Odile and Odette standing in the foyer.

"Hi, Celia," they said in unison.

"Oops, sorry," Odette said when Celia paused and looked at them. "We don't usually do the twin thing."

"Hi, guys."

"We've been waiting for you to get back," Odette said, an excited look on her face.

"You have? Why?"

"We got our mail today."

"Oh-kay." Celia glanced between them and wondered if she'd missed something. "Is there any particular reason why I should care that you got mail?"

Odile nodded, a big smile on her face.

"Well, are you going to tell me?"

Odile pulled her hands from behind her back and produced a business-size envelope. "Look!"

Celia read the envelope and lifted her eyebrows. "It's addressed to you, all right."

Odette shook her head and rolled her eyes. "Deel, would you take the thing out of the envelope!" She turned to Celia as her sister did as asked. "It's a letter from our Uncle Ezra, you know, the one who worked in the palace for your grandmother?"

"Really?" Celia's interest perked up a bit.

"We asked him about your grandmother when we saw him at Christmas. He said he'd try to put together some information for you."

"And he sent this," Odile said, proudly displaying a sheet of paper covered with messy scribbling.

Odette added, "We know there isn't a whole lot of information there for you, and you probably already know some of it, maybe most of it, but we hope there's something on there that can help you."

"Oh, thanks, guys," Celia said, taking the paper and trying to read the first line. "That was so nice of you."

Odile shrugged. "Well, we've sort of adopted you as our honorary little sister, and we thought it might help."

Celia didn't know what to say. She'd spent so many years with Aunt Agatha, who never went out of her way to do anything for her, and she'd met so many people at school who treated her like family even though they'd never met her before now. "I..." She gave up trying to find the words and just decided to hug them instead.

Chapter Thirteen

"Well, we'd better head down to dinner," Odette said, her eyes suspiciously moist.

"Yeah, see you later, Celia."

"Okay. Thanks again." She walked into her room, still trying to decipher the print on the page, and dropped her bag by her desk.

"What's that?"

"What?" Celia looked up and saw Maddie's questioning look. "Oh, this. Odette and Odile asked their uncle about my grandmother. They thought he might have some information that would help me with my family tree."

"Does he?"

"I don't know," she said, holding the paper out so Maddie could see. "I can't read his handwriting."

"Oh. That's worse than my brother's handwriting, and he's only six."

"Well, I guess I'll work on it later. Right now, I'm starved."

"So have you had any ideas about...you know?" Maddie asked quietly on their way down to the refectory.

"No, nothing," Celia said. She knew Maddie was referring to the clue in her mother's letter, but she hadn't come up with any leads yet.

"What do you suppose she hid?"

"I honestly don't have any idea. It could be just about anything."

"Do you think it's something big, or small?"

"Maddie, how would I know?"

"Well, I was just asking!" They walked in silence for a little. "How many clues do you think there are?"

"Maddie—"

"I'm just—"

"Asking, I know. But I have no way of knowing." She thought for a moment. "I would guess that there have to be at least two, since it said 'number one' on this one, but it could be fifty for all I know."

"Fifty!? You'd never find that many."

"I know."

They reached the refectory and went to find a table. "So how are you going to figure this one out?"

"Maybe I'll have another dream or something, I don't know. All I know is that the more I think about it, the more frustrated I get."

"Frustrated about what?" Kitt asked as they sat down at the table he had saved.

Celia shook her head. "Just something I'm working on."

"Want to tell me? Maybe I can help."

She shook her head again. "No, thanks. That's okay."

"Well... all right."

"It's nothing personal, Kitt, it's just..."

"Hey, it's okay. You're entitled to keep secrets from me. After all, you are the next princep."

"No, it's not—" Celia sighed. "I'm not keeping secrets. I just don't want the whole world to know about this, okay?"

"Sure."

"Know about what?" Josh asked as he came up.

"Celia's secret," Kitt said.

"What secret?" Josh said, looking at her.

"If I told you, it wouldn't be a secret, would it?"

"Ah, ha ha. Very funny."

Celia just smirked.

"She doesn't want to tell anyone," Kitt said, leaning over to Josh's shoulder.

"Oh. Why not?"

"Beats me."

"Why not?" he asked Celia.

"Because I don't, okay?"

"That's not an answer."

"Look, it's my secret and if I don't want to tell anyone, then that's my choice."

"Ah, so there *is* a secret," Kitt said.

"What secret?" Heath asked as he walked up.

Celia threw her hands in the air. "Why don't we just announce it to the whole school?"

"Fine with me," Josh said.

Celia turned to her best friend, who was watching the situation with wide eyes. "Give me a hand, will you?"

She lifted her hands in front of her. "Sorry. I'm staying out of this one."

Celia made a sound of frustration and turned back to the table. "Okay. I'm going to say this one more time, and then I refuse to say anything more. It's my business and I choose not to tell anyone, so stop bugging me about it, all right?"

"Okay." "Fine." "A-okay with me."

"But, what were we talking about, anyway?" Heath asked, a confused look on his face.

"Something Celia won't tell us about."

"Why not?" Heath asked her. She let out a low growl, and his eyes widened as he leaned back in his chair. "Hey, merrar. I won't ask again," he said, using his word for an apology.

Over the next few weeks, Celia tried desperately to keep up with everything that was going on. She struggled to finish all the big assignments her professors piled on in addition to the everyday homework, as well as trying to do research for her family tree. The piece of paper from Odile and Odette's uncle proved to be little help, as all it really had was a description of Violet, a few dates of important events, and a couple of anecdotes from his time at the palace.

With all her time in the library, Celia also tried to keep an eye out for any information about plants with seventy-seven-foot roots and at least three branches, but she had no success. She was completely stumped about the clue, and with each day that passed she got a little more tense, worrying that someone else might find the hidden object before she had a chance to track it down.

By the end of January, the deans all decided to hold their annual decorating contest in quarters to keep cabin fever at bay. They provided materials for all the students to decorate their rooms, and each coterie gave out awards for the Best Decorations and Most Creative rooms.

Celia and her seven roommates picked an Egyptian pyramids theme, with hieroglyphics, mummies, a sarcophagus, and pictures of camels. They made palm trees to go around the room, and thought they had done a pretty decent job. Everyone who saw their room said it looked great, and they were rewarded with the Best Decorations award.

One of the boys' rooms won Most Creative with a creepy crawly bug room, complete with spiders that fell from the ceiling and remote control "mice" that ran across your feet. Celia didn't spend a lot of time in their room, but she had to admit it was very well done.

February arrived with a huge snowstorm, dumping feet of snow on the campus. The walls of windows on the first floor were covered almost halfway up with drifts of snow. It made it impossible to go outside, and despite the attempts to avoid it, almost everyone started getting cabin fever.

To cheer up the gloomy students, the staff had a game night in the gym, with booths set up all over offering chances to knock down milk bottles, get a ring on a rubber duck, or pop a balloon with a dart. Celia, who had never been allowed to go to any sort of fair or carnival with Aunt Agatha (who would have found it all very distasteful), enjoyed the evening immensely, particularly since it gave her a chance to forget about everything else going on.

Chapter Thirteen

Valentine's Day meant the return of candy-grams, which students could send to each other. Last year, Celia and her classmates in Mensaleon had sent them to each other, just so no one would be left out. This year, however, Libby was busy with her new boyfriend, Aric, so she was sending a candy-gram to him, and they all decided to just skip the group candy-grams. Celia figured that would mean she wasn't getting one, but she was pleasantly surprised to find one on her desk when she returned to her room after classes that afternoon.

She opened the card, but it wasn't signed, and said simply, "Happy Valentine's Day." *Odd*, she thought. It didn't say it was from a secret admirer or anything, so she guessed it was from one of her friends, but no one would admit to sending it. Since she didn't know who to thank for her candy, she went ahead and enjoyed it, savoring every morsel of chocolate and cream filling.

As February drew to a close, Celia started getting a little nervous about the clue from her mother. It had been nearly two months and she still wasn't any closer to figuring out what the clue meant or what she was supposed to do with it. They were nearing spring midterms, which meant she only had about three months left before she had to go back to Aunt Agatha's for the summer, and she didn't want to take the chance that someone else would find the object while she was away.

The start of March also meant the next assignment for their family tree projects would be due soon. Celia still didn't have more than a couple of sentences of information, and she was pretty sure that wasn't going to be enough to get a decent grade. Add all of that to the stress of midterms, and Celia was feeling quite frazzled.

She talked to Professor Legaspi one weekend, hoping she might have some ideas about all of it.

"I still haven't come up with anything for the clue from my mom."

She shook her head. "I've thought about it, too, and I'm as stumped as you are."

Celia sighed. "How am I going to find whatever it is she hid? What if someone finds it before me?"

"Celia, if whatever it is has stayed hidden for ten years, I think it can wait a few more weeks while you figure out the clue."

"But what if I don't?"

Professor Legaspi pinned her with a look. "Your mother was confident that you would be able to solve the clues and find whatever she hid, and I see no reason not to be that confident, as well."

Celia studied her hands in her lap. "I don't know."

"What's wrong?"

"If I haven't figured it out by now, I just don't see how I'm ever going to find it."

"Are you, or are you not, the girl who's taking a full double load of classes and getting high marks to boot?"

"For now."

"What do you mean?"

"I don't have anything to hand in for my family tree assignment."

"Again?"

Celia shrugged helplessly. "I've tried to do research, but there just isn't any information in the library. Last time I found that paper from my dad in the box, but I've been through everything else in there, and there's nothing more. I don't know who else I can talk to, since there's no one left from any branch of my family. The only people I know of who knew anyone in my family either gave me all the information they have or they don't want anything to do with me."

She frowned. "Don't want anything to do with you? What do you mean?"

"Maddie's grandfather was friends with my grandmother's brother. But he doesn't like me very much."

"I didn't know you'd met Maddie's grandfather."

"I haven't." Her words were heavy with unspoken meaning.

"Ah." She sighed. "Well, unfortunately for both of us, Headmaster Doyen has been adamant that students must receive the grades they earn—no excuses. If you can't hand anything in, then there's nothing we, as professors, can do but give you a zero, regardless of the circumstances."

"But..."

"I know. I've tried everything I know of, but he won't budge."

"Then I guess that's it, then," Celia said wearily as she got to her feet.

"If you come up with anything, turn it in. Something is better than nothing."

"Okay." She wasn't going to hold her breath.

"Hang in there, Celia," Professor Legaspi said as Celia opened the door. "I'm sure things will get better."

As Celia walked back to her room, she mused that this year wasn't all that different from last year. Everyone kept telling her things would get better, and every time someone told her that, things seemed to get worse.

Turning a corner, Celia pulled up short to keep from running into the tall figure that appeared in front of her.

"Good afternoon, Miss Fincastle."

"Hello, Mr. Bazemore," she said, angling her head up to look at him.

He cocked his head. "You seem upset. Is anything wrong?"

Celia shrugged and shook her head. "No."

"Are your classes going well?"

"They're fine."

"Hm. You're a sixth-year, is that correct?"

"Yes."

"So you're working on your family tree?"

She looked at him. "Y-Yes."

He didn't miss the hesitation. "Are you having trouble with your family tree?"

"Um, a little, I guess."

"What seems to be the problem?"

"Lack of family."

"Excuse me?"

She sighed. "I don't have any family members left to talk to about my family tree."

It was his turn to pause. He gave her such an intense stare that she started to feel uncomfortable. "Well," he finally said, "surely your professors are being understanding about your situation."

"They are, but Headmaster Doyen isn't."

"How so?"

"He won't let them give me a break. He says that everyone has to get the grade they earn." She rubbed at the floor with the toe of her shoe.

"How does he expect you to learn about your family when they... aren't around?"

She shrugged. "I don't know."

"Hm." He put his hand to his chin in thought. "Let me see what I can do for you, Miss Fincastle. It doesn't seem fair to punish you for something that's beyond your control. I'll try talking to the headmaster."

"Um, thank you, Mr. Bazemore."

"You're very welcome. Have a good day."

Celia watched him walk down the hallway, a little confused. He still made her hair stand on end, but he seemed to be fairly nice. And if he actually got Headmaster Doyen to change his rules for her, that would be amazing. She turned around and kept going to her room. Maybe she had misjudged him.

Chapter Fourteen
Midterm Frustration

The Monday before midterms, Celia handed in her measly report for her family tree, hoping Mr. Bazemore had been able to convince Headmaster Doyen to let her professors cut her some slack. On Wednesday, she got her paper back with a big, fat, red zero on the top. So much for some slack.

She picked at her dinner that evening, refusing to talk to anyone. She'd never gotten a zero on anything in her life, and she didn't like getting one now. It was particularly upsetting to know that she had gotten a zero because of something she had no control over in the first place. She certainly hadn't asked to be in her position, no matter how great everyone thought it might be to be princep. She would gladly take not being chosen as princep if it meant she could have her parents back.

She sighed and drew circles in her ketchup. Not that she knew what had happened to her parents. For all she knew, they had been killed in whatever had happened when they disappeared. And thanks to whoever was behind all of that, she was stuck getting zeros on her assignments, even though she was working ten times harder than everyone around her.

"You okay?" Maddie asked.

Celia nodded, her chin on her hand.

"You sure? You don't seem like it…"

She nodded again.

"Okay." Maddie sounded anything but certain.

Celia's mood went from bad to worse that evening, and she spent her time cocooned in her bed, the curtains drawn, watching the rain that was falling outside her window until it was too dark to see anything.

The next morning, she ate breakfast with everyone, still sullen and withdrawn. While everyone else went back to their rooms to collect the things they would need for their midterms, Celia climbed back onto her bed and looked out the window again.

"Celia?" Maddie asked. When she received no answer, she said, "Don't you need to get going?"

Celia shrugged.

"Aren't you going to be late for your exams?"

"I'm not taking them."

Dead silence.

"What?" Maddie whispered.

"I'm not taking my exams."

"But, Celia," Maddie sputtered. "You have to."

"No, I don't."

"But—"

"You'd better get to your exam. You don't want to be late."

There was a long hesitation. "Fine. Have it your way."

Celia spent the morning thinking and watching out the window, where it was still raining. Maddie came back after she finished her exam, but when Celia refused to talk to her, she threw her hands up in defeat and left the room.

At lunchtime, Professor Legaspi came in. "What's this I hear about you skipping your exams?"

Celia glanced over at her. "I'm not taking them."

She lifted her eyebrows. "You do realize they're required."

"So?" She turned back to the window.

"So you'll get zeros for a substantial portion of your grade."

She shrugged carelessly. "I'm already getting zeros. I might as well earn them," she said bitterly.

Professor Legaspi was quiet for a moment. "What is going on, Celia?"

"Nothing. I just don't see the point in taking exams and trying to get good grades when I'm going to end up with lousy ones anyway, just because no one knows what happened to my parents."

"So you're giving up."

"No. Giving in."

"I see." Professor Legaspi sighed. "I didn't think you were a quitter, Celia."

"I'm not quitting. I just can't win, so why bother trying?"

"If you were having this much trouble, why didn't you come talk to me and drop your extra classes? I told you before, you don't have to take all these classes if you don't want to."

"It wouldn't make any difference. I'm failing all my sixth-year classes because of the stupid family tree project."

"So you decided you might as well fail your fourth-year classes, too? That doesn't make any sense!"

Celia lifted one shoulder in a shrug but didn't say anything.

"Did you take your exams this morning?"

"No."

"Celia..." Celia heard her take a deep breath. "Okay. I don't know what's going on, but you really need to take your exams this afternoon."

"Why?"

"Because," she said in what seemed like a very controlled voice, "a lot of people have gone to a lot of trouble to make this work for you, Celia."

"It doesn't seem to be working so well if I'm getting zeros on my genealogy."

There was silence in the room for a full minute.

"Okay. I don't have time to argue about this now," Professor Legaspi finally said, sounding exasperated. "You *will* come to my office at seven o'clock this evening for a meeting, and if you're not there exactly on time, I will come up here and drag you there myself. Understood?"

Celia had never heard her speak that way. She nodded.

"Fine." There were heavy footsteps and muttering as she turned and left the room.

Celia ventured downstairs to grab a bite to eat, and was glad to find the refectory nearly empty. She saw Mr. Morven give her an odd look, but she tried not to pay any attention. Once she finished her meal, she went back up to her bed and stared out the window again.

She knew she was being childish and difficult, but she just couldn't bring herself to care much at the moment. She was tired of dealing with everything, tired of fighting against the schemes of people like Headmaster Doyen, tired of being Celia Fincastle. She just wanted it all to go away and never return.

Maddie showed up again close to dinner time, and she seemed surprised that Celia was still sitting on her bed. "Have you been there all day?"

"Except for lunch."

"*Celia!* You skipped all your exams!? Didn't Professor Legaspi come up to talk to you?"

"Yeah."

Maddie paused. "Ohhh, boy. You didn't listen, did you." It didn't sound like a question, so Celia didn't answer. "I'll bet she's pretty annoyed with you."

"Tuh," Celia huffed.

"Can I come up there?" she asked.

"I don't care."

Maddie ascended the ladder and sat down next to her. "Will you tell me what's going on?"

Celia bit the inside of her lip, but finally said, "I got a zero on my last family tree assignment."

"Oh, Celia, that wasn't fair of them!"

"I know. But it's not their fault."

"What do you mean?"

"Headmaster Doyen has this new policy of students getting the grades they 'earn'. They had no choice but to give me a zero."

"So you skipped your exams?"

"Why bother? I'm gonna fail my classes anyway because I can't finish my family tree."

"But, Celia!" Maddie shook her head. "I guess it's your decision, but I think it's the wrong choice. You're just letting him win."

"Maybe."

"Well, in the meantime, I guess we might as well go down and get dinner," she said, moving toward the ladder. "I don't know about you, but I'm planning to go to bed early tonight."

"I have to go to Professor Legaspi's office at seven."

Maddie stopped, turned back to her, and looked at her with a raised eyebrow. "Are you going?"

Celia nodded glumly. "She said she'd come get me if I didn't." She traced the path of a raindrop on the window. "Well, actually, she said she'd come drag me there if I didn't show up, but..."

Maddie's eyes widened. "Professor Legaspi said that?" When Celia nodded, she said, "Phew. She must be pretty mad. She's usually really laid-back."

The other girls from their room gave Celia a wide berth that evening, both at dinner and once they were back in their room. She saw some of them whispering and giving her sideways glances, but she didn't say anything to them.

Just before seven o'clock, she climbed down off her bed to go over to Professor Legaspi's office.

"Good luck," Maddie said.

"Thanks."

Celia dragged her feet all the way across the school and up to the Aquilegia quarters. The door to Professor Legaspi's office was closed, but it was almost exactly seven o'clock, so Celia knocked and waited for a response. She heard chair legs scrape on the floor and then, "Come in."

Slowly opening the door, she stepped inside. She swallowed hard when she saw that Professor Legaspi was not alone in her office. A very stern-looking Higby was sitting in a chair, and a very grim-looking Mr. Morven was leaning against the window sill. Professor Legaspi was sitting in her desk chair, one hand resting on her chin with the index finger laying on her cheek.

"Sit down," Professor Legaspi said, her voice inviting no questions.

Celia slipped into the chair next to Higby, feeling the icy stares of all three adults. Silence enveloped the room and the air was thick with tension. Celia picked at a piece of lint on her pants, wondering who was going to speak first.

"Well?" Higby finally said.

Celia glanced around at the three of them, then dropped her eyes back to her lap.

"Miss Fincastle." He sounded irritated.

"Yes."

"What do you have to say for yourself?"

"Nothing."

She heard Higby suck in a deep breath next to her, but he didn't say anything. Professor Legaspi leaned forward in her chair. "We have a big problem, Celia."

"Why?"

"I think you know why."

"It's no big deal. It's not like it's going to make any difference."

"Celia, you've missed an entire day of exams. That's pretty major."

"So?"

Professor Legaspi leaned back in her chair, her irritation showing on her face. Mr. Morven looked at her with raised eyebrows. She threw her hands up in a big shrug and then crossed her arms in front of her.

"Miss Fincastle, the expectations for students at this school are much higher than skipping exams and refusing to talk about it," Higby said, a note of warning in his voice.

"And what about punishing students for things they didn't do. Is that part of the school's expectations, too?"

"We handled that last year. This is this year."

"It sure feels like I'm being punished for not having my parents around."

He drew in a sharp breath. "You know as well as I do that we are not responsible for the actions and decisions of the headmaster."

"Then why am *I* responsible for the actions of someone else? I certainly didn't make my parents disappear."

"She has a point," Mr. Morven said quietly.

"Thomas!"

He shook his head violently. "No, I care about Celia just as much as the rest of you, and she has a valid point. Rambert's new policy of giving students the grades they 'earn' is obviously aimed at penalizing one person, and I think it's clear who that person is. There is no other student at this school who suffers from that rule to the extent that Celia does."

"But that doesn't give her the right to behave this way," Professor Legaspi countered.

"No, I agree. It's rude and disrespectful. But you can't honestly say she hasn't been treated unfairly from the minute she walked through the front doors." He pushed away from the window and began pacing, jamming a hand through his hair. "She's put up with it far longer than most people would." Celia watched him with wide eyes. She'd never seen him look anything but immaculate, and now his hair was mussed and his suit jacket was wrinkled.

"Be that as it may," Higby said, "she cannot just stop doing her schoolwork. She'll be expelled. And the headmaster's been waiting for the opportunity ever since he heard—"

"Higby!" Professor Legaspi said sharply, catching his eye and nodding toward Celia.

He glanced over at her and took a deep breath. "It is inexcusable for her to purposely fail a class."

"But the headmaster is making me fail anyway!"

"Higby," Professor Legaspi said in a calmer voice, "perhaps a less authoritative attitude might help."

Celia knew it was cliché, but she thought that if looks could kill, Professor Legaspi would be long gone at that point. There were undercurrents zinging through the room, and though she tried, Celia couldn't follow everything that was happening.

"I am the girl's guardian," Higby said, indignant.

"I am aware of that," Professor Legaspi said. "However, I believe the final authority rests with Agatha Trowbridge, and while Celia is at school, you act only as a temporary guardian for the purposes of signatures and the like." Celia could almost hear Higby's teeth grinding. "And in this instance, I believe that it would be best for everyone involved if we just settle down and discuss this calmly and rationally."

Silence settled over the room again.

"So where do we go from here?" Mr. Morven asked, leaning against the window sill again.

"Well, I suppose that's up to Miss Fincastle," Professor Legaspi said. She studied Celia for a moment. "Would you care to tell us why you skipped your exams today?"

"I told you. There's no point in taking my exams when I'm just going to fail my classes anyway because I can't finish my family tree."

"Oh, this is getting us nowhere," Higby said.

Professor Legaspi leaned her elbows on her desk and rested her forehead on her fingertips. "Would you two please give us a minute?" she asked. "I'd like to talk to Celia alone."

"Sure," Mr. Morven said, setting a hand on her shoulder as he walked past on his way to the door.

When Higby didn't move, she peered up at him and said, "Please? Just a minute."

He gave her a look that Celia couldn't interpret, then stood and followed Mr. Morven to the door. When the door closed behind them, Professor Legaspi lifted her head from her hands.

"Celia, what's really going on?"

Celia looked away. "Nothing."

"I don't think so. I want to help you, but my hands are tied if you won't talk to me."

"It's just too hard."

"What's too hard?"

"Trying to keep up with everything. I keep doing all the work, but it never makes any difference. No matter how hard I try, something always messes it up, just because I'm Celia Fincastle." She said her name as if she were announcing a celebrity's arrival. "I didn't ask to be me. It's not fair."

"Celia, you can't quit just because it gets hard. Giving up is never the answer." When Celia didn't respond, she sighed.

"Celia, I walk a very fine line with you. As your professor, I am supposed to maintain an impartial distance so I can grade you fairly in class. However, as I was good friends with your mother, I feel a bit responsible for you. In addition, I find it hard to remain uninvolved. You…you're more than just another student."

Celia met her eyes and saw the truth of her words.

"It is difficult for me to fight for what I believe you deserve and still avoid being accused of playing favorites. I have worked hard to make arrangements for you this year. We've met time and time again to make sure you wanted to continue with this schedule, and every time, you agreed to keep going. I don't believe you have been pushed into this, and it is, quite frankly, a real insult to have you repaying the work we have all done for you with this kind of behavior.

"I know things are difficult. I know it's hard. But things are not going to get easier. There will always be something else you'll have to overcome. You have to decide for yourself if you are going to choose the easy way out and quit, or if you're going to work hard and rise to the challenge."

She pushed to her feet. "I'm going to ask Higby and Mr. Morven to come back in and we're going to figure out what we're doing next." She walked over and opened the door, letting the two men back into the room. Both stood behind Celia's chair while Professor Legaspi took her seat behind her desk again.

"Have you agreed to take your exams tomorrow?" Higby asked.

"No," Celia said sourly, still upset.

"Celia, I'm afraid that we're going to have to be a little more firm with you," Professor Legaspi said. "Since you won't take the exams voluntarily, I am going to have to insist you take them tomorrow, and failure on your part to follow through will mean severe punishment. Do you understand?"

Celia nodded petulantly.

She sighed before continuing. "I'm quite certain your parents would not have approved of this kind of behavior, and I feel they would have made the same decision if they were here today. I don't like playing the heavy hand, but you've left me with no choice. I'll see what I can do about making up the exams you missed today, but I've called in so many favors already, I'm not sure that people will be willing to accommodate my requests after this."

"Celia, I hope you realize the seriousness of this situation," Higby said. "I expect you to take your exams tomorrow, and I approve of any punishment meted out should you fail to follow through."

She sat sullenly in her chair. Of course they were all going to take sides against her. Of course they were going to make her take her exams tomorrow.

Professor Legaspi looked at the clock. "It's getting late and some of us have a long day tomorrow. I suggest we all get to bed." Mr. Morven and Higby nodded in agreement. "I'll walk you back to your room, Celia."

They walked across the school in uneasy silence, Celia fuming about being forced to take her exams. Professor Legaspi headed into Professor Twombly's office, leaving Celia to go to her room. Stomping through the door, Celia saw a few of the girls watching her, but she didn't speak to any of them. She got ready for bed, her anger mounting with each minute that passed.

Going back into her room, she slammed her dresser drawer shut, then slapped shut the textbook sitting on her desk. She stormed up the ladder and onto her bed, then yanked her curtains closed. She didn't care if everyone in the room was afraid of her. She was too angry to care about anything.

Chapter Fourteen

How dare they order her to take her exams? And it had to be blackmail to use her parents as an excuse! If everyone wanted her to fail her classes, then why bother taking the exams? It's not like it would make a difference!

She threw her pillow down on the bed and flopped back and forth, trying to find a comfortable position. In the midst of her shifting, something hard and heavy fell off the bookshelf and cracked her on the head.

"OUCH!" she cried, knowing it wasn't going to do any good. No one could hear her behind her curtains. She rubbed her head, feeling a small goose egg starting to swell. Turning to see what had beaned her, she saw a thick book lying on the bed near her pillow.

"Stupid...book!" She jerked it off the bed and was about to stuff it unceremoniously back onto her bookshelf when she saw the title. It was the copy of *The Roots of Renasci* she'd bought at the rathskeller on her way to school her first time. She'd never gotten around to reading it, mostly because it was incredibly long and the first page had been one of the most boring things she'd read since Aunt Agatha made her read *The Proper Use of Silverware* a few years ago.

Her mind whirled. Roots...roots...could it be? She shook her head. No, it was impossible. But...the clue mentioned... On a whim, she opened the book and flipped to page seventy-seven. She felt a tingle on her skin when she saw a page with three maps. The third branch...

Peering closer, she saw that page seventy-seven was the right-hand side of a two-page spread with maps of each floor of the main building at Renasci. It started with the fifth floor on the top of the left-hand page and worked down the floors until the last map on the right-hand page, the basement.

She tried to remember what her mother's clue had said, but she couldn't recall the exact words. She scrambled down the ladder and grabbed the notebook out of her closet, carrying it back up to her bed.

"The roots grow deep, 77 feet to be exact," she read aloud to herself. "But the third branch is the most important. For at its center is the answer you seek." She looked down at the page in the book. The third map was the basement. Was her mother referring to the basement?

Squinting at the page, she saw the auditorium on one side of the basement and the kitchen on the other. And right in the middle...

"The prop room!?" Celia looked at it again, but it said the same thing. The prop storage room for the drama club sat right in the middle of the basement. Had her mother hidden something in the prop room? And if so, how was she ever going to find it? It would be hard enough to get to the basement without someone finding out about it, let alone trying to find something in the prop room when she didn't even know what she was looking for.

Of course, she could be completely wrong and the prop room might have nothing to do with the object her mother had hidden. Somehow it seemed a bit too coincidental, though. She just *happened* to get beaned by a book that just *happened* to mention roots and just *happened* to have three maps on page seventy-seven? It didn't seem likely that it was all just a lucky break.

Closing the book and sliding it back onto the shelf, she flipped her light off and went to sleep. In the morning, she felt a little better, but still a bit gloomy. Maddie didn't seem to be in a talkative mood, so they ate breakfast in relative silence. As they cleared their dishes off the table, Maddie looked at her tentatively.

"Are you taking your exams today?" she asked.

"Yeah. I have to."

"Why?"

"Because Professor Legaspi told me I'd be in serious trouble if I didn't."

"So you're only doing it to stay out of trouble?"

Celia wagged her head. "No, not really," she admitted. When Maddie lifted an eyebrow at her, she said, "I guess... it wouldn't be fair to Professor Legaspi, since she's gone to so much trouble for me."

Maddie gave her a look of approval. "I knew you weren't a selfish brat."

"Hey!" Celia cried, lightly shoving her shoulder.

"Come on. We'd better get going."

Celia dreaded going to her exams, not because she was worried about the exams themselves, but because she really didn't want to have to face all of her professors after skipping exams the day before. Her first exam was with Professor Perrin, and she headed up to his desk before the exam began to talk to him.

"I'm sorry I missed the exam yesterday, Professor Perrin," Celia said quietly.

"Hm, well, I don't like making exceptions, but I understand there have been some extenuating circumstances in your case," he said. "Since yesterday's exam was a practical exam, I suppose we could do that before you leave here today."

"Thank you."

"I don't expect it to happen again."

"No, sir."

Celia trudged to her seat. She felt lower than dirt, making everyone bend over backwards just because she'd thrown a temper tantrum. At the end of the day, duly chastised by all her professors, she stopped to talk to Professor Legaspi while the rest of the class filed out of the room.

"Yes, Celia?" Her voice was still crisp, and Celia knew she was still annoyed with her behavior.

"Um..."

Professor Legaspi looked at her with raised eyebrows, waiting for her to speak.

"I just...wanted to...apologize."

She looked at her evenly for a minute, then picked up her bag and nodded her head towards the hallway. "Come with me." Celia nodded and followed her out the door, up the stairs, and into her office. "Did you take all your exams today?"

She nodded. "I made up most of the ones I missed yesterday, too. I'm doing the rest of them over the weekend."

"I know." She leaned against the front of her desk, crossing one foot over the other and folding her arms. "I hope you won't be trying anything like this again."

Celia shook her head. "No, ma'am."

She nodded.

"I...I'm sorry." She wasn't sure what else to say.

Professor Legaspi dropped her hands to the desk beside her. "Apology accepted, Celia. I know it's been a really hard year for you. I hope you'll choose to keep going and not give up, but it *is* up to you. If you would rather drop the extra classes, we can still remove your bad grades from your record. Your marks aren't permanently recorded until you finish the class."

Celia studied the floor. "Can I think about it?"

"Of course. There's no rush."

She nodded.

"I think it's about time for the Start of Tournament banquet," Professor Legaspi said, checking her watch. "We'd better head downstairs."

Celia stood from the chair and headed for the door. Professor Legaspi came up next to her and gave her a firm hug while they walked. "I'm proud of you, Celia, no matter what."

"Thanks," Celia said, ducking her head shyly. Growing up without her mom, she'd never really been around someone she could talk to and who would give her a hug when she needed one most. It felt good to have someone like Professor Legaspi now, who obviously cared about her.

Celia waited until after the banquet, when they were back in their room, before she told Maddie her discovery in the book.

"I think I may have figured out my mom's clue," she said quietly to Maddie.

"Really?" Celia nodded. "Well? Tell me!"

Celia pointed to her bed. "Want to come up?"

"Sure."

Once they were behind the curtains, Celia pulled the book off her bookshelf.

"*The Roots of Renasci*?" Maddie asked. "I've never heard of—" She gasped. "Roots!"

She nodded, flipping to page seventy-seven. "And look," she said, holding the book out so Maddie could see. "The clue said something about the center of the third branch. And the third map is—"

"The basement," Maddie finished, studying the page. "I guess that means you have to check the prop room."

"Yeah, but I don't have any idea how I'm going to do that without someone finding out about it."

"Hm. Well, I'm sure we'll think of something." She looked down at the book again. "How in the world did you figure it out?"

"It just sort of hit me over the head." Celia explained about the book falling off the shelf and knocking her on the head. "I still have a little lump," she said, rubbing her head.

Maddie was shaking her head when Celia looked up at her. "You are absolutely unbelievable."

"Why?"

"Just hit me," Maddie muttered as she moved towards the ladder. "Even if I didn't already know that you were chosen as the next princep, it's so obvious that there's something different about you, Celia. I think you've been given gifts far beyond the ones they teach at this school."

"Huh?"

She shook her head. "Someone's on your side," she said simply. "I can't really explain it, but there's just…something. I don't know much about the Overseer, since my parents weren't part of the demesne until recently, but I'd guess that he picked you for a reason, and he's not going to let you get out of the job, no matter what you might think."

"How'd you know…?"

Maddie shook her head and sat back on her heels. "Celia, if I were you, I would be freaking out about being chosen as the next princep. I'd probably be trying to decide if I even wanted to be princep in the first place."

"Okay, now you're scaring me."

She laughed. "No, I'm not. You're no different from the rest of us normal people, and that's how I would feel if I were in your place."

"Well…you're right."

"But I think you're out of luck, because it's obvious that you've been chosen."

"But…"

Maddie shrugged. "Like I said, I can't explain it exactly, and I don't know that much about the Overseer because my grandmother just told me about him a few years ago. But I think you're going to learn more than you ever thought you would, and I think you're in for some big surprises." She turned and headed down the ladder. "Good night," she said, leaving Celia open-mouthed and speechless on her bed.

Chapter Fifteen
The Second Piece

The rain had finally stopped by Saturday morning and the weather looked decent for the first match of the Spring Tournament. Celia had been up early so she could make up one of her exams, and she was still yawning when she went down to the refectory for breakfast.

"Morning, everyone," she said, taking a chair at the table.

"Hey, Josh," someone called as they walked past the table. "Are we gonna win again this year?"

Josh shrugged. "Hope so. We'll see."

"Your leg's all better?" Kitt asked, shoveling scrambled eggs into his mouth.

"Oh, sure. It hasn't bothered me all winter."

"Good."

"Psst," Maddie whispered in Celia's ear.

"What?" Celia asked, leaning closer.

Maddie glanced around to make sure that everyone was busy talking, then said, "I have an idea."

"About?"

"*You know.*"

"What? Oh!"

"We can get downstairs while everyone's out at the stadium. No one but the kitchen staff will be in the building."

"Good thinking, Maddie!" She chewed a bite of oatmeal. "But what if the prop room is locked?"

"I thought we might be able to ask Burnsy."

"Wow. You took your thinking pills this morning." Celia was impressed. She was still half asleep and Maddie was already coming up with great ideas.

"Why, thank you." She checked again that no one was paying attention. "I think we should try this morning."

"It's worth a shot." She took a sip of orange juice. "I don't know. It's not like we're doing anything wrong, because we're allowed all over the school on weekends, but for some reason I'm still a little scared we'll get caught."

Maddie froze and looked at her. "Not one of your hunches again."

She shook her head. "No. Just... I don't know. I guess I'm just afraid the wrong person will find out what we're doing and get whatever it is... we're looking for," she finished lamely, not wanting to say anything more in the crowded refectory.

"Well, don't worry about it."

They headed back up to quarters with the rest of their coterie to get ready for the game. On their way out to the stadium, Maddie claimed she had forgotten something, and they turned around and went back to the school. When the last trickle of students disappeared behind the trees, they carefully made their way towards the basement.

When they reached Main Hall, they had to duck behind a sofa when Higby and Headmaster Doyen came in the room.

"Higby, I'm warning you..."

"And I'm warning you, Rambert. Your policies are unfair, and you're going to lose your best student if you're not careful."

"You can't threaten me, Higby. This is *my* school, and I will make whatever rules I see fit. I will not have you coming in here and telling me what to do."

"Really? Then why are you letting someone else do exactly that?"

Celia and Maddie looked at each other from their hiding spot.

"What are you talking about?" the headmaster blustered.

"I think you know exactly to what, or whom, I am referring."

There was silence in the hall for a tense moment.

"You have no idea what you are talking about, and I will thank you very much to keep your nose out of business that doesn't concern you, Mr. Snodridge. Now, if you will excuse me, I am going out to watch my students compete in the tournament. Good day."

Angry footsteps went one direction and another pair of footsteps headed the other way. Celia and Maddie peeked out from behind the couch, saw that the coast was clear, and hurried over to the door that led to the stairway.

"What was that about?" Maddie whispered as they went down to the basement.

"I don't know, but they sounded pretty mad."

"You don't know?"

"Well, it might have been about Headmaster Doyen's new rule about grades, but I don't think that was the only thing they were talking about." She pushed the door at the bottom of the stairs open. "This way."

They tiptoed down a few hallways until they reached the door for the prop room. Stopping in front of it, Celia tried the handle. "It's locked! Did you ask Burnsy—" When she turned to Maddie she saw her friend spinning a key chain on her index finger. "You are good!"

"I know." Maddie reached around her and fit the key into the lock. There was a click when she turned the key, and then the door swung in. Celia reached around and felt for the light switch, flicking it upwards and bathing the room in a bluish glow.

They quickly went inside and closed the door behind them, then turned and looked at the room. If anyone tried to fit another thing into that room, Celia didn't know what would have happened. Every inch of available space was crammed with all sorts of knickknacks and doodads. Shelves and cabinets lined the walls, and rows of shelving filled the center of the room. Narrow pathways only a foot wide led through the room, flanked by teetering piles of stuff.

There were hats, umbrellas, books, glasses, chairs, flower pots, toys, pieces of furniture, soapboxes, shoeshine stands, large pieces of scenery, and more all over the room. It was overwhelming to look at.

Celia's heart sank as she looked around the room. How were they ever going to find anything in the mess? It seemed an impossible task.

"Well, I guess I'll take this side, and you can take that one?" Maddie asked hesitantly.

"I guess."

"Any idea what we're looking for?"

"None."

Maddie got a look of determination on her face and dug into her pile. Celia turned to her side and started checking for anything that seemed like it would be from her mom. Not having any clue what they were searching for, it was worse than looking for a needle in a haystack. They hunted for a while, checking shelves and cabinets for any hint of anything.

Suddenly Maddie screamed.

"Maddie!?" Celia hurried through the small pathway back to the front of the room and peered around the piles to where she was standing. "What?"

Maddie was rushing toward her with terrified eyes. "I saw... in there..." She pointed a shaky hand at a cabinet.

Chapter Fifteen

Celia crept forward and carefully pulled the cabinet door open. She jumped when she saw what was inside, but when she looked closer, she laughed quietly, her heart starting to return to normal. She reached in and pulled out one arm from the skeleton hanging in the cabinet. Waving it at Maddie around the cabinet door, she said, "This is a prop room. It's fake."

Maddie seemed to deflate where she was standing. "I thought... Sorry."

"That's okay."

"Have you found anything?"

Celia shook her head. "Not yet." She glanced around the room. "I wonder if we're looking in the right place."

"What do you mean?"

"Well, we have no idea how long these props have been here. Maybe they weren't here when my mom hid... whatever she hid."

"So where else do we look?"

Celia shrugged. "Anywhere that would have been here back then, I guess." She looked around the ceiling and gasped. "Like there," she said, pointing.

The basement ceilings had beams running every few feet, just like many of the ceilings at the school. Tucked next to one of the beams, Celia caught a glimpse of a small, round tube, like a toothpick holder. If she hadn't been studying the ceiling, she probably would never have noticed it there, it matched the ceiling so well.

"Help me move this chair over there," she said, pulling a tall chair towards the beam.

They dragged the chair into place and Celia climbed on top. She stretched as far as she could, and her fingertips just barely brushed the cylinder. "I can't quite reach it."

"Here," Maddie said, moving over. "Put your foot on my shoulder. Maybe then you can lean farther."

Celia carefully put one foot on Maddie's shoulder and reached for the tube again. Snatching it off the ceiling, she said, "Got it!" After carefully climbing down again and replacing the chair, they turned their attention to the holder.

"Do you think that's really it?" Maddie asked.

"I don't know. I think we'd better check it before we leave." She studied it for a moment.

"How does it open?"

"It looks like there's a cap on this end...yup, there it goes." She popped the cap off the end and found a piece of paper sticking up. Carefully pulling it out, she unrolled it and found a small sheet with the same kind of markings as the ones on her mother's letter.

"Maddie, we did it! This has to be it!"

"Great! Now can we get out of here?"

Celia carefully tucked the note back in the tube and put it safely in her pocket. They turned the light off and locked the door behind them, creeping quietly down the hallway. As they rounded the corner towards the stairway, Celia felt the hairs on the back of her neck tingle. She spun around to look behind her. In the shadowy hallway, she thought she saw something slip into a doorway, but she wasn't sure, and she wasn't going to hang around there to find out.

"Let's go!" she whispered to Maddie. They hurried up the stairs and through the deserted Main Hall. Up in their room, Celia put the cylinder with the note in her closet, her heart still pounding.

"We'd better get out to the stadium," she said.

"Let me grab my hat," Maddie said.

In a few moments, they were headed out to the stadium. On the way, they met Mr. Bazemore, who was coming back to the school.

"Good morning, Miss Fincastle, Miss Hannagan," he said. He frowned at them. "Why aren't you out at the stadium?"

"I ran in to grab my hat," Maddie said.

"I had to, um, use the restroom."

"Oh. Well, you'll want to hurry back. It's a pretty good game."

"I know," Maddie said. "But I didn't want to get a sunburn."

"Of course not. See you later, girls."

Celia glanced over her shoulder as they walked away and saw Mr. Bazemore watching them closely. She didn't breathe easily until they were sitting in the stands among the other students. Before long, she was involved in the game on the field, between Corpanthera and Mensaleon. It was a very close match, as both teams were evenly matched, but in the last few seconds, Mensaleon scored one last time to win the game, five to four.

Celia cheered loudly with the rest of the fans wearing purple, and then everyone headed inside for lunch. Stopping off at quarters to take of their jackets and hats, the Mensaleon members were rowdy and excited. They still had a chance to win the tournament.

"Come on, Maddie," Celia said, dragging her friend into her closet. "I want to know what that note says."

"Sure. No one's going to notice if we're in here for a few minutes."

Once they were in the closet with the door firmly closed behind them, Celia took the big book down off the shelf and set it on the floor in front of her. "I hope it works the same as last time," she said, holding the note in her hand as she carefully opened the cover of the book.

Soon there was a now-familiar wind blowing and turning the pages of the book. She grinned at Maddie, whose eyes had grown huge in her face. When the book finally stopped moving, its pages quivering, Celia laid the paper on the right-hand page. Sliding it around, she waited for it to melt into the page, but nothing happened.

"Hm," she frowned. "Maybe it's the other page this time." She shifted it over to the left-hand page and smiled when the paper began to move on its own. It slid into place and dissolved into the page of the book, the ink markings on the page underneath bleeding through to the top.

"Oh, wow!" Maddie breathed. "That's so churry!"

"I know, isn't it?"

"What's it say?"

Celia looked down and read:

> *Clue #2: A caterpillar sits in the sun. Ten steps to a window, look right. You see the sign; its third and last lead you to the book you want.*

"Well, another clue. Here we go again." She quickly jotted the note in her notebook, then peeled the paper out of the book. "We'd better get out of here," she said. "We don't want to make people suspicious." She shut the book and put it on her shelf, setting the note and its holder on the same shelf as the letter from her mother.

They hurried out of the closet and ran out to the foyer.

"Oh, there you are," Heath said. "We're just heading down to lunch."

"Sounds good," Maddie said. "I'm starved."

The good mood of Mensaleon lasted only until the afternoon game between Sprachursus and Tattotauri. For Mensaleon to win the tournament, Tattotauri had to lose at least once. Unfortunately for Mensaleon, Tattotauri beat Sprachursus soundly, ten to two.

Chapter Fifteen

Dinner at the Mensaleon tables was somber. It didn't seem likely that they would be able to win their second game, particularly since they had gotten the double game schedule this time, when they had both of their games on the same day.

Although they were a little disappointed at the prospect of losing the tournament to Tattotauri, it didn't stop the Mensaleon students from cheering loudly and having a good time at the night game between their team and Aquilegia. Celia sipped a hot chocolate while she watched the game, trying to stay warm as the temperature dropped. When Josh scored the winning goal, she jumped to her feet to cheer with the rest of her coterie. Soon after the game ended, everyone rushed back into the school, glad to be out of the cold and in the warm buildings again.

Maddie and Celia sat on Maddie's bed for a while that night, talking and brainstorming about the new clue they'd found that morning.

"I don't get the caterpillar part," Maddie said.

"It probably just means that the window is high enough to see a caterpillar in a tree."

"Oh, right."

"But I don't know what sign it's talking about. And the part about third and last? What does that mean?"

"Well, the good news is that it mentions a book. That should be easier to find than the prop room."

"True."

Maddie yawned. "I don't know about you, but I'm about ready for bed."

"Yeah. I want to watch the morning match tomorrow. I hope Tattotauri loses, but they're a pretty good team."

"Even if they do lose, didn't they beat our team last fall? So wouldn't they win the tiebreaker anyway?"

"I don't remember. I hope not. That would mean they basically already won the tournament." Celia tried to recall the scores from last fall, but she was too tired to think that hard. "I don't know. Good night, Maddie."

"Night, Celia."

In the end, it didn't matter whether Celia could remember the scores from last fall, because Tattotauri won their game to go undefeated for the entire tournament. Even though there was still one more game to be played—between Sprachursus and Corpanthera—there was no way for either of those teams to beat Tattotauri.

At the end of their game with Aquilegia, the Tattotauri team dragged Professor Mesbur onto the field and dumped a bucket of water over his head to celebrate their victory.

"Aw, man! What a mush!" Josh said from his seat next to Celia. "The summer tournament's in California this year. I really wanted to go."

"Maybe you'll get to go next year."

"I hope so. I want to play for some of the professional scouts."

"Really?" She knew Josh was a good player, but she hadn't realized he wanted to play professionally.

"Yeah, for some of the under-seventeen teams. You have to be fourteen to play on the teams, but they're really good experience for the college and professional teams."

"Wow. I didn't even know any of that existed," Celia said, watching the Tattotauri fans storming the field.

"Yeah. But all I got to do was go to Florida last year. It's so unfair!"

"Maddie," Celia said, holding out her hand in an invitation.

"What? Oh, right. Fairs are for pigs and cotton candy," she stated matter-of-factly.

Josh looked at them like they'd gone crazy. "Uh, okay," he said, dragging the words out.

"Can I ask you a question, Josh?" Celia asked.

"Sure."

"You're a really good Soccovolle player. How come you're in Mensaleon and not Corpanthera?"

He shrugged. "Beats me. But we can't use our gifts on the field, so it really doesn't matter what talents we have."

"Oh, yeah. I think Heath said something about that last year. Speaking of which..." She trailed off when she saw Heath approaching.

"Oh, man, my brother is *not* happy," he said, sitting on the bench next to Josh. "He really wanted to make it to the summer tournament for his last year."

"Him and all the rest of us," Josh said.

"Doesn't Corpanthera have one more game this afternoon?' Maddie asked.

"Yeah," Heath said. "There's no way Sprachursus has a chance. The whole team is pretty upset."

"Maybe I'll skip that one," Celia said. Although she enjoyed watching the matches, she didn't think it would be much fun to watch one team get steamrollered by another.

By the time the afternoon game rolled around, it was raining again, and most of the students decided to stay inside. The teams headed out to play their match, but the heavy downpour, lack of fans, and the fact that neither team could possibly win the tournament regardless of the outcome of the game caused Coach Jeuset-Partie to call the game early, declaring Corpanthera the winner after the first half.

The End of Tournament Banquet was that evening, and Celia expected to enjoy every minute of it, since she'd missed it last year. Although the decorations in the refectory were red to celebrate Tattotauri's win, it was still a lot of fun, enjoying a big meal with all her friends and classmates. As the banquet wound down, everyone realized the final quarter began the next day, and they all drifted off to their rooms to get ready for the next week of classes.

Celia looked at her calendar and couldn't believe March was half-over. It seemed like she'd just gotten back to school and now she was already looking at the last couple of months of the school year. Not that she hadn't filled her days completely full, what with all the classes and homework and projects she'd had that year. She dreaded going back to Aunt Agatha's for the summer, but she hoped Maddie might invite her to go to camp again. If not, she thought she just might ask Higby or Professor Legaspi if she could go on her own. It wouldn't be quite the same without Maddie there, but it had to be better than spending those two weeks with Aunt Agatha.

Before she could really think about all that, however, she had to make it through the rest of the year and finish all her classes. Unless, of course, she decided she didn't *want* to finish all her classes, she thought to herself as she brushed her teeth that night, remembering Professor Legaspi's continued offer to drop her fourth-year classes. She thought about how easy her last quarter would be if she didn't keep up with the harder classes. It sure sounded nice. But then again, she really liked some of the subjects from her fourth-year classes. She now knew how to send a letter with L'Auzzulla, which would let her send mail anywhere in the world, if she wanted. She didn't know anyone in the rest of the world to send mail to, but the fact remained that she could if she wanted to.

She'd also really enjoyed her Introduction to Locks class with Professor Mesbur. It was a lot of fun to learn how to open a lock just by touching it, and she thought that particular skill might come in handy one day, should she find something interesting in Aunt Agatha's attic or anything like that. She knew some of her sixth-year classmates were jealous that she was getting to do all the "fun stuff" while they were stuck doing the basics, but she was trying not to make it any worse. She went out of her way to not call attention to herself, but that didn't always prove successful.

Chapter Fifteen

Celia slid between the sheets and clicked off her light. Professor Legaspi had said there wasn't any rush in making a decision, so she put it all out of her mind as she drifted off to sleep.

Celia goggled at her paper when she got her last exam back. She thought there must have been some mistake. There was no way she possibly could have gotten these kinds of marks. She discreetly tucked her test into her binder and tried to act like nothing unusual had happened.

It was Friday afternoon, her last class of the week, and she'd been flabbergasted all week as she got her exams back. She'd kind of figured she would pass her midterms, because she'd been pretty sure she'd known at least some of the material, but her actual scores had been a big surprise for her. She still wasn't sure what had happened.

She struggled to concentrate during class, her thoughts refusing to focus on the lesson. Professor Legaspi's lecture wasn't at all boring, but Celia still had a hard time paying attention. When the bell rang signaling the end of classes for the day, Celia tossed all her books in a pile, grabbed her bag, and bolted for the door. She almost made it.

"Ah, Celia?"

She froze, then spun on her heel in the middle of the doorway. Stepping out of the stream of students piling up behind her, she moved toward the desk at the front of the room where Professor Legaspi was packing up her own things.

"Yes?"

"You got a minute?"

"Um, yeah. Why?"

"Just wanted to know how your midterms went." Celia thought her voice sounded suspiciously nonchalant.

"Uh...fine."

She looked up and Celia thought she caught a twinkle in her eye. "Want to come back to my office for a bit and tell me about them?"

Celia shrugged. "Sure."

They chatted about the day's lesson as they made their way up to the office that was becoming about as familiar to Celia as her own room. Once the door had shut behind them, Professor Legaspi set her things on the corner of her desk and turned to her.

"So, I noticed you tucked your test away rather quickly," she said. "Didn't you want to see what you missed?"

"I..." She saw Professor Legaspi trying hard not to smile. "Well, since I only missed one question..."

"Ah. And your other exams?"

"About the same."

Professor Legaspi shook her head in amazement. "Celia, I swear...I have never seen anything like it in my entire life. By any sort of rational logic, you should have just barely squeaked by on those exams, particularly the ones you had to make up in a shortened time period, not gotten nearly perfect scores!"

Celia shrugged. "I don't get it either."

She laughed. "I can tell. Nice work, though. It's very impressive."

"Thanks."

"Have you figured out your mom's clue yet?"

Celia's eyes widened as she realized that she hadn't told Professor Legaspi about the second clue. "Actually, yeah. I figured it out the night...um, after the first day of midterms."

To her credit, Professor Legaspi didn't mention anything about that evening. "Um-hm."

Celia explained about the map in the book and finding the holder in the prop room. She didn't mention her fear that someone else had been in the basement, because she still wasn't sure if that had just been her imagination playing tricks on her.

"So you found another clue?"

"Yeah. I haven't figured that one out yet, though."

"Well, good luck. Just... be careful. I don't want you doing anything dangerous."

"I won't." At least, she wasn't planning on it.

"Very well, then, Miss Fincastle," Professor Legaspi said walking around her desk and sitting down in her chair. "Have a good weekend."

"You, too." She went up to her room and dropped her bag near her bed. "Hi, Audra," she said, noticing the girl sitting in one of the armchairs.

"Hi, Celia."

"How'd you do on your midterms?"

"Okay, I guess."

"Well, don't worry about them too much. Seventh-year exams are just to help the deans figure out what classes you should take next year."

"I know. I just..."

"What?"

Audra dipped her head. "Well, you know, you did so well on your exams last year..."

Celia laughed as Maddie came in the room.

"What's so funny?"

"Audra's feeling bad 'cause she didn't do as well on her exams as I did last year."

Maddie laughed, too, and Celia felt bad when she saw Audra shrink into the chair even more.

"Oh, Audra, we're not laughing at you. It's just... well..."

Maddie came over. "It's just that Celia isn't the average student, and usually everyone fails seventh-year exams miserably."

"Really?"

"Really," Celia said.

"It's not your fault you had to come after little miss perfect over here," Maddie said, nodding her head at Celia.

"Hey!"

"Speaking of which," Maddie said, "how'd you do on your midterms?" She had a look on her face that showed she expected Celia to say she'd done rather poorly, since she'd skipped the first day and had to make up all those exams.

Celia glanced at Audra. "Um...fine, I guess." She didn't want to make the younger girl feel any worse than she already did.

"'Fine'?" Maddie leaned forward. "And what does fine mean? Did you manage to pass?"

"Well...yeah."

"What'd you get?"

"Maddie, do we really—"

"Yes, we really have to. I did rather well on my exams, and I want to know how you did."

Celia sighed. "I...uh...got mmphs on them." She tried to mumble her way through.

"What? I didn't catch that."

Celia rolled her eyes. "I got A's, okay?"

Maddie stared at her for a moment. "You got A's," she said. "On your midterms...after everything..." She threw her hands in the air. "I give up. If you weren't my best friend, I'd hate you."

Audra giggled.

"What? You think it's funny?" Maddie asked. "This girl," she said, pointing at Celia, "manages to do everything even when it seems impossible. It's absolutely disgusting." She laughed and jumped to her feet, giving Celia a hug. "I'm glad, though," she said. "I was afraid...you know..."

"Yeah, well, it was a shock to me, too," Celia said.

Maddie's stomach growled and they laughed. Audra looked at them oddly, and Celia explained, "Maddie's always hungry, and her stomach lets everyone know it."

"Oh. Well, I guess we'd better get down to dinner then," Audra said, getting to her feet.

"I like how this girl thinks," Maddie said as they walked through the door.

Chapter Sixteen
A Lost Clue

"So what are you thinking?"

Celia was sitting in Mr. Morven's office at the beginning of the next week, having her standard meeting about her classes. Professor Legaspi hadn't been able to make it, so this time it was just Celia talking with Mr. Morven. His chair squeaked as he turned to ask her the question.

She shrugged. "I don't really know."

"What do you mean?"

"Well, I like all my classes, and even though it's a lot of work, I've made it this far, and I kind of want to finish the year."

"But..."

"But it's getting harder."

"What is?"

Celia shook her head, not sure she could put her thoughts into words. "Not the classwork—that's about the same. But..."

"But sticking with the work is getting more difficult?"

Mr. Morven always seemed to know exactly what she was trying to say. "Yeah, I guess."

"And you're thinking that it would be really nice to finish the year on an easier note and not be doing homework all afternoon and evening?"

Celia nodded.

He shrugged, leaning back in his chair and wincing as it squeaked again. "I can't tell you what to do, Celia. It's really up to you."

"I know. I just don't know what I want to do."

"Things you like about both options?"

"Yeah. I like the harder classes, learning all the new stuff, but it would be nice to have fun like the rest of them."

"Well, on one hand, I can understand your desire to not have to push so hard for the rest of the year. You didn't exactly have an easy year last year, and this year hasn't been a whole lot better for you." He tipped his head the other direction. "But on the other hand, I can see a lot of reasons for you to hang in until the end of the year. The advanced training would be a very good thing for you to have, and I know a lot of people have gone to a lot of trouble so you could take those classes. Besides, you've made it through most of the year already, it might be kind of a waste to quit now." He bobbed his hands up and down in midair as if he was comparing the weight of two objects. "Tough call."

"Thanks," she muttered. "You're a big help."

He chuckled and winked at her. "Glad to be of assistance." He laced his fingers together on his stomach. "Well, you still have a few weeks before you have to decide. Why don't you keep doing what you've been doing all year until you decide?"

"I guess." Celia rose from the chair.

"You know where to find me if you need to talk to me, right?"

Celia gave him a weak grin. "Right here."

He laughed. "All the time." He watched as she went to the door. "Don't worry about it so much, Celia. Everything will work out fine."

She nodded and left the office, making her way back up

to quarters. As she stepped into the foyer, she nearly ran into someone.

"Whoops! Sorry, Celia, I'm not really watching where I'm going," a voice said.

Celia turned and saw Maybell Bluford, who was a year ahead of her, standing with a big pile of clothes in her hands. "Oh, hi, Maybell. What're all the clothes for?"

"I'm just trying to get a head start on packing." She laughed. "I'm such a procrastinator, I thought it might be smart to start now instead of putting it off like I usually do."

"Oh."

"Gotta run. See you!"

Celia watched in confusion as Maybell headed off down the hall before she headed in the same direction towards her room. Maddie, Libby, and Galena were sitting in armchairs reading textbooks when she got there. She must have looked puzzled when she reached her room, because Libby looked at her and asked, "What?"

Celia shook her head. "I just had the oddest conversation with Maybell."

"Really? Why?"

"She said she's starting to pack already. Isn't it a little early to be packing for the trip home? I mean, we still have two and a half months left!"

She watched as her roommates all looked at each other and burst out laughing.

"What's so funny?"

"You are," Maddie said.

"Why?"

"Because Maybell's a fifth-year," Galena said, as if that explained everything.

Celia shook her head again, growing more confused. "I don't get what that has to do with anything."

They laughed harder.

"Hey!" she protested. She didn't think there was anything that funny about the situation.

"Sorry, Celia, it's just . . . " Libby waved her hand helplessly.

"The fifth-years leave on their class trip in three weeks. Maybell's probably packing for that," Maddie explained.

"Class trip? What are you talking about?"

They stopped laughing and looked at her. "Didn't you notice that the fifth-years were gone for two weeks last April?" Galena asked.

"No. I was kind of busy with . . . other things."

"Wow. You must have been out of it."

Celia didn't say anything.

"Sorry, Celia, it's just that it was kind of obvious last year. It was all they talked about for weeks," Maddie said. "You really didn't notice?"

"No."

"Well, I'm sure that's what Maybell was talking about."

"Where do they go?"

Galena shrugged. "It depends. The chaperones pick a few locations and let the students decide on a final location."

"Oh. So where are they going this year?"

"Aric said they were going to Tallanton," Libby offered.

"Oh, that should be fun." "Sounds great." "Huh?"

Three heads swiveled around to look at Celia when she made the last comment. She tossed her hands in the air. "Never mind. I obviously know nothing about this demesne, so I'll just go sit on my bed." She started in that direction.

Maddie jumped up and threw an arm around her shoulders. "Celia," she said, laughing. "We're sorry. Sometimes we forget that you haven't had any contact with the demesne before. Right?" she asked pointedly, shooting a look at Libby and Galena.

"Um, yeah." "What? Oh, right. Yeah, sure."

Maddie rolled her eyes. "Tallanton is a really cool town up in the northwest. I've heard it's a little like an Alpine village."

"Oh." She stepped away from Maddie. "It sounds nice." She grabbed a book off her desk. "I'm gonna go study."

"Why don't you just study here?"

"I...want a change of scenery," she said. "See you later."

She went down to Main Hall and was happy to see it wasn't too busy. In fact, the seating area at the end near the commons was completely empty. Celia sat in a chair by the fireplace and looked out the huge wall of windows at the fading daylight. The sky seemed to glow a bluish-purple color, and a few stars started popping into sight.

She opened her textbook, but it sat unnoticed on her lap, her mind too busy contemplating other things to focus on studying.

At the back of her mind, right where it had been since she'd found out about it, was the hidden object from her mother and how she was going to find it. She'd lucked into the solution for the first clue, and she didn't have any ideas for the second clue. She didn't know if anyone else knew about the object, or if the object was even in the school anymore. Maybe someone had found it years ago and taken it somewhere. The only way she was going to find out would be to solve the clues and see what she found at the end.

Although she'd thought long and hard about the clue, she didn't have any idea what caterpillar it meant, or the window, or the signs, or the book... She just didn't have any ideas about any of it, and that was frustrating when she felt like she needed to solve the mystery as soon as possible so someone else didn't get there before her.

She also faced her continual questions about her classes and concerns about her grades. She didn't know what she was going to do. She'd gone over the options for her classes time and time again, and she was no closer to an answer than she had been when she started. In some ways it would be easier if someone just told her she had to do one thing or another, because then she wouldn't have to make the decision. But they were letting her choose, and she wasn't sure what she wanted.

Would she feel like she'd quit if she chose to drop the harder classes, or would she be glad she could focus on her sixth-year classes and her family tree? Would she feel like she had let people down after they had done so much to help her all year? How would she feel knowing she'd put so much work into her classes all year just to throw it all away at the end?

And then there was the constant feeling that she was different from the rest of her classmates. The whole discussion in her room before she'd come downstairs was a good example. It seemed that everyone—even Maddie, who hadn't spent much time in the demesne herself—knew more about what was going on than she did. She didn't know the places or people they talked about, they used words she had never heard before, and they seemed to know more about her than she knew about herself.

On top of all that was the issue of her being chosen as the next princep, which often felt like a huge weight on her shoulders or a large cloud looming over her head. Some people treated her differently just because of her future position, which she wasn't sure she wanted anyway. How was she supposed to be a leader to all these people who knew more than she did? It seemed laughable.

"Celia?" She jumped when she heard her name. Glancing behind her, she saw Odile standing there, a questioning look on her face. "Are you okay?"

"What? Oh, yeah, I'm fine. Just…thinking."

"I didn't figure you were studying in the dark."

"Huh?" Looking around, Celia noticed the sky outside had turned inky and the lights in the hall had been dimmed in preparation for the night. "What time is it?"

"About nine-thirty," Odile said, glancing at her watch. "I was just on my way back from the library. How long have you been here?"

Celia stood. "Um... not... too long."

"Well, you'd better get up to quarters. It's not long until lights out."

"Yeah, right. Thanks."

"Sure. Good night, Celia."

"Good night."

As Celia walked through the deserted hallways, she felt like the weight of the world was on her shoulders, and she wasn't sure she liked the feeling at all.

A few weeks later, Celia was sitting in the library on a Saturday morning, trying to find any information at all that she could use in her family tree. After a couple of hours, she was growing frustrated and having little success.

Her normal spot, a window seat that looked out at a lake on one side of the school, had been taken when she got there, so she was sitting at a table on the front wall of the school, right next to a window. She found herself distracted by the scenery out the window, something she didn't usually have a problem with. Obviously the book she was trying to read wasn't holding her attention very well.

Shaking her head and trying to focus on the book again, she saw something out of the corner of her eye that she hadn't noticed before. From this particular seat in the library, she could see the station and the bright blue BUS pulling into the platform. She watched the train slow to a stop, and then wait while people got on and off. She couldn't hear the whistle, but she saw it move forward and begin leaving the station.

All of a sudden, her eyes widened and she gasped. The BUS…a caterpillar…

She snatched her notebook and papers off the table in front of her and hurried out of the library. She rushed through the school, breaking into a run when no one else was around. Skidding around the corner, she took the stairs up to the Mensaleon quarters two at a time and flew into her room.

"Celia?" Maddie called as she zipped past and straight into her closet.

"Get in here, Maddie," Celia called. When she appeared at the door, she said, "Close the door and come here." She flipped through her notebook on the shelf and stopped when she reached the words from her mother's second clue. "It has to be…" she whispered.

"What are you talking about?"

"The clue! I think I figured it out!"

"You did?"

"Well, part of it. I was in the library, looking out the window, and I saw the station out in front. You know, for the BUS?"

"Yeah."

"Think, Maddie! 'A caterpillar sits in the sun'? The BUS? It looks like a caterpillar?"

"Oh! You're right!"

"But I'm not sure what window it's talking about."

"Do you think it's something out at the station?"

"It could be."

"Let's go check it out."

They headed down to Main Hall and over toward the front door. Sliding out one of the smaller doors on the side, they slipped across to the station. Celia kept looking over her shoulder, expecting someone to come along and ask them what they were doing, but she didn't see anyone.

"What did it say?" Maddie asked, looking around the small building.

"Something about a window...ten steps...look right...a sign..." Celia shook her head. "I see a lot of windows, but I don't see any signs."

"There weren't any on the outside," Maddie noted. "Maybe there are some on the platform."

They went out to the platform, trying to look like they belonged there, even though they were the only kids at the station.

"Look!" Celia said, nodding to the end of the platform. Hanging off the side of the building was a sign that said:

C-BUS STATION 4
RENASCI
STATION 5 829

"What's the 829 for?" Celia asked.

"Miles to the next stop, maybe? I'm not sure. But you've got bigger problems."

"Why?"

"Because there's another sign on that side," she said, pointing to the other side. Sure enough, there was a sign on the other end that said:

C-BUS STATION 4
RENASCI
STATION 3 886

"Oh. Well, I'll remember that one," Celia said, pointing to the first sign they'd looked at, "and you remember this one. We'll have to check both of them."

"Okay." They studied the signs for a minute until they were pretty sure they could remember them, then they headed back to the school. Celia kept checking to see if anyone was watching them, but again, she didn't see anything.

They went straight up to Celia's closet, where they scribbled down the information on the signs before they looked at the words to the clue.

"Third and last..." Celia murmured as she read the last piece of the clue. "Do you think it's something in a book in the library?"

"Could be."

Celia thought for a moment. "The books in the library are divided into sections, and each section has a number. I guess the four could be for the fourth section."

"I guess you've spent more time in the library than I have," Maddie said. "I can never find anything in there. I always ask Mrs. Romanaclef for help."

Celia shook her head. "Maddie, you're hopeless."

"Yeah, I know. So you think it's in the library?"

"It seems like a good guess."

"Well, let's go to the library, then."

Celia tore the paper with the clue and the words from the signs and stuffed it in her pocket. "I'm right behind you," she said. She grabbed a notebook and a pencil off her desk and they walked across the school to the library.

"Hi, Mrs. Romanaclef," Celia said as they walked through the doors.

"Oh, hello, Celia. Back so soon?"

"Yes," she said. "More research. I'll be glad when it's finished."

"I'll bet you will. Good luck!"

"Thank you." She led Maddie over to one of the spiral staircases leading up to the second story. "This way," she said quietly, starting up the stairs.

At the top, she turned left and went past a section of bookshelves. Turning left again, she walked halfway down the length of the walkway and stopped. “This is the fourth section,” she said softly.

“Okay. So now we check the books.” Maddie looked at the rows of shelves in front of her. “Which ones do we look at?”

Celia rolled her eyes. “Come on,” she said, going down one of the rows. She checked the numbers as she walked and stopped in front of a section. “Okay,” she whispered. “If it’s the sign you looked at, it should be in this area somewhere.”

Maddie eyed the tall shelf of books. “I’ll just let you look for it, if that’s okay.”

“Fine.” Celia pulled out the sheet with the clue and the numbers. She ran a finger along the spine of the books on the shelf as she hunted for the right one. “Got it,” she said, pulling a thin book off the shelf. “‘*Modern Uses for Handkerchiefs*’,” Celia read off the cover.

“Modern?” Maddie questioned with her eyebrow raised.

“Well . . .” She opened the cover. “At least no one will have checked it out for a while.”

“No normal person, that is.”

Celia grinned and flipped through the book. “I don’t see anything, though.”

“Let’s check the other one.”

Celia put the handkerchief book back in its proper place and hunted for the location of the other book. She checked the number on the sheet and then found the book on the shelf. Reading the title, she made a face. “‘*A History of Toenails*’. Oh gross! No way anyone’s checked that out in forever.” She flipped through that book, too, growing more disappointed as she went, until she reached the back cover. There was a small pocket glued to the back cover right near the binding of the book.

Chapter Sixteen

"Is that it?" Maddie asked.

"I don't know." Celia peeked under the edge of the pocket and saw a piece of paper. "It looks like it might be. Let me try to get it out." She carefully eased the paper out of the pocket and unfolded it, finding the familiar markings. "Here it is!" she said.

She reshelved the horrible-sounding toenail book and put the note into her pocket. "Let's go see what it says."

"Wait. Shouldn't we check something out? I mean, we haven't been in here that long. Won't Mrs. Romanaclef be a little suspicious?"

"You're right." Celia thought for a moment. "Come on."

She took Maddie over to the section where she had found the book about her grandmother. "See if you can find anything that looks like it might be about my family."

Maddie shrugged and grabbed a book off the shelf. "Okay. Here you go."

Celia looked at the book she had chosen. "'*Princeps: Good and Bad*'?" She shook her head. "Fine. It's close enough."

They decided it might look odd if Maddie was reading that book, so Celia checked it out. Soon they were on their way back to their room.

"Do you think it's another clue?" Maddie asked.

Celia shrugged. "Don't know. Probably. I guess we'll find out."

When they were safely back in Celia's closet, Celia pulled out the book and the new note. Maddie's eyes grew big again as the book vibrated and wind blew. Celia set the note on the book and it slid into place, revealing the writing:

Clue #3: You've reached the silver peak,
a purple way before you. Initially, you

know the place - but in the end, will you find it?

"I don't get that one at all," Maddie said. "Not that I've gotten any of the other ones," she added.

Celia reached into her pocket for the piece of paper with the previous clue. It wasn't there. She checked all her pockets, but she couldn't find it. "Maddie, did I give you the paper with the last clue?"

She shook her head. "No. Why?"

"I don't have it. I must have dropped it somewhere."

"Uh-oh." Maddie looked as worried as Celia felt. "What was on it?"

Celia thought for a moment. "I think it had the last clue and the information from the signs."

"Do you want to go look for it?"

"I think we'd better."

"I'll go look while you get that put away," Maddie said, pointing to the book sitting on the floor.

"Thanks, Maddie." Celia peeled the note out of the book and put everything back on the shelf. Checking to make sure she hadn't forgotten anything, she left her closet and shut the door behind her. The library book she'd checked out was sitting on her desk, and she idly wondered what made a good or bad princep. She guessed the best way to find out was to read the book.

Shaking her head to get her thoughts back on track, she left the room and backtracked their steps to the library. Halfway there, she met Maddie, who had gone straight to the library and retraced their path from that end.

"Find anything?" she asked.

"No," Maddie said, shaking her head.

"Me, neither."

"Do you think it's a problem?"

"I hope not. I hope someone just threw it in the trash."

"Well, if they didn't, and they actually managed to figure out what all those numbers and stuff mean, they'd just check the books and find nothing and give up, I would think."

"I guess." Celia was mentally kicking herself for being so careless. She only hoped it wouldn't be a problem.

Celia felt like someone was watching her, and she wasn't sure who it was. She was sitting in her Study of Touch class at the beginning of April, trying to focus on Professor Mesbur's lesson about magnetism, but she couldn't shake the feeling that someone was looking at her. When Professor Mesbur dismissed the class, she tried to discreetly look at her classmates as they left the room, but she didn't notice anything unusual about any of them.

"Miss Fincastle?"

She nearly jumped out of her skin when someone spoke behind her. Her hand on her racing heart, she turned to find Quiroz Bazemore standing next to her desk. Quiroz had dark brown hair and bright green eyes, and Celia had heard many of the other girls in her classes talking about him. He had quite a fan club among the other students, particularly the girls.

"Sorry," he said, an apologetic look in his eyes. "I didn't mean to scare you."

"Oh, um…it's okay." She looked around. "Did you need something?"

"Actually, yes. I was watching you in class today—"

"It was you!" Celia cried, feeling relieved. "I just had that feeling, you know, like someone is watching you? At least I know I'm not going crazy!"

"Sorry, again," he said, "for making you uncomfortable."

"Oh, you didn't...make me uncomfortable. I just wasn't sure if I was imagining things."

He smiled at her, and Celia began to realize why all the girls at school were talking about him. Even though she still didn't feel the need to run out and find a boyfriend, she had to admit that he was a very nice looking guy, and he seemed to have a nice personality to go with his good looks.

"Well, I'm sorry, anyway," he said.

"You were saying..."

"Right. I was watching you in class today and thinking you might be able to help me with a paper I'm working on for one of my classes," he said.

"Me?"

"Yeah. See, I have to write a paper about exceptionally gifted people in the demesne for my independent study."

"You're in an independent study?"

He nodded. "Yeah. My last school had a different course schedule, and when I got here, they told me I'd have to do some of my subjects as independent study."

"Oh."

"So I need a little help with the section of my paper on exceptionally gifted princeps. Can you help?"

Celia bit her lip. "I...I'm really sorry, Quiroz, but I'm not going to be much help for you at all. I'm kind of new to the demesne, so I don't know a whole lot."

"Oh. Well, that's okay."

"Sorry."

"Hey, don't worry about it. It was just a thought, you know, since you and your grandmother and everything..."

She shrugged. "Yeah, you'd think."

"Well, I'll see you around," he said, walking towards the door.

"Sure." Celia picked up her bag and went out to the hallway. She heard bits and pieces of conversations as she passed people.

"Man, I have so much homework, I don't think I . . ."

". . . of course I'm not going to prom with you, you . . ."

". . . poor Astoria's been in there cleaning up all morning . . ."

". . . see the shoes she was wearing today? I would have died . . ."

Turning toward the refectory for lunch, she heard someone calling her name. When she turned around, she saw Professor Legaspi weaving through the hallway and waving at her.

"Hi, Celia," she said, coming up to her. "Are you on your way to lunch?"

"Yeah."

"Can you stop by my office for a few minutes?"

"Sure."

"So, have you made any decisions?" Professor Legaspi asked once they had reached her office.

"Not yet."

She nodded thoughtfully. "You might want to think about picking one way or the other fairly soon," she finally said.

Celia sighed. "I know."

"Leaning one way or the other?"

She shrugged. "Not really."

"Well, keep thinking about it, but don't take too long. You have to commit one way or the other someday."

Celia nodded.

"How are you doing with the clues?"

"Pretty good, actually. I figured out the second one."

"Really?"

"Yeah. I found another clue, the third one."

"Where did you find it?"

"In a book in the library. *A History of Toenails*."

"The library?" Professor Legaspi sounded very worried.

"Yeah. Why?"

She closed her eyes. "Oh, this is not good." Her eyes popping open again, she pinned Celia with a concerned look. "I take it you haven't heard what happened."

"No," Celia said slowly. "What?"

"Mrs. Romanaclef checked over the library this morning, just as she does every morning."

"Okay."

"She found an entire section of books off the shelves, thrown on the floor. It's just a big mess. Books were everywhere. She's been working all morning to get them put back in order."

"Uh...oh..."

"Right."

"What...um...what section was it?"

"I believe she said it was the fourth."

Celia froze in her chair.

"Celia? Is that the section where you found the note?" When she nodded, Professor Legaspi sighed and looked off to the side. "That's a big problem."

"Why?"

She looked back at Celia with a troubled stare. "Because it means someone else knows about this and is hunting, too."

Chapter Seventeen

The Final Search

Celia felt sick to her stomach.

"Celia? Are you okay? You look kind of pale."

"I'm . . . fine."

Professor Legaspi studied her. "What's going on?"

"The clue," she croaked, her throat dry. "I had . . . it was . . . I dropped . . ."

"Celia!" She wore a look of horror. "Did you . . ."

Celia nodded. "I didn't mean to . . . and it was the one we'd already figured out . . . but I must have . . . and someone . . ."

Professor Legaspi put a hand to her head and paced around to the back of her desk. "Okay. Let's just calm down for a minute. Let me see if I understand. You figured out the second clue and found a third clue but then you dropped the second clue somewhere and couldn't find it again?"

"Well, I dropped the copy of the second clue. It wasn't the original."

She winced. "I'm not sure that's a good thing. At least the original would have been unreadable." She sank into her chair. "Oh, this is really not good."

"I'm sorry."

"No, it's not you, although it probably wasn't the smartest thing to lose that clue."

"Then what...?"

She placed her hands on the desk and leaned toward Celia. "Think, Celia. You dropped the clue and then the library gets ransacked in the same spot you found the next clue. That means someone in the school knows there's something hidden here and is trying to find it. We don't know who it is, or how they know. That clue shouldn't have been enough to tell them there's something worth finding. It should have just looked like a random sentence."

"Oh."

"Exactly." She rubbed her forehead again. "This just got very complicated."

"Why?"

"Because we have no idea who we can trust anymore," she said softly. "Your mother warned you, and you need to heed that warning now more than ever, Celia. Be very careful the information you have doesn't fall into the wrong hands. It would be disastrous if it did."

Celia nodded, her throat too dry to speak.

"If you come up with any ideas about the last clue, I want you to talk to me first. I don't want you running around the school looking for things on your own anymore."

"Okay."

Professor Legaspi sighed. "You'd better head down to lunch now. And...be careful."

Celia nodded and left the office, feeling like she had failed at the most important thing she'd had to do since she'd come to Renasci. Despite her mother's warnings, she hadn't kept a close enough eye on what she was doing, and her carelessness had opened the door for the wrong person to find the object her mother had hidden.

Chapter Seventeen

"Are you actually reading that thing?" Maddie asked a few days later.

Celia glanced at the cover of the book on her lap. "Yeah, why?"

"I just grabbed it off the shelf. I didn't think you'd really read it."

Princeps: Good and Bad wasn't exactly Celia's idea of fun and entertaining reading, but she *was* learning something from it. She shrugged at Maddie. "Well, it's kind of old, but it actually has some interesting information."

"About your family?"

"Not exactly, but sort of."

"Huh?"

Celia chuckled at the dumbfounded expression on her friend's face. "Well, it's from..." She checked the publication date. "...about sixty years ago, so it's not exactly current, but...well, it's got a whole bunch of information about the Coridans and all these theories about why they weren't chosen again. I didn't even know that a Coridan had been princep before my grandmother."

"The who?" Maddie's confusion was still evident.

"The Coridans. Didn't I tell you about them?"

Maddie frowned in thought. "Um...I kind of remember you saying something about them. Are they the ones who don't want you to be princep?"

"Yeah. Because they wanted to be picked as princep when I was...chosen." She still had a hard time getting around the fact that she apparently held some big position in the demesne. Most of the time, she felt like any other student at school.

"I remember my grandmother talking about that," Maddie said. "She's the one who told me all about you before I came to school and actually met you."

"So this whole thing with your family hating me isn't because of your grandmother, just your grandfather?"

Maddie nodded. "She doesn't say it, but I think Grand-ma-ma is actually a big fan of yours, she just keeps it quiet."

"Well, at least someone in your family likes me."

"Hey. I like you."

"You don't count."

"Gee, thanks."

"Sorry, Maddie. I didn't mean that the way it sounded."

She waved it off. "I know. So do the Coridans fall into the 'good' or 'bad' category?"

"Definitely bad. Remember how your grandfather said there wouldn't be any information in the library about the time when Violet was chosen as princep?"

"Yeah."

"Well, the book says that the Coridans were very powerful, and Manvil, the man who was princep, was…let me find it…'a cunning, ruthless dictator, who had little concern for the people who stood in the way of what he wanted to achieve'," Celia quoted from a page in the book.

"Wow. He sounds like a cheery guy."

"I know. But I'll bet that's what your grandfather was talking about."

"You're probably right. If he was that mean and nasty, there's no telling what he did. They really wouldn't want us reading about that in the library."

"This book doesn't say much more. I guess since it was written so long ago, they didn't have any information about my grandmother—only that she'd been chosen a few years earlier."

"Oh, that's too bad."

"The good news is that I know all about the princeps before my grandmother."

Maddie looked at her. "Think it's something you want to do?"

Chapter Seventeen

Celia was always surprised at how observant Maddie was. She shrugged. “I don’t know. It’s sort of like trying to decide what you want to be when you grow up. How do you know if it’s something you want to do?”

“I guess you don’t until you try it.”

“I’m not sure I can do that.” She sighed. “There aren’t any princeps in this book who were chosen and then decided not to take the job.”

“How many of them were as young as you were when they were chosen?”

She dipped her head to the side to acknowledge Maddie’s point. “Not many. Apparently it’s fairly rare for someone to be chosen when they’re under the age of sixteen.”

“How old was your grandmother?”

“The funny thing is that she was the only other princep to be chosen as a kid. She was three when she was picked.”

“And you were…”

“I don’t know, actually. Not very old, I know that.”

“Haven’t you asked anyone? If it were me, I’d be really curious.”

She shrugged. “I’ve tried, but no one will tell me anything. Every time I ask about what happened with my parents and everything, they tell me that they either don’t know anything or they can’t tell me anything.”

“Well, that’s no help. Maybe the thing from your mom would help.”

“It might, if I could ever find it.” She’d told Maddie how worried Professor Legaspi had been when she’d found out that someone else was hunting in the school, and Maddie felt just as bad as Celia about losing the paper with the clue.

“Have you figured out…”

Celia shook her head, not needing Maddie to finish the question. “Not yet. It seems like it should be so obvious, but I’m not coming up with anything.”

Maddie glanced around their deserted room, making sure no one else was around to hear. "Maybe you need another brain to help you out."

"Can't hurt," Celia said, closing the book she was holding. "Come on," she said, walking over to her closet. "See if you have any bright ideas."

Once inside the closet, Maddie reread the third clue. "I wonder..." she said. "The part about the silver peak, could that be something with a mountain?"

"Except that we don't have any mountains in the school."

"True." She thought again. "Well, there's silver and purple...does it have anything to do with the coteries?"

"Hmm...my mom was in Aquilegia, so...it's possible. If the silver was for Aquilegia, what would the peak be?"

"The peak of the roof?"

They looked at each other and spoke at the same time. "The attic!"

"It has to be!" Celia said excitedly. "But how do we get up to the attic?"

"Hm." Maddie chewed her lip in thought. "Too bad you don't have a map..."

Celia rolled her eyes. "Maddie, I'm not sure if you're brilliant or totally stupid."

"What are you talking about?"

"A map...remember the first clue?"

"Yeah. Oh! In the book! Do you think there are maps of the other buildings?"

She shrugged. "Only one way to find out." Celia dashed out and grabbed her copy of *Roots of Renasci* off her desk. She saw Libby glance her way from where she was hanging up her sweatshirt at the end of her bed. "Hey, Libby," she said, then ducked back into her closet without waiting for a response. "Do you suppose it's in the index?" she mused as she flipped to the back of the book.

"Could be," Maddie said, looking over her shoulder.

"Look, here it is," Celia said. "Page 253." She turned to the page and saw a map of all three floors of the building plus the attic. "I see the attic, but I can't find an entrance."

"Let me look." Maddie studied the map. "Right there," she said, pointing to a door at the bottom of a staircase that ran along the outside wall.

"Do you think Professor Legaspi would go up with us?"

"Why?"

"Because she's not going to let me go up there by myself, Maddie."

"You're not by yourself; you're with me."

Celia gave her a look. "I don't think that's what she meant."

"Well, let's go ask her."

"Right now?"

"Why not?"

"I suppose it couldn't hurt."

They hurried out of the closet and into the hallways of the school, which were mostly deserted since it was a sunny Saturday afternoon. Running down an empty hallway, they were slowed by a voice from behind them.

"No running in the halls, girls."

They slowed to a walk and turned to see who had spoken, and Celia was happy to see Mr. Morven striding down the hallway.

"Hi, Mr. Morven."

"Hi, Celia. You know better than to run in the halls."

"Sorry. I'm just in a hurry to talk to Professor Legaspi."

"Really? Why?"

"It's, um..."

He studied her for a moment. "Something to do with a letter you received?"

Celia nodded. "I wasn't sure..."

He nodded. "Wise move. Professor Legaspi told me all about it."

"Oh."

"I assume there's been a new development?"

"We think so. We're not sure. That's why we're going to talk with her," Maddie offered.

"I'm sorry to disappoint you girls, but she's not on campus this afternoon."

"She's not?" Celia's spirits dropped. "Why not?"

"She had a very important meeting to attend. Is there something I can help you with?"

Celia nibbled on her lower lip. She didn't honestly think Mr. Morven was the one who had raided the library, but she didn't have any way of knowing. Professor Legaspi had warned her to be very careful, and she didn't really want to take any chances after causing the problem in the first place by losing the last clue. "No, that's okay. I'll wait 'til she gets back."

"Okay. Have a good afternoon, then."

"Bye, Mr. Morven."

They split and headed in opposite directions. Maddie waited until they had left the hallway and were well out of range before asking, "Why didn't you ask him to help?"

"I'd really rather ask Professor Legaspi," she explained. "I guess I'm just being cautious after the mess last time."

"Oh. Well, when do you think you can talk to her?"

"Who knows."

Professor Legaspi hadn't returned by dinner that evening, and she still wasn't back at breakfast the next morning. When she reappeared at the staff table for lunch on Sunday, Celia was so anxious to talk with her that she could hardly stay in her seat. She waited for her professor to leave the table, but she must have been distracted, because she looked back up at the table at one point and noticed Professor Legaspi had left.

Chapter Seventeen

"I'm gonna go talk to her," Celia told Maddie as she rose from her chair.

"Okay. Can I come, too?"

She shrugged. "Sure."

They quickly cleared their dishes and made their way through the hallways and up the stairs to the Aquilegia quarters. Professor Legaspi's office door was open, so Celia knocked on it as she leaned her head inside. "Professor Legaspi?"

She looked up from a pile of papers on her desk. "Oh, hi, Celia. Come on in." She set her pen down next to the pile and smiled at them as they stepped through the door. "Hi, Maddie. What's up?"

Celia shut the door behind them and sat on the edge of one of the chairs. "We think we may have figured out the start of the last clue."

"Really?"

"Yeah." She explained the first phrase and how they had come up with the idea that it might refer to the attic over the Aquilegia quarters. "So I was hoping you could take me up there and help me look," she finished in a hopeful voice.

Professor Legaspi eyed the pile of papers in front of her and sighed. "I'm sorry, Celia. I know how much you want to solve this mystery, but I just don't have the time right now. I just got back from a very stressful meeting and I have all these papers to grade before tomorrow."

"Oh." Celia tried to hide her disappointment. "Maybe sometime this week?"

She shook her head. "I can't make any guarantees, Celia. The fifth-year class trip is coming up, and I have to fill in for some of the people who are chaperoning this year, so I need to meet with them to get caught up on the lesson plans for their classes. I'm pretty busy this week, and probably the two weeks after that."

"So, when...?"

Professor Legaspi rubbed her forehead. "The best I can do is tell you three weeks from now. I know that's not what you want to hear, but I'm afraid that's all I can offer."

Celia got to her feet, filled with disappointment and discouragement. "Okay. Well, thanks anyway."

"I'm sorry, Celia," Professor Legaspi said, turning her attention back to her papers. "You'll just have to be patient."

She nodded but didn't say anything as she opened the door and trudged back to her own room across the school. Maddie walked along beside her, disappointment evident on her face, as well.

"Well, I guess you'll just have to wait, huh?" Maddie asked as they entered their room.

"Looks like it."

But with each day that passed, Celia found herself growing more and more impatient. She couldn't help but think that she was so close to finding whatever it was that her mother had hidden, but she couldn't quite get there yet. And the reason for the delay was sitting in a silver-colored office across the school. And the more she thought about it, the more upset she became, until she finally started imagining all sorts of scenarios that she might otherwise never have considered.

What if Professor Legaspi was the one trying to find the object? What if she had known all along what was going on, and she was just using Celia to get the information about the location of the object so she could go find it herself? And since Celia had told her about their suspicions about the attic, what if Professor Legaspi was planning to go up and search on her own?

Or maybe she was helping whoever it was that was looking. Maybe she had been sent to collect information and was passing all the clues on to someone in the Coridan family.

Celia would never know, and Professor Legaspi would never get caught, because everyone thought she was helping Celia all the time.

She told Maddie her theories on Sunday afternoon a couple weeks later, who reacted with open skepticism.

"Well, those are theories, all right," she said.

"But they are possible, right?"

"I suppose...in some bizarre way, they're possible." She shook her head. "You don't really think Professor Legaspi would do something like that, do you?"

Celia shrugged expressively. "I don't know! All I know is that my mom hid something in this school for me, and I want to find it. I'm tired of everyone and everything getting in the way!"

"Then go hunt by yourself."

"But..."

"Look, Celia," Maddie said, exasperated. "If you honestly think that Professor Legaspi is helping 'the enemy'," she said, forming quotes in the air with her fingers, "then go on your own. I'm not sure I agree with your theory, but..." She shrugged, too. "Well, I guess it does seem kind of strange that she isn't trying to help you more. After all, you haven't seen your parents in, what? Ten years?"

"Eleven."

"And that's a long time to wait. I guess it's kind of suspicious that she isn't letting you go right away. I mean, if it were me, I think I'd want to know as soon as possible, too."

Celia looked out the window by Maddie's bed, where they had closed themselves off from the rest of the room. She watched a bird fly past and land in a tree, then turned back to Maddie. "I'm going," she declared.

"Going...to the attic?"

Celia nodded decisively. "I don't want to just sit around

and wait while someone else finds it, whatever it is. It's mine and I want it."

Maddie nodded once. "Okay, then. When are you going?"

She sighed. "I don't know. I can't take a chance that Professor Legaspi would notice that I'm not there for something, in case she figures out what I'm doing, so I can't go during dinner or during classes. Maybe this evening? She'll probably be busy grading papers or something."

"Do you want me to come, too?"

She shook her head. "No, it's better if you stay here. If I do get caught, I don't want you getting in trouble, too. Your parents would pull you out of school in a second if they thought I was dragging you into a life of crime."

Maddie's giggle lightened the tense situation. "'A life of crime'?"

Celia couldn't stop her laughter. "Hey! I'm just saying..."

"No, I'm sure you're right, but... well, it just sounds funny, that's all."

Celia was quiet at dinner that evening, her thoughts whirling around how she was going to get up to the attic without anyone seeing her. She heard a few people ask her questions, but she wasn't paying enough attention to form a coherent answer. When everyone filed out of the refectory after dinner, she whispered to Maddie, "I'm going up there."

"Now?"

Celia nodded. "I'm gonna try to sneak in while everyone else is coming in the door."

"Okay. Good luck."

"Thanks."

She joined the stream of students heading to the right side of Main Hall, and slipped quietly into a line of Aquilegia kids. Following them through the wooden doors marking the entrance to their quarters, she tucked off to one side and tried to remain unnoticed while she found the door to the attic, right where the map had shown it to be.

Carefully turning the knob, she was relieved to find that it moved easily, so she eased the door open and slipped into the dark staircase. Before her eyes fully adjusted to the dim light, she noticed a chain hanging in front of her, and when she pulled on it, a single light bulb lit up the narrow stairway. Glancing around the small space, she saw only a set of stairs that went up a few steps and then turned to the right. With careful, quiet movements, she began making her way up the stairs until she reached a small landing at the top. The light from the bulb barely illuminated the door in front of her, which looked big and heavy. Reaching a hand out tentatively, she tried the large, hefty handle.

It didn't budge.

Thinking for only a moment, Celia decided to put some of her lessons to work and try unlocking the door. They had only opened small locks in her class with Professor Mesbur, so she hoped she could open the large lock on this door. She set her hand on the lock and concentrated on opening it. She felt her fingers become very sensitive, as if all the nerves had gone on high alert. A strange energy seemed to fill her hands, and she thought she heard something shift inside the door. Concentrating harder, she focused all her attention on getting the lock to open, and with one final jolt of energy, she heard the lock click open. She took her hands off the door and shook them trying to get rid of the pins and needles sensation in her tingling hands.

When she thought she could use her fingers again, she tried the door handle once more, and was thrilled to find that it turned easily. She tried pulling the door open, but it didn't move, so she tried pushing it inward instead. It was heavy and only moved a few inches before stopping, so she leaned her shoulder on the door and shoved, wincing as it creaked and swung open. Standing deathly still for a moment, she hoped no one had heard. When she didn't hear anyone coming, she peered into the dark room in front of her. Stepping cautiously through the door, she waited for her eyes to adjust to the dark room.

She was standing on a platform at one end of the room. A narrow walkway in front of her ran the length of the long room. As her eyes got more used to the pitch black darkness around her, she discovered that the attic was some sort of storage area, with the room divided into sections labeled with letters of the alphabet. Each pair of letters had another skinny walkway leading to the outside wall, allowing access to the outer spaces of the room. Glancing down by her feet, Celia saw that there was nothing underneath the walkways besides beams and the ceiling for the rooms below. One wrong step, and she would fall through the floor.

Her heart pounding in her chest, she tried to figure out what she was supposed to do. She thought about the clue: "You've reached the silver peak (well, she was in the Aquilegia attic), a purple way before you." She glanced around. Of course! Purple for Mensaleon, whose mascot was a lion. Lions were cats, and the attic was full of catwalks. What was next? "Initially, you know the place - but in the end, will you find it?"

She looked around the dark room again, the words from the clue running through her mind. What did it mean? What was she supposed to do? Looking everywhere, she searched for any kind of clue that might lead her to the answer. Somehow she had a feeling that this was the end of her hunt, that she wasn't looking for another clue, but rather the actual thing her mother had hidden. But she didn't have any idea where or what it might be.

Her eyes caught the letter "A" labeling the first section. Initially… initially… Hmm… Did that have a double meaning? Was her mother referring to someone's initials? Since she had no other leads to go on, she figured she might as well give it a shot. Looking down at her feet, she stepped carefully onto the catwalk in front of her.

Although Celia was completely useless at sports, she was an exceptionally gifted student, and her talents kicked in before she really even had time to think about it. She was halfway to the first turn when she realized that she hadn't wobbled once. Come to think of it, she thought, she hadn't even thought about seeing in the dark, just waited for her eyes to adjust and moved forward. Maybe all her training was paying off.

When she reached the catwalk that led to the "A" and "B" sections, one on each side of the walkway, she stopped to think. Her mother's name was Adelle, so it was possible that she had hidden something near the "A" section. She carefully made her way to the end of the walkway, which was tricky, since the angled roofline made the ceilings slant in the storage area. She leaned to keep from hitting her head and looked for anything unusual, but she saw nothing.

Heading back to the main catwalk, she went to the next walkway, for "C" and "D". Her name started with a C, so she thought that was another possibility. Frustrated again when she didn't find anything, she went back to the center and moved on. It wasn't until she considered the next pair of letters, "E" and "F," that she got excited. Of course! EF: Elle Fincastle! She was almost certain her mother had picked that spot to hide the object, and her heart started beating faster with excitement.

She tried not to get too anxious, because she didn't want to fall off the catwalk, so she forced herself to walk slowly and carefully to the end of the next walkway. Looking around, she fought disappointment when she didn't see anything at that spot, either. But just as she was turning to leave, something caught her eye.

Crouching down, she saw something tucked along the outside wall, near the floor. Looking closer, she noticed there was a small box nestled alongside the rafter. Carefully lifting the box from its resting place, she blew a layer of dust off the top, revealing the letters "EF" carved into the wooden top. She slowly lifted the hinged lid and saw a key sitting on top of another piece of paper. Without even checking the paper, she knew this was what she had been searching for. This key had been left here by her mother, and she, Celia, had been the one to find it.

Slowly closing the box again, she slipped it in her pocket and cautiously got to her feet. As she made her way back to the center walkway, her heart jumped to her throat when she heard footsteps on the stairs.

"Well, well, well."

Chapter Eighteen
Flash of Red

The deep voice sent shivers down Celia's spine, and she peered through the darkness to see who had spoken. Her breath caught in her throat when she saw a tall figure wearing a dark cloak that completely covered his head and left his face hidden.

"So Miss Fincastle can see in the dark," he said. The man spoke with an accent Celia had never heard before; she was sure she would have remembered it if she had.

Celia gulped. "Wh-who's th-there?"

He laughed softly, a chilling, devious sound. "So naïve," he said, sounding almost amused.

Celia said nothing, her mind racing as she tried to figure out what to do next.

"As if I would just tell you..." The cloaked figure stepped onto the platform by the door and shut the door behind him, trapping Celia in the room. She couldn't get past him on the skinny walkway, and there was no way she could pull the heavy door open before he would reach her anyway.

"So, the future princep is alone...trapped in the attic...what an unfortunate turn of events." His voice suggested he was anything but unhappy about that.

Celia got an uneasy feeling in the pit of her stomach. "You're Casimir, aren't you."

He laughed cruelly. "Oh, wouldn't Casimir get a laugh out of that one."

Now she was confused. If he wasn't Casimir, then who was he? And what would he want with her? Unless Casimir had sent him… "Why are you here?"

"Rumor has it your mother hid something at the school."

"How did you know that?"

"Ah…now *that* is an interesting story," he said. "There is something in particular that Casimir has wanted for many years, but the means of getting it disappeared about the same time as your parents." He seemed to consider her as he paused. "You wouldn't happen to know anything about that, would you?"

Celia could answer that question honestly. "I have no idea what you're talking about."

"You don't?" He tilted his hooded head. "Hm. Well, someone found a piece of paper that seems to suggest otherwise."

She groaned mentally. How stupid of her to have dropped that clue! Not only had someone found it, but obviously someone who should never have known about it. She felt like she had disappointed her mother. Not only had she not kept the information away from the wrong people, but now the box and the key inside it—perhaps even Celia herself—would wind up in the hands of Casimir.

"I see you know what I'm talking about," the deep voice said smoothly. "And since that paper mentioned clue number two, it follows that there was a clue number one, and therefore a clue number three seems likely, as well. Which means, Miss Fincastle, that you could be up here for only one reason, and that is to find the object to which all the clues pointed. No?"

Chapter Eighteen

Celia refused to give him the information he wanted. No sense making it any easier for him.

"No reply? Tsk, tsk," he clicked. "That can mean one of two things. Either you haven't yet found the hidden object, and you don't want me to know that for fear I might find it before you…" He paused as if waiting for some response from her. "…or you have already found the object and you don't want me to know you have it now. Which is it, I wonder?"

"Why does Casimir want it so much? He doesn't even know what it is."

He waved an arm and the cloak flapped through the air. "Foolish girl! Do you think Casimir is ignorant about what he wants? Of course he knows what it is. And he is prepared to do anything to get it."

"Why is it so important to him?"

"Because the object your mother hid will allow him to take his proper place in the demesne and put an end to the punishing existence he has unfairly endured for the past ten years."

"How?"

He had apparently had enough. "Why, if I told you that, it would ruin the surprise, now, wouldn't it?" He took a deep breath. "Well, no matter, because it seems my objective has changed."

"What do you mean?" She didn't like the sound of that.

He chuckled. "The original intent had been to find the object before you could, a rather tricky task seeing as you found the third clue first. But now that you are up here all alone, with no one around to help you…well, Casimir would be very disappointed if I returned with only the object."

Her pulse pounded faster, something she hadn't thought was possible, it was beating so fast already. She wasn't going to make it out of that room! He was going to kidnap her and take her to Casimir and... who knew what would happen after that!

"Yes, yes, Miss Fincastle, you see, what Casimir would dearly love most is to have you out of the way so that he can become princep, as he should be."

"The Overseer chose me," Celia said with more confidence than she felt.

"Bah! Casimir is the rightful princep!"

"But—"

"Enough of this nonsense," he said, waving his arms and cutting off her words. "Now, will you come willingly?"

"Never!"

The cloaked figure lunged at her and she jumped back, her instincts kicking in and moving her out of his reach. He made a sound of frustration and grabbed for her again. She shifted just out of reach once more, but threw herself slightly off balance, and while she was righting herself from what seemed like an impossible angle, he lunged at her again.

As his hand touched her arm, there was a loud bang and a bright flash of red light that lit up the room. Before she knew what had happened, the man was thrown backwards and landed in a heap on the platform by the door. As he growled and got to his feet, Celia thought she heard a whisper in the air, but she was too busy watching the tall figure across the room to be certain.

"What's going on? What was that?" the figure asked, shaking off his hard landing.

"I-I don't know."

She could practically hear him smile in the dark, even though she couldn't see his face at all. "Well, then," he said, pleasure filling his voice, "you won't be able to do it again, will you?"

He advanced toward her again, stalking slowly across the catwalk to where she was standing. Celia tried to move away, but her back was pressed against the wall, and he was between her and the door. When he drew near, he grabbed for her again. "Got you!"

Again, as his hand touched her, this time on her shoulder, something made a loud bang and a flash of red lit up the room, revealing a cloaked figure flying through the air toward the door. Celia watched with wide eyes, trying to pay attention to everything, wondering what was going on. She heard the loud thump as he landed on the platform again, and then an echoing whisper filled the air, sounding powerful and resonant: "Intocablus..."

"What did you say?" the figure asked from the pile on the platform.

"I...I didn't."

"What is going on?" he asked again, now livid.

"I..."

"You're doing something!"

"No! I-I'm not! I-I don't know what's happening!"

He stood again and flung his cloak behind him in fury. "This is ridiculous! You *will* be coming with me!" he announced, marching purposefully toward her. He came after her one last time, reaching his hand out to grab her arm. Before his hand touched her, Celia saw a red glow, and was surprised to see that it seemed to be coming from her skin.

The cloaked figure pulled his hand back and the light faded. "What...?" He reached for her again, his fingertips brushing her skin. The red glow reappeared and a *zap* sounded in the air as his hand was pushed away from Celia's arm.

"Intocablus," the whisper echoed once more.

He backed away with faltering steps. "I don't know what's going on, but I'm getting out of here." He turned and ran for the door, yanking it open and hurrying down the steps away from the attic.

Celia stayed pressed against the wall for a few minutes, trying to get her breathing to return to normal as she waited to make sure he wasn't coming back for her. When she felt she could move again, she stepped away from the wall on shaky legs.

"Hello? Is someone up here?" Celia heard a woman's voice call up the stairs. "I heard a noise..." She thought she had never heard a better sound in her life than the one reaching her ears at that moment.

"Professor Legaspi?" she called out, her voice unsteady.

"Hello? Who's there?"

"It's me!"

"Celia!?" She heard someone's footsteps running up the stairs as she made her way toward the door. When she saw Professor Legaspi appear in the doorway of the dark room, she nearly collapsed with relief. "Celia, what are you doing up here? Whoa!" Professor Legaspi jerked to a stop at the side of the platform, just before she fell off the edge.

Celia hurried to the platform, and Professor Legaspi put her hands on her shoulders. "Celia? Are you all right?"

She started trembling, the shock of what had happened starting to sink in. "I-I'm f-fine."

"How did you get in the attic?" She crouched down and looked her in the eye. "You weren't hunting for your mother's clue, were you?" When Celia's gaze dropped to the floor, she cried, "Celia! I specifically told you not to! How could you disobey me like that?"

She tried to answer, but her teeth were chattering so hard she couldn't form any words.

"Celia?" Professor Legaspi asked, sounding worried now. "What's wrong? What happened?"

She crossed her arms and hugged herself. "Th-the c-clue...b-box...a m-man...r-red l-light...a-attacked..."

She gasped. "Was someone else up here?" Celia nodded. "Do you know who it was?" She shook her head. "Are they still here?"

She shook her head again. "G-gone," she croaked out.

Professor Legaspi gathered her in a tight hug. "Oh, Celia. It's okay now." She rubbed her back, trying to calm her down, but Celia couldn't seem to stop shaking. After a few moments, Professor Legaspi said, "We need to get downstairs and see if we can find whoever it was that was up here with you. Do you know what he looked like?"

Celia shook her head. "C-cloak."

Professor Legaspi sighed. "Of course. Well, no point in staying up here anyway. Let's get you down to my office." She carefully led Celia out the door, pulling it shut behind them, and then down the steps to the silver-colored foyer. Rushing her into the office before anyone saw them, Professor Legaspi helped a still-trembling Celia into a chair. She disappeared for a moment, then came back and wrapped a blanket around Celia's shaking shoulders.

"Th-thanks," she murmured, clutching the comforting fabric close around her and hugging it to her neck.

"Hm," Professor Legaspi said as she walked over to the phone on her desk. She turned away from Celia and spoke quietly into the receiver. After a few moments, she turned back and hung up the phone.

"Before we get into what happened up there, Celia," she said, sinking down in her desk chair, "I want an explanation. I thought I made myself clear that you were not to go hunting for that clue on your own. Why didn't you wait for me?"

Celia couldn't bring herself to look her professor in the eye. She felt ashamed now that she had ever suspected Professor Legaspi of plotting against her. It had been a stupid move to go up to the attic alone, she saw that now, not that it helped the situation any.

"Celia?" Her tone brooked no argument. "I'm waiting."

"I..." Celia swallowed hard. "I'm sorry. I...it's..."

"That's not an explanation."

"I know." Her trembling starting to subside, Celia still huddled in the chair with the blanket. "It's stupid," she admitted, pulling her knees up and hugging them under the blanket.

"It would have to be, to go up to the attic on your own."

She was too embarrassed to say anything more. She was afraid Professor Legaspi might be angry when she heard Celia had suspected her of working with their opposition.

"Celia, my patience is wearing thin," she said sharply. "I want the truth, and I want it now."

"I thought it might be you," she mumbled quickly.

"Might be me, what?"

"I...it's stupid."

"You said that. But so far I haven't heard you explain why you decided to go up to that attic by yourself."

She took a deep breath. Might as well get it over with now and not wait for a whole bunch of people to show up, because she knew someone else would be coming, she just wasn't sure who. Higby? Mr. Morven? Headmaster Doyen?

"I got impatient," she said softly, "and I started thinking maybe you were helping someone get information about the clues." She said it in a hurry, the words tumbling out.

There was dead silence from the other side of the desk.

"You were too busy to help me, and I thought maybe it was just a way to keep me from solving the last clue so that someone else could get there before me...us..."

When there was still no response, she cautiously lifted her eyes. Professor Legaspi had a stunned look on her face. It was clearly not what she had been expecting to hear.

"Professor?"

She blinked a few times, as if she was trying to get Celia back into focus. "You thought...*I*...was involved? Celia, if I had thought for a moment that you were thinking...How could you think that!?" She pushed to her feet and walked to the window, her back to the room. It was dark outside, so Celia wasn't sure what she was looking at, but she didn't want to ask. There was silence in the room for a few minutes.

"I'm sorry," Celia said again, feeling like it wasn't an adequate response.

Professor Legaspi shook her head and turned back to face her. "No, Celia, *I'm* sorry. I know you were anxious to find whatever it was your mother had hidden, and I should have made time for you to finish the last clue." She walked over and dropped into her chair again. "However, that does not excuse your behavior. You disobeyed my instructions, and that cannot remain unpunished. You have to realize the rules are for your safety, and breaking them carries consequences."

Celia nodded, saying nothing. What could she say?

"I will figure out your punishment and let you know. For now, we need to bring a few other people into this office and hear about what happened in the attic." She picked up the phone, dialed a number, and waited a few moments. She said only one word when someone picked up, "Okay," before hanging up the phone and leaning back in her chair.

It couldn't have been more than a few seconds later that there was a knock on the door. "Come in," Professor Legaspi called. The door swung open and three people came in: Mr. Morven, Higby, and a woman Celia hadn't met before. The woman had an air of sophistication about her, her auburn hair pulled up in a French twist and her navy suit neatly pressed. She seemed like she was about the same age as Professor Legaspi, with a pleasant face and a concerned look in her teal-colored eyes.

"Celia, you know Higby and Mr. Morven. This is Dr. Gemynd. Alison, I know you've heard a lot about her, but now I can introduce you to Miss Fincastle," Professor Legaspi said.

"I *have* heard a lot about you, Miss Fincastle," she said, coming up next to the chair where Celia was still bundled up with the blanket. "It's nice to finally meet you." She put her hand out, and Celia had to work to untangle her hand from the blanket to shake it.

"Um, nice to meet you, uh, Dr. Gemynd," Celia replied as she lowered her feet to the floor again, hoping she'd pronounced the name correctly.

Mr. Morven had taken his spot leaning against the windowsill and Higby had leaned against a bookcase, one arm resting on the top shelf. Dr. Gemynd took the seat next to Celia and everyone looked at Professor Legaspi.

"Is there a particular reason you called this meeting?" Higby asked.

"I must say I was surprised to get a summons to the school," Dr. Gemynd said. "I didn't figure…"

"It's not a social call," Professor Legaspi said, her voice grim. "Someone attacked Celia."

"What!?" All three newcomers spoke at the same time and jerked to attention. If not for the seriousness of the situation, Celia might have laughed.

Professor Legaspi nodded. "I waited until you all were here to have Celia talk about it. I don't know exactly what happened…" She turned her attention to Celia. "Can you tell us?"

She described going up to the attic and unlocking the door, at which point Mr. Morven looked mildly impressed. "Those locks are really hard to open," he said. "I remember being asked to open one for my finals during third-year. And you opened it on your own?"

She nodded.

"May I ask a question?" Higby interrupted. "Why were you going to the attic in the first place?"

Celia glanced at Professor Legaspi, who thankfully jumped in to answer. "She was fairly certain the solution to the final clue had something to do with the attic," she explained. "You'll remember I've told you about the clues . . . " They nodded their assent, and she said to Celia, "Then what happened?"

She told them about figuring out the clue and finding the box, then froze when she recalled hearing the voice and seeing the cloaked figure.

"Celia?" Professor Legaspi said quietly. "What happened after you found the box?"

She took a deep breath and swallowed, then tried to speak without really thinking about what she was saying. "I heard footsteps, and then someone came to the door. He had a long cloak on, with a hood that covered his face. He closed the door behind him, and said something about Casimir wanting the thing my mom had hidden." She stopped to think. "Then he said his plans had changed and now he was going to take me instead."

She heard a few people take a quick breath of air, but she couldn't tell who because she wasn't watching them. She was staring at the front of Professor Legaspi's desk, trying to get through the account without trembling, her fingers gripping the edge of the blanket tightly. "He asked if I would come willingly, and I said no, so he lunged at me.

"There was a red flash, and a loud bang, and he went flying through the air. He asked me what I had done, and I said, 'nothing,' so he came after me again. When he grabbed my shoulder, there was another red flash and a loud bang, and as he flew through the air again, I heard a whisper echo in the room.

"He came after me again, and when his hand came near my arm, there was a red glow coming from my skin. When his fingers touched my arm, there was a zap and another red flash, and it pushed his hand away. After that, he ran out the door, and then I heard Professor Legaspi . . . "

When she looked up, she saw the four adults exchanging glances, but she wasn't sure what they were trying to tell each other.

Dr. Gemynd spoke first. "You said you heard a whisper," she said. "Do you know what it said?"

Celia nodded. "Intocablus."

"Intocablus?" More glances flew around the room.

Mr. Morven frowned. "I've never heard that before. Have any of you?" The other three shook their heads. "What do you suppose it means?"

"It must have something to do with the red light," Dr. Gemynd said, "but I've never heard of that before, either."

"Curious . . . " Higby murmured.

"Yes, very," Professor Legaspi agreed. She turned to Mr. Morven. "You checked the grounds to make sure no one was still around?"

He nodded. "Antoine helped, but there was no sign of anything out of the ordinary."

"Hmm . . . " Professor Legaspi looked at Celia like she had just remembered something. "You said you found a box. Was it from your mother?"

Celia shrugged. "I don't know. I think so." She rummaged through the folds of the blanket to get to her pocket and pulled out the small wooden box. "This is it."

"What's inside?"

"A key. And a note."

"What does the note say?" Higby asked.

She shrugged again. "I don't know. I didn't look at it, but I would guess that I can't read it."

Professor Legaspi nodded. "That makes sense. You'll have to check it when you get back to your room."

"You're letting her stay here?"

She turned to the incredulous Higby. "Of course I am."

"But..."

A warning look entered her eyes. "We'll discuss it later," she said crisply. Turning back to Celia, she spoke in a softer tone. "You do have a decision to make," she said. "You can keep the box and its contents with you, but I'll warn you that we don't know who was in the attic with you. It could be risky. Your other option is to leave it with one of us, and we'll keep it in a safe place. It's your choice."

"Anne—" Dr. Gemynd started. She was stopped by a sharp look from Professor Legaspi.

"I said, we'll discuss it later."

"I think it would be wise to wait," Mr. Morven agreed.

"Celia? What would you like to do?" Professor Legaspi asked again.

"If it's all right, I think I'd like to keep it with me. I... it's from my mom, and..."

"I understand," she said. She got to her feet. "If you two don't mind," she said to Dr. Gemynd and Higby, "Mr. Morven and I need to talk to Celia about her classes for a moment. Would you mind stepping outside for a few minutes?"

"Certainly," Dr. Gemynd said, rising from the chair. Higby held the door open for her and closed it behind him as he left the room.

"Celia," Professor Legaspi said, "I'm sorry to throw this on you now, but Headmaster Doyen informed me just before dinner that you have to decide by the start of classes tomorrow if you're going to drop any of your classes. I'm not sure where *that* rule came from, but there's where it stands."

She could hardly believe they were having a discussion

about something as normal as her classes after what had happened that evening. Her mind refused to focus on anything, and she wasn't sure she had an answer for them anyway.

"For what it's worth, I think you've been doing an admirable job so far this year," Mr. Morven said, "and I don't see any reason why you shouldn't be able to finish the year. However, I understand you might want to cut back on your schedule and just try to be a normal kid for the remainder of the semester."

Celia nodded.

"What do you think?" Professor Legaspi asked.

She licked her lips. "I guess... well, I'm doing fine in my fourth-year classes. It's my sixth-year classes that are the problem, because of my family tree. But my mom's letter said this should help," she said, lifting the box she still held tightly in her hand, "so hopefully that won't be a problem anymore."

"True."

"So I guess I might as well stick with the schedule I've had all year. If I fail miserably, then I guess I'd just repeat them next year, right?"

Mr. Morven nodded, smiling. "Yes, but I sincerely doubt you'll have a problem." He shrugged. "Unless the headmaster keeps coming up with new rules... "

Professor Legaspi shot him a look, then turned back to her. "You're sure?" When Celia nodded, she said, "Okay. Then it's settled. You'll stick with all your classes. Mr. Morven," she said, turning to him. "We'll need to discuss an appropriate punishment for failing to follow the rules, and I'd like your help with that. Celia has to learn that she can't just go around doing whatever she wants when someone tells her not to."

Celia felt her cheeks grow warm as she dropped her gaze to the floor.

"Of course," Mr. Morven replied.

"However, since it is now close to ten, I think it is high past time Celia gets into bed. Would you let the others know they can come back in?" she asked him.

As Mr. Morven opened the door and Higby and Dr. Gemynd came back in, Professor Legaspi stood and walked around to the front of her desk. "Unless any of you have any other questions for Celia, I think she needs to get to bed."

Higby shook his head, and Dr. Gemynd said, "I don't." She turned to Celia. "Well, Miss Fincastle, I wish we could have met under better circumstances, but I'm glad to have met you and relieved that nothing happened to you. I'm sure I'll see you sometime soon."

"Um, nice to have met you, too," Celia replied. "Can I... ask you something?"

"Sure."

"Can you just call me Celia?"

Dr. Gemynd laughed. "Of course."

"Ready to go now?" Professor Legaspi asked.

Celia nodded and got to her feet. She tucked the box back into her pocket and started toward the door. "Oh, your blanket," she said, moving to take it off.

"You can keep it on until we get to your room," Professor Legaspi said.

Mr. Morven reached over to give her a one-armed hug as she walked past. "I'm glad you're safe," he said, his voice a little gruff.

Higby piped up from across the room. "Me, too."

Professor Legaspi laid a hand across her shoulders and directed her to the door. "Come on." She left her arm there as they made their way through the school and up to the Mensaleon quarters. When they got there, instead of taking Celia directly to her room, she turned and knocked on Professor Twombly's office door.

Once invited inside, Professor Legaspi closed the door behind them and pointed Celia toward a chair.

"Professor Legaspi?" Professor Twombly asked. "I got your message that Celia would be late for bed. What's going on?"

Professor Legaspi quickly outlined the basic events of the evening, leaving out much of the information about Celia's mother's letter and the clues, but mentioning the cloaked stranger who had attacked her in the attic. When she reached that point, Professor Twombly gasped and jerked her gaze to Celia, then back to Professor Legaspi.

"Someone made it into the school?"

Professor Legaspi pressed her lips into a thin line before replying. "We don't know. We don't have any ideas about who it was."

"But I thought we had set up..."

"Yes, but not for my attic," she said briefly, glancing at Celia, who was listening to the conversation with great interest. Had they done something to protect her while she was at school? Did they think she needed that? Why hadn't anyone told her? "In any case, I wanted to let you know what was going on. I don't expect any more trouble, but you never know."

Professor Twombly took a deep breath. "Well, I'm glad you're all right," she told Celia. "Maddie was asking about you a little while ago. You may find she's waiting up to hear from you."

"We'd better get you off to bed, then," Professor Legaspi said.

A few moments later, Celia was standing by her bed, handing Professor Legaspi's blanket back to her. "Thanks."

Professor Legaspi gathered her in a hug. "I'm glad you're all right, too, Celia. I'm sorry you had to go through that, but

I hope you've learned a lesson from this. I have your best interests at heart, even when it seems like I'm being unfair or unreasonable."

"I know."

She stepped back, glancing over at Maddie's bed. "It looks like she must have fallen asleep."

"Yeah. I guess I'll talk to her in the morning."

Professor Legaspi pulled Maddie's curtains closed while Celia changed into her pajamas and climbed up to her bed. "Good night, Celia. I'll see you in the morning."

"Good night." She heard Professor Legaspi pulling her curtains closed, too, and then she couldn't hear anything. Although she was tired, she found she couldn't fall asleep right away, her mind was full of so many things.

The man in the attic had obviously known Casimir, was working for him, in fact. How else would he have known what Casimir wanted? It was a little unnerving for Celia to come face to face with the reality of her situation. Until now, it had been just an idea, a thought that almost didn't seem real. Of course she knew she'd been chosen as the next princep, and she'd been told Casimir wanted that position. And she'd had to deal with everything that had happened last year. But it wasn't until tonight that she started to understand how serious the situation really was. Casimir didn't just want her position—he wanted her out of the way.

She wondered who that man was, and how he'd not only known where she was and what she was doing, but also how he'd managed to get into the school without anyone noticing. Were there other people at the school helping him? Chills ran down her spine at the thought. If that was the case, then she had no idea who at the school was on her side and who was on Casimir's. It would also mean that someone she'd known for perhaps the past two years was actually her enemy, plotting her downfall even at that moment. That thought was chilling, as well.

Her thoughts turned to Dr. Gemynd. She was obviously someone that Professor Legaspi, Mr. Morven, and Higby knew fairly well, and they'd all apparently talked about her before, too. She wondered what Dr. Gemynd did, if it was something connected to the school, or something else. No one had told her. She made a mental note to ask Professor Legaspi about it tomorrow, or whenever she had a chance to talk to her again.

There had been lots of little things that caught Celia's attention. Evidently, there had been more going on than she'd first realized. She had the eerie sense that lots of people kept making decisions for her without her knowledge, and the feeling grew stronger every time she encountered situations like the one in Professor Legaspi's office that evening. There was no doubt in her mind that the four adults would be sitting in Professor Legaspi's office now, still talking about her. Perhaps they'd even brought in the headmaster, as she was sure that he would have to be informed that someone had made it into the school and attacked her. She wondered if he'd even care.

That led her to wondering about the key in the box. She was too tired to go down to her closet and read the note, but that didn't stop her mind from running through possibilities for what the key opened. Was it a box of some sort? A room? A building or a house? It must be important, whatever it was, for Casimir to be looking for it all these years and to try to steal it from the school. Although Celia was curious why Casimir would want it, she couldn't help but be more excited about the promised help with her genealogy. Yes, she would be glad to get decent grades again, but her real excitement was from the fact that she would hopefully learn something about her parents and maybe some of her other family members.

With a big yawn, she closed her eyes and tried to go to sleep. It took a long time for her to nod off, and when she did, she had a restless night, full of nightmares about the cloaked man in the attic, flashes of red light, and an echoing whisper.

Chapter Nineteen

Message In A Book

After her restless night, Celia woke up early and went straight into her closet to read the note in the box from her mother. She set the key on a shelf and took the piece of paper out of the bottom of the box. Unfolding it, she found a full sheet of paper covered with the same kind of marks as the other notes. Sliding the tattered book off the shelf and onto her lap, she opened the cover and waited for the familiar wind to blow. When it came, she found herself looking at yet another page in the book, and she set the note from the box on top of the book. It slid into place, the same as the others, but something was different. The wind hadn't died down when the pages stopped flipping, and it felt as if the air around her was crackling with energy, almost like static electricity was filling the air.

She saw the words appear on the page, but just as she was about to lean over and read the letter, a blue glow started from near the binding on the book, growing bigger and brighter as she watched with wide eyes. As if being built piece by piece from the ground up, two figures made of the blue light appeared over the letter, and Celia nearly stopped breathing. The last time she had seen someone appear in that book had been when Higby had shown up to tell her about Renasci. But these two people looked very familiar to her, now that she had spent so much time looking through the box of pictures from her mother. Flickering but completely recognizable, the figures in the book this time were Celia's parents.

Her mind raced. If Higby showed up last time, and he was most definitely alive, did that mean her parents were alive, too? Was it possible they were communicating with her from wherever they had gone when they disappeared? As she wondered what she was supposed to do next, the small image of her mother began to speak.

"Hello, Celia. Since you are hearing this message, you must have solved all of my clues and found the box with the key. Well done," she said. "Unfortunately, that also means we must not be there with you, or else we would never have had to leave that key hidden until you found it." Celia saw her take a ragged breath. "We are, needless to say, merely a message, placed into this note so you can hear from us, thanks to your father."

"How we wish we could see you at this moment," the image of Celia's father said. "But since that is apparently not possible, I hope this is at least some small comfort for you."

Celia blinked away the tears that blurred her vision and focused on her parents again, trying to control her reaction to hearing their voices.

"My note said the hidden object would help you with your family tree, and it will, but it is also much more important than merely helping you finish your assignment," Celia's mother said. "The key opens the Document Vault at the palace, which contains innumerable writings of great importance. Among the papers are complete family trees for both my family and your father's family, which should be everything you could possibly need to finish your own in our absence."

"Also contained in that room are records that document the actions of a certain family by the name of Coridan," her father said. "While we cannot release the information in those records at this time, it seems likely that you will need those documents at some point, and also very likely that the family will do everything possible to make sure you don't get those records. It is very important that you use the information at just the right time, so do not rush into releasing any of it too soon. I am sure you have people around you who can help you make a wise decision."

Her mother spoke again. "If everything went according to plan, one of your professors should be a good friend of mine, and she can help you get the information you need out of the Document Vault. Be very careful about who has access to that key, and do not tell anyone you don't trust about it. No matter what anyone says, do not let anyone else keep the key for you any longer than absolutely necessary."

"Our time is short, so we have to go," he said. "Although you are only a little girl now, you'll be a young lady by the time you get this message. I'm sure we would be very proud of you, my daughter."

"We love you always," her mother said. "I wish we could be there with you."

Her father waved and her mother blew her a kiss as their images faded and blue glow disappeared. Looking through the tears that she couldn't seem to stop, Celia saw that the words on the note were the words they had spoken to her moments before. She touched her fingers to the page, wishing she could bring them back somehow, but knowing that even if she could, it wouldn't help any because it wasn't really them anyway, only their message.

She didn't bother to copy down their words, figuring that if she needed to, she could put the paper in the book again.

Lifting the sheet off the page, she closed the book and set it back on the shelf before carefully folding the paper and adding it to the small collection of notes from her mother.

She mopped her face and got dressed, then headed down to the refectory for breakfast. It was still early, and the room was basically deserted. Only a handful of early-risers were sitting at the tables, most of them engrossed in a book on the table next to their meal. They all glanced up when she came in the room, and a few of them waved at her, even though she didn't know them, but then they turned their attention back to their reading.

Celia sighed with relief. At least it didn't seem like word of last night's events had spread around the school yet. She hoped it never did. She really didn't want to deal with everyone coming up and asking her questions or trying to talk to her.

After her ordeal the night before, she found she was starved, so she piled a plate with food and sat down at a table near the front corner of the room, hoping people wouldn't notice her there. She munched on her eggs, waffles, fruit, yogurt, hash browns, and bacon while the refectory filled with people.

Mr. Bazemore came in the room, looked around, and, seeing her, walked over to her table.

"Good morning, Miss Fincastle," he said.

"Morning, Mr. Bazemore," Celia said after swallowing a bite of eggs.

He bent over and leaned his elbows on the table. "I wanted to tell you, I've been working on your…problem with the headmaster. I'm not sure I've made much headway, but I think I may have a plan. If you don't mind coming and talking at one of our staff meetings, maybe a personal plea would help Headmaster Doyen change his mind about his rules. Would you consider doing that?"

"Um…"

"Don't worry. You wouldn't have to say much, just a few words about how unfair you think it is to be penalized just because you don't have any family members around to help you with your family tree."

"Well, I guess I could do that."

"Great!" He straightened as he smiled. "I'll let you know when I need you. I'm trying for this week's meeting, but I haven't gotten the agenda yet."

"Okay."

"Have a nice day, then, Miss Fincastle."

"You, um, too."

"Celia!"

Mr. Bazemore looked up in surprise as Maddie hollered from across the room and ran over to the table. "Miss Hannagan, that is not appropriate behavior for indoors."

"Sorry, Mr. Bazemore. I was just…uh…I wanted to ask Celia about a, um, homework assignment."

Mr. Bazemore's gaze shifted back and forth between the two of them, before he said, "Regardless, I don't want to see that from you again. Understood?"

"Yes, Mr. Bazemore."

"Very well." He turned and strode to the tables of food, where he began filling a plate.

"Celia!?" Maddie hissed, whipping back around to look at her. "What happened? You weren't back by the time I fell asleep!"

Celia closed her eyes and sighed. "It's a really long story," she said wearily.

"So? Tell me!"

She glanced around at the tables around them that were filling by the second. "I can't! Not now!"

"Celia!" Maddie sounded impatient.

Chapter Nineteen

"I'm sorry, Maddie, but it's... something happened, and if word got out... I can't take the chance."

Maddie's eyes grew big. "Okay, now you're scaring me."

"Good. It's not something I'm just dying to relive," Celia muttered.

"What are you talking about?"

She shook her head. "I'm not saying anything more," she said.

"But—"

"Maddie, I really can't talk about it here. You'll just have to trust me on this."

"Okay." Now she sounded hurt. Celia watched her walk over to get her breakfast, her shoulders slumped. Feeling worse by the minute, Celia put her elbow on the table, propped her cheek on her fist, and finished off the last few bites of her enormous breakfast, which wasn't sitting so well in her stomach now.

When Maddie sat down with her food and began eating in complete silence, Celia sighed. "Maddie..."

"Don't worry about me. I just spent the whole evening wondering what had happened to you, that's all."

"Look, I'd be happy to tell you, but not here, okay? I'm sorry you were asleep when I got back there last night, but I was too exhausted to do anything about it." She rubbed her temples, her head aching from too little sleep. "Besides, I don't know if I could have gotten through it all last night..."

Maddie looked at her closely. "Something big happened, didn't it?"

Celia let out a humorless laugh. "You could say that."

"Are you okay?"

"I'm fine. Now, anyway. Just tired." She sighed again. "I'll tell you tonight, if you want."

"Whenever you feel up to it, Celia. I'm sorry I'm being such a pain."

She shook her head. "No, it's okay. But I really don't want to talk about it or even think about it for now, if that's all right."

"That's fine."

"Thanks, Maddie."

Although she was still very tired, Celia made it through the day without falling asleep during her classes. By dinnertime, she was completely drained, but she felt she needed to tell Maddie what happened the night before and that morning.

Celia decided she'd rather curl up on her own bed to tell Maddie the whole story, so they climbed up to her bed and pulled the curtains. Celia sat leaning against her bookcase, wrapped in a blanket, and began the long process of retelling the events of the past twenty-four hours.

Maddie was, of course, shocked when she heard what had happened in the attic. She gasped and put a hand to her mouth, her eyes growing big. Her eyes didn't return to their normal size until Celia told her about hearing Professor Legaspi's voice and going down to her office. She frowned with curiosity when Celia told her about the four people in the office. Celia thought she saw tears glimmer in her eyes when she told her about the message from her parents from that morning. When Celia had finally finished, Maddie took a deep breath and let it out in a big sigh.

"Wow. That wasn't what I was expecting you to tell me," she said. "And you have no idea who this guy was?"

Celia shook her head. "I couldn't see his face."

"Did you look through the cloak?"

She gave her a look of frustration. "I didn't exactly have the time to concentrate on something like that. Besides, how would I even know what to do?"

Maddie shrugged. "I just figured, since you can do just about anything they ask you to do at this school, maybe you could have tried it."

"I'll bet there was something under the cloak that would have blocked it if I'd tried anyway. Somehow I don't think this was a spur-of-the-moment thing."

"No, probably not," Maddie agreed.

"I want to ask Professor Legaspi about Dr. Gemynd, though. I've never heard of her, so why was she there for that meeting?"

"Good question. Did they say what she does?"

"You mean like for work?" When Maddie nodded, she said, "No, no one mentioned anything about her, other than that she knew a lot about me."

"Hm. That *does* seem kind of strange."

Celia gave a big yawn. "Well, I guess I'll have to wait until I can talk to Professor Legaspi. I have to tell her about the message anyway, and she's the one I have to talk to about getting my family tree out of the vault."

"Yeah, well, I think you'd better wait at least until tomorrow," Maddie said. "You look like you're about to fall asleep."

"I didn't sleep very well last night."

"I wonder why." She leaned over and gave her a hug. "Well, I'm glad you're all right."

"Thanks, Maddie."

She moved over to the ladder and started to climb down. "Get some sleep, okay?"

"Okay."

Her eyelids drooping, Celia finished getting ready for bed and collapsed on top of the blankets, asleep almost before her head hit the pillow.

"I know exactly who to talk to," Professor Legaspi said the next day. Celia met her in her office again, telling her about the message from her parents and the information she needed from the vault.

"You do?"

She nodded. "This person will know exactly what to do."

"Who is it?"

She paused for a moment, then looked up. "I'm sorry, Celia. I can't tell you that information."

"Why not?"

"Because I am unable to reveal that person's identity." She gave her a significant look. "I'm sure you understand."

"No," she muttered, looking out the window, "but I'm getting used to it."

Professor Legaspi sighed and she turned back to look at her. "Celia, I know you'd like to know everything that's going on, but it's just not possible right now. For the moment, you'll have to trust me and let me take care of getting the documents for your family tree."

Celia slipped the key out of her pocket and set it gently on the desk. Leaving her hand on it for a moment, she said, "All right," before lifting her hand off the key.

Professor Legaspi looked from the key to Celia's face. "I promise nothing will happen to it and I'll get it back to you as soon as possible." Celia thought maybe her professor understood why the key was so important to her.

While Professor Legaspi put the key into her desk and locked the drawer, Celia asked, "Can I ask you a question, Professor Legaspi?"

"Sure."

"Who is Dr. Gemynd? I mean, what does she do, exactly?"

Again, Professor Legaspi paused. "Exactly? Well, I can't really—"

"Tell me," Celia finished for her.

She looked at Celia with raised eyebrows. "Actually, I was going to say that I can't really explain it as well as she can."

"Oh," she said, feeling foolish. "Sorry."

"Perhaps you should ask her yourself the next time you see her."

"So why was she here?"

"Because...she has an important job outside of her work, and I'm afraid that's all I can tell you for now."

"Again?"

She shrugged. "I really am sorry, Celia, but you're better off not knowing everything yet."

"When *can* I know everything?"

"I'm not really sure," she said, shaking her head. "It's not really my decision, to be honest."

"Then whose is it?"

"Celia, I think you can probably figure out what I'm going to say to that one."

"I know," she said with resignation. "You can't tell me." She got to her feet. "Well, I guess there's nothing else for now, then."

"All right. I'll let you know about your family tree when I have something to tell you."

"Okay."

For some reason, Celia had thought that by deciding to stick with all of her classes, things would somehow be a little bit easier. She was wrong. As the final four weeks of classes began, all her professors decided to pile on extra homework and last-minute assignments. Up to her ears with homework and studying, Celia tried to keep up with everything, but most of the time she felt like she couldn't keep her head above water. Feeling more and more overwhelmed, Celia began to question whether she'd made the right decision, but she had no choice now. She had to finish the year.

Mr. Bazemore told her he wasn't sure when he was going to get his issue on the staff meeting agenda, so when he knew something, he'd let her know, which only made Celia feel more frustrated and discouraged. As she worked furiously for her classes, she had a thought in the back of her mind that she was going to all this effort for nothing, since she couldn't possibly get a decent grade on her family tree.

Merry, her student advisor, offered to help her out with some of her work, but there was very little she could do. It wasn't so much that Celia couldn't do the work or was having trouble with the material, but rather that there was so much work to do that she was having trouble fitting in all into her schedule, and Merry couldn't help with that at all.

As day after day ticked past, Celia waited to hear something from Professor Legaspi. After two weeks, she couldn't contain her curiosity and asked her about it after class.

"Nothing yet, Celia," she said. "I'll let you know as soon as I hear anything at all. It's . . . a delicate operation, so you'll have to give it some time. We don't want to take any unnecessary risks."

"Oh. I understand."

Another week passed, and Celia finally heard from Mr. Bazemore. Quiroz handed her a note after their Introduction to Locks class, which told Celia to meet him in the hallway by the administrative wing on Saturday morning. Celia showed up a few minutes before the time he'd specified, so she waited for him to show up.

"Ah, good morning, Miss Fincastle," he said, coming around the corner. "If you'll follow me, I'll have you wait in the hallway while I bring up the subject and provide an introduction."

He ushered her to a padded bench next to a door, then went into the room and left her waiting there alone.

Chapter Nineteen

From her seat in the hallway, Celia could hear the conversation in the meeting room clearly, but she couldn't see who was talking. For a while she paid little attention to what was going on inside, but then something caught her attention.

"What are you suggesting, Indaba?"

"I'm suggesting that the administration at this school find the courage to do the right thing."

"Such as?"

"Surely any logical person can see that it is unfair to punish a student for circumstances beyond his or her control, no?" A chair creaked. "It has come to my attention that one of our students is being unfairly penalized because of the merit rule enacted earlier this year."

"You're not suggesting we let students slide through without doing the work, are you?"

"Of course not. But is it fair to give a student a poor grade because of something he or she had nothing to do with?"

"I assume you can provide a specific example?"

"Certainly, headmaster." Celia heard footsteps, then the door opened. "Would you please come in, Miss Fincastle?" Mr. Bazemore said, holding the door for her.

She walked into the room and saw a large oval table that filled most of the spacious room. Headmaster Doyen sat at one end, and about twenty people sat around the rest of the table. Celia recognized her professors, but there were many other people there she didn't know and hadn't seen before. She felt her hands grow clammy and her mouth go dry.

"Miss Fincastle, would you please tell everyone what you received for a grade on your last genealogy assignment?"

She tried to speak but nothing came out, so she cleared her throat and tried again. "A zero," she croaked.

"A zero?" Mr. Bazemore repeated. "Why is that?"

"Because the girl didn't hand in anything for that

assignment," someone spoke up from down the table—Celia couldn't tell who.

"I agree," Headmaster Doyen said. "I saw that assignment, and she only had one sentence on the paper. Your example lacks credibility, Indaba."

"One moment, please," Mr. Bazemore said, sounding completely unconcerned. "Miss Fincastle," he said, turning back to her, "would you please tell us *why* you handed in an incomplete assignment?"

She looked at the floor. "Because I don't know anything about my family, and none of them are around to ask."

The silence in the room was deafening.

After pausing a moment to let that statement sink in, Mr. Bazemore said, "And, I assume, Miss Fincastle, that you haven't tried to find information about your family? That you just gave up and didn't even attempt to learn anything about them, and therefore had nothing to hand in?"

"No!" Celia protested. "I've spent hours in the library, trying to find stuff in books and I've tried talking to my friends, since some of their relatives know something about my family. It's just... there's not much information to find..."

"Ah," Mr. Bazemore said, coming to stand next to her and placing a hand on her shoulder. "So you've done the work, but you don't have any results to show for it, is that it?"

Celia nodded.

"And Headmaster Doyen? Members of the faculty and staff? Do *you* think it fair that this girl receives such low marks in return for her efforts?"

The people sitting around the table began murmuring and leaning over to one another to speak in a low voices. Professor Legaspi exchanged a glance with Mr. Morven and sent an unsearchable look at Celia. Celia thought Headmaster Doyen looked like he would explode. "Enough!" he said in a deep voice, and the room quieted. "Mr. Bazemore," he began in a slow voice, "I will thank you to remove the student from this meeting *immediately*."

Mr. Bazemore nodded. "As you wish," he said smoothly and steered Celia toward the door. "You can go back to your quarters now. Thank you," he said to her.

Celia nodded and set off down the hallway, but took a u-turn when she heard the door close behind her. She crept quietly back to the bench and waited to hear what would happen.

"Indaba, I am surprised at you," Headmaster Doyen said. "After what you've told me throughout this year..."

"Well, Rambert, you can't expect me to sit back and do nothing when one of the students faces an injustice, can you? Student affairs are, after all, my responsibility."

"You..." Celia heard a loud noise, like a fist pounding on the table. "I will not be intimidated into changing my rules! *I* am the headmaster at this school, and no one, not one of you, can usurp my authority. The merit rule stands and you can all inform the students that any further attempts to manipulate this administration will result in expulsion! Is that clear?"

Celia heard murmurs of assent, and decided it would be smart to clear out of there. She left the hallway and headed back to her room, her spirits low. She felt like her last hope had just been dashed. Even Mr. Bazemore hadn't been able to change the headmaster's mind. If whoever it was who was getting the information for her family tree didn't manage to get the papers in time, there was no way she could avoid failing her sixth-year classes. And with only four days left until final exams, it didn't look good.

A few more days passed, and Celia tried to concentrate on studying for her exams. She couldn't do much on her family tree, so she figured she might as well put more effort into doing as well as possible on her exams, thinking maybe those grades would offset the pathetically low ones she would get on her genealogy.

Mr. Bazemore stopped by the table Monday morning while she was eating breakfast to let her know the headmaster hadn't changed his mind, which Celia already knew, but couldn't mention. He seemed apologetic, but not overly concerned, as if it really wasn't that important to him.

On Tuesday evening, with only one day of classes remaining, Celia received a note from Professor Legaspi, asking her to come up to her office. Her heart pounded, knowing there was only one reason Professor Legaspi would be asking for her this close to exams: she must have Celia's family tree.

When Celia reached the office, Professor Legaspi waved a large manila envelope in the air.

"Is that it?" Celia asked.

"It is. I'm sorry it's not here sooner, but at least it got here. Oh, before I forget..." She unlocked her desk drawer and took out the key. "Make sure you keep that in a safe place."

"I know." Celia put the key in her pocket and then eagerly pounced on the envelope, tearing it open and pulling out a small stack of papers. She looked at the top page and smiled. "It's my mom's family tree," she said, her eyes roving over the names and gifts of every person on the page. "And all their gifts..."

"I figured your mom would hang on to that," Professor Legaspi said. "She always was a pack rat."

"Good thing, too," Celia said, flipping through page after page of information. Underneath the stapled sheets about her mother's family was the same thing for her father's side of the family. It looked similar to the rough draft she'd found in the box before, but the final copy had more complete information.

"Your father's, too?"

Celia nodded, flipping through all of those sheets and finding a small stack at the very bottom.

"What's that?" Professor Legaspi asked.

Scanning quickly, she said, "It looks like it tells what happened to everyone since they did their family trees. At least, up until they disappeared..."

"Well, you can't find out what happened to everyone since then without some sort of contact information for people, but I highly suspect that you'll find most of the people on those pages had already died by the time your parents disappeared."

"That's kind of what I figured. Otherwise, wouldn't I have gone to live with one of my other relatives instead of Aunt Agatha?"

Professor Legaspi was quiet for a moment. "Yes, that would be a logical conclusion," she finally said. "Well, you'd better get to work on your own family tree, since you don't have much time left. It's all due on Friday, so you'll have to hurry."

"Boy, do I!" she said, placing the sheets back in the envelope. "Thanks, Professor Legaspi. This should be a big help."

"You're quite welcome, Celia, but you really did most of the work to get it." She waved her off. "Now get to work!"

Celia hurried back to her room and dug right in on her genealogy. She still had to study for her finals, since she had the same hectic exam schedule she'd had all year, but she needed to finish her family tree, as it was a substantial portion of her grades for her sixth-year classes.

Professor Twombly came in to tell her it was time for lights out, but she begged to keep working, since she'd just gotten the information she needed. Although she didn't seem overly pleased, Professor Twombly finally allowed her a little longer. Before Celia knew it, Professor Twombly came back in the room.

"Celia, you need to get to bed now," she said.

She looked up and noticed everyone else in the room was in bed. "Can't I work just a little bit longer?"

Professor Twombly shook her head, her earrings slapping her cheeks with each move of her head. "It's almost midnight, Celia. You need to get to sleep."

"It is? Oh. I didn't even realize..." Celia yawned, realizing only at that moment that she was tired.

"Bed. Now."

"Okay."

Morning came early, but Celia didn't mind. She'd left her window curtains open so the sun would wake her up earlier than normal, and as soon as she woke up, she got to work on her family tree again.

At dinner on Wednesday, Celia noticed that Audra looked a little nervous. "Are you worried about your exams?" she asked.

"A little," she admitted.

"I'm sure you're going to do fine," Maddie said.

"How did you do on your ALPHAs, Celia?"

Celia frowned. "I don't think I ever saw my scores."

"How about you, Maddie?"

She shrugged. "I did okay, I guess. I'm not much good at the touch, speech, or body skills, so I was pretty pathetic at those, but I did really well on my mind and sight sections."

"Oh."

"How do you know?" Celia asked.

"Didn't you get your scores over the summer?"

"No."

"Oh." Maddie glanced at her and shrugged, then turned back to Audra. "Don't worry about it so much," she said. "You'll do fine on the things you need to, and there won't be anything you can do about the rest of it. They're not really testing your ability to do *well* on the exams, just seeing what you *can* do."

Audra gave a shaky sigh. "I don't know…"

Chapter Twenty
Good-bye Again, For Now

By the time Friday afternoon rolled around and Celia left her last final exam, she thought she was going to drop. She'd spent every single minute possible working on either exams or her genealogy, even staying up late every evening, and she was completely worn out. Two days of written exams and practical assessments including analyzing coded pictures and messages, trying to see in the dark, applying basic speed and strength theories, and hoping her letter made it from one place to another correctly with the twinkling blue light for her L'Auzzulla exam had left her beat. She'd been so busy trying to get all the information into her family tree assignment that she hadn't really had time to read and understand all of it. And at the moment, she didn't really care, either. All she wanted was her bed.

Just like after fall midterms, she dragged herself up to her bed and dropped flat on her stomach, falling asleep almost immediately. This time, however, she didn't wake up until morning, when her stomach protested the lack of dinner the night before. Sitting up and stretching to try and get some of the stiffness out of her back, Celia noticed she was still wearing yesterday's clothes. She climbed down and took a shower, then headed to the lounge to see if anyone was up yet.

Chapter Twenty

"Good morning, Celia," Professor Twombly said when Celia entered the room. "I wondered when you would get up." She was sitting on the couch with her husband, both of them sipping coffee.

"Good morning, Professor Twombly, Mr. Twombly. I guess I was pretty tired."

"Well, no wonder, with the amount of work you've been doing the past few days. I tried to wake you up so you could get dinner, but you were sleeping like a log." She glanced at her watch. "I'm sure you're hungry. The refectory should be opening any minute, if you want to go down and get something to eat."

Celia's stomach growled, and she smiled with embarrassment. "I sound like Maddie," she joked. "I think I will head down, if that's all right."

"Go right ahead."

Since it was Saturday and the school year was officially over, not even the early risers were out of bed yet. The halls were completely deserted as Celia made her way down to the refectory. With a heaping plate of food, she took a seat near the doors and starting filling the gnawing emptiness in her stomach.

"...seems odd to me..." Celia caught a snippet of conversation from out in Main Hall.

"...reaction seemed just as odd..."

"Why do you suppose..."

"...heard he had suggested it in the first place." The voices moved closer and became clearer.

"Why would he have complained if it was his idea?"

"I don't know."

There was a sigh. "I don't like the sounds of that. What else do we know about him?"

Celia saw a movement through the crack at the door and noticed two people had moved into her line of sight. She was pretty sure she recognized the voices of Professor Legaspi and Dr. Gemynd, but she wasn't certain, and she couldn't figure out why Dr. Gemynd would have come back to the school.

"Not much." She thought that was Professor Legaspi.

"I'll see what I can find out," Dr. Gemynd said. "In the meantime, I'm sure I don't have to tell you to be on the lookout, Anne."

"Always."

"Well, I'd better get going before anyone sees me here and starts asking questions."

"We really need to find a better cover for you, Alison."

"I know. But this works for now. I'll be in touch. Oh, and don't forget to let me know about plans for the summer so I can get a head start on things."

"Sure. See you later."

Celia thought she saw a glimpse of blue light, and then she heard a set of footsteps moving away from the room. *Strange*, she thought. She couldn't figure out who they were talking about, but obviously they were trying to find information about someone. Deciding her brain had worked enough in the past ten months, she pushed it all out of her mind and concentrated on finishing her breakfast.

The time between the end of classes and graduation was always a lot of fun for the students at Renasci. Saturday evening after finals was prom for the older students and the talent show for the rest of the students. Celia hadn't been in the auditorium since the school play the first week of May, and she hadn't exactly been able to relax and enjoy the show then. Now, however, she had done everything she could to get good grades in her classes and it was out of her hands, so she sat back and enjoyed the show. It was just as good as the year before, with a few new surprises from the seventh-year students, who were a talented bunch.

The annual Coterie Games Day was on Wednesday, just three days before graduation. Thanks to her classes with the fourth-year students, Celia ended up being a popular person for many events. Many of the fourth-years didn't know the younger students, and since some of the events required someone smaller who was faster or could be carried easier, they all asked her to either enter the competition with them or match them up with another student. For Celia, it was a lot of fun competing against her older classmates, particularly the ones from the other coteries. Cyn tried to intimidate her on the potato sack race, but Celia took great pleasure in beating her and finishing fourth.

Each coterie tried to pick the people who had the best skills, even though one coterie usually had a distinct advantage in each event. For Celia, that meant that she was "volunteered" for some of the events she might rather have avoided if she'd had the choice. She was sure she could have told everyone that she really didn't want to do Professor Spadaro's agility course or the paint war, but she didn't have the heart to disappoint the rest of the people in her coterie and possibly cost them a chance at winning.

A few of her classmates from Corpanthera thought they would easily beat her at the more physical events, something Celia figured would happen, too, so she was a little nervous at the start of the agility course. But once she got into the course and forgot about everything but getting through all the obstacles, she found she had a lot of fun. Much to her surprise and the surprise of everyone else, she finished second, one place higher than last year.

The paint war, where camouflage was a fair tactic, ended up being one of her favorite events. Each player was given a squirt gun with washable paint in the color of their coterie. The object was to hit as many people as possible and avoid being hit yourself. If you were hit by three other colors, you were out of the game, and the last person standing was the winner. Since she was the youngest player out there, she was also the smallest, which meant she could hide places where the rest of them couldn't fit. That, combined with her newly developed camouflage skills and a few talented teammates, left her the last player standing and carrying only one hit from someone on the Sprachursus team. It was a huge win for Mensaleon, and boosted their score by five hundred points.

Tom Carmichael, one of the Mensaleon first-years, somehow convinced Celia to help him with the piggyback Soccovolle competition, and they did fairly well. One person sat on the shoulders of the other, and the person on the ground could only play the soccer moves of the game, while the person in the air had to play the volleyball part of the game. Mensaleon lost in the final round to Aquilegia, who—oddly enough—finished last in the actual Soccovolle tournament during the year. Everyone joked they should play piggyback next year instead.

At the end of the day, Mensaleon had the highest point total, and was declared the "winner" of the Coterie Games Day competition. At dinner that evening, everyone in the coterie got to sit at fancy tables set with tablecloths and fine china and be served dinner by the Tattotauri students, who had accumulated the fewest points that day. It was a strange turn-around for the team that had not only won the Soccovolle tournament that year, but also won the Games Day competition last year.

Celia enjoyed the dinner, thinking it was probably the first time in her life that she had actually eaten a nice meal without having to deal with one of Aunt Agatha's boring meetings or gossip-fests. It was particularly satisfying to keep asking her fourth-year classmates to fetch something someone at their table needed, especially since one of their servers was Quiroz, who ended up being a good sport about all of it.

Graduation was on Saturday, and although Celia knew some of the kids graduating, it didn't bother her as much this year as it had last year. The ceremony was held outside again, although high winds made it difficult for the graduates to keep their hats on. Celia cheered for Merry when she walked across the stage, and Heath cheered for his brother, whom Celia still hadn't met. At the end of the ceremony, they all threw their caps in the air and then headed inside to escape the wind and enjoy a reception. Once the new graduates left for their party, the rest of the crowd trickled out of the refectory.

Sunday was their last day at the school before they headed home, and everyone spent the day packing up and saying good-bye. Celia was folding a shirt to pack in her trunk when she heard someone at the door to their room.

"Hey, Celia, there's a whole pile of mail out here for you."

"What? Oh, thanks, Max." She walked out and found a rather large pile of envelopes sitting in the mailbox. Sure enough, the whole pile was addressed to her, so she carried it into her room.

"Wow," Maddie said, crawling down from her bed. "That's a lot of mail."

"I know. Who do you think it's from?" Celia picked up the first envelope, opened it, pulled out a birthday card, and stared in surprise. "There must be something wrong," she said.

"Why?" Maddie took the armchair next to her.

"Because no one sends me a card for my birthday." She flipped the card open and groaned. "Of course," she said with disappointment. "Here," she said, handing the card to Maddie. "It's for you. They're probably all for you." She lifted the huge stack and dumped it all on Maddie's lap.

"What do you mean, for me? My birthday was six weeks ago."

"I know. But these are for the other Celia."

"Not again!" Maddie cried. "You mean these are all from kids at camp?"

"Apparently."

It took Maddie a full hour to open all the cards. The very last envelope she opened was a thick white one. She pulled a beautiful card out and opened it up. She frowned as she read the signature, then held it out to Celia. "I believe this one is actually for you, Celia."

She took the card and opened it. A folded letter was tucked inside and the card itself had only a signature. "*Doxa*" it said in her loopy script.

"What does she want from you?" Maddie asked, coming over from dumping the pile of cards on her desk.

"Who, Doxa?"

"No, the Queen of Sheba," she said, rolling her eyes. "Of course Doxa."

Celia shrugged. "I don't know. Maybe she just wants to wish me a happy birthday."

"Right." Maddie's voice revealed her disbelief.

She shrugged again and opened the letter. Maddie read over her shoulder.

Dear Celia,

I know this is early, but I figured I'd be better off sending it before you left than to take the chance and miss you. I hope you have a very enjoyable birthday. I'm not sure if you're ecstatic that the school year is over and you don't have any more homework to do, or if you're dreading the thought of going back to your aunt's house for the summer. Either way, try not to think about it tomorrow and just enjoy the day as much as possible.

I hope you can come to camp again this summer. It was nice having you there last year, and maybe this year I'll be a better counselor with one year under my belt. Tell Maddie hello for me, and let her know I look forward to seeing her at camp if she can come, too.

I hope your year at RAGS went better than last year. Without me there, I'm sure it had to be an improvement. Anyway, have a happy birthday and I hope to see you soon.

Warm wishes,

Doxa

"See?" Celia said, folding the letter and putting everything back in the envelope. "She doesn't seem so horrible to me anymore."

"Hello? Have you forgotten? She nearly got you expelled!"

"And? I nearly failed my classes this year. May have, in fact. I don't know yet. That doesn't prove that Doxa's the same person she was last year."

Maddie shook her head and sighed. "You're too gullible."

"No, I'm not! You're just too skeptical."

Maddie stuck her tongue out playfully at her, and Celia returned the gesture.

"Celia?" Professor Twombly interrupted, sticking her head in the room. "I just got a note from Mr. Morven. He'd like you to meet him in his office if you have a minute."

"Oh, sure. Thanks, Professor Twombly."

Celia made her way to Mr. Morven's office in the administrative wing, and found the door open and Higby sitting in one of the chairs. "Hi," she said, taking the other chair.

"Hi, Celia," Mr. Morven said. "Just wanted to go over your grades with your temporary guardian, since he won't have the authority after today."

"Oh," she said, her good mood evaporating. "Okay."

"I figured you might rather have Higby looking at your marks instead of Agatha," he continued, "given...well, everything."

Celia swallowed. Yes, it would be better to have Higby see her failing grades and not Aunt Agatha, but she really didn't want to have to see her lousy grades at all, given the choice. "That's fine."

Mr. Morven handed her a sealed envelope. "I haven't looked at them yet. I thought I'd let you do the honors," he said.

"Or dishonors," she muttered.

He made a face. "True."

Celia took a deep breath and opened the envelope. She pulled out a single piece of paper and unfolded it, noticing the same letterhead she had seen on other things from the school. Steeling herself for her pathetic grades, she glanced down the page. Her fourth-year classes were listed first, and she had gotten high marks in all of them, even the ones where she hadn't been as sure about the final exams. When she reached the bottom of the page, she nearly choked.

"Are you all right?" Higby asked.

"I'm . . . fine."

"Are they that bad?" Mr. Morven asked.

"See for yourself."

Mr. Morven took the paper from her limp fingers and scanned the page. "Very nicely done," he said as his eyes moved down. "You did fine in all your fourth-year classes, and . . . Oh."

"What is it?" Higby asked. Celia still felt numb. Mr. Morven handed the sheet to Higby, who also scanned the page. When he reached the bottom section, his eyes grew wide and he turned to look at her. "Miss Fincastle!"

"Um," Mr. Morven said, "do you mind if I call Professor Legaspi down here? I think she'll want to see this." When no one objected, he picked up the phone. They were all so shocked they didn't say anything the entire time they waited for Professor Legaspi.

When she came in the room, she looked at all of them and her face fell. "Uh-oh. What happened?"

"Grades," Mr. Morven said. Higby handed her the sheet and sat back in his chair, shaking his head.

She glanced at the page, her eyes moving rapidly until she reached the same point that halted the rest of them.

She looked up at Celia, then over to Mr. Morven. "Are these correct?" she asked. When he nodded, she gave a big whoop and flung her arms around Celia. "I knew you could do it!" she cried. Stepping back, she looked at the page again. "Wow. I must not have been the only one."

"What do you mean?" Mr. Morven said.

"Well, I can't grade exams and homework assignments any differently, but for the family tree assignments, there is some measure of subjectivity," she said. "Obviously, there are certain criteria that have to be met, but if we feel a student has gone above and beyond what is required, we can reward that with a higher grade, sort of like extra credit." She looked at Celia. "I knew how hard you had worked on that family tree, and I also knew how much time you must have spent on it the last three days to turn in something that was so complete, so I gave you a score that was nearly double what everyone else had gotten. Your family tree was just better and more complete than everyone else's. I guess the other deans must have done the same thing, and that basically negated the zeros you got on the last assignment."

"Well," Higby said, "I must say I was expecting less than stellar grades after everyone warned me about the difficulties you've been having this year. But those marks certainly aren't anything to sneeze at. Where do I sign?"

"Oh, you don't have to sign these, Higby," Mr. Morven said.

"Very well. Then if you will all excuse me, I must be going. I have some important business to attend to."

"We'd better let you get back to packing," Mr. Morven said to Celia after Higby had left. "Nice job."

"Thanks."

"Well?" Maddie asked when Celia returned their room.

"He had my grades."

"Oh."

"Actually, I got A's in everything."

"You're kidding."

"Nope."

"You're serious!?"

"Yup."

"Yay!" Maddie cheered.

That evening, Celia and her friends sat in the boys' room talking about their plans for the summer. Instead of Libby, Galena, and Burnsy, who were busy with other friends they had made that year, they had the five remaining sixth-years and Audra, Jenilee, and one of the seventh-year boys named Cameron, who insisted they call him Cam.

"I can't believe my second year here is over," Celia said.

"Hey," Cam said, "I'm just glad I survived my first." Everyone laughed at his comment.

"I think I'm going back to camp this summer," Maddie said. "How about the rest of you?"

"I'm playing in a summer Soccovolle league," Josh said. "Since I'm not going to the tournament, at least that way I get some playing time over the summer. It's not a pro team, but it's something."

"That sounds like fun," Kitt said. "Too bad I stink at Soccovolle."

"Me, too," Celia said.

"Aw, come on, Celia," Josh said. "You're getting better. Look at how well you played on Games Day."

"Yeah, 'cause I was on Tom's shoulders!"

"Well, I'm gonna sit around the house and do nothing," Heath said.

"Nothing?" Jenilee asked. "All summer?"

"That's the plan," he said, slouching in the chair.

"Heath, you slacker," Maddie teased. They all knew Heath

acted like he didn't care about anything, but he actually got good grades and put a lot of effort into his schoolwork.

"What are you guys doing this summer?" Celia asked the seventh-years.

"Not much," Audra admitted. "I don't have any big plans."

"Me, neither," Jenilee said. "I might go visit some relatives, but I don't know yet."

"I'm going bike riding," Cam said. "I'm doing a charity ride through the mountains."

"Really?" Josh said. "Sounds churry!"

"Yeah, I've been training for a while, so I hope I don't crack on the hills."

"I'm sure you'll do fine," Celia said.

"How about you, Celia?" Kitt asked. "What are you doing?"

"I'm not sure yet. I just hope I don't have to eat another prune tart." Gagging noises and comments of "Blech!" filled the room. "Sorry."

"Oh, that's just wrong!" Cam said.

"Believe me," Celia said. "I know."

Professor Twombly told them it was time for bed since they had to be moving early in the morning, so they split up and got ready for bed.

The next morning, there was a mad scramble to get everything done before the BUS left. After checking her closet one last time, Celia picked up her backpack, which held the book, the key, and the envelope from her mother with all the various notes and clues tucked inside. Shutting the door on her empty closet, she dragged her trunk out to the foyer. With some assistance from the older guys, she got her things down to the BUS and loaded into a compartment.

Going back into the school to say good-bye to all of her professors, she shook hands with most of the staff, purposely avoiding Headmaster Doyen. She didn't really have anything to say to him anyway. Professor Twombly gave her a hug and tucked a small present in her hand, wishing her a happy birthday.

Professor Legaspi glanced at Headmaster Doyen, then gave Celia a big hug. "I hope you have a good summer. If you'd like to go back to camp, we can work that out, okay?"

"I'd like that," she said, hugging her professor back.

She handed Celia a squishy package wrapped with pastel paper and tied with a frilly bow. "Happy birthday, Celia. I'll see you soon."

"Thanks, Professor Legaspi. Where's Higby?" she asked, looking around for him.

"He had to be somewhere else."

"Oh. Well, good-bye." She gave Professor Legaspi one more hug.

Her good-byes completed, Celia boarded the BUS and sat in her compartment with Maddie, Heath, and Josh. They had picked a compartment on the same side as the school, so she waved out the window at her professors gathered on the platform, then settled back for the long ride back to the BUS station.

As they hurtled across the plains at their normal super-fast speeds, Mr. Morven knocked on their compartment door and stuck his head inside. "Hi, guys. Celia, I just wanted to let you know that I'm driving you home again, so I'll catch up with you on the platform."

"Okay. Thanks, Mr. Morven."

A while later, after an impromptu birthday party in the dining car involving an unfamiliar version of "Happy Birthday" sung by everyone in the car and a long nap for all the exhausted students, they pulled into the station and piled out of the BUS.

After hugging all her friends, Celia met up with Mr. Morven and loaded in the van for the trip to her aunt's house.

Although it didn't really come as a surprise, Celia was a little disappointed when Aunt Agatha wasn't home when they got there. Without a key to the house and no one to let them in, she and Mr. Morven had to sit on the front steps and wait for Aunt Agatha to get home.

By the time she showed up, Mr. Morven only had time to drop her trunk in her room, hand her a birthday present, which he told her was actually from Higby, and then rush off to wherever it was he needed to be. Aunt Agatha seemed unconcerned.

"Well, it's certainly not my problem, now, is it?" she said before leaving the room.

Celia sighed and began the process of unpacking. She hoped she would only be staying here for a short time, but she didn't really know. Once her trunk was empty and stowed in the closet, she turned her attention to her birthday presents and the family tree information from the Document Vault that she hadn't gotten around to studying in any detail yet. As she picked up the first gift, Aunt Agatha called her down to dinner. She sighed, set the package down, and walked to the door. Glancing back at the pile of things waiting on her bed, she wished she could skip dinner with Aunt Agatha and spend the time with those things, which seemed much more interesting to her.

"Celia!" her aunt called again. "My food is getting cold!"

"Coming, Aunt Agatha!" Celia called.

She walked out of the room and closed the door behind her, knowing that it might all be out of sight, but it would never be out of mind for her. After this year, she was more familiar with the dangers she might face as princep, and she was now fully aware that Casimir wanted her out of the way. Spending time in the demesne might be risky, because it meant the Coridans knew where she was, but Celia wished she could spend the time with her new family and friends there instead of being stuck in the dreary old house with Aunt Agatha. No matter what Aunt Agatha might talk about, Celia would be thinking about other things, and starting her countdown until she could return to Renasci.

About the Author

Melissa Gunther lives in Florida where she continues her work on the Celia's Journey series. She loves to hear from readers and is always happy to answer questions, except maybe the ones about how far in the series she's written. Visit her online at www.melissagunther.com.

Books available from Melissa Gunther:

The Book in the Attic

Celia's Journey - Book 1
Available in Hardcover, Paperback, and e-Book

Key to the Past

Celia's Journey - Book 2
Available in Hardcover, Paperback, and e-Book

Turn the page to read an excerpt from

Flash of Red

Celia's Journey - Book 3
Coming Summer 2012!

Chapter One
Blue

So far, being a teenager wasn't anything spectacular.

Celia Fincastle coughed as she blew dust off a box in the attic of an old Gothic-style house and made a face when her nose tickled and her eyes watered. It wasn't the first time she'd been sent to the attic to clean and sort the mess that accumulated in the space full of nooks and crannies. As she set an old lampshade on the box, she wondered how the attic always seemed to be messy when no one ever came up there. Shouldn't it still be clean from the last time she'd been up there?

Celia had been thirteen for three days, ever since she'd come home from her second year as a student at the Renasci Academy for Gifted Students on her birthday. She lived with her Aunt Agatha, who actually wasn't her aunt, but was her closest remaining relative. To Agatha Trowbridge's way of thinking, Celia's thirteenth birthday meant she could now do more work around the house. In the past three days, Celia had dusted the library, polished the silver, prepared tea for one of Aunt Agatha's meetings, vacuumed the upstairs, washed the dishes what seemed like fifty times, weeded the garden, and now cleaned the attic.

Chapter One

She decided she liked being twelve better. It was less work.

It wasn't that Aunt Agatha was looking for slave labor, just that she honestly didn't have a clue how to treat anyone under the age of...well, fifty. Although Celia had lived with her for eleven years, Aunt Agatha had never taken an active role in raising her; she'd left it up to a series of nannies until Celia was old enough to go to school. At that point, she'd started treating Celia like the rest of her staff, ordering her around and basically making her life miserable.

Celia piled a stack of books onto a bookshelf, then turned back to the box that had been buried underneath them. Blowing her hair out of her face, she lifted the lid on the box and quickly dropped it again, planting her hands on the top to make sure it stayed down. "Ugh," she shuddered. She was sure she'd seen eyes.

Stepping away from the box, she nudged it with her toe until it was safely tucked in the farthest corner of the attic, then moved away as fast as possible. No way was she sorting through that box.

"Celia?" She turned in surprise at the sound of Aunt Agatha's voice at the foot of the stairs leading up to the attic. Aunt Agatha usually just hollered from wherever she was in the house; it was a rarity for her to actually come looking for her.

"Yes, Aunt Agatha?" Celia said, going down the curving stairs until she could see her.

"We have company," Agatha said, her eyes roving from the top of Celia's dusty head to the tips of her ratty-looking shoes. "I need you to get cleaned up and come talk with the other girls."

Celia groaned mentally. "Do I really have to? I'm still working up here, and—"

"I won't repeat myself, Celia," her aunt interrupted in a quiet but stern voice. "Five minutes," she said as she walked away from the doorway.

"Fine," Celia muttered, even though Aunt Agatha couldn't possibly hear her. She trudged up to the top of the stairs and turned off the light, then left the attic and went to her room, shaking as much dust as possible out of her long brown hair as she went. Once inside her room, she went to the closet and pulled out the last thing she would ever choose to wear, grimacing as she pulled on the itchy dress covered with flowers that Celia thought belonged on old wallpaper. The only good thing was that they weren't going outside, so she wouldn't have to put on the horrible purple chicken hat that had been inflicted upon her so many times before. Celia wondered if she could somehow "drop" the hat into one of the fireplaces at Renasci. Even if it only burned off some of the feathers, it *had* to be an improvement.

Stuffing her feet into equally uncomfortable shoes, Celia checked her reflection in the mirror. Her hair was messy, but that couldn't be helped; at least it wasn't dusty anymore. The dress looked as hideous as it felt, but Aunt Agatha would approve. It was Celia's misfortune to have had a growth spurt so that she now fit into a whole new collection of ugly outfits from Aunt Agatha, each one somehow worse than the last. The silver locket hanging around her neck looked a little out of place, but Celia refused to take it off.

She met her own brown-eyed gaze in the mirror as her hand touched the locket, thinking of not only the pictures inside but also the person who had given it to her. Only three days had passed since she'd last seen Professor Legaspi, a moment compared to the eleven years that had passed since she'd seen her parents, whose pictures sat in the locket.

Chapter One

Her gaze landed on the reflection of a pile on the floor in the corner of the room, and she looked at it longingly. She still hadn't been able to open her birthday presents from all her friends in the demesne, even though they'd been sitting there for three days. After working so hard all day, she barely had the energy to climb into bed each evening, never mind take the time to open her presents. Buried at the bottom of the pile was something else that pulled Celia's attention: her family tree. She'd finished it at the last possible second last year, just before final exams, and she hadn't been able to take any time to study it yet - a torturous thing considering she hadn't seen her family in so long.

A knock on the door interrupted her thoughts. "Celia? We're waiting for you." Aunt Agatha sounded impatient.

Celia opened the door and met the disapproving look of her aunt. "I'm ready," she said.

Aunt Agatha's eyes took in her appearance again, and this time her face settled into a favorable expression. "Very well. Come with me."

Celia followed her down the front staircase and into the front parlor, where three older ladies were sitting on the sofa and in the mauve wing back chair by the grand piano.

"Ladies," Aunt Agatha said, "I believe most of you have met my grandniece, Celia? Celia, this is Mrs. Walker, Mrs. Moreau, and Mrs. Cosman."

"Hello," Celia said, nodding her head politely.

"Hello, dear," Mrs. Walker said. "My, what a lovely dress! I haven't seen anything that nice in quite some time. Agatha, darling, you have exquisite taste!"

"Oh, thank you, Dorothy," Agatha said. "Celia, would you like to go into the back parlor with the other girls? Mrs. Moreau and Mrs. Walker brought their granddaughters along."

"Of course, Aunt Agatha," Celia said, although she thought she'd rather eat nothing but prune tarts for five days than spend a minute with any of Aunt Agatha's circle of acquaintances. Her steps heavy, she pushed through the door to the back parlor and found five faces looking at her. "Um, hi," she said. "I'm Celia."

"Oh, hi, Cecelia," an older girl with perfectly styled hair, carefully manicured fingernails, and flawless attire said with a sniff. "I'm Rosemarie, and this is my sister, Fifi," she said, nodding her head at the girl sitting next to her on the couch, who looked like a slightly younger duplicate of Rosemarie.

Celia felt her lip bleed as she bit it hard to keep from laughing. *Fifi*? Surely someone did not give their daughter such a name. It sounded like it belonged to a poodle. She almost forgot that Rosemarie had called her by the wrong name. "Nice to meet you," she said, "but it's Celia, not Cecelia."

Rosemarie looked at her blankly for a moment. "Whatever," she said, sounding unconcerned.

Celia turned to the other three girls sitting on the other sofa. "And you are...?"

The oldest spoke up, although she looked younger than either Rosemarie or Fifi. "I'm Helen, this is Emma, and that's Olivia." She pointed to each of the other girls as she spoke, and they gave a small wave when she said their names.

"Well," Celia said, glancing around the room, "it looks like my aunt left us some tea and sandwiches. Would you all like some tea?"

"Is it Earl Grey?" Rosemarie asked. "I don't drink anything but Earl Grey."

"Are they cucumber sandwiches?" Fifi asked in a whiny voice. "I hate cucumber sandwiches."

"Olivia can't have strawberries," Helen said. "They give her a rash."

Chapter One

"Um..." Celia walked over to the tea cart in the corner, trying to stop herself from running screaming from the room. "It looks like it's Darjeeling tea—"

"Then I'm not having any."

"—*but* I don't see any strawberries anywhere."

"Oh, good."

"There are cucumber sandwiches—"

"*Yuck*!"

"—*but* there are other sandwiches, too."

The other girls all spoke at once.

"I'll have a cup of tea, one lump, no cream..."

"...me one of each..."

"...only half a cup but two lumps..."

"...don't like pepper on my..."

"...really hungry, Helen!"

Celia rubbed her temples, her back to the room. Did they think she was some kind of servant? Why couldn't they get their own tea?

Ten minutes later, Celia had served each girl her requested tea and sandwich offerings, from Rosemarie's demand for one of every kind of sandwich offered to Emma's order for half a cup of tea with two lumps of sugar and the rest of the cup filled with cream.

"So, Cecelia," Rosemarie began. Celia gritted her teeth but didn't correct her. "Where do you go to school? Fifi and I attend Wellington Academy," she said, naming a well-known private school in the area.

"Oh, um...I go to an out-of-town school."

"Really? Boarding school?"

"Yeah. It's a great school. Really good."

"Oh." Rosemarie didn't sound impressed.

The door to the front parlor opened and Aunt Agatha peeked into the room. "Ah, splendid!" she said. "You girls seem to be getting along wonderfully."

"Oh, of course, Miss Trowbridge," Fifi spoke up, all smiles and sweetness.

"Yes, Miss Trowbridge," Rosemarie said. "And may I say that the sandwiches are delicious and the tea is perfectly brewed." Celia wondered how she would know that since she hadn't had any tea.

"Oh, thank you. I prepared the tea myself, of course. I just don't trust the help to make it properly, you know," Aunt Agatha replied. Celia forced herself to not roll her eyes, since Agatha Trowbridge would never deign to do something as mundane as making tea.

"Good help is so hard to find these days," Rosemarie agreed, casting a glance at Celia out of the corner of her eye.

"Well, I'll let you all continue your conversation. If you need anything, Celia can help you."

"Thank you, Miss Trowbridge," the five girls chorused as Aunt Agatha retreated into the front parlor. Celia sighed quietly and wondered how long she would be stuck here.

The conversation turned to cotillion classes and the year's debutantes, and Celia's mind wandered. She had nothing to contribute to a conversation about either of those subjects, and quite honestly didn't want to have anything to do with the things that interested these girls. As she studied the pattern on her china saucer, something suddenly caught her attention. Trying not to alert the other girls, she looked up as quickly as she dared and searched the view out the window. There was nothing there, but Celia was almost certain she had seen a flash of blue light.

Chapter One

"Excuse me," she said to the others, who paid her no attention, and she slipped through the door, across the back hallway, and into the kitchen. Hurrying over to the back window, she pressed her nose as close to the glass as possible (being careful not to leave nose prints on the window—she'd just have to clean them later) and looked around. She saw only the gardener, who was pruning the bushes in the rose garden. So what had caused the blue flash?

The door to the kitchen opened and Celia whirled around.

Read more in

Flash of Red

Celia's Journey - Book 3
Coming Summer 2012!

Made in the USA
Middletown, DE
31 March 2018